FEARLESS III

MMA SPORT & RUSSIAN MAFIA ROMANCE

AMARIE AVANT

A NOTE FROM AMARIE

Thank you from the bottom of my heart for waiting for Vassili and Zariah's finale. If you've been supporting my stories from day one, double thank you. (And if you just crammed the Fearless Series this holiday 2019 season, double thank you too!)

As an author, I always try to follow through with my promises. For this series, I almost expected not to. I'd grown to care for Vassili and Zar, and I didn't want to hurt them. Lord knows I can't harm Natasha/Cutie Pie, or the Little Bully rather. But not hurting them would mean that I'd be off my game while writing this story. Shoveling out a bland story was something I refused to do, as well. So, I set Fearless 3 aside and wrote a bunch of other stories instead.

The morning I learned my great grandmother passed away, I gravitated toward Vassili and Zar. It might sound crazy, but Vassili and Zar were my outlets. Consumed with sadness, I needed someone to hurt, and this couple was as real as ever to me. Putting pen to paper hadn't been my stress reliever in so long. Though grandmommy lived a good life (getting her wings at a blessed 101 years), the selfish part of me would've loved to have her here longer. I wanted to hear more of her stories—I could never write stories that compare to her. The pain made the words flow.

All the ups and downs Vassili and Zariah went through in the past pale in comparison to this story.

I tested them, tried them, broke them. Maybe I mended Vassili and Zar back together again . . . Okay, no spoilers.

Thank you for giving my work a chance, and I hope you enjoy it!

Amarie Nicole

SUBSCRIBE

Consider joining my newsletter to stay up to date on new releases and super discounts (especially during these holiday times). You'll also receive a free book for subscribing.

CONTACT ME

PROLOGUE

Vassili Karo Resnov

"Here's a thousand percent of transparency for you, Mr. Resnov. Zariah's weakling of a mother and I made a beautiful girl. The first time I held my princess, I thought, *God, You let us create something so gorgeous.*"

The cool evening air licks at the back of my neck. I shove my hands into my leather jacket. My wife's father, Maxwell Washington, has that cunt of a mouth of his wide open. He's leaning against the doorframe to his house. The inside of his home is immaculate, representing trappings of success. Trappings of my family as he plays judge, jury, executioner, and motherfucking warden. My wife is here. My daughter and my unborn son are here too.

"May I come in, Mr. Washington?" I growl.

"I'll be honest; the two of you made a beautiful little girl." Maxwell points a stiff finger at my chest. I'll let him keep talking, breathing for Zariah's sake.

He taunts, "My princess is crying for you."

"I'd like to see my wife," I grit out. "Hate me all your life. Let me talk to her."

1

Unfolding his arms, he gestures between us. "We're having a conversation, you and me. This goes on record as our longest discussion ever. Let's keep up the momentum. As I was about to say, Zariah will pine over you; probably more than necessary. When she's ready, I'll introduce her to some good guys."

My blood becomes lava in my veins as I speak. "You'll introduce her to some good guys. My replacement, *dah?*"

The laidback chit chat he was just using fades. Maxwell sneers, pointing another stiff finger at my chest. "You can bet your scummy, communistic ass, I am interviewing your substitute. Consider them more than worthy opponents. One of them will be lucky enough to have her. I'll vet all the candidates. One will exceed anything you could ever do for your child too."

I grab Maxwell's index finger to stop him from taking another jab at my chest. Only God Himself stops me from breaking his finger. "Keep at it, piz'da. I'll forget that you're family."

"Piz'da?"

"It means cunt. Now, I go see my wife!"

I press his hand toward his chest, twisting until he's turned around. With him out of the way, I step inside the house I'd vowed never to enter when Zariah and I were newlyweds. He'd played me with her bitch of an ex.

I'm in the middle of the foyer, ready to shout my wife's name when a sound I never will forget clicks in my ears.

Might as well be thousands of them.

Safeties are being removed from guns. A bunch of cops surround the perimeter of the room. Might as well all be crooked if they're affiliated with the Chief of Police. They've been listening to our conversation this entire time.

"Which one of you little cunts will pull the first trigger." I stare face-forward. There has to be at least ten of them waiting to ambush me. "You mudaks! You all will have to take a fucking shot at me." I point a finger to my forehead like it's a bullet. "Make sure I'm fucking dead because I am going to see my wife today."

"Look at him, so fearless," Maxwell scoffs from behind me. He leans against the doorframe again, legs locked about the ankles. The bitch thinks he's untouchable.

"Kill me and . . ." I pause, offering them the rare chance of a smile. The cocky smile completes the sentence. *You die, and everyone you know dies.*

"The Resnov way," someone whispers.

I stare into eyes—blue, brown, green. Maxwell has a diversified list of crooked cops ready to play knight in shining armor for him. If my blood wasn't boiling, I'd be flattered.

"Go ahead, threaten a room full of cops!" Maxwell comes over to me.

"Are they wearing cams?" I spit. "I doubt that. You want this shit to make the news? Cops shoot an unarmed man. Who hasn't threatened anyone? Who just wants to see his wife and kids?"

"No cams?" A familiar face moves to block the double staircase. Jackson, the cop with a history of wanting to be there for my wife, stands in front of me. His nostrils are flared, light-brown skin tinged red. An image of our first encounter pops into my mind. While driving in a police cruiser, Jackson and another cop had stopped Zariah and me. We'd been leaving Urban Kashtan, a restaurant with the best borsch, for the first time. I'd bought enough vodka to lick off all the sweet, tight spots of her body. Her ass. Her tits. Her tight, gorgeous pussy. Before we'd made it home, this bitch almost ruined our night.

"No cams?" I arch an eyebrow, ignoring the pup standing in my face.

3

"Correct. No cams, Son. That also applies to the fact that there'll be no evidence of dead, Russian scum." Washington folds his arms. "All legalities are covered."

For every cop showing his minuscule balls by way of holding heat, I have a machine gun tattooed on my forearm. I'm confident some of them would go down with me!

I sniff, keeping myself calm. "Fuck, maybe I should finish the statement. All you little bitches know the Resnov way. I die; everyone you know dies. The funeral home becomes rich! Is that what you want on your head, Maxwell? Before you die, knowing that you've caused the deaths of your little pups and their families? Make it clear to me."

Officer Jackson snarls, "So you're working for your father, Anatoly Resnov?"

"Why the fuck does it matter." I shrug. "No cams? No proof, right? I want to see my family, Mr. Washington. Make that happen before I forget how important you are to *my* Zariah!"

"Don't," comes a soft, feminine voice. The walls in the room stop shrinking in.

My hard gaze pans upward past rich paintings. My wife is at the top step, right at the chandelier hanging above. Her beautiful, brown eyes aren't as innocent as I remember. Her orbs are red-rimmed. A sweatsuit has covered every gorgeous curve that my hands, mouth, and tongue have traced over. She leans against the railing. Emotions flash across her face.

"Zariah," I breathe. All the animosity in my chest deflates. "You got to come home, baby. You are mine. We made vows."

"With an Elvis impersonator." Her tiny laugh is almost hysterical, hopeless too.

"Doesn't matter. We made vows before God." I cock my head, hard voice as soft as can be. "You and my child have to come with me. Natasha is my blood, you are mine. You have to come home. Now."

She might as well be standing right over me. A lone tear drops onto my forehead. I don't have the power to wipe it off. Doing so would be acknowledging my faults. I hate her fucking crying. Even the happy tears make me wonder. It makes my mind turn to dark thoughts about how my mom cried Anatoly a river. I contemplate on Sasha. My sister cried to so many men after they screwed her and beat me for believing she was too good for it.

I nudge my head. "Get my little girl, come down. Now."

Her sigh is heavy enough to drop her shoulders. "Vassili, did you get the divorce papers?"

Venom unleashes in my bloodstream. Keeping my cool is imperative.

"Maybe the papers are burnt to a crisp in our bedroom fireplace. Our bed is waiting for you." I stare up at her. The world around us fades. All those .9mms are ready to put me under have ceased to exist. It's only she and I, which gives me a 'pass' when I'd spoken of 'bed' and Zariah in the same sentence. Yes, I have an insatiable appetite for her pussy, but I don't disrespect her around people. After the way Anatoly had treated my mom, my mindset is screwed. Meaning, I would never touch my wife. Never hurt her with words or my hands. I'd rather leave MMA for good than insult Zariah Resnov. So, for now, it's only me and my wife here at this moment as we talk.

More tears slide down her cheeks. Zariah murmurs, "I can't leave."

"Okay, I help." My Russian accent falters into broken English. My 190 pounds of raw muscle have transformed into vulnerability. I start to move again.

The world crashes around me with a vengeance.

Jackson, who has been posted against the stairwell, puffs

5

his chest up. His eyes pierce through me. I don't regard him. He's not an opponent. He's not shit to me. I want him to hit me. To get one good lick in so that when I take off on him, he'll learn the lesson of his life. Shit, might even cost the mudak's life. I have zero respect for a person who dares to come between a man and his wife.

Without addressing Jackson, I look up at my wife. I order, "Save a life, Zar. I could kill him. Right now, even with them shooting me. Sweetheart, you would have two deaths on your head."

"Just leave, Vassili," she groans. "We can talk things through later."

I continue with, "You remember our first encounter. You know what the fuck I mean when I say, you'd also have more deaths on your head later."

"Vassili... Go!" she screams, her voice so loud it begins to croak. "You're not going to sic Anatoly on them because they're not going to shoot you, asshole. We have kids. *Just give me a moment to think.*"

I slam my forearm into my palm. Jackson jumps. I snap, "You aren't shit without a gun!"

He kisses his teeth. "You go up those stairs, you'll be the shit beneath my boot."

"I like that." I step closer to him. "You know what they say, those that can't back it up—talk it out. I'll use that line during my next match."

"Fuck you," Jackson snaps.

"I'm a killer in the cage, so I run out of shit-talk. Thank you."

So, by now, I've talked more than I ever would with an enemy. Jackson isn't aware until his body is slammed against the railing. My forearm levels across his throat. I grit out, "Next step, I snap your fucking neck." After that, the man behind me gets a swift foot to his throat. His neck snaps too.

"Maybe I'll take more of you mudaks down. Maybe you all will put enough bullets in me first. Remember, I die, everyone down here is dead. That includes you, Pops."

With my tattooed forearm constricting much of Jackson's breathing, I glance over to Maxwell. My wife's father has a hand up. Either he's ready to give the order to call off this farce, or he's executing orders for war.

" Vassili," Zariah stresses from her same spot. She's too smart to come down here. Too smart to enter ground zero because if I touch her, this charade is over. All I have to do is touch her, skim my hand over any part of her body. She'll remember just who the fuck she belongs too.

Zariah's voice is raw from crying as she says, "Vassili, your entire body is a weapon. Hands. Feet. So, go. I'll send you more papers."

"Nyet. Give me a moment to talk to you. I don't give a fuck if we have to chat in front of these piz'das!" I glare at Jackson for a moment. His heartbeat is raging against my forearm; his fingers biting against my skin. "Let me talk to you, Zar. Baby, let me talk to you."

"Vassili, it's the end of us. Don't worry. I won't abandon our children like your mother did to you."

All the venom in me fades. She won't see me. I stare up at her, eyelid twitching. She stays in the same spot, feet rooted to the ground. Our gazes connect. My look is enough to tell her that she's crossed the line. She's mentioned my mother.

7

1

Vassili
Two Months Ago, Australia

Kong's life is in my hands. My fists throb from the pounding I've given to his face, liver, and spleen. All of his vital organs are my target. I'm not doing it for the fucking belt. The Welterweight belt is at the tip of my fingers. Just a few more fights, but this one will go down in history.

All because it's Kong instead of Danushka.

My half-sibling is deranged enough to think my father loves me more. Her cunt of a mother waited a few days longer than mine to go into labor. I can feel her jealous gaze with each punch I offer Kong. Yesterday, my wife and Natasha were on their way to Australia. Her client's husband, a fucking gang member, stopped by our house. You'd think I had my sister to thank for that. Danushka murdered Noriega then . . . surprise, surprise, we learn that bitch was pretending to be my wife's ditzy friend. She's ditzy alright, ditzy enough to believe she can be chummy with me and my family. Danny's face is before my eyes as my fists slam into Kong's nose. Reconstructive surgery will be a necessity. I want to slow down and place him in a triangle-choke hold, knee-bar, or something.

I can't.

I'm not in the right frame of mind for submissions with Danushka seated next to my wife and daughter. I kick into the air with my left. The force sends my right foot flying into Kong's chest. He peddles back on the heels of his feet. The kick should've ended him, or he could just be standing there in a daze. With crazed eyes, I decide to put him down. Pulling power all the way through my toes, my punch slams into his nose.

BLAP. His nasal bones cave. Sweat drenches my muscles as the referee lunges in front of me. Kong's legs cave. He drops, with the ref on top of him. With him down, I climb up to the top of the cage, straddling it. My gaze searches through the crowd. Fist pumping in the air, I glare through a sea of mudaks to find my wife. Eyes sparkling, she blows me a kiss.

"I fucking love you!" I mouth.

Danushka pumps her hand near Zariah's face, breaking our connection. All the hot blood coursing through me runs cold as I remember the chat I'd had with Zariah before the match. She said to focus, to keep my mind on the game. Something dies in my soul at the thought of that cunt Danushka sitting with my daughter, my family.

I move my leg back over, toward the inside of the cage, and jump down onto the blood-painted canvas. The referee is still hovering over Kong, waving an ammonia-inhalant beneath his nose. With a hungry glare, I watch; dark thoughts rove through my mind. Deadly ones.

My heart barely slams against my chest. Adrenaline raw, I

stare through the ref as he continues to rouse the fighter with smelling salts.

He. Won't. Wake. Up.

But my mind is frozen to this moment. Kong laying, sprawled on the floor, means nothing. MMA means nothing.

Danushka did that to me. She killed my love. Maybe Kong died, maybe he's in a deep sleep for now. Fuck him; he was a means for me to get out my aggression. One day, Danushka will meet a worse fate. My hands hang at my sides, I smile at the thought of just how much pain they'll cause my sister. My callused fingers will feel her pulse stop. For now, fuck MMA.

"You put him in a coma," Vadim groans. The cement walls behind him are almost the same color as his ashen skin. We're in a dusty, old dressing room. While the old man can't fathom how Kong is still in a dream state, I feel nothing. My coach rubs a hand over his fallen face. "Come alive, Vassili. You-you put him in a coma! What the fuck is wrong with you?"

"Nothing!" I start to lunge at him. I'm a fraction of a foot away when the fear in his gaze stops me. This can't be happening. Vadim had the respect of my family ages ago, since I was a little mudak who had a bone to pick with the world. I take two steps back, rubbing my neck. I gesture again to play it off. "Nothing, Vadim."

Nestor gazes at me; he's too much in shock to speak.

A little while ago, the smelling salts haven't done their fucking jobs. Kong's wife's shouting slams through a sea of people.

"You tried to kill my husband. You—"

I have been in a daze the entire time. Nestor has to enter

the cage. I probably look like a bitch, handholding, skipping, shit like that as my team leads me through the crowd. The flashback fades. With hands in fists, I issue quick pops against my skull.

"Fuckkkkkk!" I roar. That's enough to make me come alive and remember my first love. *What the fuck am I without MMA?* I ask, "Is he dead?"

Nestor shrugs. "Let me text Yuri."

"Nyet!" I growl.

The Ukrainian cocks a brow, shoving his phone back in his pocket. "Why not? You asked if he died?"

Because I need Yuri and Mikhail at my wife and daughter's side at every fucking second. They have to keep watch while Danushka is around. This is something I can't talk about with my training team. My broad shoulders lift in a half attempt at a shrug. I grumble, "I don't give a fuck if he's dead. He should've been prepared to fight!"

"Don't be a shit-head," Vadim snaps.

"Injury goes with the territory, mudak!"

My coach steps toward me, bushy brows pulled together. The lion in me is ready to send him a few feet into the cement wall, but I allow my hands to hang at my sides. I need to feel the weight of them there. The numbness that had taken over me when I'd punched Kong's lights out is returning with a vengeance. The delight from watching him *stay down* starts to pull me under, to transform me into someone my wife doesn't know.

I need to focus on her beautiful face. I need to remember our daughter's laugh and keep moments like this for Danushka.

Not sure how much time has passed, but when I blink, my family has entered the room. Zariah paws my cheek. I start to push her away, then notice Yuri's still holding Natasha. My one-year-old is prepared to topple out of his arms to get to me. So, he keeps scooping her back up. Mikhail is at his side. Danushka too. I can tell Malich's oldest is trying his best to stay away from my sister. Mikhail, Yuri, and I—we're fucking dead right now.

I still can't fathom how Mikhail has gone from "God and Church" to being ready for murder. The death of their brother, Igor, has changed us all. While I am making moves to recreate a connection with his father, my Uncle Malich, I haven't noticed how hard it's hit me. Not until I got into the octagon. Of course, it has been bad from before.

It's worse now. I find myself pawing at Zariah's ass; my breath is at her forehead. Her dress is so tight that my dick is ready to slam straight through her wet pussy. Pressing my cock against her, I grip her ass, bringing her closer.

"That's love," Danushka clucks in agreement.

"Vassili." Zariah steps back in her stilettos, looking up at me. Her brown orbs track over mine. We've had arguments about how she wanted to fuck faces at parties—I've always refused.

"I'm good, girl." I step back. I pull her waist to me again. I press my lips to hers and kiss her like the piz'da of a father had kissed my mom. My tongue darts into her mouth, all the way down her throat. She moans, melting to me.

"Mmmm." Zariah presses her head against my chest. "I'm not used to all of that PDA stuff."

Tipping her chin, I whisper against her lips. "Tonight, my cock is going straight between those two chocolate cheeks of yours."

"Vassili." She slaps at my arm. With a sigh, she changes the subject, saying, "We argued our way back here—"

"I did all the arguing," Danushka says.

"Don't you speak!" My index finger goes straight to her forehead. "Don't speak to me."

"I love pain, big brat." She chuckles. "Don't stop . . ."

My eyebrows pull together. A million things are wrong with her request.

Zariah plants herself between us. Nobody seems to notice or care about Danushka. My wife says, "An ambulance took Kong almost an hour ago."

An hour . . . How could that be? Vadim had been arguing with me, and then I'd blinked. Now, my family is right before us. It couldn't have been an hour.

Zariah licks her lips in trepidation. "We have to visit the hospital to check on Kong."

"Or do we?" Danushka asks.

"Vadim, Nestor." I turn to my team. "Can you guys go see if the place is cleared out?"

They exchange looks before heading toward the double doors. Natasha lunges herself into my arms.

"Cutie Pie," Yuri growls, catching her at the knees so that she doesn't fall face-first.

I grab my daughter. She feels good, soft, innocent. I almost want to send her home to Zamora Hankins, my wife's mother. I don't need good, soft shit right now. I need to put Danushka in her place.

My sister speaks first. "Nyet, no time for Kong. We'll send him flowers if it behooves you, Zar. We have to get to Italy. Horace is awaiting us."

"Fuck you, fuck that mudak that you brainwashed into marrying you." I place my hand over Natasha's ears. "Fuck everything about you, Danushka."

"Are we done with the toddler squabble? That piz'da, Kong, may have taken one too many hits from you, but me," she pauses. With a wide grin, Danushka opens the tailored blazer she's wearing. The pearl handle of a revolver is shown for a split second. "Remind me that we're blood, *brat*."

Mikhail is in her face in an instant. It's so quick I jump

back, pressing my daughter to me. I can't fault him for wanting to put her down in front of my seed.

Yuri grabs his arm. "Not here, Brat!"

"Then where, Yuri, Mikhail. Where?" Danushka's faux blue eyes trackback across them all. She was born with brown eyes, is taller, and built like a fucking ox. Now, for Horace, my father's once assassin has become a fuck toy—just as postal. "Where the fuck do you plan on biting the hand who wants to feed you? To help your family become invincible like we once were. The Bertolucci's—"

Mikhail's arm moves in a flash. I have to hand it to my fat cousin Yuri because he's even quicker. Danushka's mention of the Bertolucci family retaliating on ours, which led to their brother Igor's death, has crossed the line.

"Alright, Mikhail." Zariah presses a hand to his chest. "You're better than this, than her."

I watch her tiny hand against his suit. He wore it yesterday while driving like mad to get to Zariah before Noriega could murder her and Natasha. Only, Danushka arrived at our home first. One devil died. The other is glaring up at her cousin.

Zariah's tiny hand moves with every hitch of breath he takes.

"Don't do it, kuzen," I say. Although I'm all words right now, if Mikhail attacks, we all attack.

"Thank you, brat." Danushka nods at me. "Honestly, time is of the essence. Kong is of no importance. It's not our fault that he was no match for a Russian bull."

I gaze away from her as she compliments me.

"We still must meet with Horace."

"Why?" I growl.

"Our father's death is of the utmost importance to the Bratva. Now rather than later, I always say." She brushes a manicured hand over her tailored suit, grooming herself at the mention of murdering our father.

She wants to be king. She wants me to be the substitute who sits at the table of seven and pretends to call the shots. She wants me to be a fucking robot who speaks her words, but the dead don't speak.

Zariah

The last 36 hours have zipped by like a whirlwind. It's taken over three hours for us to leave the convention center. Media outlets have surrounded the place, craving a statement from Killer Karo. When we finally enter the suite, Yuri and Mikhail go to the room on the far side. Danushka claims the couch. Vassili holds a cranky Natasha who rubs her eyes and whimpers. She's a bully without sleep.

I slip off my stilettos as Vassili places Natasha into a crib borrowed from the hotel. Reaching behind me, I start to undo the zipper of the couture dress my new "best friend" bought me. If Danushka weren't threatening my life after my encounter with Noriega, she would've placed me in the best-friend zone. This trick acts like the past couple of days haven't transpired.

Vassili's callused hand goes over mine. He stops me from unzipping the dress. Stepping behind me, his sweaty scent infuses into my nostrils. He still hasn't taken a shower since the fight, though he did wash off the bit of blood on his marble face. Now, I have no qualms with how he presses his lips at the nape of my neck.

"Vassili, should we take this party into the tub," I murmur. My breath hitches in my throat as the zipper moves titillatingly slow down my back. Cool air teases down my spine, then my husband leaves a trail of soft kisses. The sensation becomes a ribbon of a moan in my mouth. "Baby, we should . . ."

"Nyet," he grumbles from deep in his abdomen, moving to his knees. I reach out for the column at the foot of the bed while my knees turn to jelly as his kisses fall toward my lower back. "Tonight, I will worship this body, in all its glory."

I shudder, having lost my voice. My feet move a fraction of an inch as he removes the dress from my curves. Heartbeat slamming in my ears, I wait for his lips to caress the small of my back that leads to the meat of my ass. He doesn't. My body is flooded and invigorated by how his mouth has tasted me only a few times. Damned him.

"Vassili . . ." I whimper just as my husband pops up.

I'm spun around and pressed against the column so swiftly that a yelp doesn't have time to catch up. Vassili presses his body to me. He leans forward, kissing the curve of my neck, his tongue swirls around that spot. He's swirling so perfectly that I move my hips, widening my stance, my treasure is as jealous as can be.

Natasha's breath starts to taper off in her crib. I groan, "Babe, let's go . . ."

"Nyet," he finally says. "I promised to worship you, worship this body." His fingertips trail down the arc of my side cleavage. His gaze roves over my face. I feel an inescapable pull towards his lips, even though my body is now achy and fully supported by the column. His fingertips continue their decline along the shape of me. His low

Russian voice is hardly an audible rumble. "Worship all these beautiful, dark sweets, in all your glory," he growls. "But I'll do so in all my glory."

Conjuring all my energy, I exhale then lean forward. My lips meet his and warmth blossoms across my chest, tingling and rippling all over me. "All your glory?" The words tumble from my mouth, hardly audible. In a daze, I ask, "Hmmm, that means you're fucking me now?" *Please don't stop touching me.* I wait on bated breath. Damn him! I'll take this man dirty as hell. He's a Russian god to me.

"Dah," Vassili replies, pulling the compression shirt over him.

There I go, using the column as my support again. I lean my head back, hungry eyes viewing art. Every inch of his body is dripping in tattoos, muscles. My mouth pools at the thought of seeing him naked, but he stops from removing his pants. I've known Vassili for just shy of a decade, and everything about him is still the greatest: sex, touch, love. Amazed, I shake my head a little.

Like he can read my mind, a cocky smile flashes before my gaze as Vassili descends again. He sinks into my arms, his mouth taking to mine. I drown in the taste of him. Our tongues dance, colliding for so long that I'd happily die in this moment, in his arms.

"Fuck," my husband says, coming up for air. His heartbeat hammers into mine. I lean back against the column again, feeling damn near tipsy off of his mouth.

He moans from down low in his abdominals while snatching up the golden, shimmery dress.

"What are you doing?" My eyebrow arches.

"It's a dress fit for a queen, my queen. And I'm the mudak who never did a thing to deserve this, so I have to prove otherwise." With tender hands, Vassili helps me back into the snug-fitting designer outfit.

19

"You deserve me," I murmur, as his hands smooth the dress back over my hips. The entire movement has my brain going delirious and my pussy screaming for attention that we're doing it wrong. But no. We are doing this so, so damn right. My husband is reinventing foreplay with the focus he gives my body. He kisses my shoulder, smoothing the shimmery material over my ass.

"No," I moan when he begins to zip me up. He stands. My eyes are ablaze with curiosity. If I could've seen myself now, I would swear I'm smiling at him like I am 18 again. Back then, Vassili scared and enticed me at the same time.

He steps back, again, my body wavers beneath his heated gaze. Shaking his head, the look in his gaze tells me never to change. "Girl, if I could get you pregnant right now . . ."

Innocent heat flutters across my cheeks. Damn, Vassili's staring at me like this is the first time. I chuckle softly, pressing my hand over the gold material covering my flat abdomen. Delighted, I murmur, "Vassili, I'm having your baby. Happily pregnant again by you. You're so crazy, boy. So, so crazy."

Shaking my head, I rise to the tips of my toes to taste him again. Vassili cups my cheeks between his palms, his dark orbs are smoldering even further as his eyes rove across my face. He presses a kiss to my forehead. "Shit, girl, you look so good in that motherfucking dress. I'm about ready for you to come out of it again."

I laugh from deep in my body. We can both be committed in this second. Feels like happy drugs are pulsating through my veins, happy drugs, and a few shots of Resnov Water. The fighter, *my fighter*, slaughtered a man in the cage tonight, then he treats me infinitely better than I could ever imagine a man treating a woman.

His square jaw nudges behind me. "Remove your panties, get in bed, ass all in my face."

Moving my hands behind me, I start for the zipper of the shimmery material. But his palms are over the back of mine again. Vassili's warm breath sets my skin on fire.

His voice is passionate, slow as he says, "Did I give you orders for the dress?"

"No, but I thought the entire scenario was to get me out of it, again," I whimper. Though I won't voice that I'm torn between loving every single second of us doing so, I'm also torn by wanting us naked in a flash.

His hand clamps softly over my throat, ceasing my defiance. All those giddy moments that remind me of falling for him flee. All that's left is hard passion.

Vassili's stone-carved, handsome face leans in until his lips are a breath away from mine. Half elated, half terrified that I'm in trouble, I wait for his reply. Punishment, praise, whatever he offers, comes with attention; it includes *him worshiping me.*

"You want to be worshiped tonight, girl?"

His hard, Russian tone and those delectable words unravel the past 36 hours. The image of Noriega holding a gun to my face and Natasha's face has been whisked into oblivion. All that's left is desire sparking across my entire body. Damn straight, I have a mouth that knows every angle of my man's cock; it also knows how to say too much. So, I moan my response, nodding slowly. He offers another squeeze. This one takes my breath away.

"Khorosho," Vassili tells me 'good' in Russian. His voice becomes a low, rasp as he orders, "Lift your dress up. Lift it just enough, girl. Enough for me to see the bottom of that meaty ass and those fat pussy lips."

Like a chameleon, the good fighter vanished, leaving me standing before the guy *I knew* was bad the second I laid eyes on him.

I have never felt so good in a dress. I owe that to Vassili, that and the fact that he makes me feel perfect in my own dark brown skin. He's right, the garb fits every inch of me, elevating my beauty to its own Black Queendom. Pressing my hand over my shimmery dress, I start to inch it upwards. Vassili steps back in the grand bedroom. His thick, muscular body owns the entire area as he watches me. The expensive material glides up my curvy, dark brown hips.

"Panties first." He sniffs.

I slide my panties down and entice him with the sight of me lifting my tight dress. The material hugs where the apex of my sex meets. The bulbous part of my ass is on display, lips glistening. This man can get me off with a smoldering gaze.

"Stop."

Following his command, I await another order from the fighter. My inner and outer folds start to jump, dancing in anticipation.

He gestures toward the bed. "Climb up, move slow."

When I turn around, a subtle hitch comes from his throat. I clench the sheets for a second. My limbs are unsteady. The air is cool against my ass, against my pussy that's peeking between my cheeks as I climb up toward the headboard. To be honest, I love the smell of Vassili after a match. We've joked about it before. He's a sportsman. I don't care.

"Hold formation, Zariah," he says.

My nails are imbedded in the ultra-soft sheets now. I expect a swat to my ass, but Vassili comes over. I can feel the warmth of his mouth as he breathes in my pussy. I clutch harder as he presses his lips against my throbbing labia.

"I missed you," he tells my pussy. My slick walls spasm. The warmth of his breath, reminding my treasure of how lonely it is without his dick.

"Vassili," I murmur.

My husband curses under his breath; a low rumble of a growl sends shivers along my spine.

"Shhhh…" Again his breath sends tiny thrills against my slit. "I remember drinking a fifth of vodka out your cunt, Zar."

Callused hands cup my flesh as he rubs my ass and hips. He explores my dark brown curves while eating my pussy from behind. His hand slams down at *that* very spot. At the same time, pain radiates across my skin, Vassili's tongue plunges deep into me.

Heaven flashes before me. "Fu-fuck, Vassili. Oh, do it again."

"I do it again, Zar, it has to hurt more."

My lower back curves. His palm continues to slither over one ass cheek and then the other. A hard breath comes from Vassili. His mouth moves faster than before, licking up all my juices as I rock. My body cums on his stiff tongue.

My body sags. The first orgasm was enough to leave me depleted, but I wouldn't dream of falling out of position on my hands and knees.

Grunting barbarically, he pulls out of his sweats and drops his trunks. I gawk. There's n shame in my desire for my husband. He picks up the belt that must've been discarded at some other time. My gaze flies over the colorful etching of tattoos in his arms as Vassili weighs the belt. The belt slams down onto my ass cheek. With it, an imaginary inferno strikes my skin. He holds up the belt, poised to offer another strike, but stops. With the left side of his lips cocked, Vassili drops the belt. His hand comes down over my ass crack and pussy. His fingertips offer a surprising sting against my clit. Hand cupped, he continues to spank my pussy. Delirious delight clouds my brain.

"More, Daddy," I beg.

There isn't an ounce of pain, only pleasure as it builds. I welcome the eruption of my cumming in his palm.

He continues to smack until my pussy creates a sing-song sound of the wetness he covets. "That's right, Zar. Get that pussy wet for me. This little spanking has my entire hand soaking wet."

As the sound continues, I clutch the sheets again. Vassili slides down beside me, his colossal frame commands much of the bed. He holds up his candy-coated fingers and palm, then slides them across my cheek.

"Hey," I gasp, though my tongue dips out for a taste.

While commanding the entire bed, Vassili reaches up, grips a fist full of my hair, and licks the wetness from my cheek. He fists my hair, bringing me close enough to lick my cheek.

I move from my doggie-style position until I'm sitting on my bottom. I take in every brick that's come together to make his body. He's staring at me again, the way any woman would crave for a man to desire her. I'm lost in his mesmerizing eyes, cheeks burning once more like I'm new to this. Like my first time.

I notice how quiet the room is, aside from Natasha's dreamy sigh. Vassili holds up his wet hand. He paws his cock, massages his balls, and arches an eyebrow. That look tells me I am ready to service him.

My eyes fly to his erection, soaring like a friggen skyscraper in the city. I clasp his cock with one hand, ready to deep throat him. The back of my hand sears with pain as he slaps it.

"Damn you, Vassili," I growl, a giddy chuckle still riding through me too. The second my tongue tastes his salty cock. I proceed to deep throat him. No hands per his silent, almost lethal request. The back of my hand continues to prickle in pain as I knock my throat with his lengthy erection.

24

"Relax your jaws," he replies.

I start to look up at him. His stiff Russian accent is different. Not by much, but I wonder how Kong's ordeal has heaped onto everything else. My tongue massages the veins on the sides of his fat cock before I pull him back inside of my mouth. Not an inch is left inside of my mouth. I'm full of cock as I suck with vigor. I catch a rhythm, twining my tongue around his hefty girth. His cock hypnotizes me enough to take the beast to the head. An ache begins between my thighs. With my mouth working him hard, I fuck myself happy too. Another orgasm is ready to drench down my hands when—

"Good, good." He flips us until my face is smothered in the pillow and his cock is knocking at my tight ass.

With a naughty laugh from deep in his abdomen, Vassili moves so quickly that my back arches. His cock spears deep inside of my pussy. My eyes roll back in my head.

"Oh shit . . ." A deep, low groan vibrates across my tonsils. "Yes, yes!"

My pussy walls quiver, attempting to strangle his cock as he hits it from the back. Part of me wants my pussy to put a death grip on his piece for him to cum in an instant. The other part of me is in ecstasy that this night will continue to last until the first light. While he strokes my valley with his manhood, I reach between us and work my clit.

"That's right, fuck your little clit," Vassili groans, transitioning from endearing to full-blown alpha.

I sigh, submitting this moment to memory. While on top of me, his chest crushes my back. Vassili's powerful body is running along me. His strong hands cup my ass and glide across my curves.

"Vassili," I purr from deep down in my throat, drowning in another orgasm.

"Zar-iii-ah," he groans. "You're so fucking wet, girl. Don't make me do it. Don't make me cum yet."

The orgasm torpedoes. My teeth bite down into the pillow. A million sparks torture my body. I want to beg Vassili to cum. I'm speechless, can't open my mouth except to moan.

"Nyet, not yet." Vassili's hand clutches the back of my neck, and he moves his dick like a piston. It's faster and faster so that he can please me longer—when I could never be happier. The heaviness of his magnificent erection stretches my slick walls so good, satiating my entire body. Vassili is all dirty grunts and cusses as he works his way deep inside of me.

I glance back at him. His muscles compress and relax with each rapid thrust. Licking my lips, I slowly start to work my ass against him. Tears blur my vision.

"Vassili," I scream. He's clamping down on my clit as I cum all over him again.

"Fuck, Zar, keep trying to milk my cock," he groans.

His words sound like pure erotica in my ear. My ass claps hard against his taut body. His balls thrust at my leg. I work my clit with the same power his dick drives through my body. "Damn, I'm cumming, Vassili, I'm cumming."

My face falls forward. His thrusts reach deep into my throbbing walls. My legs are too weak to hold me up. Vassili reaches forward, clasping the back of my neck, forcing his cock into me. I have to turn my face to stop from suffocating.

"Oh my, oh shit," I start stuttering as he begins to explode. Vassili yanks me up and plants my face against his groin, offering me the taste of life.

My eyes peel open. Across from me, Natasha is still sprawled in the crib. Her sheets have been kicked down to her feet in the middle of the night. I turn over in the bed, almost expecting to be disappointed.

Why? I'm not sure.

Vassili's dark gray eyes—he swears they aren't gray—are peering up at the ceiling. He glances over at me. "You okay about all of this?"

I hide a smile. "About what?"

The sex was so good, so mind freeing last night that moments pass before the rest of our 'current' lives dawn on us: Danushka, Anatoly, all the drama from his family. I say, "You were Doctor Jekyll and Mr. Hyde last night. First, you reminded me of the day I fell in love with you—at first sight. That should never have been possible; then you gave me rough sex and . . ." I groan, licking my lips. "How long have we been asleep?"

His mouth presses down on mine for a deep in-love kiss. "An hour, Zar. *That was good.* And you know I'm not talking about that, girl. I'm talking about, Danny, Noriega, and—" His words transform into a low, seeded roar.

"Hey, don't go all Hulk-Smash on me, Vassili. I knew what you were referring to. We *are* a team, so I focused on the good stuff." I reach between us to graze my fingers over his square jaw. We haven't addressed Noriega, not in the slightest. How do you mention a dead man when someone else is a more significant threat to your life? Skimming the line of his chiseled features, I say, "Last night was perfect. Every single second I'm with you, I'm so happy, baby. You saved me, Vassili."

3

Vassili

Why the fuck does she have to say that?

That's just it. I didn't save Zariah. Never deserved her. Last night I might have been able to blind my wife for a moment with good dick, but dark times are coming.

Yesterday, I was a world away when my wife and daughter needed me the most.

My mother abandoned me and my sister, Sasha.

My baby sister got it worse than me.

I've finally gotten something to call my own—Zariah, Natasha, the little boy that's just starting to in my wife's belly. My wife's stomach is still flat, but she has to be giving me a son.

We'd had a massive fight after Igor's death. I'd left her to fight with my father and didn't keep up with the cases Zariah has taken. She's a homemaker now—but she doesn't know that yet. The fight dug its roots in me. It made me feel unsteady, and I didn't follow through. She'd said, *"Vassili, you go away to fight in Australia in three weeks. I dare you to run off before then. I will find you and drag your ass home. Now, do you want to see the ultrasound? That's your gesture to me that you plan to take care of our home."*

Instead of taking care of our home, I am headed to Australia. I'd left my life, my most valuable possessions at home, so that Zariah could handle a case.

She and my daughter are my home. These things cannot happen again. Once Danushka is handled, I will see about anyone else affiliation with Noriega. Hell, that bitch of a half-sister might be hard to shake. I'll have to reach out to my father before then, reach out, and not tell him that his own daughter has a hit on his head.

He'll think I traded teams though I've never been a fan of him, the Bratva, or her. For now, I concentrate on Zariah. She thinks I saved her.

Fuck, I did nothing.

"How?" I ask.

My wife smirks. "Thank you works."

"That bitch saved you from Noriega. She brings it up every chance she gets."

Zariah clasps my jaw. "The night before last, I arrived with Danushka. You and I didn't get a chance to talk, Vassili. You had the match . . . Your win got overshadowed by Kong."

"I'm not thinking about him," I growl.

"Okay, let's talk. I'd rather have waited until we were not in bed. Maybe we could have skipped this whole discussion about Danny. Maybe she will disappear. But she's irrelevant?"

I scoff.

"You want to know why?"

"Nyet," I mutter, shrugging my shoulders.

"Because she's one person. One vindictive, *emotional person*. Who taught me not to fight with emotions, Vassili?"

Rubbing the back of my neck, I consider how I'm not all that confident my wife is a match for Danushka. Should I tell her so? Fuck no! I mumble, "I did."

"That's right, you taught me, Vassili." She cups my cheeks, looking up at me. "You're a beast in the cage, and you've trained me to fight too. She's our opponent. We're a—"

I roll off her.

Here we go.

The "we are a team" bullshit got me into the latter situation with her. I set my mouth to grant her every lie she needs to hear, but the words don't come out.

Zariah bolts up into a seated position, reaching out for me. "Vassili?"

We will never be a team. Well, unless that shit has anything to do with teaching Natasha or my son with a sport. Other than that, I don't need her by my side when I handle *my* family.

"Baby, we haven't had a moment alone until late last night. Thank you for sharing a lovely night with me, but you brought this up. So, we're at that point where it's imperative that we discuss how to get rid of Dan—"

"Zariah," I growl. My heart is ready to implode in my chest. I never wanted her around another Resnov, to begin with. Only me and only blood—the kids we were to have. I lie, "We will figure something out together. Not here. The bitch is in the same place. Let's wait till we get home. Alright?"

I only needed this lie to get her off my back about Danushka. Other than for her safety, I'd never lie to Zariah. My cousins and I need to have a chat. We can't do that with Natasha and Zariah here. My family needs to go home under the protection of someone.

Mikhail and Yuri are sitting on stools, leaning across the pony table when Zariah and I walk out of our bedroom. Natasha is on Zariah's hip. My wife presses her hands over Natasha's ears and nudges her chin to Danushka. The bitch is out cold on a pullout couch. She's indecent. I glance away and gag.

"We should . . ." Zariah begins to whisper, pointing at the front door.

Natasha squirms and pushes at her.

Yuri holds up an index finger. We can leave right now. The look in Mikhail's eye warns that leaving isn't his top priority. Months ago, I found out Danushka had sent me emails about a deceased fucking cop—who *wasn't* a fucking cop. It was her attempt at a brain fuck. It had taken Yuri's father ages to find her. Malich exhausted all resources before Danushka reached out. I have to keep an eye on my older cousin, Mikhail, the doctor. He's liable to forget all the preaching and praying he's done in his life. He'll fuck all that good shit up for his baby brother, Igor.

"Don't leave on my account," Danushka says in a muffled voice. "Oh, and Zariah, I thought you'd be the last one to suggest such a thing. Shame on you, friend."

Zariah stops toddler boxing our daughter, who's winning the fight. "We were heading to breakfast . . . *leave us all alone.*"

I grip her about the waist. The fucking attorney in her was ready to debrief me a while ago with a meaningless pep talk. My lips land against her earlobe. "We're a team, Zar," I mumble in her ear, hoping to God that I sound legit.

"Can you cover yourself?" Zariah grits at her now. I've kept my gaze away from the little psycho, so I start over to my cousins.

Yuri whispers to me, "Can you leave Zar and Natasha with—"

I give a low growl, "Yuri, how the fuck can you ask that?"

"We need a game plan," Mikhail grits.

"I'm sorry," Yuri caves.

His big brother glowers at him now. The strong front they'd had a second ago has disappeared.

"They're friends," Mikhail whispers back. "As far as Danny's word goes, Zar and Natasha have to be safe. Let the girls have a day shopping before *we* go to Italy. While they're away, we can figure out how to get Danny and Horace. Kill two birds. . ."

Zariah gasps.

All of our eyes go toward her, even Natasha. Danushka holds out an iPhone.

My wife blubbers, "Th-that . . . that . . . that . . ."

Danushka turns toward us, using a throw pillow between her chest and still fisting the phone. "My brat, Grigor, has . . . Excuse me, Vassili, I mean *our brat*—"

"Half," I grumble.

"You think Grigor is some little shit. He's a sharpshooter. Anatoly never knew how important his son was to the Bratva because he was stuck dangling on your balls. Everyone thought Grigor was the brains. Vassili, you are brawns. But me and Grigor—we're brawns and brains. And that's why you're going to help us kill—"

"Zariah, what the fuck?" I cut her off as Zariah holds her hands over her face. Her fingers are trembling.

Danushka glances at the iPhone, and then rolls her eyes. "I must've clicked out of the video application. As I said, Grigor is a sharpshooter."

Zariah exclaims, "Gr-Grigor murdered one of the secretaries at our law firm. From across the street!"

My half-sister pats her shoulder. "Sheesh, sweetheart, you act as if you weren't less than a foot away from a body. Hello, we left Noriega's body to one of my husband's men. You know death, *now*."

"How many men does your husband have," Yuri asks.

Silence ensues as everyone now turns to him. He shrugs. "I thought I'd try it. Zariah tried it earlier. Why not, eh?"

"Oh, cousin, my husband has so many men on his team. We couldn't possibly vet a seat on the Seven—Anatoly's seat —without foot soldiers."

"Well, now we know," he gestures. "Lots of men."

"And Anatoly has removed his blessing from your father, Malich. Yuri, you should consider joining—"

"The fuck he has," I growl. "My . . . my . . ." Shit, I almost called the mudak, my pops. There's a first time for everything.

Danushka places her hands on her hips. "You meant our father. And how do you know, curious minds are inquiring. How are you aware that Anatoly still has a place in his cold, stony heart for his brat?" She places an arm around Zariah.

There's a slight gleam in my wife's eyes. She wants to know too. There's no way in hell I'll mention that Anatoly has come around a time or two. It dawns on me. I went to him last month—it ended up with Zariah and I fighting. So, my wife can't fault me for a visit she knows about. "Anatoly still backs Malich. I spoke to him."

"Brawns, yeah, that's what you have." Danushka laughs, stepping toward me. "You listened to our father."

My hand grips her neck. "Brawns? Huh? What else do I need besides brawns to end you, bitch?"

Zariah tugs at my arm. I slide her hands away from me. Natasha is at her side, attempting to pull me from Danushka. The bitch gasps for air as my little heart falls on her bottom. Natasha scampers up. After reading all those baby books, I can only pray to God Natasha is too young to remember me choking the life from her half-aunt.

"Stop, Vassili," Zariah screeches. "Yuri, Mikhail, make him stop!"

"Why?" Mikhail growls my word as my grip around Danushka's neck tightens.

Zariah gasps, "Grigor's sniper rifle is on your father—Mikhail, Yuri. Your father! Grigor is ready to strike!

Fire burns across my skin. I woke up on the wrong side of the bed this morning, the side where confidence ruled. The side where obliviousness worked. The side where I forgot not to underestimate my fucking half-sister.

4

Zariah

I have been selective with my words. These past few weeks, nightmares have plagued our family. So, I endeavored not to blurt out that I saw a live-streaming video of a tiny red dot in the middle of Malich's forehead. He's been in a somber mood in his bedroom. Danushka warns that it's punishment for joking about leaving her at the hotel a few minutes ago. Now, I reach down and bite the bile back into my throat while helping her stand.

Danushka's body goes flush against mine. The silk blouse she's wearing is hardly buttoned; it presses against mine. Tiny breasts warm against me, nipples hard. Her breath sends creepy waves across my cheek.

She murmurs, "Thank you, friend."

The coupling of her actions and the look in her expensive "blue" eyes sends vomit burning a line up my throat. With a gulp, I reply, "You're welcome."

I glance over at Vassili. He's huddled with the guys. They're the team I should be a part of, but with a sociopath at my side, I have to bide my time before I can help my family. The glint in my gaze tells them not to act.

No form of retaliation will help Malich, while Grigor is in a rented mansion across the street from his. The term rock and a hard place mean nothing. We're fucked.

The sun slams down on us. The scent of fish guts doesn't churn my stomach anywhere near as much as Danushka does. Seagulls swoop low, squawking around in search of food. The wooden planks shake with each move we make. Vassili plucks Natasha up into his arms. He starts to pull me near him, but Danushka grips me on the opposite side, pressing us hip to hip. Now, my husband won't touch me. At the end of the dock is a ruined fisher's wharf. Standing before it is a man with a square-shaped face. A group of men is around him.

Horace Molotov.

"That's my Horace, Zariah. I underwent the scalpel almost thirty times just to catch a man like him." She bats her faux blue eyes again, and I'm left to determine if she believes he's handsome. He does exude power, even from twenty yards away. She continues to drone on, "Shorter, skinnier, higher cheekbones—I did it all for his attention."

With a pep in her step, Danushka runs ahead, toward him.

"Who is he?" I ask.

"He was your father-in-law's right-hand man," Yuri shares. "That mudak got the seat at the seven that our father declined. One of the first, who isn't blood to have a say."

Mikhail continues with the quiet rage he has going, and I suspect Vassili isn't in the mood to talk.

We continue, although very slowly, heading toward the pier. I scoff. "It's clear Horace no longer needs that seat."

"Zariah." Vassili steps before me. "I'll have a word with Danushka. She'll send you and Natasha home."

My hands go to my hips as I stare at him. "No, that won't work because the second I leave Danushka's side, you'll forget that you have a wife, a child, and a growing baby to return to. Either things are going to go your way and 'light's out for Danushka.' Or shit ends badly . . ."

"And lights out for my father," Mikhail huffs.

They exchange glances. The plans they'd cooked up, while I entertained Danushka all the way to Italy, are hidden by marble-carved faces.

"I'm the attorney, Vassili-baby. The fucking mediator—until we find a true opening. Let me do this." I start ahead as Danushka calls out for us. I don't require my husband's response, don't need it.

"My darlings," she says, clapping her hands together. I slip against her side, taking her awaiting arm. Horace holds his hand out.

"Mrs. Resnov." His fleshy lips hardly move as he locks gazes with mine. With Vassili over ten yards away, he says, "You and my wife are so beautiful together."

With her arm around me, Danushka strums a few fingers down my cheek. She purrs, "We truly are. After my father's death, the three of us can celebrate in one of my rooms. Drinks, lingerie, games. Or the four of us, though I doubt Vassili would . . . Zar, would he?"

"No," I stutter, almost positive that she's mentioning group sex. Yet, this might be the first time in my life that I opt not to read into someone's statement.

"That's too bad," Horace says with a grin. He starts past me, prepared to shake more hands.

37

Vassili looks him up and down. "Put your fucking hand down, mudak! I know exactly who you are. We all do."

At his sides, his cousins also have their square jaws held high.

Horace clears his throat. "Well, perhaps I should reintroduce myself. A new era is upon us, Vassili."

"What are your plans?" Yuri gestures. "My entire family has seats at the seven. My uncles, my aunt—"

"Nyet, not precisely," Danushka cuts in. "No woman truly has a seat at the seven, Yuri. Our aunt's husband has that seat. Malich forfeited his seat, now my husband has it."

He chuckles. "How many piz'das is this guy married to? Because I've gone to enough of your weddings Horace. No divorces. Danny, I thought you had balls. Now you're just a little blond piz'da on his payroll with a momentary title."

Those doctored eyes of hers cloud with tears. "Don't make me cry, Yuri. You're the nicest cousin I have . . ."

"Yes, don't make my wife cry, Yuri," Horace grits. "Grigor is ready to put down your father at any given second. Play nice."

Vassili hands me Natasha and moves to his face. Mikhail's stiff-arm pushes me even further back.

Vassili growls, "Horace, keep making threats.You'll find yourself in an unmarked grave before you can blink."

The men behind us begin to edge for the back of their blazers and suit jackets.

Horace's entire body tenses.

"Alright, guys," I cut in, hoisting Natasha on my hip. Her bright brown eyes glance around, anticipating an action she shouldn't ever be aware of. "Let's talk out a game plan. You want your father dead, Danny. He's never been there for you. Vassili, I presume the same scenario, different story. Let's hash out our plan."

5

Vassili

Over the years, Anatoly and I have shed each other's blood. My knuckles have throbbed after more fights with him than any opponent in the octagon. The last time I choked him, craving to dominate the last of his life source, I had reason to stop. My cousin, Simeon, would've done me in. At the time, I'd have met my maker and reaped the consequences. Heaven or hell. No problem.

But I can't do him in. No matter how many years Anatoly shaved from my mother's life, I can't do it.

Horace has us all seated around the table. Natasha is asleep against my chest; her breath is at my ear. It's all I need to remind me not to be numb to the entire situation and go off. Zariah was on the right track when she'd mentioned playing mediator. I can almost see myself to the point of ending it for all of us if Natasha was not in my arms right now. As an impatient man, I'd have fought until my last breath. Instead, I'm seated and hugging pure innocence. My left hand clasps my wife's thigh under the table.

"Before we get shit started," I begin. "Horace, you look at my wife the way you did when we walked up, I'm liable to forget—"

Danushka cuts in, "Grigor—"

"I'm liable to fucking forget about Grigor having a sniper rifle," I finish in a growl. "I'm liable to forget all the wrongs my *mudak* of a father has done and kill you instead."

"I will respect her as if she were my own *babushka*." Horace's head dips. "Now, I would've rather we all meet at one of my homes in Moscow, but I'm sure Anatoly has received word that you're all here with me."

Yuri shakes his head. "Don't think we're working with you, yet. We may not grant our blessing for Anatoly. We may stay out of it."

"You can stay out of it then," my half-sister spits. "My brat and I have everything covered."

First, I assume she's speaking of Grigor. This delusional idiot smiles toward me. All the muscles in my body melt as I ask, "What's the plan to murder our father?"

Horace grimaces. "We're old friends, Vassili. Let's start with strengths. My new life coach swears by it. Setting a foundation with our strengths will solidify our relationship; after which, we can chat executing various outliers that would weaken said relationship."

"What the fuck do you mean, various outliers?" I ask. Mikhail is seated on my opposite side. I purposefully took the spot next to him. If he snaps, we're all dead.

"We won't extinguish everyone in the seven," Horace advises. "Anatoly's family. Simeon's mother and father—his entire family must expire. Also, you all may not be aware, but I have a very good friend in the Seven now. His name is Don Roberto Dominicci—"

"Nyet!" Yuri shakes his head. "That can't be true!"

"You'd dismantle an entire operation?" Mikhail rubs his temple. "It's blasphemy for an Italian . . . "

"It's the Bratva," I cut in, agreeing with him. "There are no Italians at the Table of Seven."

Horace grins sheepishly. "He is the first Italian at the Table of Seven. I inducted him myself."

"You don't have that right," Mikhail scoffs.

"Dominicci is a billionaire, so . . ."

"So?" Yuri wouldn't get it if it bit him in the ass the fact that Money is King. These idiots are blinded by power, with a few screws loose in their brains.

Horace laughs. "So, we will rule as one, with capital and physical force. We are not all lucky to be born as a Resnov as you see." He nods toward Zariah.

Danushka's face brightens with a smile. "The future is diversified. I, for one, am happy to advocate for interracial relationships." She plucks up Zariah's hand, holding it high.

"This is bullshit," Yuri mutters about Danushka ruining everything.

My wife rolls her eyes removing her hand from Danny. "I take it. I'll be the token black woman of this shindig."

"Black people don't—" Horace cuts himself off.

"Finish your statement," I growl.

"Yeah," Zariah chimes in with a chortle. "Maybe you should since the Bratva has become a multicultural establishment. How do I inquire about a discrimination policy?"

"Oh, friend." Danushka laughs along with her.

The chair scrapes the cement floor so hard that one of the wooden legs snap off. I lunge from my seat. The fighter in me feigns for something to break, someone to break.

Yuri's eyes are questioning. We've exchanged very few words while entering the room. Those fucking words have gone something like this: *We're all pussies.* At this moment, we can't turn alpha and rip Horace and his crew a new hole.

Don't worry about Danushka. She became dead to me the second she came for my wife and daughter. I can taste her demise. Not now. We are fucked.

I'm a Russian bull who's consumed a bathtub filled with vodka and haven't gotten drunk. Tonight, vodka and champagne are poured freely. Though Horace is hiding out from my father, he's rented a villa inland for us to stay. That bitch-sister of mine is delusional enough to believe we're at a family reunion. Zariah and Natasha leave the main hall first, followed by Mikhail. For the most part, Danushka has kept one of her girls on Yuri and Mikhail in an attempt to stop us from communicating. She grants him mercy when Natasha becomes fussy.

I move across the mocha-colored clay tile, my boots padding the ground as my vision sways. The new glass of expensive champagne in my hand becomes the catalyst for my loss of reality.

What if Zariah decides this world isn't for her? The Resnovs, though I've kept her from, are like kings and queens. Aside from Danushka and Horace's half-brained power trip that will crash and burn, I've steered the bad away. All the Resnov heirs are marked. That mudak, Anatoly Jr., my father had attempts on his life when he was a kid. I grip at the stairwell, recalling how paranoid he can be. Even with enemies gunning for him, he still sits on top.

I feel someone watching.

With a groan, I turn so slowly that Mr. Overstreet dominates my mind for a second. The bastard was beating on Zariah's mother, Zamora. I ambushed him in his car one evening, and he couldn't quite turn around without peeing in his pants. I turn, and my boot misses a step. Letting out a tipsy chuckle, I slide to sit down on the stairs, staring down at an Italian.

"You keep following me, and I'll kill you!" I point my index finger, not quite meeting its mark. The motherfucker won't stop swimming before me.

"I . . . I have to," he stutters, staying on the bottom step.

"Sergio, Sergio?" My gaze narrows, and I rub at the stubble along my jaw.

He seems ready to backpedal, regardless of my sister's orders. Though he stays put, he licks his lips and asks, "Who is this Sergio?"

Rubbing a hand over my face, I mumble, "I killed that bitch a thousand times for my wife. You can't be Sergio . . ."

"No-no, I'm not. I have to ensure that you abide by the rules."

In a flash, I'm down the stairs separating us. "Rules, what rules?" My forearm slams into his throat as I continue to clutch the champagne. I bash his face in with a left hook.

"Don't follow me!" I growl the words my father often spat into the wind. Nobody would be following us from one whore house to the next.

"He's following you, brat." Danushka appears at my side. Her fingertips strum down the side of my jaw. I push at her, but she stays there. "You should do something about it."

I sniff. "Then you send a message to that piz'da, Grigor."

"He's our brat, Vassili. Grigor wouldn't hurt you or what belongs to you. However, I suggest you do something to him," she points to the Italian, "...for following you." She stops caressing my jaw to grab the bottle of champagne from my hand. With a flick of her wrist, the bottle crashes against the wall near the Italian's head.

"Wha-what are you doing, Ms. Molotov?" he stutters. "These are your orders, your husband's orders!"

My forearm crunches against his throat, and I push him all the way back to the wall.

"You'll learn to join us, Vassili," Danushka purrs, holding out the neck of the bottle. "Why not now, brat? Consider it a peace offering."

Drops of champagne dot my boots as I take the jagged bottle. I press it into the man's stomach, imagining that it belongs to Danushka. His arms come out, slapping and popping, offering all the little swats that a bitch would. My dark gaze is wrought. I can't kill my half-sister yet, so he will have to do. After stabbing the bottle into his abdomen a few times, I continue holding him with my forearm. I jab and jab at him.

"Yes," Danushka shouts. "Yes. This is beautiful, brat." She grabs his chin; his brown eyes are questioning and filled with agony. "You're the first to see such beauty. Vassili and me!"

At the sound of her whiny, elated voice, I crack his neck.

The dead Italian falls at our feet.

I take a few steps back. This is a dream. No, this is a fucking nightmare. My knuckles are embedded with a few pricks from broken glass. I press my lips to the back of my hands and bite out the biggest shard.

"I could wash you," she says.

"Nyet," I growl. Something about my half-sister is broken. I don't mean the half that's willing to murder our father for notoriety. Her blue eyes are gleaming in lust. I start up the stairs.

"Vassili," she calls after me.

"What!" I glance back down at her. I'm halfway up the stairs, at the same spot I was when I got the paranoid feeling.

She tosses up a fresh bottle of champagne. "You're not ready for us to have the perfect night yet, Brat! We will one day."

"The fuck we will, Danny. You've always been a weird,

little shithead." I point two fingers at her. "Once you put Anatoly in the grave, I'm out."

Her head tilts. "I love you so much, Vassili. Maybe I'll never let you go."

I've already turned around. I continue up the steps with the new bottle of Dom in my hand. We were ten years old when Danushka first climbed in my bed. I punched the bitch in the throat and climbed out. Shortly after, Anatoly sent Sasha and me to the home of another one of his whores. Up until now, I've assumed she might have tried to kill me. That mudak, Anatoly, made me paranoid enough to believe it.

But now . . .

I shove that thought into the back of my brain. Along the corridor, I notice Mikhail lurking in the shadow. He comes from the darkness. The faint illumination from the skylight shines down on him.

I place my hand on his shoulder. "You good, kuzen?"

"Nyet."

"Are you going to fuck it up for all of us?"

A few beats pass. Like my wife, Mikhail can get lost in his thoughts for so long that I don't expect an answer. He mutters, "Nyet."

I shrug a little. "Go read your—"

"Nyet! I will not read my Bible. I will not pray till that cunt sister of yours is dead."

I give his shoulder another squeeze and let go.

"Was Yuri slamming his cock in one of her whores?" he asks.

"He's still drinking." I rub the back of my neck. "We're on Horace's turf, Mikhail."

"You said that before, and I won't play the part." He starts away from the bedroom that my wife and daughter are in. I hold out the uncorked champagne, but he sidesteps that as well. Mikhail mumbles something about a security camera in

45

the hallway. He enters one of the extra bedrooms for the night.

Jiggling the handle of the door, I find that it's locked from the inside. Since Natasha may or may not be sleeping, I whisper, "Zar?"

A few seconds later, the door is opened. My wife is dressed in cotton pants and a long, white tee, clothes that tell me there won't be any sex tonight. We can get to that later.

My eyes are drinking her in from head to toe, searching for any signs. Hurt, pain, I don't know what the fuck to expect when it comes to having her here. I can't keep her *safe* in this place!

"Vassili?" Zariah cocks her head.

I blink.

"Oh my gosh, you aren't listening to anything I say," she grumbles. I'm worried about my wife, and she's trying that one angle that I won't let her have: team. There's no way I'll let her help us out of this shitty-ass situation. But I listen to her reflect, "Do you think Mikhail and Yuri should sleep in the same room as they did at the suite in Australia?"

Her eyes are alight with questions. My wife will do anything to keep the peace. I tighten my jaw so that I don't end up saying something stupid. Something that will have the attorney arguing with me too.

"I appreciate Mikhail's unwavering loyalty. Vassili, he stood outside this door for three hours. I'm still not convinced he'll contain himself. He's liable to . . ."

Head dipped down, my mouth goes over hers, tongue darting inside hers, I close the door behind me, bringing Zariah's tiny waist with me. I lock it. Last night, I loved my queen. I needed to fuck her and show her that all the nightmares coming to us at every angle mean nothing. I needed to clear her fucking mind. Now, I need her love to free me. Though I won't allow her to help me fix things, I have to

46

know that none of these mudaks can put a wedge between us.

In a half-second, the pants and sweats that stole her frame are on the floor. Royal purple bra and panties still cover everything I desire.

I look her deep in the eyes, my thumbs massaging the inside of her wrists. My lips go to her delicate fingertips, her palms, that quickening pulse. "No matter how dark shit gets with my family, Zar, you won't leave?" My massive chest tightens. Not that I'd ever let Zariah go, I covet the words. She stays because she wants to and not because I've become my father.

Drag her ass back.

Lock her up.

Keep her for all time.

My lips press against her wrists again, and I say, "You'll never leave, Zariah?"

"I—Vassili," she murmurs. "Why would you ask me that?"

"Say it, girl. Say you'll never leave."

47

6

Zariah

In my attempt to connect gazes with Vassili, my brown orbs flit back and forth. Those obsidian marbles of his mirror a past that has died a long time ago. I can see his mother. A woman that I've never set eyes on, attempting to flee Moscow and flee his father.

His tender actions throw me for a loop. The lips of my labia are throbbing for him. I stare at his face, those gorgeous eyes and that chiseled jaw that was set stubborn earlier today. All I see are the couplings of a madman.

Fire burns my skin as his mouth grazes my wrist, and he repeats the same question that he had moments ago. "You'll never leave, Zariah?"

"No. No." I clasp his face and feast on his mouth. My mind has been in attorney-mode, ready to help my husband create a defense. Now, I stand before him, bare to the emotions he never shows me. I can almost touch his vulnerability. Never thought it possible, but I'm content in it because it makes the beast human. Throat constricted, I stare into his eyes and say, "Never—never, Vassili."

Vassili's heavy hand goes to the back of my neck. He presses me away. "I don't like that word. *Never*," he says, his Russian accent thicker than it's ever been.

"Vassili, you're hurting . . ."

He stops clasping the back of my neck, and now Vassili is cradling my face. His callused fingers and palms are abrasive, yet tender as he holds me as though I am breakable. His thumb traces the curve of my cheekbone. The touch is so light that my soul burns for him to kiss me. Damn, those kisses he offered me last night left me splayed against the bedpost. I beg for that with my gaze, needing it. Intuition keeps my feet rooted against the ground. Don't lead, Zariah, I tell myself. Let him dominate. He needs this now.

I anticipate the barbarian who is well-versed on how to fuck me senselessly. Vassili needs to take a deep breath, and that means a good, hard screw. Anticipation scorches my skin as I wait for him to lead.

With Natasha asleep in the center of the bed, Vassili presses me against the wall. A fiery of kisses trail down my neck while his hands skim over my shirt. Those damn heady kisses leave me breathless. Save for my thong, I'm naked before his searing gaze. I'm plastered against the wall, chest-pounding, nipples taut, and waiting for a good fuck.

"Tell me you're mine forever," his husky voice is low, lethal.

Body burning with desire, I murmur, "I belong to you, Vassili Karo Resnov."

Vassili says nothing. Something flickers in his gaze. He moves closer to me, his ropy body crushing mine against the wall. Damn, I need him to undress too. My husband teases my bare skin with his hands while every part of me aches for his lips again. He palms my curves before bringing his hand to the apex of my sex. I lean harder on the wall, beneath his dark presence. My pussy sets off like fireworks waiting for a mere stroke of his fingers. Vassili's warm breath plays at my lips.

"Say what I've told you to say," he commands, his fingers clawing into the skin at the inside of my thigh.

"I'm yours, forever," I murmur.

Now I realize the flicker in his eyes is from anger. It crashes. He's pleased with my response as his mouth plants against mine. The king of my world descends with a kiss to my collarbone to a nip at the side of my cleavage. His tongue swirls over my nipples as he works his way down. It isn't until the beast is on his knees that I notice his fingers are still clawing the inside of my thigh. Vassili clutches my hip and brings it over his shoulder.

His lips press against the dark brown welts he's made. His mouth moves inward. My hands go to his hair, fingers prickled by his buzz cut. I touch the back of his neck as he presses his nose against the silk of my thong. He rips the shirt down the middle, eyes hypnotized by the sight of my pussy. Never removing his hot gaze from me, Vassili's torn shirt is tossed behind him. My fingers savor the intricate tattoos on the planes of his broad shoulders as he breathes me in.

"I'm fighting for more moments with you, Zariah," he says, his fingers running up my hips. He tears my panties from my frame. "I need you always to appreciate what I do for you, for our daughter."

With his face pressed against my valley, I find it hard to assure him of my love. My hand kneads the back of his neck. Vassili needs to hear that I'll never leave, never let him go. I don't ever want to. My husband's aura is brittle one moment and pliable the next. No matter how steely he can be, I'm tethered to him. As his lips press against my heavy clit, I make more promises than I'll ever be able to keep.

Yes, I'll love him all my life. Concerns still prickle at my heart, such as, how much time do we have on this earth if there are more Danushka's and Horace's in the world craving a piece of us.

My head falls back against the wall. His tongue darts past the slickness of my slit, slamming upward against my g-spot. The heat from his body burns against me, sparking fire throughout my chest. My heart urges him to fill any achy void between my thighs.

My brain screams.

"Vassili," I groan, weak in the knees.

He hefts my other leg around his shoulder; my entire body gets pinned against the door. A shutter of moans claim me, and my fingers dig into the flesh of his shoulders. Climbing over my first orgasmic wave, I rock my hips and pray he doesn't suffocate. On his knees, Vassili grazes his teeth against my tiny bulb. He catches a rhythm that damn near shatters me. He alternates to darting his tongue as deep as it will go inside of me. Gaining leverage, my husband's fingers bite into the soft flesh of my hips.

Pain and pleasure blur. The hurt feels so fucking good. And the good is my euphoria. The mini symphonies have clashed, starting to build in my toes.

Fuck, this one *will* break me.

"Vassili," his name tears through my lips as cum floods out of me. All my desire unleashes on Vassili's face. He slams my back against the wall. Though I'm still straddling his face and shoulders, my hands lift up, splayed against the wall. My body goes slack, and I'm a trembling mess, all because he ate my pussy like his last meal.

Sensations detonate, and I push at Vassili's face. The orgasm is too intense for any sort of sensation. I try to escape the onslaught of his thick tongue, but he's power personified. The licking has turned into biting as Vassili takes to the inside of my thigh with his teeth.

"Nyet," he grunts. His mouth engulfs the lips of my pussy, causing more spasms.

"Oh, fuck! Please fuck me," I beg, voice exhausted from whimpering and murmuring. My limbs dangle over his back, toes locked underneath. My arms fall at my sides. Vassili pulls me down from his shoulders and stares at me through intense darkness eyes.

His massive chest slams against mine, heart battering my own. The way his fingers thread through my hair warns that I'll feel pain even before he offers a good tug. Damn, I can't complain. Vassili has lavished my body with pure pleasure. I'm putty now.

With his thick lips coated in my juices, Vassili growls, "Remember when I told you your pussy tasted like water?"

"Oh yes," I huff, walls shuddering for more at the thought of us.

"I need this water to survive . . ." he says.

A gasp escapes from my lips as his mouth descends on mine, demanding and rough. Now, I'm back in the predicament we were in earlier. Stuck between a rock and a hard place, Vassili has always been my rock. My spine slams against the wall as his cock spears deep into my wet valley. Fireworks of desire and sparks of pain weave through me. With each assault of his cock soaking wet from my pussy, my spine crashes against the wall. His cock slams straight through me, punching at my gut. I take every hit with a shout loud enough to reach heaven.

"Vassili," I scream, voice trembling.

His teeth graze my neck before dissolving into my skin. Hot tears slither down my cheeks as I cry out, "More, more, more . . ."

The Russian bull riding me rams his cock inside of me. Every intense thrust sends my pussy walls convulsing, attempting to keep his magnificent erection inside of me. The assault lasts until my back is bruised, and my pussy is satiated with his hot, searing seed.

He's devoured me, ate me like he was dying, and then screwed me as if my pussy were the antidote.

Vassili

natoly is a mudak, and I am too. When Zariah first
became pregnant, I set aside "Crime and Punishment"
by Fyodor Dostoevsky and a shitload of MMA text on strategy. All those girly ass parenting books became my meat. I
snuck every single book Zariah had because, like fucking
hell, I was going to be prepared for my firstborn. Learning
how to be a better father became my food. If my wife had
read a particular book first, I'd rip out pages, which implied
that we are like our parents. Burn that shit. Have nothing to
do with it.

Those fucking pages have come back to bite me in the ass
as I awaken to see tiny bruises along Zariah's back. My first
thought is to pick her up from the pallet we made on the
floor and place her on the bed next to Natasha. That's not the
man I want to be. Fuck her and set her aside. Some of those
baby books—the ones with clout—remind me of who I could
be, not the shitty past.

My lips press against the purple blemishes dotting Zariah's back. Shit, I had her spine slamming on repeat against the wall last night. She said nothing and took all this pain. The only word roving through my mind is: mudak. That's what I am. The world I was born into has predisposed me to that. No amount of baby books that tried to teach me otherwise matters, for the sake of my daughter—matters.

Mouth tasting another parcel of pain that I've caused, I consider the truth. I have to let them go. The thought is almost enough to kill me.

Let. Them. Go. My wife, my daughter, and the seed that's barely taken root in her belly is my son. And I am the mudak who should let them go before I—

"Mmmm, you stopped," Zariah's murmurs in a throaty voice. "Don't stop."

"I hurt you last night," I snap before I can think better of it. "Now, you don't want me to stop?"

Zariah turns around. Her dark brown gaze is twinkling. She starts to speak but presses her mouth against my chest. Her breath is warm as she yawns. "Sorry."

Anger begins to rise over me.

What the fuck does she have to be sorry for?

I'm the mudak. I can still see the humbled look on my mother's face. When someone hurts you so bad that you can't do anything else, you humble yourself. That's all she knew before she broke. Patience. Humbleness. Sorry.

Now, Zariah's breath is puffing toward my jaw in tiny statics of laughter. "Damn, Vassili. I remember a time, feels so long ago, that your full name was 'Vassili, you're an Asshole.'"

She pauses from her laughter in an attempt to include me. I grip her cheeks. "What's so funny?"

"*What's so funny*," she parrots in an awful attempt at my accent. After a few seconds, Zariah presses her lips to mine. "You are my everything, Vassili. We've had this conversation before. If you want to fuck me, then please do. And if you

55

want to make love to me and call me queen, I'll love you all the same. Last night, we screwed."

With not an ounce of emotion in my voice, I reply, "I'm leaving you, Zariah."

The first slap is free. I grab my wife's wrist. Her left-hand juts out. I grab that too. "Zariah—"

"You-you sounded serious! Don't make me hate you, Vassili. Don't get lost in those dark-seeded thoughts of yours." Her volume is hardly a whisper, but the words sting.

"Nyet, you're the one who overthinks shit, Zar. And, *dah*, I am serious."

Her arms start to wrap around my body. I push her away. She whimpers, coming to her knees. In a half-second, Zariah's attempt to straddle me lands her in the array of blankets on the floor. "Think, Zariah." I grip her forearms and hold her down. A tiny lioness roar comes from her. Had I not been serious, this shit would be funny.

Those pretty brown eyes of Zariah's simmer. She closes them a second before tears begin to roll down the sides of her face.

"*Think*, girl," my voice is harsh again.

"I'm your wife," she mutters.

"I don't need one of those. Not right now," I grit out.

"Marriage is love and-and—"

"Compromise," I sigh. "I love you, Zariah. But I can't play house with you. Fuck compromise, girl. This isn't working for me."

With her eyes closed, she murmurs through gritted teeth, "We were never a team, Vassili. I hate you so much. I hate you—I hate you—I. Hate. You."

Though her tormented soul has me magnetized, I look up. Our daughter is sliding her feet and legs off the side of the bed. In a flash, I'm up and helping her down the lengthy platform.

"Good morning, Cutie Pie."

"Daddy love, love," she flexes and relaxes her fingers, doing sign language for 'milk.'

My bruised heart is momentarily knitted together. While teaching Natasha Russian and English, I picked up some sign language. It's another suggestion from those parenting books that label me a mudak. I smile, "You want milk?"

"Can we talk?" Zariah's voice hardly reaches across my shoulder as Natasha and I walk away from her.

"Nyet."

"Vas . . ."

"Nyet!" I growl, still headed toward the bedroom door with our daughter. Natasha looks up at me with bright eyes, repeating my word with the same force. Her beautiful fucking smile almost does me in.

The door connected to the bathroom slams shut behind her. The pallet where I fucked my wife last night looks like a disarray of us as I walk right over it.

"Let's go see about some milk for you, Natasha," I say, planting a kiss on her caramel forehead. With my baby girl in my arm, I unlock the bedroom door. Before I open it, I decide that a conversation with my daughter is in order. This may be the last time we have a chat in a long while—at least until Zariah gets over her fucking emotions. In this reality, shit isn't safe for her.

"Daddy did something stupid," I tell my kid.

"Daddy?" Her long lashes kiss her cheeks as she blinks at me.

Not a man moved to tears, I chew my bottom lip. Not ever. My little girl will never see me cry, although Natasha is my closest confidant after my broken patella. "Daddy broke mom's heart a little while ago. I pray that God will bring you someone who won't do that shit to you. Not on purpose— because I'd kill him and ask God's forgiveness later. Also, not by accident too. You don't need a husband like Daddy, Cutie Pie. You can do better than this. Better than us."

She chuckles. "Cutie . . . cutie pie."

"That's you, girl." I press my index finger into her chubby stomach. "That's you. Our little chat isn't just about husbands. Any man who hurts you answers to me. Got that?"

My little doll laughs again. I glance around, only to realize we're still rooted at the door to the bedroom. I'm torn between the family I coveted all my life and what's better for them. I open the bedroom door, and we start out. "Let's go get your milk—"

The door to the en suite bathroom bursts open. Zariah struts out. Jeans and a crumpled blouse cover her body. She grabs Natasha from my arms. "I'll get the milk. *We're leaving now.*"

I grab her arm. "Can you take a moment and fucking think, Zariah."

"I have!" She shouts, then her eyes aren't meeting mine. I turn around. At the bedroom door, Yuri's about to make a retreat. Zariah puts our daughter in his arms like she's a bag of potatoes. With her hands on her hips, Zariah growls. "For seven years, I stuck to my guns, Vassili. Turning around was something I shouldn't have done. Guess I shouldn't have said *never* last night!"

"Zariah," Danushka sighs, exiting a set of double doors at the farthest side of the hallway.

Now we have a fucking audience.

"I'm leaving him, Danny," Zariah sniffles. "Good luck with the parent-icide."

"Aw man," Yuri stares at her. "Look, Zar. We can all talk this out. You're family; you're my kuzen now."

"No," she snaps at him. "Yuri, you're a murderer. Vassili, Danny, all of you. I'm done wi-with all of you."

Danushka's eyes narrow. "We're survivors, Zar. I thought you understood that."

"Whatever you say, Danny! I thought I married a man who wanted nothing to do with you people," she sneers. "First, I get introduced to you," she nudges her chin at Yuri. "Next, your fucking father. All of Malich's family. Even Danushka. There's no end, is there, Vassili? I don't want this anymore."

I lean against the wall, one ankle locked around the next as I watch Zariah. History repeats itself. This is Vadim's Gym, day one—love at first glance for me all over again.

This time though, it's better to let her go than to fight for her. To fight and keep her safe.

"Zariah, I guess you're like Taryn now?" Yuri sniffs, his puffy jaws set in disappointment.

"Yes, and my goodbyes were overdue." Zariah shifts Natasha to her opposite hip.

Danushka steps in front of Zariah and my child. With a hungry gaze, I watch.

"Natasha is a Resnov, you know." Danushka shakes her head. "I'm disgusted with you, Zar. You hurt my brat. You're supposed to be my best—"

"Danny, don't waste time on my old bitch." I run a hand over my buzz cut. "I've had the same piece of pussy for way too long. Where are the girls Yuri had last night?"

Zariah stares at me, Natasha too. Her smile freezes on her face.

"I can have—"

"Not those bitches, *sestra*," I smile, calling Danushka 'sister' for the first time. "Tell those bitches to find more bitches for me. The only *leftover pussy* I had is now leaving."

8

Zariah

My daughter and I have been sent home, arrived in a super jet, left in business class. I'd called my mother while we sat at the airport in Italy. If there's one thing my mom can do, it's coordinate the time for arrival. She's hitched a flight from ATL. She's been worried about the repercussions of Kong's coma. He still has yet to awaken. With an overnight diaper bag in one hand and Natasha sleeping in my other arm, I start through the terminals of LAX. Sunglasses shade my red-rimmed, swollen eyes. I meander through the airport as I did after finding out my husband accosted an 'innocent' man. In that, I hadn't known the bastard was avenging the assault of my mom.

As we descend the escalator, my hot, tired gaze tracks the crowd of people sifting through luggage. Across from them is an area of seats. Part of me wants to smile when I see my mother, already seated with her luggage. The real me just wants to crawl into a tiny ball and scream until my lungs and throat bleed. She stands, grabs her rollaway, and starts over to us.

"Oh honey," my mother groans, plucking Natasha's limp body to her chest. My daughter opens one eye, peeks at her grandmother then returns to her slumber on Zamora's shoulder.

"Mom, why didn't you catch a Lyft? I could've met you at home."

"No, no." She waves me away.

With Natasha out of my arms, I grab her rollaway.

"Hey, don't you need to get your luggage?"

I blink a few times, opting not to mention that Danushka sort of kidnapped us. I'd worn the most designer digs I've ever had in my life. "The luggage was lost when we arrived in Australia."

"Oh, baby. Well, Sammy's here. As a matter of fact . . ." She pauses from talking to me to pull out her phone. "Hey, yeah, she's here . . . Yeah, Cutie Pie too . . . Thanks."

I simper. "It's the middle of the night. How—Why is Samuel here, Mom?"

"Because I called him. He's called you too, you know." She walks with me toward the barrage of sliding glass doors. "Your brother called. Everyone I know is calling because of that Australia incident."

"Yeah, well," I grumble as the doors swoosh open for us. "You know, Momma, you're the only one I called. My cellphone is off."

We continue out into the warm summer night. Part of me wants it to rain so that I can cry again as I pull off my sunglasses. My mom drags me along to a designated area. I notice her expression the instant she's found Samuel through the haze of rides. Her disappointment plunges into the abyss of nothingness. She waves him over, and his convertible glides before us.

"I apologize, Zar," he starts out, dressed in a navy suit against his super-dark skin. He has a few gorgeous shades on my father. Though his white-teeth gleam in a smile, he rubs my back with sympathy. "I was just leaving dinner when Mora called. I would've gone home and switched rides."

"Do you have a car seat?" I ask voice strangled.

"Yes, ma'am." He takes the overnight diaper bag. "Mora, let me get this stuff in the trunk, and I have a hug for you too."

My mother stops herself from giggling; her skin flushes red as she holds Natasha and pats her back. "Oh, no. Don't hug me, Sammy. I came running. No shower. I was cooped up on that flight all evening."

Samuel and Zamora, who love to call each other by their nicknames, stop to chat. I take Natasha and squeeze us through the back of the passenger seat. Once I have her buckled and settled in, I sit opposite her. I grab my designer glasses from my purse and then stop. How ridiculous do I look already? The ride to my home is filled with silence until my mom speaks.

"Okay, so . . . when is Vassili coming home?"

I chew my lip, infuriated by her comment. My mother is as oblivious as my father has always said. "Never."

"Zariah, you two are grown-ups. You've entered into a relationship and now have a daughter to consider," Samuel reprimands.

"Thanks for the reminder, *Dad*," I mumble to myself. My father's ex-best friend, my mentor, and the guy who signs all my paychecks is right.

"Oh, hell, no, Zar." My mom chimes in. "I'm not having any of that. I refuse to believe you've been slapped around or called out of your name and taunted by him."

"Nope." I almost sneer. Well, I was taunted before we left.

My mom kisses her teeth. "Whatever the hell you two are

going through can be worked out! Or does it have anything to do with Kong?"

My lack of response becomes Zamora's reason to latch onto our past issues. I'm reminded of how vital Vassili's fights are. Images of his torn patella after fighting Gotti cross my mind, and I still can't respond to my mother.

In a soothing voice, she says, "Sweetheart, your husband has a demanding career. He has fans and enemies. They all want to have their say about the fight. Sounds overwhelming, Lord only knows how much. As far as I'm concerned, Vassili gave his best performance. The other guy may have been on drugs or something. You have to stick by your man's side."

Ha! Stick by your man through thick and thin. Far as I'm concerned, we are about the most loyal women on earth. Or maybe that's just the petty bone in me prepared to dominate. With a sigh, I say, "Momma, can we stick a pin in it for now?"

The next morning, I awaken to the scent of bacon. I roll over in bed. I never knew how massive it was until Igor died. While Vassili's heart and soul were a thousand miles away, I'd curled into a tiny ball in the center of it. I sit up, reminiscing about how his return led to our last fight.

The double doors are open. The sunlight streams in from the skyline right outside of the room. I grab my iPhone and power it up. A symphony of buzzing goes off in my hand. Pulling in oxygen, I open the voicemail application. My thumb scrolls over an endless succession of messages. Most of them are from Tyrese Nicks, the newest attorney at Billingslea Family Legal. Just as I start to click on the first one, a call comes in.

It's none other than the culprit himself.

"Zariah?" Tyrese's voice is a touch deeper than usual and more endearing than I've ever known.

A flurry of tears wash across my cheeks. Why did he call me so many times? "Hey, what's up? Oh my god, is Felicidad okay? How are the children?"

"What?" The sound of air rushing in the background, and then what I assume is a door closing. "No, there's nothing wrong with them. Ms. Noriega and her children are safe. I was . . . ahem, Noriega is missing."

Yup, dead in a ditch somewhere, compliments of Danushka. "When did he go missing?"

"I take it you haven't listened to any of my voicemails."

"No," I start to tell him we can talk later when I'm at the office. *If I go.* The naïve card is a little easier to finagle when I'm not standing in the counselor's face. "My phone has been off a few days. What happened to that thug?" I wince, at my choice of words and inability to feign shock. The gang member and cartel runner is no longer a threat to my clients. *Our* clients. Tyrese forced my hand when I took the case for his wife, Felicidad Noriega.

"Somehow, he got out of Twin Towers." He mentions the correctional facility in downtown Los Angeles. "I was calling you repeatedly about that until I saw you were in Australia. I started to call you after the mob at the event center. So, this Killer Karo and Kong thing . . . Hey, when are you going to stop me from talking. I figure I'd go on until you cut me off."

Through the receiver, I can feel his smile and see his dimples deepen. We make a good team whenever we work with Felicidad to keep her and her children away from Noriega. Kneading the nape of my neck, I try to reply, "Can we not talk about that?"

"Alright, I understand the husband is not a topic of discussion—ever. You sound a little off. Zariah, is something wrong?"

I laugh through the tears now. "Ha, I'm not your client, Tyrese."

"We're friends."

"We're not," I grit out. Vassili and I are on the outs, but I'd rather slit my wrists than do anything to harm the love I have for him.

My husband's voice is in my ear, and he's saying the worst words I've ever heard him say. *"The only leftover pussy I had is now leaving."*

Although he's said those foul words, no more than 24 hours ago, that same friggen mouth stole my breath. My Vassili has said, "I'm fighting for more moments with you, Zariah. I need you always to appreciate what I do for you, for our daughter."

That bastard gave up on us!

Instead of hearing the sound of my husband's voice, another man jokes with me. "I refuse to believe we're not friends, Zariah. You and I almost got capped by the Dos Locos Gang."

His chuckle is as smooth as the bourbon and whiskey my father coveted when I was a child. I lick my lips in trepidation. "I'm getting a divorce, Tyrese. Will you draw up the documents?" I pause from telling him that he's also every checkmark on a man that I could've married.

"You want me to create divorce documents for you? Have you tried counseling?"

"Boy, you flirted with me relentlessly on the first day that we met," I chortle. "No way in friggen hell do you care about any attempts to save my marriage, so save it."

"I don't like to see you sad."

"Yeah, there you go. Crossing the fucking line, Counselor."

"Zariah, you're a very gorgeous woman. But I'm not an idiot—"

"What, you don't want to be in a coma by flirting?"

"No. I can handle myself." Again he offers a laugh, one that sounds good right about now. "I, honest to God, don't like to see you sad. I appreciate how you've changed my outlook at work."

"Oh, yeah? The plan. Work with the infamous ex-DA Samuel Billingslea at his cheesy, family-oriented law firm. Check. Bulldoze your way up to head DA in Los Angeles, I remember. No check yet. That's fine; these things take time."

"I'm not that asshole anymore, Zar—"

"Keep me posted about Felicidad. I don't know if any of Dos Locos will retaliate against her on Noriega's behalf . . . if they think she had something to do with it. Bye." I hang up. Shaking my head, I growl at myself. How stupid did I just sound? How would Felicidad have anything to do with her husband's death? The bastard planted fear in her heart. He kept her alienated from her family in the States. He had the backing of a Mexican cartel in her hometown. I climb out of bed, ready to start the beginning of the week.

I should've taken my ass to church yesterday, I consider with a sigh. I turn on Mandisa and pray that her Christian music will keep my mind off Vassili. For even a half a second.

9

Vassili

More whores than Anatoly keeps on rotation are surrounding me. Not a single one has on a top. Tits of various sizes and shades are in my face. Seated on the couch, I push a girl from my lap. A tattoo artist makes himself comfortable in a leather rollaway chair before me.

Danushka is here too. She's in some sort of lacy, see-through bodysuit. She grabs the girl that's sulking away from me and plants a hard kiss on her mouth.

"Okay, out!" she shouts, slapping the whore's ass. "All of you out."

The artist sniffs, looking me over. "You don't have any space."

Danushka's thumb drags across my pec. "He has space. Right there. What are you getting, brat? Another machine gun? Cats near the kremlin?"

"Nyet." My gaze burns through her. She's like a fly, the kind that keeps coming back after you thought you'd murdered it. "Cor Ne Adito." I spit the words.

"Khorosho." She smiles.

With a shot of vodka at his lips, Yuri pauses. "What the fuck does that mean?"

"Oh, my inquisitive cousin, I forgot you're not that bright like my brat." She chuckles. *"Don't rip your heart out.* It's Latin."

I turn in the seat. "Try to use the same style as this text on my back, eh?"

The artist nods.

Yuri grunts. "I don't like the meaning of that. It's dumb."

"You're dumb, you fat fuck," Danushka spits.

"Who you calling—"

"Look at you," I cut him off, glaring him up and down. "You are a fat fuck, Yuri."

His cheeks almost puff up like Natasha's, though his are covered in tiny hairs. He glares at the two of us. "Vassili, kuzen, we go home now. Malich didn't raise us to disrespect our women. Fuck this slut."

"She's my sister!"

Danushka sits back, a grin on her face.

Yuri scoffs. "She's the devil. And you don't need no motherfucking 'don't rip your heart out' bullshit on your back."

I growl, "What happened to Zariah is like Taryn?"

"I . . ." the fucking teddy bear mutters, "We all hurt each other's feelings yesterday."

With a smirk, I stare up at him. "Where's your self-respect, Yuri?"

"He's no Russian bull. He's not." Danushka kisses her teeth.

"Just because I refuse to bash your face in like any other man would..." Yuri wags a finger at her, "doesn't make me any less of a man. Vassili, you are my brat! You're not her brat. You are mine."

I flex my arms, chest puffed up, and focus on where the newest addition to art is going.

Yuri's fingertip comes toward me as if he's going to jab me in the forehead. The artist moves out of the way. My forearm swipes over his in the nick of time. I bring his arm beneath mine and twist. I'm up from the chair in seconds, while Yuri's back is to me. His fleshy cheeks jiggle.

"Get off me," he grunts, "You mudak!"

"Stop being a piz'da," I growl in his ear.

From her seat, Danushka lifts a little and pulls out a pearl-handled gun. "Brat, he is our blood, but alas, it is your call. What should we do?"

"You want to shoot me?" Yuri's jaws shake with fury as he shouts.

"We would probably have to kill Mikhail when he comes down the stairs. Or I can send word to do it in his sleep." Danushka lets the trigger-guard twirl around in her finger. "All your call, brat."

"You and Mikhail get the fuck out of here," I roar into Yuri's ear. We're not strangers to a brawl. After fighting for Zamora Haskin's boyfriend, we ended up in the slammer. There was too much testosterone roaring through us when we fought.

Yuri turns around. He doesn't even make an attempt. "I'm supposed to be your manager, Vassili. We should be sending flowers—some shit to Kong's family. You, mudak, you should be sending flowers to your wife. Flowers and fucking choco- lates. You're entertaining whores. Did you sleep with them last night?"

"Nyet!"

"I don't believe you."

Danushka snarls. "My brat doesn't owe you shit, Yuri. Get going."

Ignoring her, he stares at me. "I don't believe you. Okay,

so I fell in love with a whore. Taryn was a trick. Maybe I do shit like that on occasion, but you, Vassili, you." Yuri shakes his head. "You love Zariah. *You're my brat!*"

He lunges himself at me. His fat head slams into my rib. I flip over the low seated chair, landing on my feet. Yuri isn't that quick on his toes. A vase goes crashing to the ground with him on top of it. I hold out my hand. He slaps at it. "Fuck you, Vassili."

"Fuck you, Yuri." I stare down at him.

"We are brats!" His breath is heavy as he clambers to his knees and up to his feet.

The glimmer in his eye causes me to duck before he reaches out. He stumbles over his feet. Too angry to fight. At times, my cousin has been known to get a few good hits in before the takedown, but not today. The mudak acts like Zariah and I are his parents, and we're getting a . . . Divorce.

Fuck, I hadn't thought about that. Pride won't allow me to sign those papers, no matter what. The devil on my shoulder reminds me that's another way I'm like my father. We're both unwilling to let go of the best love we've ever known.

Yuri swipes another arm out.

I offer a rare smile and wink. "Don't do this, Yuri. You look like a fat, fucking idiot."

"Oh, I do?" Again, pure emotion moves him. Like he tried to do, the tip of my index finger pushes at his skull with enough force to set him straight. Well, my strength and his emotion. A crowd is around us. Mostly Italians but a few loyalists turned traitor on Anatoly for Horace. My eyes land on Mikhail.

A solid left bounces from my jaw. I wriggle my jaw. Yuri follows up with an uppercut. I block. My right fist slams straight into my cousin's forehead. All the hatred in Yuri is dead to me. He's sprawled out on the ground.

"He's sleep," I tell Mikhail. "Take this fat fuck, and the two of you can go home."

My oldest cousin's skin tinges red, his jaw set. Danushka continues to twirl the shiny gun in her hand.

"Don't make the mistake of thinking my brat made a request," Danushka says in a soft voice. "Nyet, that was a command, Mikhail. And because your little fat brother is asleep, I'll send my car to the airport. If you leave without being a thorn in my side, I'll pay the *coach airfare* too."

Mikhail's voice is a low rumble. "Fuck you, piz'da."

My sister laughs. "You know, traveling coach is the cheapest it gets. So that just means, now you find your way home. Guys—"

"Don't touch him," I grit out. If these mudaks help Yuri out, by way of tossing him out like trash, Mikhail will die today too. He's not having it.

I snap, "Get your brat and go, Mikhail."

I reclaim my seat.

Danushka settles back, and I don't even turn around to watch them leave. "Should we send for the girls again? I feel like this tension needs to ease, Vassili. I'm sure one of them can please you while you get your tattoo."

"Nyet. I just want to get it done. Girls later."

10

Zariah

O ur first night as husband and wife returns to me.
Vassili kneeled and worshiped my body, and I got the
perfect taste too. How sweet my pussy was as it peppered my new
husband's colossal cock and spurred my addiction. My slick, wet
walls climbed off the most massive erection I'd ever seen in my life.
I scooted down and threw my lips around the crown of him. All the
sweet juices surrounding his shaft glossed my mouth.

His voice was delectable, and he groaned while my tongue toyed
with the jelly I'd offered. My lips and pussy were magnetized to his
dick. A heady delirium surrounded me. I couldn't determine where
I wanted his hot semen to go. I applied pressure around his dick,
working my lips down to his balls. I continued with the cock-
sucking fest until Vassili's fist yanked at my hair. His hands
claimed my hips. Electricity flew across my skin as my walls
plunged on him.

A deep, low laugh came from his powerful abdominals,

rumbling against my inner thighs. "You look like you're in heaven, Zar," he'd said, sitting up somewhat. The action forced more cock into my pussy, widening my slick walls for him. "You don't know heaven yet, girl. I'll take you there tonight."

Arousal enveloped me as I worked my hips. Vassili's swollen cock caressed every inch of my valley. We were going to screw until his cock made me go blind. His fingernails clawed into my thighs, and I welcomed the piston club as his cock jumped in and out of me. My tits bounced; my ass looked gorgeous behind me. And what looked gorgeous before me? Mounds of muscles and tattoos, and my hot Russian beast. He worked me so hard my pussy ached for split seconds at a time before swallowing his cockhead and welcoming him into me.

"Oh shit, baby, I'm not going to make it," I screamed. The slick, sensitive folds of my pussy clamped down around him in an attempt to hold him there. Shit, I had lost every ounce of my mind. In that single moment, I prayed to keep him right there, fucking deep inside of me. There was so much power in my pussy as it orgasmed around him, squeezing and squeezing him.

"Fuck," Vassili groaned. He stopped pumping me up and down. He'd said the most beautiful words a man could ever say, "Suck daddy's cock, Zar."

With my walls attempting to milk him, I climbed down and tasted all the good we created.

Floundering for air, I awaken from the dream I've had for over two weeks. My body is in an erect position on the bed; sweat clings to me. A few tears begin to twine with it before I drag myself from the bed.

This is hell. This is the hell I chose all because Vassili Karo Resnov drew me back to him like a moth to an unquenchable flame.

Like a robot, with no heart in its chest, I do all the things that strong black women do. A shower burns my skin, helping to further wake me up. A little while later, I put my hands together to pray over the table before I eat a wholesome breakfast.

"So, Mom, I know you had a cruise to go on…"

"It's almost autumn." My mom waves her fork at me. "I don't know why my high school friends wanted to go on a cruise at this time. Those cheap heifas."

I push my lips up into a smile. "Yeah, but your version of cheap was one of the most expensive cruise liners."

"Yup. Couldn't afford peak season. Honey, I got the insurance. I'll cancel in the nick of time. Don't worry, either. I'm only waiting to do so because they're going to have words for me. They can have those words while they're flying to Miami."

"Oh, mom," I groan, picking up my fork. "Just go."

"Then who's going to watch Cutie Pie? Taryn is unpredictable. Her hussy of a mother—"

"Momma, the 1950s called. Hussy has to go into the time capsule. Let it go."

With a snigger, my mom washes down the pancakes she made, by way of a large glass of orange juice. She proceeds with the same attitude and the same tired, old storyline. "The hussy had her tits all out around my ex-husband. Listen, I'm over Maxwell. Done deal. But there's a bro code, the same as there's a *sistah girl code*. That bitch—"

"By all means, revert to hussy." I almost smile because my mom and *colorful* bad words don't mix. Zamora Haskins is the light in my dreary life. I can't smile because my heart is in the pit of my stomach. I reach over and pour a few more cheerios onto my daughter's table.

"I'm staying. Besides, Sammy is coming to dinner tonight."

"I have dibs on Samuel Billingsley, Mom. He's my mentor. Not your flirt buddy."

"Girl, that man is a dark chocolate dream. He could be both. He is still willing to do an intervention for you and Vassili."

"You can't still be team Karo," I scoff.

"I'm team Killer Karo and Team Vassili—my son. I refuse to believe he's done"

"We've had this discussion."

"No, I've had this discussion, you get all tight-lipped. Humor me, Zariah. Who is the culprit? You. Him? Who!"

"We've changed." I'm up from my chair, the robot in my brain has enough fuel to move forever.

Move and not think about Vassili.

Doing so is the hardest task I've ever had. My lips press to Natasha's forehead. And instantly, I'm floored by the thought of him not seeing her. Sure, she's been cranky, but he *cannot* see her...

With my purse over my shoulder, I head toward the side hall. The garage is at the end of it. I toss over my shoulder, "My coworker has the divorce papers ready for me to review today. This discussion is final."

"You need Jesus," is all she will say.

Much of the day passes by before I head into Tyrese's office and knock on the door.

"Come in," he calls out.

Upon complying, I'm given a shock full of eight-stack! Tyrese is seated at his chair, pulling into a royal blue polo. "One of my clients' children spit up on me at court today..."

My eyes are sliding up to his warm brown face and those damn dimples. When I reach his eyes, they're sparkling.

Hands on hips, I snap, "Well, you could've said just a moment. Or something."

"I think I covered the *or something*." He winks. "It's lunchtime. Where would you like to go?"

Nowhere. Food tastes like shit while the love of my life is in a different country, with a deranged sister, and whores galore. Of course, I don't share that. I offer a shrug. "I have a Lean Cuisine in the freezer. I'll pass."

"Forget Lean Cuisines, Zar." Standing up, he starts to place his wallet in the back of his slacks. "Miss Zamora is from the south. I know you like better meals than—"

"Mr. Nicks."

"Oh, hell no, Zar. I'm no longer Mr. Nicks. We've had this conversation before." He wags a finger.

"Keep doing that, I'll bite it off."

"Is this sexual harassment?" He places a hand at his chest. I turn to leave. Tyrese is around me in seconds.

"I'm not in the mood," I bite out. "Anyone could've completed the divorce documents for me. I could've done them myself—" and *cry all over the paperwork.* "But I asked you ..."

"Why?" He cocks a brow.

"Why what? We-we aren't compatible anymore."

His dimples deepen. "I meant, why me? Why did you want me to help you, Zariah?"

I stare through him for a moment.

"I offered—"

"An intervention? Thanks! You're not the first."

"Yes. You strike me as the stay married forever type."

"What kind of statement is that?" I grit out.

Tyrese shoves his hands into his slacks. "It's an assessment. Alright, no lunch. I looked over your assets and created two documents. You sure you want to dissolve your relationship and walk out with nothing?"

"Positive."

He sucks in his bottom lip, chewing on it a bit. "Zariah, are you afraid of—"

There's a commotion in the front of the tiny firm. The man has a Russian accent, deepened by emotion.

My eyes narrow slightly, catching the familiar voice. "I have to…"

"You can tell me anything." Tyrese clasps my arm, his thumb massaging over my skin.

"Zariah!" I spin around to see none other than Yuri! He places his hands on his knees, breathing erratic.

"What's wrong?" I start out of Tyrese's room, but he's offering my in-law a bottle of water.

The innocent, teddy bear takes it and sits down at his desk. At first, I'm livid at my coworker's manipulation. The damn attorney is trying to be nosy. A sinking feeling lines the bottom of my gut.

"Yuri, what happened? Is Vassili—"

Vassili

They say keep your enemies closer. I've never had a problem with that. As an MMA fighter, submissions are king. I go to war in the cage, and then I put mudaks asleep. I keep them close until their breathing tapers off, and their muscles are putty in my hands.

Or they tap out.

But there's no fucking way in hell I wanted to be this close to Danushka. The bitch is continuously at my side. If I were in my right mind, I'd think that her plan for me to have the seat and for her to give the orders was bullshit. Just something she'd said. There will be no seat for me at the table of seven. Won't be a table for this cunt either.

Now we're seated around the table. Me. The bitch. Horace and Don Roberto. The Italian has this look about him. Like he was passed over for the motherfucking Godfather movie.

My gaze is across the room. My mind is on my wife. Where is she? What is she doing? How much does she hate me right now? Shit like that.

"We would like to open up a few more seats, Vassili." Horace clears his throat. "What are your thoughts?"

My thoughts? That you're imitating my father and doing a fuck-over job at it. This isn't the Bratva, not with an Italian. I glare through him. So far, they treat me like a king. "Open all the fucking seats you want."

"You're still boss of all bosses, brat. Well, you and I." Danushka smiles.

"And this piz'da has a seat at the Resnov *Bratva*?" I glance at the Italian. What is this, a little gang?

"Young man, I am fluent in your language. Do not call me a cunt," Don Roberto says.

"Do something about it," I growl. The old man should've waited until I really said something about him in Russian. He looks at me like I'm the idiot, but I'm not stupid enough to share that I am fluent in Italian too. His problem was showing his hand too soon. He won't know I speak his language until he needs to know.

Don Roberto scoffs.

"Now, now, boys," Danushka purrs. "We are setting the foundation for our new relationship. The first order of business, Vassili. Do you have any idea where our father is hiding?"

"Dah. Nyet. Fuck, I don't know. The mudak was slippery when we were kids, Danny."

Her gaze glues to mine for a few beats. "Well, it tseems our father is afraid of us, Vassili. Ha! Simeon is missing, too. What are your thoughts on our cousin, Simeon?"

My heavy shoulders lift a little. "You mean besides Sim's face looking like a dog's asshole."

She laughs again. My hands tighten into fists beneath the table, nails digging into my skin. I have to play the fucking comedian.

"He does, doesn't he?"

The door opens with a rush of air. A lanky Russian who traded teams comes rushing into the room. He breathes heavy, saying, "Horace, I have—"

"Why are you here? Who said you could disrespect us!" Danushka says in a steady voice, cutting in.

He apologizes to her, and then turns to me. "Horace gave express orders to let you all know of any updates on the fighter?"

My chest tightens.

11

Zariah

"Let's chat in my office," I reign in the fear that I felt when asking about Vassili. A split second ago, my heartbeat stopped. I didn't consider Tyrese when asking if Vassili was safe.

"Dah, that sounds better." Yuri looks between the two of us. Something flashed in his gaze, and then he gestures to the empty water bottle in his hand. "Thank you."

"Tyrese Nicks, Esquire. Here, allow me."

Though he holds his hand out for the empty bottle, Yuri places the bottle in his left hand, then offers him a firm shake. Firm enough for me to notice the blood being snatched from Tyrese's fingertips. I'd wondered if Yuri came to his conclusions when entering Tyrese's office. Instead of tossing an accusation my way, he follows me out.

Once in my office, I close the door. Yuri sinks down onto the couch in my office. He rubs his hand over his face as I lean against the front of my table.

"How you holding up, kuzen?" he asks.

"I'm alive. What's wrong with Vassili? Is everything alright between him and Danny?" Heat builds in the corner of my eyes. The tears that I told myself had no business staying there, clouding my vision for a moment. The hot torrents tumble over.

Yuri leans forward, wide-legged. "Dah, he's still with the bitch. Zar, don't you cry over him. He's . . . he's an idiot."

"How are you?" I chew my lip. Yuri became a good friend of mine the day Vassili allowed him around me. My protective husband had nothing to worry about. Although his haste to enter my office is disconcerting, I ask him again, "Are you okay? You left Vassili?"

"Nyet! That idiot got rid of me and Mikhail."

"Should I take that?" I gesture to his water bottle. "You seemed like you weren't ready to part with it."

"Oh, yeah." He hands it over. "I don't trust attorneys, Zariah. Well, I trust you. Not the rest of these mudaks. I don't need anybody with my fingerprints. So, you'll make sure that gets to the trash?"

"Definitely. When did Vassili part ways with you all?"

"A day or two after you, Zar. So, you haven't been chatting with him?" Redness flushes across his chunky cheeks as he asks, "The two of you are done?"

I give a small nod.

Yuri's eyes close, and his hands scrub across his face. After a groan, he sits forward, addressing me. "We have to get Vassili back, Zar. We have to make sure nothing happens to my brat. *He is my brat.* Not hers. She's a manipulative snake!"

"I know."

"My father..."

"Oh, Malich," I murmur. Igor has yet to rest when Danushka ruined things. "How is he? I should come by?"

"That's a good idea. You and Natasha drop by. Malich wants nothing to do with the entire 'snatching up kingdoms,'

81

power trip that Danushka is on. He's lifting his protection from Vassili." He paused, biting his knuckles. "I've called my brat over and over. I tried to tell him."

Clutching a hand to my chest, I ask, "Malich is . . . He's done with Vassili?"

"Done." Yuri nods. "I should be done too, but— the two of us have to save him. Mikhail told our father that Danushka's antics were the reason Igor died. You know, Igor was my pop's favorite? Even if he wasn't, Vassili picked the wrong side."

"What would happen to him?" I ask in response. A river of tears flood down my cheeks. "Yuri."

"We both know how this ends, Zar."

"What will we do, Yuri?" I sink onto the couch next to him. My hand burrows into the cushion, breaths becoming pants. "What *can* we do!"

"We're fucked, kuzen. Malich is done waiting for Vassili's response. He will connect with Anatoly. That's assuming Vassili's father isn't already aware of their coup."

"I thought Anatoly went into hiding?" I ask. If Anatoly has gone into hiding, it would appear that Danushka has the upper hand, right? Where I'm from, if you're confident enough to believe you can win a fight, there's no reason to hide. This isn't an old fashion street fight. "Anatoly's not in hiding?"

"They're brats, Zariah. Anatoly has no reason to hide from Malich. Now, he has reason to go after Vassili. Danny is happy right now, coming up with plans. Though, she doesn't have as many loyalists as Uncle Anatoly. Right now, he's taking a tally of how much that bitch and *my* kuzen are screwing him over. He's good at waiting, watching and checking off how much he will do . . ."

A few days later, I bake a Russian Honey Cake from one of Sasha's recipes that Vassili says he'll never forget. I've asked him countless times why he refuses to write down any of his dearly departed sister's favorite dishes. In response, I received a grunt. One time, I'd stumped him with the notion that he should pass it on to Natasha. No grunt or response came my way, but I could tell he was considering it. I silently pray that I have done the cake justice from memory, and then dress Natasha in her best.

"Oh no! We're all supposed to go out to dinner tonight," my mom says, watching me latch a white gold cross around Natasha's neck. Malich had given her the necklace at her Christening. Though the ceremony was held at my mom's church in Atlanta, he'd completed a few customary Russian rites. All I can hope is that her great uncle remembers as much for when we head over there tonight.

Not for Natasha's sake. Yuri already confirmed that my daughter and I are neutral in the ordeal. Regardless, even if Vassili's making all the wrong moves right now, I will fight for my husband.

What about when there's nothing left . . . The vile thought worms its way into my mind.

"Should we all go?" My mom asks.

"Huh?" I blink away from Natasha, whose fat fist is pawing softly at her necklace. With the closest attempt to a smile, I offer Zamora my undivided attention.

"Should we all go?" she repeats. "I know that Sammy has been included in your Sunday dinner tradition with you and Vassili. Sometimes they're at Malich's. Should I ask Sammy to come? Then we can all talk about Vassili."

"About what?" I snap. I'm instantly reminded that I'm my father's daughter. "Sorry, Mom."

"Child, you get a pass. Given the circumstances." She huffs. "Maybe every so often, Vassili needs time alone."

"Mom, don't do that. There's no such thing as giving a man an inch when it comes to you. Zamora Hankins, you're always ready to give him a mile." I lower my voice as if Natasha is aware of where this conversation is headed.

"There's a difference between a man hitting on you and needing a moment..."

"Mom," I grumble.

"Space," she snaps. "He could need space. We can ask his uncle Malich if this is a trend in their family. Hell, this could be a Russian thing. And you, my dear, married a Russian. You need to learn about their customs."

Feels like water is becoming white noise in my ears as I fail at making my case. "I've known Vassili for a decade, Mom. It's not an annual trend or something he does every ten years. We didn't make it."

"*Didn't make it*, my ass. You're not divorced yet. And you said you'd have your coworker draw up the papers days ago. You're having second thoughts."

"Don't keep Sammy waiting on my account." I wink. Yup, that little action made me seem a bit psychotic. So far, my melancholic remakes have had mom texting me devotionals at work. Now, she lifts her eyebrows. "We didn't schedule this dinner for me, Zar. But for us to have the chat you refuse to. We thought with wine. . ."

"I get it," I chuckle, cutting in. "You thought with wine, candlelight, and the ambiance. Hmm, I'm stopping there. Maybe I don't get it. Momma, please get ready *for your date with Sammy.*"

An hour later, Natasha and I are in an affluential area where Malich has owned a mansion for ages. Who knows if he remembers the man he was before Igor died? Yuri shared that it has taken years for his father to be molded back into that man after the death of his wife. Malich has to remember he's the one who has every family member he knows at his house for dinner. Before anyone leaves, they come to see him, telling him their needs. He's the patriarch. The provider.

But when I pull past the wrought iron gates, only two imports are in the lot. Yuri's SUV and Malich's late-model Mercedes. My heart falls. Did Mikhail return to the ER? I would give the doctor a call, but he wasn't the same since his brother's death, either.

I get out of the car and open the backdoor. Natasha is latched into her convertible car seat. The puffy tulle of her dress is extra dramatic around the belt straps. I pull her out.

"Mommy, love," she tells me.

I offer her a quick, puckered kiss. "We're here to see Uncle Malich. You ready to see your uncle?"

"Albina!" She shouts the name of Igor and Anna's two-year-old daughter. She was almost the same age as Natasha is now when I first met her. Malich had opened the door with Albina in his arms.

"I hope little Albina's here too," I murmur, pressing my lips to Natasha's forehead for one more good luck kiss.

The door opens, and Anna stands there. She's dressed in black, which makes her skin fade. The dark undertones of the lack of the right vitamins and lack of sleep are viable beneath her skin. Anna hugs me and then takes Natasha from my arms.

"Albina will be so happy to see you, Natasha."

She starts into the house; I shade my eyes. The walls are

sky-high, but not an ounce of evening light gets through the velvet drapes. With my eyes adjusted to the dark, I lock the door.

"Zar, go ahead in the kitchen. Malich is waiting for you."

A lump of trepidation is in my throat. I ask, "Will we all have dinner?"

The ghost of a woman offers a faint smile. "I'll send Natasha and the girls down shortly."

My heart sinks. Anna's the prime example of the worst-case scenario when falling in love with a Russian mobster. "You sure you're not hungry too?"

"Thank you, Zariah, but I am not hungry."

"Vodka?" My smile shakes as I watch them ascend the steps.

"Nyet. I'm sorry."

I head down the vast area, with its out-of-date furniture, and into the kitchen. Malich is seated at the island. He has a butcher's block in front of him. None of the pleasing aromas that generally come from the kitchen surround me. Nothing is the same.

I hear hustling down the steps. A few moments later, Yuri is in the room. "Pops, you said you'd book—"

Malich comes to life, eyes startled until he glances at me. He contains his anger. "Zariah, you came."

"Hi," I murmur, hugging him.

Like Anna, he's lost some weight. His skin is pallid.

Malich asks, "Where is Cutie Pie?"

"Anna took her upstairs to visit Albina."

"Those two are best friends, I see," his response is friendly enough but lacks the care I grew accustomed too. "I've started to cook."

"I don't smell nothing, old man," Yuri says, heading to the wall oven. "You've been down here for ages, muttering about what's for dinner. What exactly did you cook?"

"Yuri!" Malich's fist slams onto the table. From my assessment, he has to have been standing at the island for a very long time, his mind far away from here. "Son, why don't you whip something up for us all, seeing that you have no career. No aspirations!"

Yuri stares at him, eyebrows snatched in confusion. "Dad…"

"You're no longer *managing the situation,*" Malich mocks the same words that Yuri would tell Vassili when my husband says he's the manager. "You're a grown man, son. What is your contribution to this family?"

"I'll cook," Yuri huffs. He retreats toward the refrigerator then comes back. "I'm not some bum who does nothing, Pops. Vassili needs time to think—"

Malich cuts him off with the wave of his hand. His voice is grave and low as he threatens, "Say *that* name again, son."

I gulp. Malich still has enough heart to offer me half of a smile as signal that I'm *not* banned.

Not like Vassili.

Zariah

The scent of coffee beans rouses me from dark thoughts surrounding my husband. I'm seated at a large table toward the back of a knockoff Coffee Bean & Tea Leaf in LA. The light from the front windows shimmies across much of the room but barely reaches me. Shades cover my eyes again. At least this is a bright, early LA morning. Samuel has a monthly meeting here. The tiny café is away from the office, and the carrot cake is the star of the place. Us attorneys are on rotation each month to arrive early and claim the largest table for our group. My stilettos dangle from the high-seated stool. I glare at all the other patrons who think this table is a free for all. Lucky for me, my aura is dark enough to keep the rest of the folks in need of a 'pick me up' from testing me.

My mom texted me during my dinner with Malich that Samuel would come to the café this morning in my stead, I declined. Leaving the house while the sun had yet to say 'hello' worked. I needed to flee my mom's presence by any means. Poor Natasha, she misses Vassili with a vengeance, and I snatched a kiss while she slept this morning.

It's 7 am and an hour left before the rest of the attorneys will trickle in when Tyrese steps into the establishment. The summer sun creates a halo around his warm brown skin, classic suit, and Italian loafers. Women are mid-sip of their drinks, and a few are even jamming carrot cakes in their mouths when they stop to stare. All I can think about is the token times my white-thug of a husband donned a suit. No matter how Vassili acted the last time I laid eyes on him, old school R&B broken heart songs ain't got nothing on me.

Tyrese removes a pair of sunglasses that cost more than anyone is wearing in the room. His gaze slithers across the customers; thick lips pull upward once he finds me. Or it's my imagination. Tyrese has been with Billingslea Law Firm for a little over two months, so he's aware that we all meet here and at what time. Last month, he was put on the calendar for November and was reminded to arrive extra early. But that was for November—not the start of September. This is my month.

"You're early," I quip. "Had I known, you could've taken this month and yours too."

"I wanted to talk to . . ." His palms start for the backs of my hands.

"Talk." I press mine into my lap.

"Zariah, I'm concerned about you." Tyrese groans. "We haven't always seen eye to eye."

"Now that we've *teamed up* on Noriega's case," I pause, aware of how I gritted out the word. *Vassili and I were a team.* Removing my glasses, I pinch the bridge of my nose. I pray to God that my eyes mirror him and not the frayed emotions of my heart. "Tyrese, I'm not divorced yet."

"That's what we need to talk about." He leans closer to me. "Your safety concerns me."

I snort. "You think—"

"Fuck," he mouths under his breath.

I track where Tyrese is now staring. My assistant, Lynetta, is strutting into the coffee shop. I murmur, "Well, if everyone was going to come early, I could've been fashionably late."

Without laughing at my watered-down joke, Tyrese arises from his seat. He places his hand on my shoulder, the thumb strumming across my skin. "Can we talk about this later?"

"No need."

"Then, when are you going to view the documents that I drew up for you, Zar?" He glances at me, wanting a quick response. All I can offer is a shrug as Lynetta moves through the crowd and toward us. Tyrese pulls out her seat. She proceeds to flirt relentlessly until the entire team has arrived.

Friday marks a few days shy of three weeks since I've seen my husband. Lord knows how many times I've hovered over his contact in my phone, with the urgency to tell him about Malich. Anatoly must've known Danushka was after him when she and Horace forced us all to Italy in lieu of Russia. All Malich did was blot out my name and Natasha's from Anatoly's shit list.

So, I sit in my office all day and call to check on Natasha each time my thumb hovers over Vassili's number. When it's time to leave, I glance into Samuel's niece's office. Aside from him being my mentor, his niece was another reason I'd passed the bar on the first go. Connie isn't there. I bite my lip. For the past few days, I've walked out with her to deter Tyrese from asking me about the documents.

The smoggy heat descends as I open the door. Tyrese is

coming out of his office around the perimeter; his pace is quickening. "Zar," he calls, in a respectable, firm tone.

Removing my phone from the pocket of my skirt, I pretend to be unaware and answer an imaginary call while stepping outside. I've just taken a few steps from the front door when a Bentley with blackout tint stops parallel to me. The luxury vehicle is so close that the heat from the engine singes against my skin.

"Hey, Zariah," Tyrese calls out as the window zips down.

"Get in," a man with a clipped Russian voice orders. Standing at my full height and with the car so near, all I can see is the outline of his custom suit. The outline is fitting of the Incredible Hulk. He's a little larger than Mikhail, and nobody else in Vassili's family comes to mind. Who the hell is he?

With Tyrese worried about my 'safety' around my husband, I play this cool as a cucumber. "Just a sec, sir."

"I said get in," he growls.

But my legs are already strutting back toward Tyrese, who has made it out the door. "Oh, um, yes?"

The driver's voice is deathly low, "Get in or he dies."

"Okay," I growl under my breath. "Give me a moment."

Plastering on a smile, I weigh my options. Piss off the stranger, who I owe absolutely nothing to. Or give my colleague another reason to worry.

I walk back toward the building. Alright, poppa didn't raise no fool. Of course, one doesn't turn their back on a threat. If the stranger desires to do me any harm, I might as well include my partner in crime—when it came to the Noriegas.

Tyrese stares past me as he attempts to get a good look into the car. "Who's that?"

"Family," I gulp, then plaster on a smile. Intuition tells me that this is the truth, so I shrug and repeat, "My husband's family."

Tyrese's light brown gaze zips across my own as if at this moment, he wishes for his words to sink in. He touches my biceps, rubbing them softly. I don't push away like I'd done at the coffee shop. I'm too afraid to tell Tyrese about my fear. Because one, my husband made me fearless. Two, regardless of if whoever sent for me is team Danushka or team Anatoly, I have to know what's going on with Vassili.

For all the times my thumb has hovered over his contact, I've called him a thousand more times. It's always at night when desperation suffocates the life right out of me. When I'm too exhausted to analyze our last moment together. When I need him like my next breath.

"Yes?" I clear my throat, realizing Tyrese hasn't said a word either.

"That's your husband's family, Zariah." His grip on my arm becomes a little firmer. "Please tell me you're safe."

"Stop being paranoid, Mr. Nicks," I murmur, unable to catch the hitch in my tone. "I'm dissolving a relationship with my husband, the same as half the human population. We have a daughter that his family adores."

"And they're pulling up to your job like this?"

"Yes."

"Where's your car?"

I stop myself from glancing over my shoulder. Shit. From his stance, I can tell that the attorney is ready to grill me. When I started walking outside, was my car in the lot? Had whoever sent for me 'removed' it from the equation so that I'd take the ride—nice ride. I chortle, removing his hands from my arms. "Have a good weekend, Mr. Nicks."

My coworker stares at me intently as I turn in my heels and strut back to the car. After the fiasco with Yuri, Tyrese shouldn't see the fear engulfing me. My palms are sweaty, my knees weak. I open the front door and climb inside.

"Good thinking," the man's voice wraps around me like smooth steel. I haven't even looked at him yet, but I offer Tyrese another wave and smile while shutting the door. I sit back almost too afraid to get his true description. I inhale deeply and another scent rouses me. This one doesn't couple well with the beast seated beside me. I start to turn my head.

"Don't look back yet, sweetheart." The voice is deep, kind. Deceptively kind. His cologne infuses in my nostrils, offering a pleasant, calming scent. A marriage of masculinity and luxury warn that were the two of us friends, I'd be safer than I've ever been.

From the corner of my eye, Tyrese is leaning against the door, still watching. And I'm seated, face forward, intelligent enough to heed the words of the man seated behind me.

"I had hoped to meet you under different circumstances. Better contexts, my daughter."

The fine hairs on my arms ascend. My brain issues various commands for me to take my next breath. Needing oxygen to speak, I suck in a dose of air and murmur, "Anatoly?"

"That, I am. Sweetheart, you may look back once we leave the parking lot. If it pleases you," he continues. Every word he says is marred with an erotic tone. He isn't even saying anything sexual for goodness sake. He sounds like the devil when compelling a woman to the delights that hell offers— first. "If you prefer, once we are away from here, Simeon will stop and allow you to get in the backseat. We are going to your home, so you are aware. Also, your vehicle is waiting for you at home. Please, my beautiful Zariah, don't worry. Do let me know if you have other questions, I may be able to answer them."

"Th-thank you," I stutter. Rubbing a hand over my

forearm in self-comfort, I take a look at my husband's cousin, Simeon. His sister is Anatoly's younger sibling, and she has a seat at the table of seven. My breath hitches. He looks nothing like Vassili said!

Simeon's face is not the rear end of a dog, not in the slightest. His gaze is dark as sin. His face is chiseled gold. He's beautiful. Devastatingly handsome . . . just like my Vassili. He has to be a few years younger than my husband. Simeon reminds me of when Vassili and I first met like he's more beast than man. I almost smile reminiscing on how my fighter for a husband softened for me.

"Wow. So, you're family, too?" I ask him.

Simeon curses under his breath. The exit that he's attempting to navigate also leads to that dreaded Hot Chili's drive-thru line. Hungry Los Angelinos still don't know how to act and as usual multiple patrons are blocking the exit with their cars.

"You're going to want to . . ." I gesture with my hand, in a friendly tone. "Yes, that's how you do it, *fam*."

Simeon grunts more, without acknowledging the help I offered. Hell, maybe he didn't even get that 'fam' was subliminal for him to treat me as such. Although Simeon looks like my husband, he chills me. Almost like when you look into the eyes of a serial killer on a news segment. He scares the *fuck* out of me.

Anatoly says, "While we leave this forsaken lot, my Zariah, I must be blunt. You are not to fraternize with Tyrese Nicks outside of work. Do you understand?"

His voice still sounds like sex. As if he should be having all his conversations with any other woman in this world— not his daughter-in-law, but while in a bed.

"Oh?" I cringe, offering said daft response.

"He is what you call a bad man."

The lawyer in me shines through, "You know him?"

"*Krasivaya*, I'm a very powerful man. I know everything about him. *The attorney.*" His delicious low voice transforms into a rumble of a laugh. What did he mean by the attorney? Simeon has stopped the car. "Now, please, if you will. Come sit next to your new daddy."

I thought my knees would give out when I opened the door the first time. I rely on my hands, they move from the handle to the top of the passenger door, assisting me with standing. My hands go to the backdoor, holding me up. There's no such thing as a request. He formed his words as such. 'Now, please if you will,' were niceties in a world engulfed in darkness. There's no such thing as me obliging him either. I open the door. In the back seat, right on my side, Anatoly is seated.

"Oh, I . . ." I start to close the door to move around to the other side, but his hand catches mine. His fingers envelop my hand fully, and again, he doesn't have to say anything in that sexy tone of his. He's hardly moved toward the middle seat when I'm pulled in behind the passenger seat. The door is yanked shut. The king of the Bratva's body is pressed against mine, and he looks almost just like my husband. The car starts again.

I stare at him for a moment forgetting who he is. Vassili surrounds all my thoughts. I miss him with all of me. Anatoly's hand is against my cheek, his breath tickling my lips.

"How did my son throw you away, Krasivaya?" he asks lips a fraction from mine. He begins to call me beautiful in Russian, again and again. One hand dips between my thighs, and the other goes behind my neck, pressing my lips to his.

A resounding smack sends a hard dose of ice through my veins. I stare at him, his chiseled jaw burning red beneath the skin. My palm is on fire from the blow. The desire in his eyes obliterates.

Fuck, I'm dead . . .

"Anatoly," Simeon grits out. I don't know if his nephew is warning him from the kiss or urging him to punish me. I stare, wide-eyed, waiting for any retaliation.

"You still love him?" Anatoly sits back in the chair. His hand clamps between my thighs again. Though my sex responds, I try to push him away. His fingernails chew into the flesh at the inside of my leg, locking on to me. "You still love him, answer me, girl!"

"What happened to krasivaya?" I cackle, still working at removing his hand. My fingernails dig into his wrists. We're both on a mission to draw at each other's life source.

"Do you still love my blood?" With the question, his hand ascends another notch.

"Anatoly!" Simeon breaks.

The car stalls. A flurry of honking and cussing flash toward us.

"Do you still ..." Anatoly repeats his question as I grow nauseated. His palm rises another notch, the inside of his hand brushing against the silk of my panties.

"Mrs. Resnov, you will have to answer him," Simeon barks at me. "I will not save you."

The beast without a mask confuses me. Save me? Simeon thought of saving me? The other monster, the one in an angel's disguise, clings to my thigh.

I growl. "Yes!"

"Good." He lets go, his fingers tweaking across my sex before he removes his hand. "Let me know if I should kiss away the hurt, daughter."

Anatoly sits back in the chair, undoing the top button of his suit. He places his hand to his nose. I glance at Simeon, whose eyes are shot, with a rage that I don't understand. Why is he angry? This bastard was a second away from raping me. This bastard is his blood.

I cross my legs, keeping them as shut as possible. Taking a deep breath, I focus on ceasing the trembling of my spirit. Then I ask, "Do you plan to harm me or my daughter? My-my daughter? How is my car at home? My mother and my daughter are—"

"Relax, krasivaya," he mutters. "Your mother and Chak Chak take a walk around this time of day at the park. Next, it's cupcakes or donuts at the bakery around the block. We have all the time that we need."

"All the time we need for what, Mr. Resnov?"

"For me to know if you are worth my blessing."

13

Vassili

"Did you touch her?" I growl. My first words are supposed to be for my wife. All my attention should've been for her. I am supposed to apologize for following through with our plan and letting her leave in Italy. I am also supposed to kiss her and tell her that I miss her more than any MMA technique I ever learned.

My gaze tracks from Anatoly to Zariah to Simeon and back again as they trudge down the hallway and into the sitting room. I'd just sat down from an attempt at burning a hole in my wife's favorite oriental rug. I'd been pacing back and forth. I wanted to go get my wife. She fucking belongs to me. As I paced, a million wild thoughts slammed through my brain like a freight train. Now, I'm up in seconds, her favorite throw coming undone as I tear it apart. "Did you touch my wife!"

Zariah sighs. "Vassili, stop ruining our furniture."

"Listen to your wife, *moy syn.*" Anatoly winks.

Zariah moves before him as my fist flies. I stop a fraction from her face. "Don't. Ever do that," I growl, fist-shaking.

Her hand goes to her hip. "We need to talk."

Simeon moves toward the coffee table and plucks up a shiny, red apple. He groans, realizing its fake.

Anatoly seems to be waiting for a fight, but glances at my cousin. The one who saved his life so many times before. The three of us end up fighting, or Simeon wins by default. And fuck no, not because he's a big mudak. We all end up bloodied. He usually stops us all with a gun to my head.

The cunt, who I'll never call father to his face, shrugs. "Ah, no fun? No anarchy? Well, I had that protein shake for nothing."

"So, this is how the two of you say hello?" Zariah glances between the two of us. "Fighting and glaring?"

"Dah, he's a disrespectful child." Anatoly sniffs. "Simeon, you hungry?"

He nods.

I glare at Anatoly and order, "Be gone before Zamora returns with my daughter. And if Danushka has someone watching…"

"Pah, they're not as equipped as you're giving them credit for, *moy syn*."

My father's eyes are all over my wife as we head toward the double staircase. Just his gaze is enough to send venom shooting through my veins. But the two mudaks head toward the garage.

As we walk up the steps, Zariah's body calls to me. I reach up and skim the inside of her thigh.

"Don't even think about it," she grits over her shoulder.

Before I can finish laughing at her warning, I've gripped my forearm around her waist and scooped her hips. All that ass spills over my shoulder. She dangles in my arm as I continue to climb the step.

"Vassili, you asshole! You wanted me to *pretend* to start divorce proceedings, I should!" She seethes. Her arms flail behind me, and her legs kick the air in front of me. I could've held her in my arms, but she's pissed off.

"Why the fuck did you wear a skirt today," I growl.

"Asshole," she says, issuing an onslaught of slaps until she feels unbalanced and has to grab my head.

In the bedroom, I close the door and fling her onto the bed. *"Why did you wear a skirt?"*

She starts to rise, but I press her chest until she's flopping back on the bed. We do that a few times before Zariah comes to an understanding that she's to stay there.

"You're mad about a skirt?" She lifts the edge of the material before pushing it back. "You have nothing to be angry about, Vassili!"

"Did he—"

"Want some leftover pussy," she spits out.

I stand back, hands at the top of my head. "We had to sound convincing, Zar."

"Fuck convincing! You didn't even give us a chance." She starts to get up again. Her hand dashes out. A resounding smack slams across my face. I take it, and then I push her back onto the bed.

She sits straight up. "Not a single chance to work this out together. Vassili, your father was the last case scenario! But you fuck me stupid, give me a plan that may or may not be necessary. After two hours of sleep, you execute that plan—a fail-safe! Hello, it means, try a few tactics first, not dig straight in. I have never been so angry with you, Vassili. Never."

"I apologize," I reply, attempting to stare straight into her eyes.

"I'm not ready to compromise." She pings back up, her hands flying. I grab both her wrists, spin her around, and now the two of us are on the bed. My hard cock spearing her ass.

With her face against the sheets, Zariah screams. "I am so mad at you."

"Okay," I bark. "You have the right to be. Can we talk?"

Beneath me, my wife has all the pent-up aggression that I once had while waiting to get into the cage. She snaps, "So mad I could—"

"I'm trying not to be a mudak, Zar."

She flies off at the mouth with, "You are! You're a mo-deck!"

I smile at Zariah's mispronunciation of the word. It's not time for me to correct my wife on the language because her entire attitude needs changing. I clasp my hand at the back of her neck. The fury in her burning the inside of my palms. "Girl, if you make me rise to your level of anger, you will not like it."

"You never need me, Vassili…"

Times like this make me wish I hadn't shaved my Mohawk. I need something to tug. Something to hit. But I'm lying in a soft bed with the woman who belongs to me. She's dead-on about one thing. I'm too much of a *mudak* to tell her that I belong to her too.

Instead of reassuring her like I've done a thousand times before, I roll over and onto my side of the bed. After a few more moments, Zariah lays back onto my chest. I disconnect myself from her sniffles. Looking at her reminds me of my mother.

Zariah burrows her face into my chest. I'm about to thread my fingers into her hair when she asks me another question that reminds me of my past. "Did you play your part with Danny? *Screw all the pieces of ass* she had at her disposal for you?"

———

"Anatoly, did you fuck her?" My mother growled. "I'm begging you to hit me. Hit me!"

His hand zipped out faster than I'd ever seen. Blood spurted down her nose.

I moved in front of my dad. I was so little he almost gave me the kick that was meant for my mother's stomach. The one that would've murdered Sasha before she even had a chance to survive...

With one hand clinging to her swollen belly and the other was around me, she snapped. "Hit me, Anatoly. Hit me and hit me and then kill me because I'm not in the mood for this."

"You're pregnant," he growled. Still, I was invisible, and he almost tripped over me to get to her. "You fucking piz'da, you want me to kill you?"

"Nyet!" I screamed, my cheeks shaking.

"Dah!" she sneered.

"All because I have enough love to give to some other piz'das. You want me to kill you?" He seemed to notice me then. Bent down to my level, he pulled out a gun. My three-year-old hands drooped as he offered it to me.

"This cunt wants to die, Vassili. She's selfish. You want to stay with your mama? I know you do, moy syn." He tipped my chin up and down for me.

"Please," I cried.

He stopped forcing me to nod and clawed his fingers into my skin. "I won't murder your mama. Maybe she's begging me to kill that little fucker in her womb."

"Anatoly," she spoke. All the animosity had fled from her tone. "I'm—"

"Too late for apologies. You want to die, and you want the Resnov in your belly to die? You want me to kill my own blood. Or have you been having a little fun too, slut?"

"This is your child..."

"Vassili's my child." Anatoly moved me around until I faced her. His arm draped over my shoulder. "This is my child. My son. I don't have daughters, bitch. Who is that in your belly—"

"You have Danushka. This is Sasha!" I blurted as if reminding him of the name Mom and I chose meant a thing.

He spun me around. "Like your babushka, Vassili?"

I nodded. Tears gleamed in my eyes, but my lips pulled in a smile. "Dah. We named her after Grandma Sasha."

My father spun me back around, drape an arm over me. He gritted out, "You naming the kid after my mom, slut?"

"She's your child, Anatoly."

He pressed the barrel of his gun into my hands. I'd wiggled and tried to pull away, but his fingers clawed into my wrists. He forced me forward until the barrel of the gun pressed against her growing stomach.

"Cock back the hammer, moy syn!"

I shook my head, a torrent of tears in my eyes, blinding me to the sight of my mother's fear.

"Cock the motherfucking hammer, Vassili." His words rang in my ears. "I'll have a doctor patch up your mama. She won't leave you—can't leave you, even if she wants to. Cock it before you get the spanking of your life!"

I did as told.

"You done asking me if I'm cheating on you, slut?" he asked my mother.

"Did you have fun cheating?" Zariah asked again. Her chortle pulled me away from the worst part. My father had given me the beating of my life. At least, my mom and Sasha were safe for the moment.

"I played my part," I mumble, still dazed by the memory. All I know about my mother is *pain*. Every thought connecting to her is an example of the man I never wanted to be.

The flashback continues to call to me, but Zariah's entire body tenses. What the fuck did I say? I'd been in a daze. What did I say?

"What?" I ask, trying not to sound like I don't give a fuck, though a part of me still clings to the memory of how Sasha never had a chance.

"You did what you had to. You *played* the part." She sits up.

I grab her to another round of her physically attacking me. "Kisses, Zariah. I kissed a few women. Watched a few more than when we were alone—nothing. I didn't cheat."

"Hello, you kissed women but didn't cheat! Let me kiss another man, Vassili. You make me insane!" She scampers across the bed.

The nightmare still clings to me. I glare at her. "Insane, that's fine. As long as you know who owns you, Zariah, you can go fucking insane!"

"You are an asshole," she says, lips trembling.

"I've heard that, girl. The last night I was with you, I asked you a question." I get out of the bed and go sit on the lounge, facing her. "I'm not fucking you right now, Zariah. So, I'll ask you the same motherfucking question again."

"Oh, does screwing me while inquiring make me prone to lying? Is that what you think! What question, Vassili?" She sits at the edge of the bed, feet dangling. "All I remember was orders and threats during our last night in Italy."

"I asked if you could turn back time, would you?" My breath catches. Fuck, I don't need her noticing that. All she's ever known was my undisputed confidence. "Would you?" I roar.

Zariah's shoulders jolt. With tears streaking down her gorgeous dark skin, she glares at me. "Don't you ever ask me that, Vassili. The answer will forever be no. We have a baby girl, Vassili. I'm giving you a daughter or a son! There's a tiny seed growing in my belly," she grits, clutching at her flat abdomen. "So, ask me this shit again, I will try to fight you myself! There's no such thing as turning back time because I'd fall for you every time. Our lives are hard right now. I'd still do this over. Do it all over. Every second!"

My chest broadens with oxygen. I get up from my seat, limbs heavy. In front of Zariah, I move to my knees and press my mouth against hers.

"Khorosho," I mumble.

The mudak in me that's just like my father wants to say more. To say that her response was nothing to me. That regardless of her declaration, either way, she would forever be mine. I'm a fighter and not some piz'da who uses his mouth to threaten. I back my shit up with action. The type of response *she* craves.

My mouth moves from her lips to her jaw, down the length of her neck. When my lips press against the pulse of her neck, Zariah lets out a moan. My left hand drags into her flat-ironed hair, gripping the strands while tugging. Her pulse taps against my bottom lip, I sink my teeth into her flesh, sucking and biting.

"There isn't a single reason for me to cheat, Zariah. Everything you have makes me crazy." I suck at her neck, leaving a sign of my love there. "I love that mouth, your walk, your ass. I'm addicted to finding more reasons to put a smile on your face. I own you." *We own each other*.

"Oh, Vassili," she moans.

"No reason for me to look at another woman, girl. You have water between those fucking thighs, all a man like me needs to live on."

The thickest thighs I've ever known splay further for my muscular frame. My lips travel down to her breasts. I reach around her and tear the seam of her blouse then unhook her bra.

Leaning back on my haunches, I order, "Get undressed."

My heart booms inside of my chest. It beats hard as fuck as Zariah slides to the left side of her hips, pushing her skirt and panties down at the same time. Her curvy frame lifts on the opposite side. My hands skim up her legs, meeting hers as she gathers the material. I yank it off for her, then I'm leaning back again. Like a tiger whose next meal is the feast of its life, this mudak needs a moment to contemplate *how* he plans to dig in.

I'm going to beat this pussy up, TKO it. Before that, I'm going to break those glossed, fatty lips down slowly with my mouth.

Zariah's gaze flickers with desire, fear, and craving. "What should I do . . . Vassili?" She almost stutters as she did on our first time. Her first time. She'd been so innocent, and she still is.

"Sit there," I tell her, returning my gaze to her sex. I groan, "Damn, you're getting wet for me, and I'm not even touching that pretty pussy. You want me to touch it, don't you? Drink all that water?"

Her hands fly to the sides of her, clutching the edges of the bed.

I chuckle softly. "Don't worry, girl. I'll touch it. Before I do, Daddy has a request."

My wife's full lips hardly move as she begs, "Please . . ."

"Keep that ass planted on the edge of the bed. Put your heels up on the edge of the bed too. I need to see more of that pretty pussy, examine your clit, your folds. See how wet you get while I watch," I reply, though my attention is not leaving that gorgeous pussy of hers anytime. Zariah does my bidding. Her thick thighs press against the sides of her. Her breasts are right there in the center, followed by a tiny stomach that I'm eager to watch grow. That tiny waist of hers gives way to her legs shoved close to her body. What's between those legs and pretty feet is all I ever wanted.

While I'm eyeing her pussy like a hawk, I watch those fatty folds begin to twitch a little.

"Vassili, this is torture. Your words, you're eyeing me, it's killing me. You can screw me, make love to me, or—or—or do something!"

"Shhh." I place my finger at my lips, gesturing to her sex. "Me and this pretty pussy haven't had a chat in a good amount of time. I can't just beat the pussy, not yet. We have to connect."

Again, her lips quiver. I'm not even thinking about blinking while staring at the glistening folds. My cock strains against my pants.

She groans, "We don't have time for—"

"Don't say another word, Zar," I growl. My gaze has yet to leave my pleasure. I lean forward, and Zariah exhales. I lean back.

"Vas—"

"Shhh, girl," I grit out. I look up at her, and she has a silly smile on her face.

"I really hate you, Vassili."

Wagging a finger at her, I warn, "You fucked this entire process up, girl. Let's start over. Pretty Pussy, are you—"

"Oh, hell, no! You aren't having a conversation with my lady bits." Zariah starts to press her knees together.

Leaning back on the floor, I fold my arms.

She resumes position.

"Remember when I showed you off in the mirror, Pretty Pussy?"

"I—"

"This is a conversation between me and Pretty Pussy," I

grit out. "Sorry about that, Pretty Pussy, some people lack respect."

Zariah's lips purse and she stops herself from all the arguing that she's accustomed too. She wraps her arms around her knees, but my pretty pussy is still on deck at the edge of the bed.

I lean forward on my knees, then press my thumbs between Zariah's slit. Her hands go behind her, and those hips curve; back arches, offering me more pussy. With my thumbs all glossed up from her outer folds, I press back the flesh and get a good look at her cunt. I lean forward even more, and she sighs again. It's one of those 'thank you' sighs where I know I won't have to hear her shit talk.

My lips touch her clit. I'm 190 pounds of muscle, but I do that shit with such finesse that her legs tremble on either side of my biceps.

"Fu-fu-fuck, Vassili," she squeals.

My wife has my lips so glossed up that I wouldn't be picked out of a lineup.

"I knew you missed me, Pretty Pussy," I groan. "Wet as fuck at first touch. That's what I've always loved about you."

"I love you too, Vassili," Zariah chuckles.

"Shhh, sweetheart. I'm having a private conversation.

"Then you keep chatting and add some penetration, licking and sticking and chatting. How about that?"

My breath lands against her sex as I laugh heartily before Zariah can continue arguing, my entire mouth plants across Pretty Pussy. My tongue darts deep as my mouth dances around her cunt.

"I love you. I love you, I loveeeee you," Zariah groans. Her silky, soft fingers clasp at the back of my neck as my tongue flicks and coats inside of her honey. The lion in me growls against her sopping wet flesh. And that growl is enough to unleash more sugar as she comes all over my mouth.

"Oh shit, oh shit," she murmurs, voice hardly audible. Her hips roll around on the edge of the bed, fucking my tongue slowly. I lean back on my haunches again, my fingers digging into the flesh of her ass, bringing Zariah with me.

"Oh," she yelps.

Not paying her any attention, I move around until my calves are no longer over me, and I'm lying on the floor. Zariah straddles my face. I can't breathe. That's okay. It goes with the territory of being a professional in the MMA world. She can come again and offer one more fuck face that I can't see now—at least. With her knees on the ground by my ears, Zariah works hard for her release. Somehow, I've sopped up some of her juices rolling down the side of my face and then my thumb plunges into her ass.

My cock barks in my pants. Fuck, I should've undressed first. The beast is calling me all kinds of idiots and dumb-fucks in Russian as I work her hole. My dick loves her dark brown cakes, and it can't get to her.

Zariah erupts on my face. The instant her body tenses up, she yelps again. Now she's face down on the ground.

"I am not in the friggen octagon, Vassili," she groans. "This takedown was illegal."

"Shhhh…" My chest is against her back, and I lift myself on to one hand to unbuckle my pants. Fuck shoving them down. The blue balls I've suffered for weeks will be the death of me if I go another second without busting into her pussy. So that's exactly what I do. Eyes rolling back in my head, I sit in Pretty Pussy for a second. Pretty, tight, wet, drug, fuck yes. My brain stops. My muscles relax, and I sit there in her cunt. This is what life is made of. The world can fall apart around us, but I'd kill a motherfucker first before I leave these wet walls.

14

Zariah

H *ell to the no!* Vassili's cock slammed straight through my pussy. At the moment, it was enough for my walls to milk him for all of his worth, but I'm not done with him.

His hungry gaze had my neither regions spazzing like crazy. Now they're insane. My fingers clench the plush rug, and I slap my ass cheeks against his muscular frame. The Russian fighter is built like a brick. We are going to cum until our bodies are bathed in his seed.

"Give my pussy a little more, Killer Karo," I growl, ass slamming back, my pussy gobbling his dick.

That rouses my husband because his hands claim my thighs, and he pumps hard enough that I have to stop helping him. I steady my knees and forearms as he thrusts deeper into my valley than I ever thought possible. His breathing becomes heavy, sounds so good to my ears.

Understanding my plight, Vassili pulls out. "Clean me off, girl. You got my dick so wet . . ."

"Mhhhh," I'm moaning like Thanksgiving dinner before

I've even placed my lips on his cock. Vassili sinks back onto the floor again, his back against the bed. I slither my tongue around his stiff, erection, taking extra care to stroke his deep veins. There's nothing like a man with a veiny cock that grows to infinity. After I've licked off the sweet taste of me, I pull him into my mouth. Damn, he's at the back of my tonsils, and I wish I had more room to give him. Half of my husband's cock is going cold. I place my hand around the base of his shaft, and he growls.

It's the pure, animalistic growl he gave earlier. The one that set fireworks off my pussy lips before he even touched it! Fuck. An orgasm rushes down the inside of my thighs. I remove my hand from his cock and continue sucking.

"That's right, Zar, get Daddy good and clean." His deep voice is silky and hypnotizing. "Don't you ever use your fucking hands on me, beautiful. You're better than that."

I almost pause. Vassili Karo Resnov is a cocky, confident bastard.

"That's enough. Get our lubricant," Vassili nudges his square jaw to his nightstand, the one that's clear over on the opposite side of the bed. How. The. Hell. Will. I. Get. There.

As I sit on my hip, Vassili grabs my hair, and he glares at me. "Get the lubricant, Zariah."

My eyelid twitches. I pop up from the floor. In record speed, our ultra-comfy mattress has become my obstacle course as I bound over it. I yank the top drawer out, grab the lubricant, and start to climb back, but Vassili is seated on my side of the bed. His hands are behind his head. He hasn't broken a sweat. His abdominals and massive chest are hardly moving while I work to catch my breath.

He gestures for me, then bites his lip. I climb onto his cock, handing over the lubricant.

Vassili presses a hand across my throat and squeezes it delicately. "Thank you, girl."

"You're welcome, boy," I reply, timing my aggressive response with just how sexy I feel while grinding on his cock.

"Keep working that pussy for me, Zar." He peppers my neck with kisses. "Next, you'll work that ass."

"I am working my ass," I offer him banter with a flutter of my eyes.

"Not the way you will be when I tell you." He offers a rare smile, but not the one I love. It's contrite and snarlier than anything.

With my body sliding up and down Vassili's, I continue to let my juices flow on his cock. He sits up, and my hard nipples drag across his hard chest, titillatingly slow. I realize that I've been moaning so much that it almost hurts.

My heart is filled with love. Vassili's hand skims across the side of my breast. The delicious feeling of his hands on my body dies as he sets me on the bed. I lay on my side, watching him coat his magnificent cock with gel. He gestures for me to move positions, and I'm now in reverse cowgirl.

"Now, you can work that ass . . ."

I glance back at him, straddling his legs, but I pause. "Huh?" Alright, that sounds stupid. Of course, I'm aware of what my husband wants. And yes, I've had his thick, white cock in my ass, but only when he's fucking me from behind. The control he's offering scares me.

He drags his fingertips across my spine. He orders, "Do it."

My mind flashes to Anatoly for a moment. A smooth, kind voice had clashed with actions that vastly deterred from it. I shove his father away from my mind as Vassili's palm presses against my back.

"You got this," he says, his voice returning to the nurturing coach I love.

I start back, aligning my anus with his lubricated cock. The cool gel feels good.

"Fuck your clit, Zariah; it'll clear your mind."

Feeling more like a team than we have been in the past, I skim my finger along my tiny pearl, press inside of me, and gather more gush. With my fingers coated, I caress my clit. Next, I realign my ass with his cock head. Measuring my breathing, I start to work his crown against my sphincter. This is all a mind fuck, a sensual, carnal mind-fuck because he's done this before.

The control part is what scares me. When it comes to sex, I trust my husband with my body more than I trust me. He's well versed in the language and taught me everything I know. A feeling of bliss sends goosebumps sparkling along my forearms as I work my ass down on his massive cock. I move into a squatting position, lick my lips, and concentrate on my husband's happiness.

Then I do something I should've done from the start. I stop giving a damn about my emotions and focus on him.

He's breathing. It's a phenomenon. The fighter can run five miles, TKO a slew of men and then take one influx of oxygen. His breathing is steady, heavy, and does something to me. In a squatted position, I press my hands onto my knees and pop my ass up and down. I breathe in the scent of all the sex we made with each thrust and work his cock in my ass.

"Oh shit," Vassili growls.

"Cum in my ass," I shout the words before they even came to fruition in my mind. My ass continues to pump his cock. "Cum in my ass, Vassili."

He screams my name, my ass gripping his cock as a volcano of hot seed sears into me. My pussy quakes, making my tiny asshole hurt. I revel in how his dick spasms inside of my ass. Heart slamming against my breast, I hold the position. My thighs are weaker than they've ever been before, but I take pride in keeping them up. After his eruption, I lay back on Vassili and breathe.

"I missed you so much," he murmurs in my hair.

Pressing my hand over my drumline of a heart, I smile. "I've missed you, too."

With my eyes barely peeling open, I reach out for Vassili. A coldness creeps into my heart. His side of the bed is empty. Not even warm. I whimper.

"Don't you dare cry," a baritone voice calls out.

Beam wider than the sunshine, I turn around and sit up. Vassili is seated on the chaise, wide-legged. My bright smile falters at the sight of him. Yesterday evening, he'd been in the same spot, daring me to deny this life that we've built together. Daring me to say that I'd start over and go a different path. Gulping down my worries, I ask, "You've been thinking?"

He directs a thumb over his shoulder. "I watched Natasha sleep for a few hours, then . . ."

"Oh, Natasha," I groan. Somehow, Simeon and Anatoly have worked it out so that my mother and daughter were out all evening. Vassili explained that they had some sort of text scrambler and sent a few messages to her from *my* number. She took Natasha to a Disney movie and dinner on the grounds that I needed time alone. "I know you've missed her, Vassili."

He looks away from me like he did for the first couple of times I mentioned his sister. It had been over a year before he even talked about his mom, so I smile softly. "We'll fix things, baby. We have to—"

"You're going to live with your dad."

I chortle. "Whatever, Vassili."

He's fisting something in his hands, then he tosses it over. It's a burner phone.

"Same passcode as I used to have on my other phone, Zar. You know, before the techy facial recognition bullshit."

Snatching up the phone, my eyebrows pull together. I tap in the code.

"Look at the text messages, Zar."

"I am!" I snap, although I wouldn't have known to do so without a prompt. The text application has been modified. It's not a regular Apple app. I press on one that says, "The Bastard." The blank face emojis that are a part of the name is exactly like I had re-entered my father's number. I scan through the text messages.

"I'm getting a divorce . . ." I read the words.

In a slow, clipped voice, Vassili growls, "Don't say that shit out loud. Please, baby, it's the worst thing that could ever happen to us."

"Who-who wrote this? This was sent to my father's number," I murmur. "Why would we tell him I'm getting a divorce, Vassili! Wh-why! Danny is the only person who needs to believe we're breaking up. Who wrote this!"

His jaw clinches. "You sent it."

"Vassili, don't fuck with me." I hold the phone in both my hands. No matter how heated my flesh is, I can't break the damn thing in half.

"I wrote it, Zar. Your father misses you. Technically, just this morning, the two of you had a good text conversation. He asked if you'd call him to talk about the dynamics of you going home. He'll be there for you when I can't, baby. Think!"

"Fuck you," I screech, pulling the covers over my body.

"Shhh..." He says. "Your mother is a few rooms over. She

115

doesn't know that I'm here, Zariah. Everyone must think
—*know* that we—"

"Fuck you, Vassili," I snap again. "So, we're getting a
divorced."

"I said, don't say that, Zar." Though he's making an order,
his voice seems to soften. He's been right there, across the
way from me this entire time. Till this precise moment, he's
felt as far as he'd been for weeks. "We have to keep up
pretenses—fuck, that's the worst thing I've ever said. Zar,
baby, we have to . . ."

"Divorce," I grit out then chew my bottom lip. "Oh yeah,
it's a 'pretend' divorce. Also, you ordered me not to say as
much. Granted, all these rules are your rules. Yet, you can't
stomach your game plan. I can't live with abandonment.
Can't live with me kissing another man. Fuck you-fuck you.
Triple fuck you," I whisper, tears slamming down my cheeks.
"What are you up to, Vassili?"

He glares at me. An imaginary shield keeps him from
jumping on me and forcing me to shut my mouth. Like I'm
possessed, I continue with, "What are you doing? You tell me
that I need to be safe from Danny! I don't know shit—Yuri
knows even less! What are you really up to? Preparing for the
throne? You'll become your father's successor! Is that what
you're—"

Vassili is off the chaise and on top of me in seconds. My
wrists are above my head. He places his hand firmly over my
mouth. He growls, "I need you to calm down. Do you got
that?"

Once he removes his hand from my mouth, I whimper.
"Yesterday, those requirements of yours came with an apology. Not today? Fuck you a thousand times, Vassili."

"Why you mad?" His Russian accent amplifies and transforms into broken English.

"You said we were a team. That Anatoly was a fail-safe—

not the fucking plan, Vassili. You were supposed to go to your father last! Then you—then you send me home before we—"

His palm claims my lips again. "You said this last night, Zariah. If you don't stop crying right now, *I will leave.* You make me leave and you won't know anything at all."

I swing out. My arm hasn't even hit a trajectory of a few degrees before his hand clamps down on my wrists. I'm sinking right before my husband's eyes, and he doesn't even offer a hand. Vassili Karo Resnov has always saved me.

He's saved me from the torture of murdering my best friend's ex, Sergio.

He's saved me from spending years as an attorney with a life of monotony.

He's saved me from the belief that love wasn't worth it.

Or is it?

15

Vassili

My cock is swollen between us. While Zariah cries, I remind myself that I'm not the mudak who will fuck her as tears stream down her face. I shove one part of my genetic make-up to the background and attempt to cling to rationality.

"Talk to me," I clip out the words.

"You don't care what I have to say," she sniffles.

I lean on my elbow, pinching the bridge of my nose. *You aren't your father's son*, I tell myself. You're better than that piz'da, a billion times better. There's a rage in my soul. I need obedience. I need her to shut the fuck up and listen to what I have to tell her. Her cooperation is of utmost importance. Zariah's compliance means Danushka wouldn't find out I fucked her over for my pops. Of course, I fucked that bitch over for Anatoly. He means nothing to me. My existence comes from him, so Danushka means less than nothing.

The only woman I've ever let hold my heart breathes softly in my arms. Too many weeks have gone without her. I concentrate on gathering all the patience I can muster. "Talk to me, baby."

"You wouldn't answer my calls, my texts."

"We had this chat, Zariah, while I fucked you in Italy. No calls, no texts. Nothing."

My weight crushes her luscious body, clamping her arms down at her sides. It helps me feel her muscles, know when she might attempt to flee. I ask, "Anything else you'd like to tell me?"

"Will you tell me everything? Keep me in the loop?" At my lack of response, Zariah's bottom lip protrudes, compelling me to have a taste of her mouth. I kiss my wife, and her body is putty beneath me. When she's about to run out of air, I let up.

She mumbles, "I missed you . . ."

"Me too, girl," I snap. *C'mon, Vassili,* I tell myself. My hand skims across her face. "Okay, I know, I know. I miss you and Natasha. I miss our life. When this shit is all over, I'll make it up to you. Now, I have to leave before everyone wakes up."

I start to kiss her, and she turns her head. "No, Vassili. I want you. *I want you right here.* Mad. Happy. Fucking me. Making love to me. If I can't have that, then I need space. If I wanted *'Disappearing Acts,'* I'd pick up the book by Terri McMillan. Tell me your plan, Vassili."

"Zar—"

Her breath strokes across my face. "This isn't a typical situation, *Vassili.*"

"Alright, we discussed that the night in Italy, too."

"Yes, you had my back slamming against the wall. You hurt me—"

Guilt burns in my veins, I cut in, "I'm—"

"I loved it," she groans. "The pain also solidified the fact that you can't always be with me."

"Nyet. Fuck that. I could be a million miles away and still

be with you. I'm with you, Zar." I sit up from on top of her, bringing her with me. "You have to get that through your head. While we're apart, I am *for you, with you.*"

She sits back against the headboard, clasping my pillow in front of her, and then she huffs. "At least you get to play the savior. I'm an attorney; I fight in the court, you fight in the cage. Vassili," she groans, "I won't be able to relive what happened the day Natasha and I left you last. Please, let me into the loop. "

"You are," I reply.

"I'm not. Yuri came to my office," she pauses to bite her lip. "He's taking it bad. This is the worst 'new normal' ever. What do you want from me? Can't we tell Yuri?"

I tell her how Yuri and Mikhail parted ways with me.

Zariah sinks back against the pillows. "This is too much, Vassili."

"It is what it is. Malich knows. Mikhail knows too, sweet-heart. Yuri, he's too soft, wears his emotions on his sleeve. Not Mikhail. My cousin would've tried to fucking kill me if he knew I fought Yuri and chose Danushka. Mikhail knows, and Yuri can't play the game."

"You could've told Yuri," she replies. "He's miserable. He's your best friend, your brother."

I groan. My cousin definitely got to her. When Yuri growled about being my brat before I took him down, shit almost broke me. Out of all my half-siblings, I could deny having a brother my entire life. Not Yuri. He *is* my *brat.*

"Look, baby, it sounds bad. The fat fuck doesn't have it in him to have a role. Zariah, now I need you to pack your things. Natasha's too. My father has agreed to keep you safe, but you won't be around him alone. He refused to help unless I allowed him to meet you on his terms. That's the single reason I allowed him and Simeon to pick you up from work."

"I get it. Everyone's showing their balls."

"Unless I tell you that Anatoly is coming around, you run. *You won't be around him alone,*" I parrot like a fucking idiot. I connect gazes with her, needing my words to penetrate. "Got that?"

"Yes."

Feeling my abdominals tangle into knots, I ask, "Did Anatoly treat you right?"

"Yes," she growls.

"You sure?"

"Ha," she chortles. "If I'm to be around another sperm donor, you'll have to believe me, won't you?"

I stare at her for a few beats, recalling how I'd forced her to respond to me yesterday. Would she have a do-over for her life?

It didn't matter what she said. Change the past, not change the past. It all meant nothing.

In no world in which we've crossed paths would I have let her go. I feel myself clinging to the dysfunctional reasoning that drove my father mad in the past. I'll have to believe in her while she's with that mudak, Maxwell Washington.

16

Zariah

For a second, my husband had become tense during our discussion. After which, I welcome the cocky bastard that I'd grown to love as we have, what I assume would be, one last quickie. Vassili fucks my body, directs his own porno, and has me laughing as he talks to Pretty Pussy.

And then he's gone.

After a shower, I wrap a terry cloth towel around my frame. In the bedroom, I stare at a black, willowy dress that I've picked out. Tears form in my eyes and not for the reason that they should. The secretary Grigor murdered with a sniper rifle would be laid to rest today. Her body has been held in the morgue for three weeks. Samuel has pulled a few strings to have the murder investigated. Though it's still labeled as a freak accident. The odd circumstances surround a .50 caliber bullet and a 1.3-mile distance. Tears burn my eyes, and the black dress burns a hole into my soul, darkening it.

Loud arguing ensues. My ears perk up, and I grab the silk robe draped around the back of my chaise, slipping it over my naked body, I hardly have it tied when I open the door and start down the stairs. At the bottom of the steps, my mom stands at the towering front door.

Hand on her hip, Zamora growls, "Who do you think you are?"

"Mom!" I shout, rounding the bend where the double staircase meets toward the bottom.

An authoritarian voice that strikes me as almost familiar reaches out to me. "Ma'am, I am here to complete a safety check—"

"Safety check for who?" I gasp, flying toward the door. The mornings are beginning to cool off for fall, so I wrap my arms around my chest as the air chills at my nipples.

Two officers are standing in the doorway. On is white with a smattering of blond hair and uneasy blue eyes. The other is light-skinned with a broad nose and lips. I've seen him before.

"Officer Jackson," I murmur. Images from the night when Vassili and I went to dinner flood my mind. This had idiot stopped us to ensure I was safe.

The narrowing of his eyes lessens and becomes a smoldering brown as he glances me over. "You remember me?" The blood underneath his chiseled features is highlighted with embarrassment.

"I do," I grit out.

"Well, what do you know, she's safe!" My mother snaps.

"Can we chat?" he starts to gesture for me to follow him across the fragmented stone.

I stay put. "Not necessary."

Jackson licks his lips, and then he stares at my mother before returning his attention to me.

"Who is this man?" my mom argues. "I have your badge number too."

He smiles at her. "Like mother, like daughter."

"What's the reason for the safety check, Officer?" I ask as he appears to be interested in carrying on a full-blown conversation.

"Your father sent me. Do you need any help packing your things?"

"So, you're the movers, huh?" my mom chortles. "Wait, did he say father? What?"

"You can tell him that Natasha and I should arrive this evening, thank you." I slam the door in his face. Forcing a deep inhale, I spin around to give my mother my attention. "Unfortunately, mama, I have to spend a few—"

"You're going to your dad's house, Zariah? Why?" she replies, flustered.

"I heard Vassili's in town," I offer the rote response he gave me. "He has press coverage at Vadim's Gym to—"

"Good, let's go get your man."

"*To* discuss Kong's coma and another anticipated fight if he won. Also, I have a funeral to attend. I'm dressing for it now."

She looks me up and down. "This is what's wrong with young people today, not willing to fight for their relation-ship. You tell me right now, Zar. Has he hurt you in any way? Because either, we are going to pray together that God blesses the two of you, or we will pray that God blesses me not to try and murder that man!"

"Mom!"

"Well, I've gone three weeks under the assumption that your marriage is dissolving for no reason. Tell me," Zamora implores, reaching out to rub my arms. Her palms are warm through my silk robe, and I sigh.

Dammit, Vassili, I contemplate. He told me to be believable, say whatever is necessary. I bite my tongue, unable to sell out my husband.

"Then I'll see you for church tomorrow. Lord knows that Maxwell won't fight for Natasha to have a stable childhood home. After, we can catch up with Vassili. He will give you some sort of explanation, I can promise you that."

The black dress is a fraction from dragging across the lush green grass as I stand toward the back of the crowd. Tyrese is standing at my side; he pulls an arm around my waist.

"Are you okay?"

"I'm alright, Ty—Tyrese," I murmur. If that's his nickname, I sure as hell don't need to be saying it. The scent of him was so welcoming for my bruised heart.

"You can call me Ty," his voice dips a little deeper.

With my sunglasses on, my focus is on the soulful sound of "Take Me To The King." The weight on my chest lifts momentarily as I praise God. Then it's over, and I notice that Tyrese hasn't removed his arm from around me.

He says, "So, wherever we go after here, let's skip out a little early."

"Can't."

"Zar, I need to talk to you outside of the confines of our job. Will you let me? You have my cell, yet you don't answer my calls or texts."

I chuckle quietly at the thought of how I'd mentioned the same words to Vassili earlier. Nodding, I reply, "I will. Not today, though. I'm moving back in with my dad."

He starts to hold me tighter, but I start into the crowd of people before us. Tyrese is on my heels. I stand next to Connie. Samuel is on her opposite side.

"Hey guys," she whispers to us. She's not wearing glasses, and her light face is puffy red.

I offer her a one-arm hug. Tyrese offers her a head nod, edging his way between me and another person who might be family. If memory serves me correctly, I've seen a picture of the young guy on the secretary's desk.

"You're moving back with your dad." Tyrese's lips almost graze my earlobe. "You're afraid."

"I'm not," I mutter under my breath.

"Let me be there for you," he pleads.

I look at him intently for a second. A soft wind bristles past, sending a splay of my freshly pressed hair into my face. I push the tresses back, still staring at him. He eyes me curiously as I murmur, "I know who you are now, Tyrese Nicks."

His head cocks a little.

"I know," I mouth to him again, letting it sink in. We met at the beginning of the summer. Tyrese Nicks couldn't hide his revulsion of my last name, though he insisted that we knew each other. He had the perfect cover story.

Lt. Sullivan was a serial killer cop my father refused to assist the then DA Samuel Billingslea with collecting enough evidence to prosecute. Although my father wasn't Chief of Police then, he, along with the rest of the LAPD community, were of no help to the prosecution. That day Sammy became my mentor. Tyrese chose that pivotal point in history to pretend that he knew me. Like Danushka, who hid in plain sight, he used me. He said he knew me.

He did not.

Maybe he's IA. Internal Affairs should've been sniffing at my father's door years ago.

Maybe he's a Federal Agent.

It doesn't matter because my husband needs my help, and Tyrese is the man to do it.

17

Vassili

The speed bag torpedoes, zipping in circles at the speed of light. My knuckles continue to drum across the leather, sending it volleying around. I'm running on fumes. I didn't have a second of sleep last night. The images from my nightmare past threaten to spill over into reality. The shit I told Zariah so she could understand my history pales in comparison to the thoughts that torment my mind. Crap that I haven't even recalled comes swarming back into my thoughts. I'd held Zariah tighter, focusing on her soft body and how at peace she was with my arms around her. When that's not enough, I've spent a few hours in the nursery, watching the slight rise and fall of Natasha's back as she sleeps.

Sweat drenches down my back and chest as I offer the speed bag one last slam. The chain breaks, and the damn ball zips across Vadim's Gym. Across from me, the fatheads at the weight station stare. They don't show me the love that they once did when I was a hotheaded fighter. To be truthful, that love Vadim's crew showed dwindled the second I walked into the room this morning. Just like earlier, gazes follow me as I start to retrieve the ball.

The Three-Headed Monster plucks it up from the ground. He's still terrified of my wife. She's still afraid of how she embarrassed herself with our Sergy, who wasn't the Sergio that needed his life snatched away.

"You good, brat?" Sergy asks.

"Khorosho," I mumble, taking the ball.

"Nyet, no fucking khorosho," Vadim's strained voice zips out in a steely tone.

"Fuck," I mutter under my breath and turn around.

He pulls a cup of coffee to his lips, eyeing me like an enemy as he looks over the top of the rim. Nestor, the Ukrainian, is at his side. My sparring trainer chews on his bottom lip, eyes everywhere but on mine.

"You want to talk?" I gesture toward the stairs. "Nestor, you too. Let's all talk."

Vadim points a stiff finger. "Nyet. You're done here, Vassili. Kick rocks."

Hostility and lack of sleep roar through me. "What do you mean, *I'm done here?*"

"Last I saw you, Mr. Resnov, was almost a month ago in Australia. First, I assumed you were done, now I insist you're *done here.*"

"Okay, I see. You want to have your cunt wide open." I stalk past him. "See you in your office."

Vadim chuckles. "Nyet. Everything I say, everyone can hear."

I spin around as he slowly does as well. Only, he's addressing everyone in the gym. "This little shit here bucked up on me after a fight—"

"The fuck I did!"

"You did." Vadim pauses from staring at the men who've worked out here for ages. Half of them are too afraid to give us all their attention. The others eye me warily.

"Vassili got right in my fucking face like this after the match with Kong." Vadim's wrinkled hand is pressed an inch away from his nose. "I've known the shit's grandfather, Anatoly Senior, since I was sucking on my mother's tit as a wee babe. This Shit who put a mudak in a coma gets in my face. He disappears. My gym doesn't stand for shit like that. Vassili Karo Resnov, you are dismissed."

I shake my head. "I'm not leaving. Try me, old man." I move a few paces to a weight bench. Seated wide-legged, I glare up at him. "Make me. You too, Nestor." My glare dances across the room, and I punch a stiff fist at my chest while threatening them all. *All you mudaks make me leave!*"

The wrinkles on Vadim's face part ways as he looks me over. "Who has the title, Vassili? Who has your mother-fucking belt, you little shit?"

Fuck, I wonder, *who has my belt.* My first love was gone from me for the past 22 days. Not an entire thought was to be had for it unless one of Danushka's roaches had an update on Kong. My teeth rake over my top lip as I consider the UFC match that occurred a week ago. I knead my neck. In the past, I've watch every motherfucking fight. Zariah would be wrapped in my arms, joking about all the testosterone on the television and how she needed me. Then I'd fuck her good before returning to watch every angle of every fight.

Rhy stands next to Vadim.

"You?" I growl.

"Welterweight UFC champ," he brags. I'm used to the ass face spitting words at me with his cunt wide open. Although today, there's not a snarl in sight.

"What should you say?" Vadim asks.

My eyes fly from the ass face to my coach.

"This gym is built on support, Vassili."

I place a paw at my chest and chuckle. "Coach, you want me to say congratulations? That's what you want? Or Rhy."

In an instant, my nose is pressed against my enemies. "Mudak, you must want me to threaten you. You must want me to promise that you won't be having that belt for too much longer."

Vadim sniffs. "That's between the two of you, Vassili. Also, you'll be needing to find a new backing, because we aren't behind you anymore."

"I'm going to hold onto it longer than the last guy," Rhy snarls. "As a matter of a fact, I'll hold onto it longer than that *weak ass, wannabe Russian* who gave it to that roach, Gott—"

He doesn't see it coming.

My fist slams into the side of Rhy's face. Gripping his shoulder, I bring him down as my knee assaults his mouth. A few of Rhy's teeth go flying. With my hyper senses, I note at least three, one canine.

"You all are done with me?" I start toward the weight bench I was sitting at, chest puffed out as I uproot it from the feeble bolts holding it down. The bench goes tumbling. That isn't enough. I slam my fist into the mirror, relishing the sound of it crashing. I turn on the crew that is supposed to have my back.

I was five years old. My dad had to be looking much like I do now. Nyet, worse. His face was splattered in blood. My mother's blood. Sasha had done something—something that reminded him of another man. Something that made the paranoid thoughts swarming in his head gather and collect. He'd asked my mother for the thousandth time if the little bitch had a different father. His fists flew across her face . . .

From my peripheral, I can see myself in the cracked

mirror. The knuckles on my left hand drown in blood, much like the vision I had long ago forgotten.

"In my office," Vadim growls.

Like the dead coming back to life, Rhy flies into a seated position, shaking his head. He starts up. Nestor stops him.

"Keep him here," my coach growls at the Ukrainian.

"I'm going to murder you," Rhy screams at the top of his lungs as I follow Vadim up the steps.

Wiping my knuckles on my boxer shorts, I follow Vadim past the old boxing ring and into his cluttered office. At least, he hasn't removed my shit. Hordes of memorabilia and pictures of championship matches surround us as I slink down into a chair.

I want to start over.

I've asked Zariah that, but it's me who wants this world we built to crash and burn. She's been sitting in my spot on our first encounter. I had claimed Vadim's seat while he was out. I'd worn her down relentlessly. Right about now, that day could start all over again. I'd make the same moves. Allow her space to focus at Spellman and then Berkeley. I should've gone to get her myself. Fuck Yuri. Fuck my entire family. I'd have kept her away from them all.

When I blink, Vadim is writing something on one of those receipt thingies that he gives to the newbies who meet the standards enough to work out here. I've always worked out free, but that doesn't mean Vadim hadn't eaten when I did way before my sponsorship.

He crumples the thin paper a little and tosses it at me. I catch it. "What the fuck, Vadim?"

"Those are the three different places that I barter for when equipment breaks. I want a new mirror, and I don't give a damn if the bench still works. You're getting me another one."

"Okay." I shrug. "You're done with me?"

He scrubs his face with wrinkly hands. "You done being a piz'da?"

"Dah." Vadim bursts into laughter. He gestures toward me. "I'm supposed to school you on my prized Welterweight Champ. Rhy had his cunt wide open, didn't even see your left hook. So, how can I school you when Rhy needs to shut his mouth and see what's coming."

I laugh too. "Remember Kyiv?"

"Dah," he nods. "You had that fight with the mudak who said he fought bears for a living. There's only one other Russian UFC fighter I've ever seen footage of doing that. Rhy is a liar. The guy in Kyiv was a liar."

"Khabib," I mention the fighter in a different weight class than me. He's the only one who fought fucking bears. "Those were good times, Kyiv."

"Good times. Rhy is barely Russian, shit; he's a little German. And to tell you, you are not Russian, blasphemy." Vadim leans forward in his chair; he shakes the smile from his face. "Dumb rookies like Rhy aside, you need to know one thing. Next time you get in my face, Vassili, I will kill you."

"I doubt that, old man. You have my word, though, there won't be a next time," I grit out.

"Khorosho," he mutters. "It's better that way. I don't need your father coming after me. The Resnov blessing is right there, right below God. Now, I need the little shit I met on the first day to return. He was a fighter, Vassili. Not a hoodlum running around with more ties to the Bratva than his blood."

"You know what's going on?" I gesture, at a loss for words.

"The second I saw Danushka in Australia, I knew you were in a bind. Does Anatoly know the two of you are fraternizing?"

He seems to be holding his breath, waiting for my response. I nod.

"That girl has a death wish then."

I groan. "I'm waiting for Anatoly to finish Danny. To get it over with."

"Nyet." Vadim shakes his head. "That mudak has never changed. When he was a boy about the age you were when Malich first brought you to me, he watched two dogs fight. They were Ovcharkas. Massive motherfuckers like at Black Dolphin." He mentions one of the toughest prisons in Russia. "The one dog killed the other, and he took two slugs to the victor."

For a moment, I chew my lip in thought. The MMA world stole my heart when I found out it had strategy. A strategy meant that no matter how you tweak shit if you followed through, you'd be golden. I can't fucking stand people that are unpredictable. Danushka might seem like it. After all, her cards are on the table, the bitch can be cut down.

My father.

He's another story. What compelled the mudak to drop his winning Shepard dog? The dog showed promise. I ask, "Why?"

"Because the winner killed the one he loved." Vadim rubs a hand over his mouth. "He has this habit of seeing how far something or someone will go. When that person has made all the moves they have at their disposal or Anatoly's past the point of no return, that person meets his demise. A fucking death that makes the pit of my stomach upchuck into my throat. So, while you're consorting with Danny, keep that in mind. Anatoly is making a tally of every wrong—eh as if he hasn't lived a life needing vindicating."

"I'm doing it for him," I mutter the truth.

In no world would I lift my hand for the piz'da. Even

when I left for America with Anatoly's blessing, he asked to have a hand in The Red Door. I gave Malich all the details of how Anatoly wanted to be involved in my lounge, and that was the end of it. I did this shit for Anatoly, for the Bratva, and my wife doesn't know it yet . . .

18

Zariah

T he repast is held at a soul food restaurant. Tyrese and I skip out. Now, his Maserati swoops into valet at an stylish boutique hotel that boasts an exclusive lounge. He's out of the car, handing over cash, and rounding on me in seconds. There's an intensity in his gaze. Not the kind I've grown accustomed to when his eyes would glue to an outfit that hugged my curves.

Tyrese's gaze reads one thing: He has to know *how I know*.

Alright, I'm not aware of exactly who he is. As an attorney, I'll bait the truth out of him. I didn't bust my ass in law school for no reason. The handsome black man will break for me, and once he's broken, he'll be on my team.

Our team.

Team Vassili and Zariah, because I'm not team Danushka, nor am I team *Rapey* Anatoly. He holds out a hand to help me out of the car. I ignore it. Tyrese's muscles pull in. He offers half a laugh.

"You are going to talk to me, right?" he asks, shutting the

door and coming to my side. "If you're the Zariah I've met on a few occasions, we'll get nowhere."

"Oh, we will get somewhere." I turn on him so very close to his face. "Mr. Nicks—or whatever your name is, you will tell me everything."

"I can't." He chews his lip.

Taking a few paces back, I then strut toward the door and into a lobby of marble and glitz. I've had dinner here with my father and a few of his friends before. With my clutch grasped in hand, I start into the room. Tyrese loops his arm into mine.

"We'll take a table for two and send the specialty wine list. Not the regular one," he tells the hostess.

I blink a few times. He's offering Will Smith from the 'Bad Boy' series vibes. Like a rich boy cop. I grew up around cops, I should've sniffed it on him earlier. I allow him to guide me. Men need to feel like they're in control. He has a few more seconds before I snatch the reigns. The hostess starts to a table. Tyrese moves past her and pulls out the chair for me. I claim the seat, then the bastard descends across from me.

"You took me to a very public place, Ty," I murmur, my voice as lush as the select wine list that's on its way to us. "Why? How will we share our thoughts with others surrounding us?"

His mouth perches into a half-smile, the left dimple on display. "I can't tell you, Zar. I honestly brought you here for a good drink, and if you're willing, you can tell me more about your husband."

My heart sinks. I assumed Tyrese was here for my father.

Not Vassili. Although mentioning an infamous serial killer/cop case like Lt. Sullivan was his way in, I should've expected this.

"No drinks." I lace my hands before my flat abdomen. "I still love my husband, Tyrese."

His entire façade tenses ever so slightly. "You're afraid of Mr. Resnov enough to move back with your father. Take that into consideration . . ."

A server in a stiff white suit steps up to us.

"Bourbon whiskey," Tyrese orders. "You sure you don't want to preview the selection?"

Though I'm not mentioning my pregnancy to Tyrese, I snort. "You were playing a part, Ty. Flirt to get the information you need. It's no longer necessary."

The server clears his throat, not interested in tidbits of our conversation.

"That's it," I tell the server, who walks away.

He places his forearms on the white linen and leans forward. "I wasn't flirting to get information out of you, Zariah. You are one of the most beautiful women I've had the pleasure of meeting. The second I landed eyes on you, I swore to myself that I'd remove you from the Resnov snare."

"What do you think you're saving me from?" I lift an eyebrow, smiling sweetly.

"More than you know."

My mother declined a ride to LAX, saying she plans to stick around. She also reiterates that church is in the cards for us tomorrow. If there is one area my gorgeous, kind-hearted mother doesn't play, it's church. I can remember so many times sitting in a pew at a shotgun house of a church down in Georgia with her family members. I'm playing with the devil now but come tomorrow, I'll meet her there. Maybe I'll even ask her what friends she's staying with. She's livid with me, bags packs, and Uber ready.

Now I'm seated in the front seat of my SUV, glaring at the side of my father's luxurious home. Along the side of it, my old balcony warms my heart to memories.

Vassili came to me even before I knew I needed him, he was there.

"Mommy?" Natasha rings out from the backseat, right before the good old times can pull me under.

I blink, and there's a police cruiser pulling in front of us. Rolling my eyes away from the sight, I glance into the rearview mirror. "Are you ready to see Gramps?"

She displays a few teeth in response to the singsong of my voice.

As I get out, Officer Jackson does as well. His biceps are flexed as he closes his door.

"Where's Hutch?" I joke.

"Hutch?"

"You're Starsky. Listen, if you want to kiss my father's ass, then you have to know the oldies. Shaft won't work, he rides solo all the time. So, you must be Starsky, and you left Hutch. I take it you have to be the in-charge. The other guy was so fresh behind the ears. He's not yet used to the fact that his dream of saving lives and keeping the street clean is all a fallacy."

I pause. He doesn't respond to my "ass kissing" reference.

Jackson nods slowly. "That's what you think of us? The LAPD gets enough backlash from people whose cellphone cameras show part of a scenario. You're the daughter of the Chief!"

"Not all cops are created equal, Officer Jackson."

"Call me—"

"Jackson," I grit out. After a second, I look up at him through thick lashes, recalling that I'm in the middle of a "nasty divorce."

"I-I," I touch my forearm, displaying a false level of

vulnerability. "I love my dad. He just didn't think that–that I made a good decision. Kind of sucks when he's right."

Part of me wants to screech that this is all acting, that I desperately want to go home.

Jackson's eyes become liquid gold as he looks me over. "I can understand that more than you know, Zariah. I thought I married a good . . . um. Do you need any help with your things?"

"Yes, I appreciate it." I unlock the trunk of my SUV and then go to the back door to get Natasha out.

Once she's on my hip, I glance down the street.

"What are you looking at?" Jackson latches the trunk door. He comes to my side, but I shrug.

"I thought I saw a car—um." Fear clutches at me. Vassili wants me here for my safety. While he's working Danushka, they're friends, and I'm his enemy. Knowing the psychotic woman, any friend of his is an enemy of hers too.

Jackson stops glaring in all directions when I start up the curb.

"I'll talk to your dad about increasing patrol in the area."

"No need," I tell him because I crave with my entire being that my husband will crash through my balcony. Well, not crash through, but I'd really love to see him sooner rather than later.

"I'll do it anyway." Jackson holds Natasha's Disney-print rollaway on top of my designer canvas print. He follows me up the intricate paved steps.

The door bursts open.

With arms wide, my father's pearly-white teeth pop against his dark skin. "You have no idea, Princess, how long I've waited for this moment."

Yup. He's been waiting for me to fail. Little does he know, once I have Tyrese Nicks on my side, that slimy agent will forgo my husband and the Bratva. Nicks will sink his teeth into my father and other crooked cops in the LAPD. I'll hand him the evidence that the force refused to provide Samuel when it came to LT. Sullivan.

I allow myself to be enveloped into arms that have harmed my mother. When he leans over to kiss Natasha's forehead with the same lips that cheated on and cursed my mom, I allow that too. One day soon, my father will pay penance for all his wrongs.

19

Zariah

On Sunday morning, I start the day with the Lord's Prayer and an onslaught of kisses to my daughter's smiling face. My palm roams over my flat abdomen. I can hear Vassili telling me not to "baby" our son. I'd retort that maybe God has blessed him with another girl to keep safe. My heart isn't set up to reminisce on my husband because I have plans to set in motion.

"Shhh . . ." I tell Natasha, planting her on my hip. Her ruffled, yellow pantsuit matches the dress I'm wearing. I start down the stairs, my jeweled sandals wedged into my purse. Of course, I'm conscious of every sound my bare feet make, the drumming of my heart. I silently curse myself for having my one-year-old as a partner in crime. I stop right outside of the door to my father's study, and all the oxygen in my lungs depletes. Maxwell must've gotten up from the bed. The faint sound of footsteps above sends me and my little angel fleeing toward the kitchen.

Okay, Zariah, I tell myself. This is the worst time to

initiate the search for any illegal activity my father has been up too.

I n the kitchen, Natasha bangs copper pots on the ground. Without a highchair and a playpen, I need the sound of her constant ruckus to know she's safe. I keep one eye on her, another on the hallway, and another on the fresh, raw potatoes I'm slicing. Yes, that's more eyes than I have. These are hard times. Like any man, my father loves country potatoes. I've got T-bones marinating, for steak and eggs too.

In cotton pajamas and an aristocrat's robe, my dad appears once the steaks have begun to sizzle on the iron-grill. I move away from the stove, a hard smile on my face as I hug him.

"Good morning, Dad." I kiss his bristled jaw.

"Good morning, Princess." He looks past me, eyes the food approvingly, and goes toward Natasha. This is the part I hate the most. My daughter is too young to 'fake the funk.' A term my mom and her cronies used in the past. As he pulls her up off the floor and into his arms, she doesn't push away or catch an attitude, which is her MO. Her innocent, chubby fingers paw at the evil man's face. Too bad she doesn't have a copper pot in her hand. Had she "BOPPED" him on the head, I'd have scold her now and gifted her with French Fries later.

"You two headed to church soon?" my dad asks, grunting faintly as he reaches down to place Natasha back near her symphony.

"Yes."

He rubs the back of his neck, then leans his elbows on the glossy counters. "I should go to church today. Lord knows I've been blessed in my career for over thirty years."

Not on your life, I consider, smiling at him. Mom's

143

gunning for an intervention with Vassili and I. Since my husband and I are acting so bizarre, I doubt that adding Maxwell to the mix will help. She has holy oil, holy water, and one of those prayer cloths in her arsenal. It hurt to her core when I mentioned coming here.

"Uh oh," I hasten toward Natasha and squat down. My thumb roams over her mouth. There's a tiny bit of slobber on her face. There always is. My stomach muscles churn as I play it off. "Are you coming down with a cold, Cutie Pie?"

"Is she?" My dad's eyebrow raises as he squats beside me. A second later, he's breathing heavy and standing to his full attention. "Grandpa is too old for this, Princess Natasha."

"Do you have any Vicks Vapor Rub?" I ask, determined to set a scene. Feels like I've been tossed to the deep end of the pool. My mom wants me to make amends with Vassili. He will literally kill me if I bring Natasha around him . . . with Danushka nearby. Hell, I could kill myself for allowing our baby anywhere near Danny after she held a gun to my daughter's head.

My father is the lesser of two evils.

"How about I stay? I'm not dressed, I'll look after Natasha." Dad says, searching through the cupboard. "Having her around people, with her onset of sniffles, isn't a good idea."

I hesitate as he hands over the Vicks.

"Princess," he pauses. "We haven't been close since you . . . you married—"

"He's still her father." I stop from balling my fist.

Maxwell nods. "It's taken you coming home for me to understand that you have feelings for the guy. The same as I'll always have feelings for your mother for the blessing of children."

Bullshit, I stop myself from chortling. My return has *cured* Maxwell Washington of his innate hate for my husband. I

144

lick my lips because this has presented me with a good enough moment as any to create a few stipulations. "I'm glad you understand, Dad. While Vassili and I are divorcing, I need you to promise that he's not on your radar. That neither you nor any officers of the law will hound him."

"We are peace officers."

"Ha." I relax my tensed muscles, jut out a hand, and grin. "Dad, Vassili and the *daughter you love* have created a little girl. . ." I stop myself from mentioning that we also have another baby on the way. Clearing my throat, I add, "We made this little girl. I can't have him harmed."

He clasps my outstretched hand. "Got it."

I squeeze—as if the action does anything. "No following Vassili, Dad. Leave him alone. No harming him or giving orders . . ."

"Zariah, I don't appreciate what you're inferring . . ."

I chuckle. "Dad, I'm an attorney who covers all the possibilities."

———

Later on, I pick up my mother at one of her old friend's homes. Old 'girlfriends.' Back in the day, the terms 'besties' and 'homies' was out—'girlfriends' was in. While I pretend Natasha is coming down with a cold to keep her safe from Danushka, Mom's friend waves at me from the front door, with crumpled Kleenex in hand.

My mother slides into the car, dressed in jeans and a shirt. Now, this is a far cry from how we grew up. Ruffled dresses, itchy stockings, lengthy slips. Though my mom became more lenient with the years, she's not that friggen indulgent. I glance her up and down as she pulls an antibacterial gel from her purse and rubs her hands.

Zamora lays her head back with a sigh. "Lord, I've been

145

waiting for you to come to get me. Girlfriend says it's fall allergies. If I catch a cold Zariah, I'm-I'm . . ." My mom stops speaking as she digs through her purse again.

"What are you looking for?" I try to glance at her, but I'm pulling onto the main boulevard.

My mom's palm covers my vision for a split second as she does a quick oily cross on my forehead. We've been in this scenario before. Where I swerved, and we almost died since Momma is two parts filled by the faith and one part goofy. At least, today, I'm prepared.

I mumble, "Oh, I figured."

"Heh, did you prepare for this?" she asks, flicking her now wet hands at me.

"Yup," I laugh, wiping the dribbles of holy water from my cheek while one hand is on the steering wheel.

"Did you—"

"Yes, mom, where is your holy rag?" I grin at her.

"I don't know what you think is so funny."

"Sorry, I appreciate your support," I reply. Any prayers Zamora has lifted to heaven on my account have rained down as mercy in the past few weeks alone.

"Turn here."

"Turn?" I arch an eyebrow, following her directions. Instead of veering left near a shopping center that leads to the church, we start toward an industrial area. "I thought we were going . . ."

"No." She plays with the Satellite Radio until an old Kirk Franklin song comes on.

"He's Able," she sings, shaking her head. "Yes, He is. Zariah, we're not attending church today. Vassili is at the convention center in an hour. We can catch up to him before or after the PR set."

"What?"

"Did I raise you to respond in one-word sentences?" she snaps.

"Okay, Mom," I cringe.

She scoffs. "How will we get the two of you back together? Huh, Zariah? I need you to try. This is cause for getting down on your knees, praying to God. Not acting like your marriage is some sort of sham. You don't know what divorce feels like. You don't need to."

"Who said anything about . . ." I groan. Had I told my mother about divorce? Of course, the term divorce was meant for everyone who can negatively impact us. Danushka, definitely. My father, for even more obvious reasons.

"Samuel told you?" I ask.

"Yes! One of your coworkers helped you draw up the papers. Why not do them yourself?"

Because, like Dad, I need Mr. Nicks on the same page, I stare at her instead of uttering the words out loud. "Mom, everything will work out."

"In the name of Jesus!" She snaps.

I murmur her words, with no desire to alarm her any further. Life would be so much easier if people like my mom or Yuri were in the loop. They're invested in our future. I open my mouth to tell her the truth, and then I huff.

2 0

Vassili

Questions fly at me from various angles. I sit on a stage, rubbing my knuckles against my lips. Nestor does a shit-job of fielding the ones I have refused to answer and giving the "okay" for others. Vadim is on the opposite side of me. The old man is becoming angrier by the second.

My coach is desperate to save my brand. I won't say this shit out loud, but Yuri was always good at managing the situation.

Across from me are cameras, lights, people. Too many fucking people. I'm not a people person. Vadim believed this would be better than addressing fuck-offs like Alex on the Sports Network. The coach thought this open venue would help.

"We would like to know where you went after Kong went into a coma?" one asks.

"Well," I pause for effect. Vadim coached me not to give them Killer Karo. He said give 'em Vassili—the real guy. "The entire ordeal came as a shock. Kong is a man with a wife and a family. I am too. While we all go into the cage because this is a game, it never became more real to me until that second . . ."

For a man not interested in having long conversations, I realize I haven't answered the question.

"I needed to take a moment away from the spotlight. That may make me sound like a selfish guy, but I have so many young fans in the world. I had to give myself time to realize what I've done and to respond in the way that aligns with the role model I strive to be."

Through the crowd, my eyes connect with my wife. I'm going to kill her. She's here. The worst place for her to be. Unable to tear my gaze away from Zariah, I continue. "I'm not the same Killer Karo who stepped into the octagon a decade ago—who talked too much. I needed a moment to deal with..."

My voice is strangled. An infrared beam from Grigor's rifle is right between Zamora's eyes.

I start to stand, pulling the earphone from my ear that cut down on the background noise. My words ringing in my ears, blood rushes like the mighty Volga River. Voice raw, I conclude the entire conference with, "If I, if I could take it back, I would . . ."

Maybe I mean Kong.

Maybe I mean knocking him the fuck out.

Maybe I'm referring to the deal I made with that bitch—my sister.

Vadim took over. He had to have noticed it too. The fucking light between Zamora's eyes that would've snuffed her out in less than a second. I sit in the passenger seat of Vadim's old school Cadillac. Nestor and the rest of our team have the same confused looks on their faces as Vadim had when I brushed them off in Australia.

I grit out, "You drive slow as fuck, old man."

"Nobody's dead," his voice cracks. "Keep that shit in mind, Vassili. Be the calculating fighter, not the fighter that bashes in skulls."

"I'm both—I'm going to do both the second I cross paths with Danny. I will calculate exactly where to bash her motherfucking dome in, knock her lights out!" I growl. With a quick move, my forearm slams into the palm of my hand. Nyet, I don't want to do that to her. She'd be knocked out the second my steel arm crashes against her jaw. I flex my knuckles and fingers. I want her to be aware of every second it takes for me to kill her.

His ride starts up the hill that leads to the mansion Danushka and Horace own in Hollywood. "Listen, Vassili, you need me—"

"Vadim, I don't need—"

"The fuck you don't! You need me to coach you on how far you can go with that girl. Keep in mind that Anatoly isn't interested in her dying by your hand because he hasn't . . ." In Russian, he shouts the words 'given the fucking order.' As if my coach thinks the translation to English wasn't going through my thick skull.

Chest puffed out, my fingers curl into fists. My callused thumbs rub over my powerful, curled fingers. *Fuck Anatoly, fuck his orders, fuck . . .* I slam my head back against the seat and roar.

"Khorosho, get all that shit out now, Vassili. Talk it out with the piz'da because she spared your old lady's mother." Pulling the keys out of the ignition, he pats my shoulder. "That means she needs you."

We get out, slamming the door behind us. Water

continues to rush in my ears, but it's not my blood that's threatening to erupt. Two fountains are on opposite sides of their home.

I need Vadim here more than I can imagine. I'm playing by Danushka's rules until my father is ready to strike. Every second in her sight ruins me for the MMA world. I could see myself slaughtering more fighters, wanting to kill them all to get my hands on my sister until I can wash my knuckles in her blood.

Double doors that could almost touch the sky are open. Instead of her guards, the bitch saunters out, arms outstretched. "Brat!"

Also, I hate it when she calls me brother.

I give her the stiff arm. My palm presses hard against her forehead. No matter how hard the bitch swings, she can't throw a jab. Danushka doesn't even try. Her blood-red mouth is set in a smile as I ask, "Where the fuck is Grigor? Have the two of you lost your fucking minds?"

"I thought it was you who had lost your mind." Her fingers are soft as she wraps them around my wrist. She gives a leisure tug, pulling my hands toward her swan neck. "You want to choke me?"

Vadim is at my side. He stops short of making a suggestion—like he does when I'm in the cage. His eyes cloud with confusion as he stares at her.

"She likes it." I move so quick that Danushka's chuckles taper off. My forearm slams into her throat, and she's back against the left door. "You like fucking with me, Danny?"

Her teeth grit into a grin. "We could really *fuck with* each other, brat."

My fist stops right at the tip of her lips. She doesn't even flinch. She kisses my knuckles, and I move away from her. My hand is ready to grab a tuft of my mohawk. It hasn't been gone long enough. I'd be fucking bald if I still had it.

"Young lady," Vadim clears his throat. "This is your blood, your brother."

I've never seen my coach so flustered. Is he saying I'm blood, so she'll stop metaphorically fucking with me or, in a literal sense, stop attempting to?

"Yes, he is." Danushka drags a finger along his jawline, blue eyes teeming with desire.

"I'm married," the coach gulps. "He is...your brother is too."

"I'm getting a fucking divorce, Vadim," I blurt.

The old man stares at me as if my statement isn't working in my defense. Danushka is weirder by the second.

"Awesome," Danushka bats her lashes. "Once we catch up to Anatoly, take him out, and you're divorced, then we—"

"We what?" I growl.

She offers a silly laugh. "We reign as King and Queen . . ."

"What happened to your husband?" Vadim speaks, flustered, running a hand through his thinning hair. Probably something he hasn't done in ages, but she brings out the worst in people.

She presses herself to him, peppering kisses along his jaw and then whispers something in his ear. I gulp down the vomit in my throat. His eyes widen, he nods.

"L-Let's go!" Vadim's voice grows hard as he works to steady each word. "Let's get the fuck out of here, Vassili."

"See you all soon." Her manicured fingers wiggle.

In the car, Vadim clutches the steering wheel. A curdling throat sound comes from deep in his throat before his cheeks puff. He opens the door and lets it all out.

"Danny has that effect on me too," I growl.

"She wants Horace dead too, Vassili. She *wants the two of you* . . ."

"Don't fucking say it."

He rubs a hand across his mouth, then mumbles, "Jesus, I can't say it!"

"Good."

"You tell that wife of yours to keep her ass away until this situation is handled," he reprimands.

My head falls back, jaw set. "I told her already."

"Zar and our little Bully need to be away from this—all of this shit. You told your girl to start the divorce process, dah?"

"Dah."

"Send them somewhere, Vassili. They are family. Send them somewhere and have Mikhail or . . ."

A flurry of my fist slams across my chest as he whips his ride in reverse and moves away.

"I can't have Mikhail do anything now! Danny believes Malich and Anatoly are divided. She's got eyes on the hospital. Mikhail has returned to the ER; everyone is playing life as usual. Except for me!" My fist continues to King Kong across my chest. *"Except for me and my motherfucking family."*

He huffs. "Should I talk to Zar? We can't let anything happen to her."

"I can handle this by myself," I growl.

"Nyet. I've coached you for over a decade. Kept you from flying off the handle when a couple of refs *called it* with their eyes wide shut. Kept you in line. This might be the hardest fight of your life, Vassili. I'm not going anywhere.

Zariah

'Don't come to see me,' roamed through my head. Vassili left that text message from an "unknown" number when my mom and I had started toward the car. She's been complaining that he didn't see her when she waved her hands, cutting them across the air. Almost two months have passed since he'd disrespected me in Italy. It has been about a month since Anatoly set my heart on fire with fear, only for Vassili to remind me of what love felt like.

Contemplating how every part of my being adores and misses my husband, I shift in a rocking chair. Natasha's burrowed against my chest. My growing baby has started to make his presence know. My stomach is a tight, slightly protruding rock. Maybe Vassili is right. He's predicted a son.

Heart clutched in my throat, I concentrate on Natasha's soft breathing and cling to her warm body. I glance around the new nursery. What had been my older brother, Martin's bedroom, then a storage room, is transformed again.

Maxwell has surprised us with the room. A convertible

crib of beautiful mahogany. A princess-like treasure chest is filled with developmentally appropriate toys. He'd done it all for us to stay.

To make this our home . . .

To stay for as long as we so please.

All I crave is to fly into Vassili's arms.

"You miss daddy," my voice croaks. I plant a kiss on the top of Natasha's curly hair.

"Maybe she misses Taryn?"

Blinking a few times to stave off the glossiness from my eyes, I glance at the door. In a suit, Maxwell stands there. For all the crimes he's committed, he has the nerve to put on an empathetic façade.

"Taryn has her pretty much all day," he says. "Pretty Princess could miss her."

"Dad, she misses Vassili." I stop myself from the innate need to remind Maxwell of my child's bond. Don't need my father initiating his own plan of attack. "If you and Mom had divorced while I was so young . . ."

"Okay, Zariah." He holds up his hands, palms out. "I get it. She's innocent in all of this. I hope her naivety doesn't trickle over to you. How are the divorce papers coming along?"

I chew my lip. Might as well have plunged myself into an interrogation room down at the precinct. The dynamics fit me, saying that I don't know how to find the bastard to serve him the paper. That's the usual "excuse" for most people. Since Vassili hasn't reached out, I haven't bothered Tyrese with executing my request for a divorce. It almost feels like if I have him served, that makes this farce real.

I reply, "Nicks has been busy."

"While you're waiting for your co-worker to draw up the payers, reconsider the date I suggested?" Again, I'm eyed like a criminal. With a smile on his face, Maxwell adds. "Jackson's swinging by shortly for a chat with me anyway."

"Oh, what kind of chat? Business?" Damn, the lawyer in me has no problem taking the "A" out of Q & A. I clear my throat. "I could, but Natasha's restless tonight."

"What are grandparents for?"

I smile, arising and setting Natasha down onto her stubby feet. I almost pluck her back up as she takes a few stumbled steps toward him. My ornery father is more than willing to meet her the rest of the way. He scoops her into his arms.

I've been tempted to sneak Natasha away from my father and Jackson. I'd found the three of them in the kitchen after dressing in ripped jeans, a blouse, and blazer. If only she could share what they'd chatted about, but that was the professional in me. Needing to work all the angles.

Jackson and I stroll down the Universal Boardwalk. A multitude of people passes by on either side. We stop at the Voodoo Donut shop. We grab our items, sit at a table outside next to the famous Voodoo gingerbread man, and watch people.

After a little while, I ask, "So . . . How is it with my dad as a boss?"

His vanilla and pistachio covered donut is an inch away from his lips when he lets out a chuckle. "I'm that awful company?"

"No." I pause to take a breath. I try not to imagine myself in a courtroom. Albeit not badgering a witness on the opposite team, it would be nice to get some useful information out of Jackson.

"I get it. Your dad was insistent about this date. If you're anything like I was. . . I must've searched divorce attorneys a thousand times before I took the plunge."

The edges of my lips pull up, just enough for me to play the part. "You forget one thing. I could've created my own documents." I bump shoulders with him.

"You don't think you'd need an outside factor, Zariah? Someone to fight for your half… visitation, stuff like that?"

Fat chance, asshole, I think with a smile. "I considered it…" I try to segue our conversation back to him. "How did you pass the time after your divorce?"

"Work helped."

Bingo! I clear my throat. "How did you get so close to my father? You're still on the beat?"

A little something flickers in his eyes. I expected push back from Jackson, but he says, "Nope. I was promoted. Kissed a few asses to get out of the uniform the boys in blue wear."

"Hey, I thought women loved men in uniforms," I pause from rolling my eyes at the cliché. "You kissed my dad's ass too?"

"For the past three months I've been D1," he says of recently making detective. "I know how he likes his coffee. I always spoke up during debriefings. Made all the relevant suggestions, volunteered to work in the worst areas."

Now my brain is on overdrive. Thoughts slam through it. *How did Jackson make detective? Was it legit?* The things he's named are good ways to be seen by higher-ups at the precinct, but I'm stuck.

It's almost ten at night. I've checked in on Natasha and talked myself out of a shower so many times before I pull myself into the bathroom. Like a Spike Lee flick, I'm moving around no thought to it. In the shower, I start to scream, but nothing comes out.

I snatch up the Bath & Body Works. In my haste, I drop the loofah. Mouth gritted, I leave the damn thing on the ground, lather the soap in my hands and begin to wash.

"Years later," the sexiest Russian voice ever permeates my thoughts. "You still haven't learned how to work that pretty pussy in the shower…"

Eyes brightening, I search through the haze of smoke that my steamy shower had made. I breathe out, "Vassili?"

Vassili

She'd been frustrated as fuck when I come into the bedroom. I'd left her alone for a few minutes. Shit, I'd left Zariah alone far too long. Tonight, I'd left her alone while Natasha and I were at the window to the nursery. My daughter and I watched her mom return home with the mudak. It took something out of me not to go downstairs and give the cop the same action Kong got. It took even more out of me to put Natasha back into the crib that her sorry excuse for a grandpa bought.

My baby cried for me. Her happy chuckles went straight to tears. I hid in Natasha's closet. Zariah had come straight upstairs, giving me a reason to believe the mudak didn't taste my wife's lips.

Listening to Zariah sing a lullaby calmed the frayed nerves, settled my muscles. When she'd gone to change, Natasha's fat paws for hands clutched at the crib. She held herself up and waited for me again.

I made a few promises that I intend to keep only to find Zariah in the shower muttering under her breath. She rubbed her sudsy hands over her body all wrong.

Didn't show her luscious dark skin any of the love it's grown accustomed too. Her disrespect for her sexy curves reminded me of the first time I came to see her after murdering Sergio. She'd been trying to fuck herself because she'd *met me.*

She'd been doing it all wrong.

Rubbing a hand over the back of my neck, I say, "Years later. You still haven't learned how to work that pretty pussy in the shower."

"Vassili..." her breath catches in her throat. That beautiful throat of hers needs to be glossed with my cum right now. With a wide-legged stance and my hands in my jean pockets, I stay on the fuzzy rug.

The glass door swings open. She clings to me. The pent-up air I didn't even know I'd been holding in my lungs releases.

My wife is loyal. My wife belongs to me, despite the bull-shit game we're all playing for Danushka and Anatoly. Her hot, wet body cleaves to me as if she won't let me go. Even if I order her to. Water drips from her hands as she loops them behind my neck. My shirt is all wet, jeans dampening.

"I called you so many times," she murmurs.

"I thought about you a million more times than you called, Zar," I groan.

Clasping her hair, I wonder if she's crying. I can't see that shit right now. Happy tears, sad tears. The fighter in me doesn't know how to differentiate and doesn't give a fuck to try. She's still clinging to me. One arm at a time, I shove off my leather jacket, then I rip my shirt. My pants are shoved down as Zariah's mouth presses against mine.

I don't dare look into her eyes. Confirm her tears. Instead, I walk backward until we're both in the shower. The water washes away the truth I refuse to see.

Her straightened hair zips into natural curls.

"Much better."

"Much better?" Zariah cocks an eyebrow in confusion at my words.

I'm not mentioning the shit I hate. The shit that reminds me that I'm more like my father, and she's more like my mother than I'd care to know. Always crying because of him. I clasp the back of her neck. "Tonight, we're going to do all the same shit we did from our first night together—"

"But we didn't have sex, Vassili," she groans.

"Don't talk back, girl."

She sighs.

"I'm the one that gets to say *but*. I'll cum inside that pretty pussy when you can't take it anymore."

"Oh, Vassili," she purrs.

"First, fuck yourself like you did when you didn't know I was watching, Zar. This time you know how it is to be filled with my cock." I rub my thumb over her lips. "That mouth, that pussy, that ass. You know good and fucking well, Zar. So, touch yourself. Do it with love."

"Okay." Her voice is delectable as she roams a hand down the center of her breast.

"Nyet. You don't understand yet. If you don't touch yourself right, then I'm not cumming in any of those beautiful places made for me." Though my voice is hard, there's no way in hell I'm not filling her up tonight. She'll pout and learn just how beautiful it is to watch me *watch her.*

"I—"

"I'll cum, and you'll watch with envy," I lie.

Delicious anger flashes before her eyes. The attorney in my wife is ready for a challenge. Her tongue darts out, gliding over her lips. I crave this. The hard lust and determination in her will become our perfect night.

This time, when her hand slides across her breast, she tweaks a nipple. Fuck, half of me feels like a mudak for not

160

doing it for her. The other half of me is on fire for not having her in so long.

Little does my wife know, I haven't fucked her in so long. I need all this foreplay so that my cock can slam deep, go long.

With the water streaming down on her heavenly curves, Zariah places her foot on the shower seat. She spreads her thick walls. I gulp down the desire riding through me as her fingers disappear into her cunt. Her mouth sets, lips tense, pretty face filled with determination.

A fierce growl rolls through me as I watch her fingers fuck deep into her pussy. I step forward, and her breathing intensifies, pace falters. My paws press into the flesh of her ass, I stand so close my hard chest crushes her nipples. I whisper against her ear, "You almost stopped, girl. Now you have to be punished."

My words leave her heart bursting against my chest. I rub my hand across my bristled jaw, fighting the animal in me; the animal that wants to leap out. To fuck the rules and have her this very second. With a smile, I reach between her legs and grab her pussy. My fingers massage at her fat folds. I slip my arm around her and crush her with my body while showing her how to work her clit and her lips at the same time. "Do it like this for me, Zar."

"Shit . . . Shit . . ." She pants, biting down on my shoulder, body trembling between my arms. "Ye-yes."

"You," I tell her, kissing her lips with each word. "Taste. So. Motherfucking. Good." My mouth lingers at hers, fist snatching a shock full of her hair. "Do it right this time, or you continue to suffer." *Baby, don't make us suffer.*

I sit down on the ledge of the shower, leaning back, I watch Zariah gaze over my muscular body. "Get to it, Girl."

She places her foot on the ledge beside me.

"Open that pussy for me, Zar."

With trembling fingers, she does it right this time. She pushes back her thick ass lips so I can see that little hood, I reach forward and kiss her clit. Zariah moans deep, steadying her hand on the glass.

"Work your pussy," I growl.

Holding her lips open, Zariah lets her finger dip inside her cunt. She strokes her core. I reach up, giving her pussy my middle finger. With her fingers and my one finger stretching her walls, I teach her the erotic rhythm. Slow and delicate. I know my wife is on track when her hips start working on our fingers. I reach to the side and bite down on a juicy curve where her ass meets her hips. She rides harder, grinding down, moaning and groaning.

"You look so beautiful fucking yourself." I sit forward this time, letting her leg hook over my shoulder just as she's ready to cum. So, I can drink the feast she's made. My tongue dives in, lapping her up like a dog.

She doesn't have a second to come down from her high when I'm standing, pressing her breast against the glass. My hand swats hard at her ass, sending her back arching. I drive my cock into her core, balls slamming against the inside of her thigh.

"Dayyyyum!" Zariah tries to clutch at the wall as I sit deep in her pussy. Then out, and then gliding into her. I grab her arms from over her head, bring her elbows behind her. Now, I have the ultimate power as I thrust into her. Her ass claps back at my every thrust. My solid, rough body holds tight to her delicate one, and I stake claim to the thickness of her ass. My heavy erection gives her pussy the beating of its life.

2 2

Zariah

"Say you'll stay." I fall into Vassili. My pussy spasms out of control after all the attention. His ropy, strong arms beckon me as he holds me in the bed. The fighter becomes my haven as I catch my breath, my heart slamming against his chiseled chest. The hard beating of it is the only power I have over him. "Vassili, please say you'll stay."

"Zar . . ." Vassili mumbles, his Russian accent thickening by the second.

"The man I married was invincible," my voice trembles. I close my eyes, and then apologize for the low blow.

Callused fingers glide across my jaw. Vassili's thick, pleasing mouth presses against my lips. "Girl, you didn't give me half a second to respond. I'll stay for—"

"Yes," I screech at the top of my lungs and then glance around wide-eyed. The balcony door is open; the night is set off by a half-moon. There's not a sound, and it's after midnight. I assault his face with kisses and try to keep my glee under lock and key.

"Zariah," he grabs ahold of my neck, not squeezing but enough to gather my attention. "Listen to me. I'm staying the night, but you have to do something for me."

Dread swallows me whole. "Please, can it not have anything to do with your family?"

Vassili's dark gray eyes become stark black for a moment. He licks his lips. "Zariah, you're my wife. Let me change my tone here, girl. You will do what needs to be done. Understand?"

I start to climb off my husband. His hand stops skimming my neck and he grabs the fat of my hips, locking me in place.

"No lip. Promise me now that what I have to say, you'll do," he grits.

"Yes," I snap, attempting to slap at his chest. His hands snake up from my hips, and he locks my wrists. My pristine education growing up reminds me that my husband is king of the takedown. Vassili's leg locks around mine. Somehow, he lands on top. Except, my face is in the pillow, and his miraculous cock is piercing at my ass.

"Zariah, you talk back too much." The only love he's showing me is the caress of his breath against the nape of my neck and side of my cheek. "We got shit to do, girl. What did I say to you from the beginning? What did I tell you that one night in Italy?"

"You're doing this for us," I murmur. My mouth is muffled by my attempt to suffocate myself with this feather pillow.

In Russian, Vassili grits, "What?"

"You're doing this for us," I reply more assertive this time.

"That's right. For us. I love you, Zariah." Vassili scoots down in the bed, his mouth pressing against my spine. Each descent lands another kiss against the center of my back. Each one is more delicate than the last.

I squirm, needing the coach in him to coax me toward whatever shitty goal he has for us now.

My back arches and Vassili's lips plant against my puckered asshole. His tongue begins to slither around and wedge between my cheeks. My pussy, though achy, cries for him. I bite down on the very spot of the pillow that was helping suffocate me a few seconds ago. My moaning and groaning increase a few octaves as his tongue darts into my ass. Vassili presses his thumbs into my pussy, slamming at my g-spot.

As he sleeps, I cry. One of those silent cries where it hurts so bad that the sound refuses to exit your mouth. This morning, I awake to salt streams dried on my cheeks and loneliness creeping into my chest. He's left a note.

Wearing designer sunglasses and my favorite cheery, yellow dresses, I head to work. I drop Natasha off with Taryn and swing by Panera Bread for bagels for the entire office. When I arrive, I stop at the front of the building. The clerical staff come from their cubicles, Connie too, as I put out various cream cheeses with the bagels.

"I thought I smelled heavenly carbohydrates." Samuel's niece moans as she plucks up a cinnamon bagel.

"What's the occasion?" Tyrese's luscious voice comes from behind me. With my emotions unraveled, I smile up at him.

"Hey, I think I promised you bagels when we finished that thing," I murmur.

His brown eyes lock onto mine, approval sparks across his gaze. *That thing* is my divorce.

"What thing . . ." Connie begins. She's had a crush on our

coworker for the longest time. Yet she stops glancing at the two of us to squeal as Samuel enters Billingslea Legal. He has bags with one of our favorite southern restaurant emblems on the side.

"Chicken and Waffles for Ty and clerical, Connie and Zariah, I've got you covered too."

"Black Santa," Lynette chortles, helping him with a bag.

"Well, I guess you can all put your bagels in a zip lock baggie for tomorrow." I shrug, recalling that I'm supposed to play the part that my husband gave me. A woman on the verge of divorce. Vassili requested to be served while he's with Danny. He and his sister have established a relationship. It includes a Russian restaurant on Friday evenings.

"Zariah, get over here," Samuel calls after me as we head toward the break room. Tyrese attempts to catch my eye contact. I'm sure he prefers more clarity, due to my ominous statement. I'd been so wishy-washy since Vassili asked me to initiate the divorce last month.

"We can talk later," I mumble to him as we all 'round the corner. The break room has a coffee table with two couches parallel to it. Across from it all is a lengthy table with cheap chairs. Most of the folks who love to grub have grabbed the to-go boxes and have claimed the couches. Samuel's eyebrows press together. He hands me the box with my favorite French Toast.

"Why are you so happy?" I plaster on a smile, needing to make an inquiry with him before all the tattered nerves in me begin to crash.

Samuel is all white teeth against his gorgeous dark skin.

"That's a look of a man in love," Connie says of her uncle.

Our boss rubs a hand over his face. "I plead the fifth."

Dang, I consider my mom for a moment. In this sucky ass world, Samuel only ever loved one woman—his wife. She and my mom were good friends. After she died, very young, my mom always mentioned that Samuel was "falling out of love" with another woman. She'd been joking. Had to be. She and dad were meeting for another first double date with Samuel. My mentor has crossed paths with a swarm of gorgeous women since. I kind of thought Zamora and Samuel were getting close.

"Well, does *she* call you 'Sammy'?" I grit out beneath my breath. For my mom, for my current circumstances, hell, I *am* acting like a certified hater.

A few minutes later, Samuel sits at the table with me. "Zariah, can we all get together?"

"Who is we?" I drown the perfect French toast in more pecan syrup.

"Me, you, Vassili. Ms. Mora, if you'd like?" he huffs.

Tyrese settles down across the way. "You're still in mediation, Zariah?"

Samuel glances at him, almost like a father would when someone speaks accusatorily to his child. He clears his throat. "Yes, they're working it out."

"No, we're not," I grumble, almost calling Samuel 'dad' like I've done on occasion. When I do, he backs off.

"Alright," Tyrese shrugs. "I'm helping Zariah with the process—the divorce process that is. This is family law. Who wants to draw up the papers for themselves?"

"Zariah, not as your employer but as someone who cares a great deal about you," Samuel begins, "I suggest you take your time."

"I have to," I grit out.

"Why do you feel that you have to?" he asks.

Tyrese chortles.

I do too. "Sammy, don't offer the spiel like some would-be client coming into the office. I'm dissolving my marriage; it's the best thing that could happen to me."

I rise from the table. The workers at the couches have all

stopped shoveling food in their mouths to glance at me as I walk out. I can hear Tyrese telling Samuel to 'allow' him. I'm halfway to my office, and in a few short strides, Tyrese has my arm, he guides me inside and shuts the door.

He's close as hell to me, his eyes sweeping across my face. Something akin to trepidation crosses his face. He inquires, "You're not playing me, are you?"

"What the fuck?" I gasp. "What do you mean, I'm not playing you!"

"At the funeral, you blew my cover, Zariah. Then we have drinks—"

"You blew your cover, Tyrese, or whatever the fuck your name is."

He rubs a hand at the back of his neck. "I'm going to share something else with you."

"Why?" I gasp. Under any other circumstance, I'd take any information he'd give me. My entire agreement to return to my father's home was to implicate him, hell, the LAPD as a whole if necessary. It would be nice to have a federal agent on my team, but this has been a hard day. Very hard day, and it's not even 10 am yet.

"Because I want you to understand the severity of the Resnov Bratva, Zariah. Maybe you and your husband are clashing. Maybe he put you up to this. A man like him has to understand that I'm not the only Fed who is interested in putting him and his family down."

Leaning against the door, I gulp. "Okay . . ."

"Approximately two years ago, you married Resnov."

"Vassili," I murmur.

Tyrese leans against the front of my desk and crosses his arms. "I had an inside man at The Red Door."

Unable to contain myself, I spit the truth. "That place is legit."

"It wasn't until you married a Resnov, Zariah."

Pinching the bridge of my nose, I feel inclined to agree. Instead, I blink. "Okay."

He laughs softly. "Brilliant, how you chose your words. That inside man doctored numbers . . ."

The thought clicks in my head as to who he is speaking of. The first night Vassili and I reacquainted, he'd gone into Malich's office and came out livid. Later, we found that a female bartender had been the perpetrator. "She's dead."

"Yes." His head tilts, his gaze searing through me. "You knew her?"

"I did not. She was a bartender. She was skimming money and—"

"Yup, the bartender. Karsoff was working with us and working us all." Tyrese huffs. "Karsoff was the only opportunity that we had into The Red Door. We learned about how Malich *and Vassili* Resnov were sex trafficking women. Bottle service was the bottom line. Had Karsoff not gotten greedy, she would've helped us take at least two slimy Resnovs off the streets. Maybe more."

"I'm a Resnov," my tensed lips pull into a sneer.

"So, you don't want a divorce?" Tyrese's eyebrows knit together in distrust.

Damn! With my hips swaying like the ocean, I step toward Tyrese. I stop once his cologne sifts into my nostrils. The faint sound of his breath hitches is at my ears.

"I still love him, Tyrese," I say, pressing my hand against his chest. His skin is warm beneath his linen shirt, warm and taut. I glance up at Tyrese through my eyelashes. "I'm still in love with my husband. That aside, divorce is best for me because . . ."

"Has he—" his deep voice is steady and measured. Tyrese's knuckles skim up my biceps. "Has he done anything to you?"

"Not physically." My throat clutches for a second, I hate

169

myself for the deception. I'm not willing to bet on how good this Federal agent is since we've been able to see through each other thus far. Well, I wasn't able to see through him until recently. Taking into account how Nicks and I helped Ms. Noriega and her children, I have a gut feeling about him. I need this ally. Vassili and I need this ally more than my husband can ever know. So, I let my eyes water with misguided tears.

He clasps my hands that are at his chest, his thumb roving over my wrists.

"I'm supposed to be your new angle," I say. "Since Karsoff is dead, you wanted to use me to get closer to my husband?"

He licks his lips with a nod.

"I have something better for you."

We're so close that Tyrese's strong abdominals pitch as he laughs against me. "You have something better for me than ridding the streets of any Resnovs."

"Any Resnovs? I bet if you had Anatoly Resnov . . ."

I glance up through long lashes into sparkling, hungry eyes. I can almost feel his cock rising against my stomach. Yeah, that is Tyrese Nick's biggest motive.

"You know where he is?"

"Not at all times," I shrug. "He's on America's Most Wanted—tippy top of the list, right?"

"That's not the only list he's wanted on. Interpol for starters."

"Then help me help you, Mr. Nicks."

"How?"

I back away. "Tyrese, it's logical to say that when it came to Ms. Noriega's safety and the gang that came through here, we connected."

"I'd like to see that you and your daughter are safe."

I stop myself from clutching a hand across my stomach.

"So, as I'm learning about you, you're learning about me. I need your help on something first."

He takes a few steps forward. "What? How can I help you?"

"My father."

Eyebrow arched, Tyrese stares at me. "Is he alright?"

"Yup, Maxwell Washington is doing very well." I plaster on a grin. "Chief of Police."

"I know."

"Running the biggest gang that the West Coast has ever seen."

Tyrese begins to lean against my desk again. He folds his arm, eyes shaded in thought. "I don't . . ."

"I'll prove it to you; you help me clean these streets. Then . . . once I'm divorced," I pause again. That damn lump forming in my throat once more . . . then I deceive him. Albeit, only one part of my statement is a lie as I say, "I have a soft spot in my heart for my husband. Always will, but I'll help you find his father."

We begin to shake hands, he yanks at me, pulling me to him. He licks his lips, dimples at the ready. "Do not cross me, Zariah Resnov."

"I'm pretty sure you understand that if you cross me, that you will have not only marked my life but yours too."

171

23

Vassili

The speedbag torpedoes the tips of my knuckles, sending it spiraling around in a flash. With all eyes on me, I stop myself from obliterating the damn thing. The people that were once *my* people at Vadim's Gym haven't said a single word to me since the fiasco with Rhy. The little bitch has a vice grip on my championship belt. Even if I hadn't tossed a haymaker at him last month, they'd have to pick sides. A brand has to choose between its two biggest franchises—there I fucking said it. Apparently, Rhy became a franchise when Gotti snatched my belt and showed the world about my knee.

Vadim had first agreed that I'd train with Nestor, and he'd train Rhy for a match between the two of us. Now, I have disrespect against me and a bitch who's afraid to lose his belt. I've disrespected Vadim. The old man is over it, not the Three-Headed Monster or any of these mudaks.

The speedbag lobes in the opposite direction as I issue one last cross with my left fist. I rub my warm right knuckles against the bristles of my jaw. My mind is on the wraps that I didn't put on my hands when I turn around. Everyone's gaze flies toward their individual machines. Those thick necks, square heads mudaks won't say shit.

I glance over at Rhy. He's five minutes into my time with Vadim.

"C'mere, *moy syn*," Vadim calls out, calling me 'my son' in Russian. When my father does that, it's a different mother-fucking situation. The Old Man was there from day one, nobody else.

I nudge my chin as my cell phone vibrates in my pockets. Zariah has called me nonstop from a blocked number. My good girl doesn't understand that we will get to us later. I'm surprised to see a text from Danushka.

The Bitch: Having fun working out?

I start to slide the iPhone back into the pocket of my sweats when it vibrates in my palms again.

The Bitch: That Bitch better fight you.

I start to chuckle. Funny how she's given Rhy the same name I've given her. Three dots ping on the iPhone as my delusional ass sister appears to be typing. So far, I've learned that her marriage is open. Horace is banging girls some-where in Europe while she's sleeping with all the men on her team. Maybe Grigor—her full-blooded brother.

But she can't be fucking him all the time because Grigor stays within a sniper's radius from me. Anatoly's still depressed about how Grigor crossed him for Danny. All our lives, Grigor was his brains. I was his brawn—even though I never lifted a fucking finger for him. The bastard is delu-sional, too. Except, he plans to hand Danny, Horace, and Grigor their asses.

Nyet. I'll do in Grigor. He marked my mother-in-law's head with a sniper rifle.

When the time comes, I'll do in Danushka too. The Bitch

creeps me out, and I only trust myself to know that she's dead.

Instead of more text messages, Danushka has sent a few screenshots of social media. That Twitter thing that Yuri use to handle for me. Damn, I miss my kuzen. And the rest of those sites that my closest kuzen once managed. It's been two months since we've said a single word to each other. I think about shooting him a text but begin to read the different posts.

The MMA world is on fire with the fact that the commissioner reinstated me, even though Kong is still in a coma. People on Twitter are gunning for Rhy with GIFs about him running from me.

She has to have spent a reasonable amount of time *screenshotting* all of them. I slowly scroll, another message pops up from her.

The Bitch: We can make him fight . . .

The Bitch: One way or another

The Bitch: Or . . .

The Bitch: If he dies, who gets the belt by default?

Though I hadn't anticipated responding to her, I reply, "Leave it," and push it through. The iPhone goes off more in my fisted palm as I head toward the cage.

A tiny moon darkens beneath Rhy's eye. I never had a shiner last so long, but he's a different breed. Not a real Russian. I'm a bull. He's a cricket—loud and useless. Vadim clucks his tongue. The takedown between Nestor and Rhy ends. The little shit doesn't even offer his teammate help. Nestor rolls over in his padding and gets up.

I pull out of my sweatpants with tight trunks holding me in.

Rhy grunts as I begin to weigh down my hands. He doesn't step foot into the gym without his T-Rex hands wrapped up. He whispers that only "dummies" don't prepare for practice.

"We all can't have precious, dainty fingers," I shrug.

"Close your cunt, Vassili," Vadim shouts.

I glare through my coach. We both know that the little shit-head masked his words. Gripping the side of the cage, I climb up and over, landing on the canvas with a thud. Nestor offers me a nod.

"Don't say shit to Rhy," Vadim orders under his breath, though he smiles at me and pats the back of my neck.

I sniff.

"He's sensitive, dah?" he shares under his breath, pretending to check my wraps.

"Who's sensitive!" Rhy calls out.

Damn, how did he hear us? The idiot has one cauliflower ear—hardly lifted off his career but he's sporting that nasty ass ear of his. And he's standing a few yards away.

"You choose! Vadim, you choose now! Me or *that!*" Rhy shouts to Vadim. He scours up the cage, straddles the top, then does a backward somersault landing right in front of me. Showoff.

I rub the bridge of my nose, thinking, *don't try me. Don't fucking try me, piz'da. Don't try me, you little mudak!*

My mind goes to Zariah, and that doesn't help one bit. The craving for her controls me enough to have Rhy in a hospital bed on life support next to Kong. Then I think of Natasha as Rhy argues with Vadim to pick between us. To throw me out like he said he'd do weeks ago. A half-smile brightens my face. The Little Bully has helped me from matching his aggression.

"Why you smiling?" Nestor asks.

"What?" I rub a hand over my face.

"Why are you smiling," Rhy parrots.

"Rhy," Vadim says in an attempt to calm the moment, "We should all talk in my office—"

"Nyet! Nyet! Nyet," the fighter's fists jar at his chest.

Now, Nestor knows why I'm smiling because he chuckles under his breath. There's nothing left for Rhy to do but fall onto his tummy and have an all-out temper tantrum. I can almost hear my *kuzen* shouting that the *piz'da* isn't from Russia at all. He acts like a little Pasadena brat.

"You pick, Vadim, you choose between him or me."

"How about you two fight!" The Three-Headed Monster says.

"That's a good idea, Sergy," I nod.

"You say you can wipe the floor with Killer Karo," he points a finger at Rhy. "Make some money—do it!"

Nods and 'dahs' from half the weight team trickle over.

Chin up, Rhy steps toward me. Let him be on guard. I stand there, hands loose, chin down. He can have the first strike. I'll allow that.

"I'll fight you. I'll keep the belt too," he spits the words.

"We can set something up," Vadim sighs. "Nestor, you and Rhy . . ."

"Nyet." Rhy sniffs. "I will only work with you. Why would you give me to this fucking Ukrainian—"

"I'd rather work with Vassili, eh." Nestor rubs the back of his neck. "I've got a baby on the way at home, no need to deal with one at work."

Rhy stares incredulously at all of us. He gawks at all three of us before heading to the door of the cage. The rest of the men have made two lines that lead him toward the door.

Sergy is the first to give him the one-finger salute on his way out.

"That means you two are good?" Sergy asks.

All eyes fly toward me. *Could I have pegged them wrong?* They have always been Team Killer Karo. Shit, these days feels like only my wife is behind me—and that's okay. You don't disrespect Vadim's Gym, even if you're a mother-fucking Resnov. They were all waiting to see that the coach and I were good again.

"Khorosho," I nod.

Vadim wraps an arm around my shoulder. "Long live the King!"

E very other second, I pull the tie away from my Adam's apple. Bright lights click rapidly to my right and to my left candles glow. Danushka sits across from me as we have a window seat at Urban Kashtan.

"These are good times, brat." She reaches across the table to grab my hand.

To keep away from her touch, I grab the bowl of borscht. I press it to my lips to drink some of the broth.

She murmurs, "One day, when you and Grigor are on better terms, we will all come here."

"He's an outsider, right?" I glare as she puts the bowl down.

"Nyet," Danushka's eyes twinkle. "Hey, I need you to keep smiling. You're out on the town with—"

"My sister." As much as I hate to give her the title, it's a reminder for her crazy ass.

"Dah. And you have a crowd of reporters and paparazzi outside. They're in love with you too. They want to hear how you'll put down that little bitch, Rhy, is it?"

"Dah," I mumble.

Danushka turns toward the window. The bright lights flash harder, hypnotizing her. She offers a pageant wave. The bitch turns her hand into a fist, symbolizing the fight that I'm consigned to with Rhy. He's blasted on social media that I need to be 'prepared,' and a bunch of other words that he assumes was ominous. His little cunt is all wide open. It's a shame that he's made MMA all about his mouth and not backed it up. I'll keep quiet, sign a contract that works for me too, and then put his ass to bed. I'm too old for shit-talking. I'm at a time in my life where I'm ready to pounce.

Add Rhy as a submission.

Squeeze Danushka's neck until her fake blue eyes pop.

Beat Grigor to death with my hands.

Check. Check. Check.

"Karo, Karo, will you fight Rhy?" one of the reporters starts into the entrance of the restaurant.

A tiny babushka that is seated at the door wags her gnarly finger. Her voice sounds like dust as she threatens, "This is my place! Get!"

I'm up from my seat. Danushka begins to move out of her chair, but I gesture for her to sit back down. The skirt she's wearing is too fucking short, and I'm not ready for all of my food to come back up.

"Respect this establishment," I tell the guy. "You want a soundbite, give me a card."

He offers me a business card before heading back outside.

I turn toward the babushka that I've never had. She's always welcomed me into her restaurant. My palms glide along her warm skin, and I press my lips to the creases at her forehead. Damn, I wish I had a grandma for Natasha. "I'm truly sorry."

"Nyet," she waves my apology away. In Russian, she says, "You are a good boy, Mr. Resnov. You've helped keep my doors open, found more customers."

I kiss her forehead again, then notice behind her down the hallway.

It's the ugliest motherfucker I've ever seen in my life. After connecting gazes with me, Simeon starts into the men's bathroom of the Urban Kashtan. The old school restaurant slacks off in this department. I follow. Seconds later, I'm breathing in piss as I look at his ugly ass face.

"Why are you here, Simeon?"

"Paid that reporter to step inside. Get your attention, without Danushka riding your wee balls." He stops in the center of the room. There are old, yellowing stalls on the right, and two porcelain sinks with the rusted finishes to the left.

We stand at the same height. He's no cousin of mine. Just a lap dog for my father, and occasionally, he uses those choppers on someone. Not me. I'd put his ass down. Unlike Rhy, I'll match this mudak glower for glower.

Simeon asks, "Update on Horace?"

"Nyet."

"You lying to me, kuzen?"

My mouth pulls into a tense smile. "Want to *ask* that question again, Simeon? Ask me if I'm a motherfucking liar. Do it, with *your wee balls*?"

He shrugs. "I'll ask you this: Do you know *who your motherfucking family is*, brat?"

"Brat?" I chuckle. "Out of all the bitches Anatoly has impregnated, I never considered anybody brat. Not until I got close to Yuri, Mikhail, *Igor*."

"Igor was vindicated," he grits.

"His death shouldn't have happened, Simeon! You were my father's right hand. Grigor was the left. Why didn't you keep tabs on Grigor, huh? You say, do I know who my family is? What the fuck? You're a Resnov too, oh I forget. Anatoly let you play leader since I chose not to."

"Dah, you're right. You should've been at Anatoly's right shoulder. You could've kept an eye on our—on your brat! You would've known that Grigor and that little piz'da out there weren't loyal. Your lack of loyalty killed Ig—"

179

My fist goes flying. I'm a seasoned MMA fighter, but I take the bullheaded route. My fist slams into his teeth. I want to knock every one of them out of his mouth for saying that I had anything to do with Igor's death. For every brick I issue, Simeon tosses one back in my direction. He's left-handed. I have specialized training for mudaks like this.

I slam my forearm out; his chin slides to the left. My other hand takes quick body shots to his liver. I'm set to annihilate it until his left bounces off my chin. The hit leaves my spine ready to disconnect. I'm heaved back against the porcelain counter. It cracks against the wall. I go falling toward the silver-rusted piping beneath it. Simeon gathers leverage.

"This is all your fault, Vassili," he growls, his fists slamming down.

"Is it?" I grip the back of his neck and break my forehead against his.

Fuck. My vision swims around. His head is massive. The head-butt did a little more in his favor than it did for me. My hand chops against his windpipe. The bear doesn't stop letting his fists fly. I press my knee up and into his junk.

Okay. *Dirty.* I know. Now, ask me if I fucking give a damn. *Nyet!*

Simeon is whizzing laying in a pile of piss, as I jump into a standing position.

"You big bastard." I laugh down at him as he pulls out a gun.

He cocks the hammer, licking the blood from his lips. "You little shithead."

"Do it." I kneel, placing the middle of my eyes between the barrel. "Do it. You want to be me, kuzen, eh? Dah? Do it!"

And he does.

It clicks. He's laughing now, though I haven't even flinched. Simeon stops grimacing at the pain against his balls and pulls out the clip. "Empty, brat. I am more loyal than you."

My hand clamps across his throat. "Say that shit again?"

That hard blow to his balls has miraculously faded. Simeon lifts his hand. I begin to squeeze him with both hands now, and he tries to work his forearms between my arms to break the chokehold. His massive face is red.

I grit, "Tap out, kuzen."

Bighead. No brain. He continues to work his forearms up between my hands until he gains leverage. I quickly release his neck and take ahold of his hand to pull him backward and onto his stomach. He twists until we're both on the ground again.

The door opens.

A Latino with biker shorts and a fanny pack stares between us.

Without missing a beat, the guy asks, "Which one of you is Mr. Resnov."

"We both are," Simeon declares since his mother kept her maiden name.

The messenger rolls his eyes. "Which one is Vassili, Vassili Resnov?"

"That'll be this piz'da right here," Simeon says, patting my shoulder.

The messenger takes a few steps in and lets a manila envelope float down toward me. "You've been served," he blurts before leaving.

Simeon and I lean against the toilet stalls. Again, I'm reminded that grown-ass men aim like toddlers as I crack my back. He does too.

"Feels good," my cousin groans. "We are too old for this shit, Vassili."

"We are. Danushka is right out there," I grit out.

"Danny loves the limelight. She won't come in here." He gets up, holds out a hand.

For the first time in my life, I find myself taking the hand of my nemesis. I get up. "No luck on Horace. Okay?"

"Dah," he groans. "I hate America. North America, South America. I want to go home."

The beast then chews his lips as if he's considering his words.

"Are you keeping an eye on Zariah and Natasha?" I ask. Out of our entire lives, I have never asked him anything before.

"Dah, dummy. They're at home with her pop. Could never be safer with the Chief of Police." He points a stiff finger at me then gets to chewing his lip again. "Vassili, they'll be home all night. We still need to talk."

"Nyet," I grit, aware of how this conversation will proceed.

"The Bratva is very important, Vassili. One day, if you'd just give Anatoly the same attention that you've been giving Danushka this entire time and—"

"Hello, motherfucker," I grit out. "I'm only giving Danny attention at Anatoly's insistence. Nyet, not even for that. I'm waiting for him to lift the protection order off her head because I'm going to take her out! Go tell that to the boss."

He shrugs. "Okay, you know that Anatoly wants Danny, Horace. I'm doing in Grigor. I have too, we were close for so long . . . I . . . need to feel his blood."

I stare at Simeon for a moment. Aside from arguing, we've never had a real conversation. There's a soft knock at the door. The Bitch is ready to go. I toss my index finger to my lip to quiet my cousin. He glares at the door then moves toward the last stall in the bathroom. I go in the opposite direction, open the door. Danushka peeks inside, icy gaze tracking as much as she can see.

She gasps, "The fuck happened to you?"

"You see a messenger come through?" I think fast.

"Dah, he better be worse than you."

I breathe easy. She saw him come in, but luckily for us, all the guy who served me the papers must have hightailed it out of the ally exit.

"He knew karate," I shrug.

Danushka can't understand that I have a blackbelt in various forms. Fury burns red across her throat. She opens her leather jacket to display a pearl-handled gun. "We should catch up with—"

"Nyet." I clutch the papers in my hands. "That bitch had me served, and she was smart enough to have someone who can fight do it. I'll give her that."

"You're getting divorced?" Her eyes transform into Azul gems. Danushka leans against me, rubbing a thumb across my jaw, then licking the blood from the padding of her thumb. "You said it, brat, I didn't believe you. For that, I apologize. Now, we should celebrate. Girls? How many girls could we fuck?"

My stomach slams into my throat. "Nyet. Not tonight." *The only female I want is my wife.*

Where the fuck is Horace? Once he's found, this farce can end. Pretending to cheat on Zariah and become the whoremonger I once was isn't too bad. Danushka isn't satiated by a little bit. That greedy bitch always wants more.

She wants me—for us to be kings.

24

Zariah

"So, Mom, where have you been staying . . ." I tiptoe over my wording. My entire plate is full, and it's not with the trimmings for Thanksgiving dinner. Vassili's family and putting my father in his place have controlled much of my thoughts. I was dropping off Natasha with my mom, at her oldest friend's home, I learned Ms. Zamora Haskins has been spending her nights out. *Please don't let it be another Mr. Overstreet, dear God, please!*

My mom tugs a computer gaming toy for toddlers from its new casing. In retrospect, I should've seen the signs. She's happy.

Happier than she's ever been.

Samuel too.

"It's Samuel..." I blurt. When he said he was dating again, the part of me that's grown accustomed to the world falling had assumed the worst. Winner, winner, chicken dinner! Her eyes light up. I gasp, "You're the other woman—"

"The other woman!" Mom grips at the thick, plastic

casing so hard that it tears. Wow, I've only been able to open packages like that with scissors.

"No, not the other woman." I sink down onto the old school, flowery couch in her friend's house. "The woman. The woman he fell in love with after his wife died! The woman he's tried to stop craving this entire time!"

She beams. The red, hot fire beneath her light skin begins to soften into a blush. "He . . . I . . . Sammy and— we've . . ."

"Momma, give me a happily ever after, pahlezzz. My life sucks."

She blinks, still flushed.

"Sammy is the reason you stayed after leaving my house. Also, you're the reason he brought soul food for breakfast the other day?"

"Well, I told him not to go in on that particular morning," Zamora stammers. I can pretty much read that her statement included her laying in his bed while doing so. Clearing her throat, she asks, "Zariah, can I tell the story, or are you hell-bent on badgering the witness?"

"Natasha," I scoop my daughter up from the bouncer. "Tell your grandma that she's not the witness, she's the defendant."

"Daddy, daddy," is all Natasha will say.

I sink back down onto the chair.

Lips pursed, Mom plucks out the instructions for the reading tablet Samuel bought Natasha. Mom mumbles, "Oh, so you're not going to question Cutie Pie about why she's mentioning Daddy? I'm the only one who has to take the stand."

"You're also about to be held in contempt, Ms. Zamora."

She glares at me; I stop and am reminded that my mom was born in the South. I offer an award-winning smile. "Mom, I've always thought you and Samuel made a great couple. Throughout the years, you'd hate on any woman he was preparing to bring by for a double-date with you and Dad."

"Argh, you have to mention him?"

"Please, tell me how it happened." My thumbs rub the back of her hands softly before removing the educational toy from them. "How did you and the brilliant Samuel Billingslea make things right?"

"Well, I've been in love with him since I can remember." She stops speaking in trepidation to fidget with her fingers.

"I know. Again, for example, I must use the hours you'd take to get dressed for double-dates that included two other persons." I taper off my words, so she doesn't have to hear me mention Maxwell.

"I met him first," she murmurs. My mom pulls Natasha up and holds her. Zamora is the only one who the little bully will let cuddle with her, without squirming away. "We crossed paths in college. I know everybody loves to say you're stubborn and smart like your dad, but I was in my undergrad. We took a few Political Science classes together. Lower level stuff. Same study group."

"Did this study group include only two people?" When my mom beams bright, I chuckle. "Poor light skin people. God didn't make you for keeping secrets."

"Hush yo' mouth," she cackles. "Well, y'all dark skin people. God made your skin so mesmerizing. I stared at that man. Every second he looked into a textbook, my eyes were glued to the darkest of chocolate. I mean Wile E. Coyote, *Hungry Eyes*, eyes bugged out. All of that!"

"Hungry eyes? Okay, so you did a little dirty dancing with him, is that why you never spilled the beans?"

She clears her throat and shakes her head no.

"You sure, Ms. Mora," I try to take on Samuel's tone of voice.

"Not in college. I did two years, Zar. The scholarship I

had was not reinstated due to a cut in funding. Out of state tuition was no joke, had to take my ass back go Georgia!"

"Momma," I groan, having recalled that she did about two years of college in the past. Dad joked about how she pulled enough classes to obtain an Associate's Degree. "What happened?"

"He wrote letters."

"Okay?" I gasp.

"I got a job." She laughs. "Same rib joint we all went to after Vassili saved me from that ass of an ex of mine. Different name."

"And the letters," I reply, telling myself to focus on my mom. The love story reader in me is roused. "What happened? He stopped writing?"

"Yes. He stopped. I suppose after writing five of them without a response that I'd stop too."

"Have you no shame?" I say exasperated, although in an attempt to be funny.

"Humph, so much shame that I couldn't bring myself to respond. Six years later, I was out here visiting with my old crew. I always came every summer. This time, I did a California Roll at a stop sign."

"Damn, Daddy stopped you?" I groan.

"Yup. Ruined my life. I should've thanked him for a ticket instead of his number. A few months in, I found out that Samuel was a public def—"

I cackle, "Public Pretender, say it ain't so."

Finally, my mom smiles with me. "Girl, he took the joke out of that title. Advocated for a lot of young, black men. Moving on up, George no Weezy…"

"No . . ." I shake my head. "No, momma, no. You didn't!"

"Yup. Fast forward a couple of months. Zar, girl, you tell me you remember all the trouble I went through during our double dates after his wife died. Well, I'll tell you. I spent a thousand hours getting ready for our first double. Maxwell said it would be special. My girlfriend wanted me to-to call it a day with your father."

"Dang, there would be no me or Martin."

"No," she mumbles. "I invited *my girlfriend* on the date. Maxwell invited Samuel. The same night I introduced Sammy to my friend in Cali—God rest her soul, your pops proposed. Killed two birds with one stone that night."

My smile is more genuine than it's been in a while. "Well, I'm so glad, Mom, that your serendipity has started over."

"Can you do me a favor?"

"Sure."

"I'd like to take Natasha this weekend. Sammy hasn't had a real day off work in ages. Sure, he travels a lot for conventions and building knowledge. We'd like to do a few enriching activities. You know he's a Brainiac. We're heading up to Washington. I might be able to convince him to go to an amusement park or two. There's also a hands-on museum there, can we take Natasha?"

"She'd love that." *Also,* I consider silently, *it will be the safest place for her.*

———

It's a crummy Saturday evening. My husband has been served, and our little heart is boarding an airplane. Kicking off my house shoes, I move through the upstairs portion of my childhood home. Maxwell is downstairs. Almost ten of LAPD's finest are here. I'd texted Vassili that now was the best time as ever to swing by—for us to really play our part.

It makes more sense that, on my end, he still wants to be together. Although he doesn't respond to my text message, this scenario will also work for my mission with Tyrese. I've taken down every name of the boys in blue that are in the kitchen talking with my dad. This isn't something they can readily explain on the stand. Sure, there's a football game on. But they're in uniform—on the job. I'll send the list of names to Tyrese, maybe one of them has stepped out of line, and IA has tried to call them out?

I'm about to call Tyrese to see if he can assist with a search when there's a knock at my bedroom door.

"Yes?" I call out, sliding my phone into my pocket.

Jackson peeks inside before opening the door. "I had the feeling you didn't want to watch the game with a bunch of guys, so I brought you up a sub."

My father's perfect substitute hasn't flirted with me in the slightest. I almost glance away from him, feeling a stream of guilt for wishing harm on him and his entire team of goonies. "Thanks."

I get up from the seat and grab the plate with the half sandwich and Lays chips. He pulls a Coke from the pocket of his uniform.

That's another warning sign?

If they're all here to watch the football game, why is everyone dressed up? Feels like they're on the clock.

The doorbell rings, it's followed by banging on the door that's hard enough to bring it from its hinges.

"Stay here," Jackson orders.

Stomach lodged in my throat, I stand in the doorframe of my bedroom. My hand goes to my chest. I pray to God that my father follows through with his agreement to me, to Natasha. This would be the worst time for him to show his true colors. I hear bickering coming from the front door. The television is off. All of my father's soldiers haven't made a peep as Vassili asks to come inside to talk with me. He has to make this quick. This scenario that my father has to see can't be viewed by Danushka or Grigor. This is all a means to give my father "closure" and to confirm that he won't show his hand while Vassili and I are separated.

"Here's a thousand percent of transparency for you, Mr. Resnov. Zariah's weakling of a mother and I made a beautiful girl."

Shit, he gets to play the tired husband who misses his wife, meaning I'm the cold bitch. For the next few minutes, I listen. Tears drip down my chest as Maxwell mentions his replacement.

When the Resnov Way is mentioned, my heart implodes in my chest. I pray harder as Jackson asks about Vassili working for his father.

My husband spits, "No cams? No proof, right? I want to see my wife and my kid, Mr. Washington. Make that happen before I forget how important you are to my Zariah!"

"Don't," I speak up, unable to contain myself any longer. My fingers curl around the railing, and I glance down at him. A case of vertigo steels me for a moment. Stomach-churning, heart wrenched free from my chest, I stare at Vassili. Nobody else is here as he says, "Zariah. You got to come home, baby. You are mine. We made vows."

I'd give anything in this world to leave with him right now. Though, in a detached tone, I snap, "With an Elvis impersonator."

"Doesn't matter. We made vows before God."

As he speaks, my tears begin to fall again. Everyone has a notion of my husband, that he's bad. He's a Resnov. My father just called him communist scum. Samuel called him riffraff before they had a single conversation. But my husband is a praying man. Funny, before him, I had my mom and father as models for what love is.

And I sure as hell didn't believe in such a word. The L word was a fable.

But my husband prays before every single match. He's a

good man. He has faith. We must have all the faith in the world that my father, Danushka, everyone who is against us, sees what they need to see. Which is why I proceed, without my heart in my chest. I disconnect myself from Vassili. I brush off his threats. His arguments with Jackson. Even when he pins my father's lapdog against the wall, and I can only see guns pointing toward their direction.

I switch off because Vassili required this of me.

"Vassili… Go!" I croak. "You're not going to sic Anatoly on them because they're not going to shoot you, asshole. We have kids." Shit, I hope nobody notices how I mention that I'm pregnant. My body shakes as I continue to fly off the handle with, *"Give me a moment to think."*

There's a muttered conversation between Vassili and Jackson. Then my husband is motioning, "Next step, I snap your fucking neck. After that, the man behind me gets a swift foot to his throat. His neck snaps too. Maybe I'll take more of you mudaks down. Maybe you all will put enough bullets in me first. Remember, I die, everyone down here is dead. That includes you, Pops."

My gaze tears toward the floor as I'm still unable to see Jackson and Vassili. I glare at my father. His hand is up. What is Maxwell signaling for? I can't have that happen.

Voice raw, I remind my husband, "Vassili, your entire body is a weapon. Hands. Feet. So, go. I'll send you more papers."

"Nyet. Give me a moment to talk to you. I don't give a fuck if we have to chat in front of these piz'das!" He comes from beneath the staircase, standing next to a pillar by the front doors. Every part of him calls to me as he says, "Let me talk to you, Zar. Baby, let me talk to you."

His handsome frame clouds my gaze as tears flood harder. Seconds later, I say the words he told me would work. The words that would make my father believe we'd separated and keep me and Natasha safe during these times. Fuck, these words will ring in my ear until the end of time. I've always said that emotional abuse hurts the most. Physical scars will fade over time. Words cling to the mind, poisoning thoughts. He'll hate me for this one day. Not now, because he asked this of me. One day, he'll forget why we're fighting and only recall these words. I crush my husband's spirit, with my words. As I say them, they echo in my ears: "Don't worry. I won't abandon our children like your mother."

Vassili

Okay, I've said the bitch wasn't there for me and Sasha. My kid sister was passed around like candy in a whore house because our mother went on the run. Anatoly could give a fuck. For Zariah to mention my dead mother's faults. It was everything I told her to do. Everything that could break me.

I stare up at her. On the inside of her, a dam of tears is at the ready. Shit, she'll break any second and forget that this is what we have been training her for: the motherfucking TKO, and I'm her opponent.

For a split second, it's just the two of us again. I need to tell her to stay strong, to play the fucking game. This game doesn't have one thing to do with us. Jackson's glower is enough to remind me to stay in line too.

The cop gulps in air as I consider my wife. Khorosho, he doesn't know that this is all a performance. A fight. A match. Bullshit.

"You want to keep me from my kid?" My Russian accent

slides on extra thick. I'm speaking out my worst nightmare. My words thunder out, "My kid, my kid, *moi deti? Nyet!*"

"Yes." Zariah stops clinging to the railing to place a hand on her hip. That mouth of hers has always been meant for trouble. That mouth would've been the death of her if I'd let her talk the same shit in the Italian gym that she had in Vadim's while searching for Sergio. Damn, she looks so hot defying me—well in everybody else's eyes.

"That can't happen." Over my shoulder, I shoot out a sure promise, "I'll see my kid, Zar. You all have a nice day until I make that happen."

I barrel past Maxwell and to the door. The sun is no longer there. Fuck, I'm welcomed into the cold. My little boy is growing in her belly. My daughter is probably arriving in another state—far away from me. I never thought this would be with my blood being away from my side. I start for my ride, remembering the time I'd caved to Zariah for a fight in Kentucky while she was pregnant. The only other time I'd left her and Natasha for the octagon, with no intention of them coming, was when Juggernaut became a notch on my belt in seconds. Cutie Pie was a newborn, and that had been the reason.

A weight slams against my chest as I slide into my Mercedes truck. I look up at the side of the house and toward Zariah's balcony. She's not there.

For a split second, this isn't a game.

I snatch out my phone, my thumb hovers over my wife's contact in the blink of an eye.

"Don't be a mudak," I mutter to myself. Can't bitch up now. Can't call her seconds later. Before I can click out of the contact, the screen lights up.

She's calling.

Heart squeezing in my chest, I press the away button.

Then I'm dialing Yuri, my brat, though he's not on that

page anymore. As I swoop out of the parallel position, I wait for him to answer. I'm a few blocks away when his happy ass voice chimes in, but of course it's voicemail. *C'mon, Yuri, you're too good for this shit.* I press the button to redial him.

"Dah?" he snaps through the receiver as I head past a Chevron and zip onto the freeway onramp.

"I went to see Zariah," I growl, fisting the phone in one hand and navigating through traffic. Even speed doesn't help me.

"I sent over some papers for you to sign," he takes on a business tone.

"I just mentioned, Zar. Aren't you supposed to be team Vassili and Za—"

"Smart Water isn't dropping you and that's after I managed the fucking situation. Maybe you don't know about that. The manufacturer for Killer Karo clothing almost breached contract—handled that. Some magazines wanted a soundbite—managed that. All the deals that were about to fall through since you went to Italy after Kong was announced in a coma. Oh, shit, I went to Italy too. Good thing some-fucking-body got me sent home like a fucking dog with its tail between its legs. Maybe I was smacked in the head so hard that I forgot about that shit for a second and managed everything. I *managed* all these situations!"

His volume increases. I'm tempted to take the damn phone off the speaker. Teeth bared, I annunciate each word, "I'm sorry, brat. You home?"

"Dah, home. Nyet, brat!" The call disconnects in my ear.

———

Ten minutes later and my wife has called me a thousand times. I'm parked in front of Malich's home. I can hardly stare at the front lawn where Anna lost it in front of the cops. All of this was the Bratva's fault and I'm working for the Bratva. With a hard sigh, I call him again. "Yuri, come outside, brat."

All the cuss words in our native tongue come barreling out of his mouth, staggering on top of each other. I hear a few grunts and then see a flash in front of the upstairs window that belongs to my cousin's bedroom. The phone hangs up again, but I have the feeling that beneath the attitude, my fat ass, softy of a cousin is still . . .

"Shit," I mouth, stepping out of my Mercedes truck.

Where is my fat ass, softy cousin?

Did I ever say that Yuri and I look alike?

Lights from the front of the house skip on due to his movement, putting the bastard in the spotlight. Yuri isn't what Zariah's bitch of a friend, Taryn, once called a teddy bear. He's a beast. He's a beast like me. Two months did this to him.

In a wife-beater and basketball shorts, Yuri flexes deltoids that he never had before. He slams his hand across his chest. "Dah, all those hours on the phone chatting up people, handling the situation, I went hungry."

"You didn't just go hungry, Yuri." I hold out my arm to hug him. How the situation has reversed. I was never a hugger. But he's no longer that bitch's cuddly bear.

His voice grows hard, "I worked out so that I could—"

I sidestep a hook made for my jaw.

"Heh, cute, kuzen." I let out a laugh when half of me wants to make things right. And all of me is stuck on my wife. "You spent what? Six weeks juicing, eating lean meats, and a few pushups later—"

"Nyet, it was a little longer than six weeks!" Again, he comes for me with a punch that obliterates the air.

Shit, if air could hurt, then it'd be in pain. I pat the side of my face. I laugh, "C'mon, kuzen, I don't feel a thing. I suggest you take on Simeon. You can pretend you won because the bitch is ugly anyway."

"Oh funny, eh? What's funny to me is that you and Sim look like twins!" Yuri squares his shoulders, elbows tight. He does all the things that Vadim taught—everybody else but me at the gym. Shit, I knew the stance while walking in there. This time when my cousin tosses a punch, I grab his arm and spin him around.

I press him to me, locking him down. Most of his body-weight is mine to control. "Listen, brat, and I do mean brat. You said you were my brother before I even claimed you a couple of times when I came out here." I mention when we were children. My memory is spotty. I have that bitch of a mother of mine to thank for that. Who would want to remember all the times she let Anatoly and his men slap her around . . . all the times I failed her too? But I can remember half my siblings hating me for being the oldest. The other half not so much. And then there was Yuri. The brat. My brat because he said so. "You said I was your brat, Kuzen. You said that shit so many times before I even acknowledged you."

Teeth gritted, Yuri seethes, "Then don't acknowledge me. Take your ass back to Russia."

I stop myself from squeezing his arms back behind him more; it would dislocate his shoulders. I do him one better. I pop him on top of his head. "You are my brat, Yuri."

He argues, "You're like one of those jocks in those high school movies. Everybody loves you, well, I hate you."

"Hate, kuzen? Your mother said don't say that word years ago."

"Don't mention my dearly departed—"

I pop the top of his head again; he struggles against me. Yuri starts to throw his head back in an attempt to bash my nose. I move quickly enough for the takedown. I grapple around on the grass and have him in an anaconda choke. There's lots of muffled breathing as he struggles.

"You're my brat, Yuri," I growl, waiting for him to tire himself out.

The lights bleep back on along the lengthy house as Malich approaches us. His arms are folded. He brings death with him; all the mourning that I don't have a second to consider is wrapped around him. I almost don't look him into the eye. The night Igor died, we were in front of the hospital. My uncle—the man I would've gladly called father —forgot I was blood. Malich Resnov didn't want me around anymore, but I'm his big brother's son. He can't toss me out on my ear.

"Stop, son," Malich stresses.

"Nyet," Yuri strains, his tone stressed by the exertion of his body. "Dad, you said—"

"I said what you needed to hear," Malich snaps. "Let him go, Son."

"We . . ."

Malich groans, "We're all on the same team."

Yuri laughs for a second, seemingly unaware of the tension. His father repeats himself.

My cousin continues to laugh hysterically as his father tells him a few times the same words over and over. My muscles begin to exert from holding him in the anaconda chokehold this entire time. He's got to have lost his mind, to have the energy to laugh with his lungs crushing.

Finally, Yuri says between laughter, "That's why Mikhail didn't help me fight you in Italy?"

"Dah, he knew."

"Dad." Yuri raises an eyebrow at his father, grass lines pressed against his face. "You all knew? All of you, but me?"

"Now, you do!" Malich barks.

But Yuri is seized by more laughter. This time, it's not

psychotic; this time, he's at peace. There's the fat fuck I know with a jolly face. My cousin can forget that someone cursed his mother when he feels like he's been let in on a secret. His smile falls. His voice is a low rasp, "Zariah hates you right about now?"

I realize that I should let him up. My cousin is stupid enough to take the pain when he's curious and worried about something. Somehow, he's invested in my marriage. I start off him. "She's acting like it."

From below, Yuri has lost the elated shock and starts to strain against me. I tighten my hold as the anger begins to rise in him. He snaps, "Acting like it? Why do you think? Dad, this mudak called Zariah . . ."

"Yuri, stop," Malich says.

All the resistance flees, and I jump to my feet. A skinnier, more muscular Yuri, breathes heavily as he lifts off one knee and then the other. He rubs the stalks of grass from his cheeks.

Malich orders, "Yuri, if you are to be king then . . ."

You need to grow the fuck up, I mentally finish my uncle's statement. Yuri has too much heart and emotion. So, I do just like my uncle, and fold my arms, glaring at him.

My cousin's gaze squares against me then at Malich. "Dad . . . I didn't . . . We haven't told Vassili this."

"He knows, son." Malich comes to my side and places a hand over my shoulder. "Vassili doesn't give two shits if you take over the Bratva once Danny is put down.

"This, this . . ." Yuri starts breathing heavily. "This is all a game?"

Vassili

My cousin has asthma. Igor had diabetes, but Yuri Resnov had asthma. Also, the fat fuck is a little too nice to be king. He grew up with a good father and not the devil, for example. Yuri, Mikhail, and I sit around the table in the kitchen. Food wafts through the air. Tonight, Malich is at the stove, bringing yet another dish before he settles down next to his oldest son.

"I pulled a double in ER today," Mikhail sighs. He holds up a spoon of borsch. "Now, I plan to eat until I fall face first in this bowl."

His father claps his back, pleased at his eating. When we come up with the plan, it brings Malich back to life.

"You've wanted to tell me for a long time, brat." I nod to Yuri. "Malich will make you king."

My cousin shifts in his seat. "Why didn't anyone tell me that you knew?"

"Why?" I cock a brow. "Because you would know that I'm not fucking playing the game for Danny or Anatoly,

Yuri. You'd be best buddies, and we didn't have time for that."

"Okay." Yuri smiles, and I have to get used to him doing so with a slimmer face.

Malich smiles at his son. "Yuri, you will be the peace-keeper of the seven, one day. You manage Vassili in and out of the cage. Once we get rid of all the parasites and the Bratva is back in Resnov hands, then you will sit on the throne."

Mikhail nods, giving a Biblical perspective. "My brother will be like King David and King Solomon."

Not interested in the Bratva, I ask the million-dollar question. "Yuri, do you want this?"

Malich stares at him. "Son, you tell me. I always wanted out—from day one. Albeit, I've been thinking." My uncle stops talking to look at both his sons. "Igor is gone. Nothing in this world will return him to us. Before any of you were born," he pauses again. This time, including me into the fold. "Your grandpa ran the Bratva. He was fair. He went into poli-tics, started to sow seeds. Anatoly Senior weighed his options and considered what was good. Yuri, you are good. So, is this for you?"

I stare at my cousin. He's done some stupid things in his life, like wanting to marry Taryn. We're all over the place. I'm playing Danushka against my father. Malich says he saw the light since Igor died, but I don't know. My eyes lock onto Yuri. Does he want this or is he managing the situation based on how Malich calls it?

"I have to go." I stand up. "Danny is meeting with Don Roberto."

"What a disgrace!" Malich slams the side of his fist onto the table. I start toward the kitchen exit, as he continues to rant. "Italian roach. See, Yuri? This is another reason why we have to take over. With Anatoly, we are not safe anymore.

With Danushka, it's all the same, yet she would let some Italian join the Bratva, it's blasphemy!"

I never understood it either. Danushka let Don Roberto into the fold, aside from him being the richest man in Italy. The Bratva has gotten into bed with influential people around the world, but to let him sit where Russians sit. To drink from our cup and give his opinion like a Russian. It's unheard of.

Guess it doesn't matter much because Danushka's eyes dance before my vision. They're already bloodshot from me squeezing out her life-force. And she doesn't even know it yet.

It's after midnight when the elevator at The Red Door zips open on the roof level. The fires are glowing, and my heart bleeds for Zariah. Exiting the elevators, I square my shoulders and head over to a table to the far side of the roof. My gaze tracks the number of people inside. Danushka smiles up at me. A goon is seated next to her. Two men with their backs to me. One is in a Fedora; I know he is Don Roberto. His spine isn't as erect as the other. I start past the spot where I drank from my wife's pretty pussy. My heart clutches in my throat for an entirely different reason. *Is the man beside Don Roberto Horace?*

Once Horace returns to the fold, it's game time.

When the side of his face comes into view, I notice that he's another roach. Fuck! I come around the table. Hell, I prefer to sit next to the cockroaches then claim the seat on the opposite side of my sister. Her manicured hand glides up the sleeve of my leather jacket.

"Come, come." She smiles at me, taking a stand. "This is Vassili Resnov, my brother."

Don Roberto stares at me then dips his chin. "Ferrara." He nods to the roach, who stands up wearing expensive Italian digs. "An associate of mine."

I shake the Italian's hand and plaster on a smile. Look, I never had a problem with Italians, not before my wife's Sergio. After an Italian murdered Igor. I want to bash in the face of every Italian male I see.

"An essential associate." Danushka winks.

"Oh, like you're the second richest man in Italy?" I offer a cocky grin.

"Almost," Mr. Ferrara says. He's got deep ridges in his skin but doesn't look like he's had such a hard life as Don Roberto. Money probably brought him into their gang. For a second, my mind returns to Yuri. He doesn't want to be king, I can understand Malich's point of view. Malich will guide him, much like Danushka's stupid ass believes she is guiding me now. Malich will set the table of seven back in order.

For a few hours, we drink Resnov Water. They smoke cigars and talk. All I see before me is my sister's bloodshot eyes.

27

Zariah

My eyes jolt open. Something warm and muscular is beside me. I've learned what it feels like to live a cold and lonely life, so I peer through the dawn of an early morning. The sun hasn't even thought about dipping over the horizon.

"Don't scream," Vassili's voice is low and gravely. "I'm so fucking tired."

As he speaks, I can feel his entire body drain of any remnants of energy. I ask, "How long?"

"About twenty minutes of sleep. Your door is locked, so don't ask."

I chortle a little. "Don't ask if my door is locked, or don't ask you never to leave?"

A groan comes from my husband's massive body.

"Or don't ask you . . ." the giddiness of him being here has passed and all that remains is desire. "Don't ask for you to touch my body."

"Give me an hour. I'll make it all up to you." His voice is

so deep that a smile burns across my cheeks. I remember one time sounding like Count Dracula because I couldn't imitate a Russian voice. While he begins to fall into sleep, I nestle closer to him. As close as I can get. I'd been ready to start the day now that Vassili was here, but somehow sleep clings to me too.

A few hours later, I grouse awake, feeling eyes on me. Again, a hard dose of electricity goes off in my nerves. I'm in such a state, so accustomed to lonely, that I stir around anxiously. Vassili is sitting on the bed with his back leaning against the headboard. Somehow, I'm using his thigh as a pillow. His cock pops against my forehead, but I stare up at him and rollover.

"I-I said some awful things . . ." I murmur, remembering how I mentioned his mother. Though he'd asked me to, an apology chokes my throat.

He places a finger to his lips. "Your pop is here, Zariah. We don't have time for you to cry."

"I wasn't going to cry," I whisper. "I don't like this, Vassili. I want to come home and for us to be a family again."

His hand glides behind my neck; he massages there. Then he fists his cock with his other hand. "Nyet. Stop talking. Suck my cock and drink up, Zariah. You'll feel better."

I climb to my knees, my ass going to the air and my mouth sinking down on the crown of his thick cock. This isn't the time for throwing soft kisses against the base of his long, fat shaft. I suck with the enthusiasm of a woman who has a will to survive. My mouth begins to ache instantly. It takes sheer dedication to learn the angles of him and to remember how to move my mouth around his thickness.

With my pussy pulsating between my thighs, I slobber all over Vassili's dick. Once my mouth is slack, I bring him to the back of my throat. The Russian beast fills my mouth to the brink, slamming against my tonsils. Vassili places his hand at my neck, quickening my pace. Up and down. He pulls me up so I can love the mushroom-shaped crown of him. My tongue slithers over his hardness, gliding the taut ridges of him. A moan comes from his massive chest. It gives me the confidence to pull his massive erection as far down my throat as possible. With each caress of my mouth over his steel shaft, I begin to knock hard at my tonsils.

"Fuck," he groans as I continue to assault the back of my throat with his dick. His moans are so deep, so erotic.

I flick the head of his cock with my tongue. My tongue blazes all around the base of his shaft, writing my name.

"Zariah," Vassili says, fisting a handful of my hair. Before I can purr, my tonsils are bruised. He slams my entire mouth down on his dick again. My hot, wet mouth envelopes the monstrosity of a cock.

"That's right, suck Daddy's cock." With the force of his hand at my neck, his dick plunges deeply with each word.

The sounds of my sucking and stroking become wet and messy. I'm sucking Vassili's cock like a Super Slurpee at the AM-PM convenience store. His white seed is already ingrained in my mind. I want an entire belly of the Russian fighter's cum swimming in my gut. The walls of my pussy shudder, desire coating my thick folds. With my body on fire for him, I'm pulled into a trance.

I crave my husband's cum with all my might, and then something beautiful happens. Every thick muscle in my husband's body tightens beneath me. A flood is unleashed into my mouth.

Vassili's fingers clamp into the back of my neck, and he holds me there. "That's right, girl. Drink all Daddy's cum. It will make you stronger."

Sometime later, I hear talking coming down the hallway. A woman's voice. Berenice's voice. My father's old secretary is on her way into my mother's room. She's telling Maxwell that the lunch they just ate was good. On key, my stomach rumbles.

"How are you still hungry, girl?" He paws at my cheek. "That tummy's full of cum."

I kiss his lips. "Sure is. While it's given me the courage to . . ."

I almost mention my father, which might sound weird. Mentioning Maxwell Washington while we're talking about my belly full of my husband's cum. I almost dare to tell Vassili everything about my plans for my father. Loving dark eyes stare at me. I glance away. He doesn't need to know yet.

Smiling back, I add, "It's *almost* given me the courage not to get out of this bed and go raid the fridge. Vassili, promise not to leave while I'm downstairs."

I hold up my pinkie finger. Vassili takes my hand and kisses my pinkie finger.

Twenty minutes later, the coast is clear. Vassili's sex gave me confidence. I almost head toward my father's office, but instead, I saunter down the steps. In the kitchen, I grab a silver tray and pile it high with a few of the subway sandwiches from yesterday. I add a veggie tray that has yet to be opened and a few bottles of water and head upstairs. Balancing the feast in one hand, I push open the door with the left.

My heart sinks to the pit of my stomach. Were our son

larger in my womb, he'd probably be doing somersaults attuned with my despair.

"In the bathroom, girl," Vassili calls out.

"How did you . . ."

I hear a slow rumble of laughter as I close the door to my bedroom. Vassili comes out of the bathroom and holds up my phone. A tight frown smears across his face. A case of anxiety that I never knew heaves against my chest. Damn, I recall how shitty my Saturday afternoon was supposed to be. It all revolved around another man.

Tyrese Nicks and I scheduled to meet an hour ago. My gaze shifts to the digital clock on the wall and then to the hardness of Vassili's face. I'm late . . . he could have texted me.

"Look at Natasha. That's daddy's girl," Vassili says, chucking the phone at me. "I don't think I could even match that pouted face."

I take a deep breath and catch the phone before it can slip through my fingers.

A call comes in from none other than the agent himself. I press the away button and place the phone on 'Do Not Disturb.'

Vassili fucked me sideways before leaving. We were screwing so hard when my father and Berniece returned from God knows where. We had to take our party to the rug on the floor. Now I have rug burns as I dress for the evening. Not sure what compels me, but I dress in all black. Ripped jeans, a designer blouse, blazer and stiletto booties. I'd taken a Lyft.

Now, with one foot in front of the other, I meander through the hotel lobby where Tyrese is staying.

I can't believe I've been his target this entire time all because of my last name. Emotions on empty, I slip inside of the marble and gold encased elevator, heading to the top floor.

"This is not a good place to meet someone when you're married," I mumble to myself, clutching an alligator tote.

Along the hallway, the door to each hotel room is much further away from the next. I stop at the right one, knuckles poised to knock when Natasha and Vassili flood my mind. *Loud rap was in my ears. Vassili was in a wheelchair. Our daughter used his shoulders to hoist herself up and wag around her thick-diapered butt. They were so happy. I can remember how sad I was, wishing that his patella would shift back into perfection.*

With my fist a fraction away from the door, I determine that happiness doesn't need to be just around the corner, I could've been happy then.

Happy that a bum knee was the extent of Vassili's problems.

Happy that my husband loves the two of us with all of him.

Happy that Natasha can shoot me a frown after I turned from the rap.

Happy she is so fat and so healthy.

But I am not happy. I am sad for reasons I can't remember. That's the day Danushka crossed paths with me.

My phone rings. Speak of the devil. Hell, I'm wearing all black, feeling myself for a second, so I answer it, "What do you want?"

Danny sneers, "Vassili loves to get his dick sucked, doesn't he?"

"Wh-why are you talking about your bro-brother's member, Danny?" I mutter, sorely thrown off by her statement. Does she know we are still together? Did Grigor watch us through the window this morning?

"We were friends once, Zar. While your loyalties have been on the decline, I've continued to look out for you. Check your phone, *krasivaya.*"

The call disconnects just as the front door opens. Tyrese smiles at me as I glance at my phone, "I thought I heard talking. How long have you been standing here?"

I clutch my chest, letting out a stifled sob.

2 8

Vassili

An Hour Earlier . . .

I'd pulled into the mansion that Horace and Danushka own. My eyes zeroed in on a Rolls Royce that hadn't been here this morning. Did it belong to Horace? The finish line zoomed through my mind as I let myself in, only to see Danushka in the foyer.

She was sitting at a chair, legs wide, head in her hands. She'd looked up at me and spat the words, "Look at you, getting your cock sucked . . ."

The phone in her hands somersaulted toward my face. I caught it in my fist. "What the fuck, Danny? You are crossing the line!"

"I said I trusted you, but you proved me for a fool," she growled. "Grigor's still watching you. He was watching you and Zariah a little while ago!"

My chest heaved as I started toward her. Fuck waiting for proof that Horace was home. I was going to murder this bitch, now.

As I lunged at her, I felt a prick at the side of my neck.

"Welcome back, Vassili," Horace's voice came from behind. Then, I was dead weight . . .

Rope strains against my chest, biceps, hips. I'm gritting down on terry cloth when my vision swims into focus. Blond hair is draped over my lap. Very light blond hair. I start to heave when I notice that it's much longer than my sister's.

"Look at her," Danushka's voice calls out to me.

I glance around. I'm in her room. The fireplace is aglow. She's wearing one of those lingerie pieces that I never fail to shred off my wife's body.

"Ssss-ssss--," I try to tell the blonde to stop, but my cock is wet and slick.

"Isn't she a beauty?" Danushka pulls the woman's face up. "I bought those lips for us."

I start to strain against the rope; then I stare at the woman. No life is behind her blue eyes. Not an ounce of it.

While the woman continues to suck my cock, my sister pulls up a chair. "I can remember being a girl. Your mother had to buy us all the gifts. It was during one of your parents' peace treaties." She reaches over, strumming her fingers through the girl's hair, and helps guide her head up and down my cock.

Bile slams through me, charring my throat but stopping there.

"Your mom brought us gifts for New Year's. These little matryoshka dolls—those were mine. While the boys got good, good gifts. I got fucking dolls." She reaches down, flicks at my cock and kisses the side of the girl's face. "This one looks like the dolls that I never wanted. Looks just like them, all but her lips. Her lips weren't as pretty, I made them pretty because *I had the power to.*"

The shock I didn't know was holding me tight begins to

dissipate. I begin to shift in the seat, attempting to break the legs of the chair.

A gun is pulled out. Danushka places it to my head. "All she's going to do is get you ready to cum, then you'll cum for me."

"Ffffff . . ." I growl.

"You aren't attracted to me yet, Vassili." Danushka pulls an arm around herself. "I can change myself for you." Her gun goes to the woman's dome. The blonde is high on something so strong that she continues to slurp at my cock. "Horace loved her until I *became* her. My measurements are her measurements. I became her height. I had ribs removed to thin me out! I am this bitch!"

I glare in shock. My sister has always been brown-haired and massively built. We all are. Now, she's not, and the woman latched to my dick is the reason why.

Danushka lifts the blonde's hair, but her face lulls. "Sweetheart, does it feel like he's about to cum? Vassili, please nod when you're about to cum."

A vein in the side of my neck is about to burst.

"Why? Why do you ask? You and I." Danushka points the gun back and forth between us. "We are kings and queens. Let me show you." Danushka sways as she walks toward the door and opens it slightly. She speaks something in Italian; her voice is too muffled for me to hear. The double doors open wide. Men come in dragging a body.

Horace's body!

"He dropped you. I dropped him. Permanently. Ahem, Horace was still in love with her." Danushka places her gun into his slack mouth, laughing as she moves the barrel back and forth. His lifeless lips are pliable to each stroke of the barrel. "While I was making moves, Vassili, Horace was with her. She's already a zombie now, and he still loves her— Excuse me. Loved her."

"Mmmmmgggg—" I growl into the cloth constricting my mouth as the doors close again.

My cock is still being worked by the drugged-out blond.

I glance back over and Danushka slides a phone into my face. "Look, I sent Zariah a picture of you and this little matryoshka doll. No need to worry about her any longer. I think she gets the picture—metaphorically speaking. We Resnovs are meant to fuck and screw whoever we want to! I was okay with Horace sleeping with this doll, but that was always until I had you."

She points the tip of her gun at the blonde's head. The girl looks up at the instance her brains go soaring to the left side of me. The sight killing all the stimulation she'd caused my cock.

"Damn," Danushka rolls her eyes at the sight of my cock going limp. "Well, I got this."

She starts to kneel before me. I bring my head forward, connecting with Danushka's nose. The force of it also sends me toppling over on top of her. My entire body is restrained, and I'm in a fucked over position. My forehead continues to slam into her face. Nose, mouth, shit, my forehead rocks against hers as I shift myself around.

I expect her goons to come marching into the room, but there's silence. My head slams into Danushka until her face is a bloodied pulp. When I feel like the bitch is down for the count, I stagger to my knees, pushing up awkwardly and moving toward the wall.

"Shit," I growl low in my throat. If I break out of this chair, the Italians that are surrounding this place will hear me . . . half of me doesn't give a fuck. The other half wants them to come so that I can try to murder them. Once I get my body free. I slam into the wall—once, twice—the doors burst open.

Two guns zero in on me. Moments later, the leveled silencers fall to the ground.

"What's happening here, brat?" Yuri says, eye twitching at the sight.

Danushka moans.

Mikhail puts his gun into the back of his jeans and comes toward me.

"Did she . . ." Yuri begins.

"Don't," I grit out.

Mikhail cuts the ropes with a knife then turns away. I zip up my pants.

"Please don't tell me this orgy included . . ." Yuri stops speaking to gag. "Fuck, should I say Horace or your sister? I don't understand what happened here. Maybe I'm too innocent to know."

"Yuri," I growl.

"Hey, this is enough traumatizing shit to have me eat my weight in Ben & Jerry's," he shrugs.

"You good?" Mikhail finally mutters. "Jesus . . ."

"I'm good."

He turns around, getting a good look at the place as I go toward Danushka. I get down to her level.

"Br-brat," she spits up blood. "Brat, wait."

Voice raw, I snarl, "Why?"

Her lips are covered in blood as she mutters, "I love you."

"Shit, I've never loved you, girl."

Her faux blue eyes flutter open. Licking her bloodied lips, Danushka says, "I've always loved you. *Loved.* I wanted to be you, *wanted to love you.*"

I place my hands around her throat.

"You sure you don't want us to handle this?" Mikhail places a hand on my shoulder.

"Because I don't have a problem killing this bitch." Yuri chuckles.

"Nyet," I growl, beginning to squeeze.

"Your mother," Danushka moans.

All the muscles in me begin to cave. I have imagined this a thousand times, yet my fingers refuse to squeeze tighter around Danushka's neck. She mentions that dumb story about my mom buying her matryoshka dolls as a child. Half my memories of my mother are tainted, the other half lead me down a dark path.

I listen to my sister's words. She reminds me of more than I'd ever want to know. Secrets long forgotten.

With tears burning my eyes, my hands flex around her scrawny neck again. After Danny's revelation, part of me wants to apologize for sending this bitch straight to hell.

2 9

Zariah

My gaze is hard, like one who refuses to let a single teardrop. My bottom lip is racked over by my teeth, and Tyrese zeros in on that. He licks his lips, eyes me eyeing him, and looks away. So far, he's been polite. There is no way in hell I can walk into his place and not let the cat out of the bag. That cheating cat. My husband.

Can't claim that the photo is doctored. Can't play the wife who refuses to believe what her own two eyes witness. Can't pretend the entire ordeal is nothing and hide my phone before he gets a single look in.

Tyrese downs his drink. "Fuck," he says underneath his breath "You're pregnant."

I blink away tears.

"Zariah, you've always known how to celebrate a winning case." He holds up a vintage whiskey. "I thought we'd celebrate with this when you were ready to fully let him go, but . . . how far along are you?"

"We're not discussing that," I grit out, glancing away.

"Alright, I can't say that I know what you're going through."

"Then don't." I shake my glass of cranberry juice, the cushion he's using for the drink I sorely wish I could have.

Tyrese's brown eyes wash over me. Those dimples know when to run and hide because his orbs are laden with sympathy. "Alright, no more chatting about the husband. I just want to remind you, Zariah, I told you about the girl who was our witness. How she should've been our way in, until you."

"Yeah," I reply. "She got greedy and fell in love with money. The same thing happened to me. I got greedy and fell in love with the guy . . . the guy who was supposed to be my momentary reprieve after reserving all my hours for college." I begin to mumble, realizing we're still about to talk about my husband. "I put all my eggs in one basket, handed it to Vassili Karo Resnov."

He sighs for me. "You fell in love."

"Like that girl. Instead, I fell in love with a man instead of money. Now I'm dead too."

He comes out of his seat, kneels in front of me. "You're not dead, Zariah."

"I'm so dead," I murmur. Thoughts swarm through my mind. Wild ideas that align with my father's credo. Thoughts that dictate how replaceable Vassili Resnov is. Danushka played me? Every few seconds, a belief contrary to what slapped me straight in the face, seeps into my mind. "I'm so dead, dead, dead." *Dead because if I leave him, it lifts Anatoly's blessing. If I leave him, I leave my heart with him . . .*

"You're worried that he'll hurt you for leaving him? You never admitted it." Tyrese plants himself between my legs, his breath skimming across my cheek. Damn, how did he get so close? He's drinking. I can't. He's tipsy, bent on emotion. I'm pregnant, broken, and drowning in my emotions.

"Zar, I remember when a car came up to Billingslea legal. You were scared out of your life."

Eyebrows zipping together, I ask, "When Noriega came?"

"No, the fucking Russians, Zariah." Now his fingertips skim across my cheek. "Those dirty Resnovs. Vassili thinks he owns you. They all do."

"Yeah," I murmur, letting the pain lead.

"Zariah, I can't say I understand this separation between you and your father. You say he's a crooked cop. I'll still assist you with that, but let's save that for another night. Right now," he says, offering another reverent rub to my cheek. "I can keep you safe. You and Natasha."

A half-second becomes a million years as his mouth brushes against mine. Moonlight streams into the room, and I push back from him. I groan. "No, no."

My hand weighs down like a brick and hardly meets its mark. I stagger up from my seat and move. I'm treading through imaginary water as Tyrese is in my ear. His voice is the comfort that I wish I didn't need as he asks me to stay.

"No," I growl. "This was . . . this was a mistake."

"No, it wasn't, Zariah! You and Vassili—that's the mistake. The biggest mistake you've ever made. Shit, I'm starting to believe the rift between you and your father has more to do with that mistake than anything else. Let me help you."

I cackle, finding my tote, pulling it against my body before stalking toward the door. "You said you had something to share, Mr. Nicks."

"Not tonight."

"Whatever," I grumble, my hand a fraction from the doorknob before I try to turn.

"Let me at least call you an Uber."

"Yeah . . ." I nod in agreement.

"So, wait, then?"

"In the lobby, and I can do it *myself*."

By the time I hit the lobby, I've got a Lyft on the way. Needing the fresh air to promote some semblance of normal, I decide to wait outside. The only valet is seated on a stool at a podium near the exit. He asks if I'd like some company. I shake my head, continuing through the sliding glass doors. After a few minutes, a midsized SUV pulls up about ten yards out. The ultra-white lights blinding me. I click on the screen and confirm that I have a midsize SUV—dark blue. With the lights blaring in my direction, I start toward it to confirm that it's the right color.

Then my phone rings. The ringtone dedicated to none other than my husband.

Wow, so now he's calling me. My mouth is set to ask him to explain himself, I'm about to press 'accept' when the back-door slams open. My unanswered phone clatters onto the sidewalk as I'm tugged inside. Before I can blink, the front of my blouse is torn open, a mouth assaults my breast.

"St-stop . . ."

"Not so fast," the man places his forearm against my throat. I glare into the darkness through prescription glasses. He's got a clean-cut look about him, but filth blares through. The man moves his forearm a fraction of the way as he asks, "You know who I am?"

"Grigor." I tremble.

He chuckles. "Nobody ever gets it right on the first time. You're smarter than I pegged you for, Zariah."

"Wh-what do you want from me?"

"One measly little fuck. Enough to shove it in Vassili and Danny's face." He presses his forearm back against my throat. "Enough to show them what it's like to be put in second place. Oh, and you die. You obviously die after the fuck."

"Why?" I hardly get the word out, recalling a few tips my father taught me. Gather your surroundings while pretending to pay attention to the assailant. Stall.

"Danny loves him. *She loved me.* She thinks I'll always be there." He fists his hair with one hand. "I've always been there. I worked for that bastard for her. Loved her. Loved her before she changed herself. Loved her first before anyone else loved her. Loved her!"

I almost forget protocol as his words fly like sprays of spit into my face. "Who?"

"Danushka! Never mind, you're as stupid as I thought." His legs squeeze around mine and he bites my nipple.

Glass sprays. The window comes crashing in. My eyes zip shut at the last second. A hand zips inside, grabs his throat. Another hand is holding a silenced gun. Two tiny puffed sounds are emitted before Grigor's body falls limp onto mine.

The door opens. He's thrown off of me.

I gape at Simeon. Damn, he *resembles* my husband.

My fingers are out, shaking. Simeon stares at them, placing my discarded iPhone into my hands like he isn't sure of what else to do. His gaze slips to my breast. He groans, buttoning my blazer before I can even think to do it.

"You good, dah?" Simeon asks.

"No . . ."

"I think you are." He sniffs.

"Nnnnn . . ."

"You have to be okay, Mrs. Resnov. You're breathing— you're okay." He holds out a hand and helps me from the back seat. Simeon escorts me to the front seat of the SUV. "Get in."

"Wh-why?" I stutter.

"Dead body, stolen vehicle. You gotta be fucking with me, Mrs. Resnov, you know why."

I climb in.

I expect the door to close in my face, but he removes his jacket first, places it over me then jogs around to the driver's side. Simeon mutters to himself, reaches to the backseat, grabs the keys from Grigor's pocket. My head turns slowly. I watch as he places his fingers into two tiny holes at the side of his cousin's head. His fingertips are soiled in red blood. He rubs the crimson liquid around, studying it in interest.

I stare.

"We all have our delights, Mrs. Resnov. Because of you, I didn't *enjoy* this." He pulls away from the curb.

"I'm sorry you had to murder your cousin for me," I grumble.

"You ruined the *how*." Disappointment mars his gorgeous features.

Fear prickles up my spine. So, the bastard wanted to kill his family. The apprehension is enough to break me. Instead of caving in from his hard glower, I match it. "So, we're going to hide the body and the car?"

"Nyet, I'll do it. You'll get a ride home. You aren't in the right frame of mind to drive yourself. Or you wouldn't have been waiting for a car at *a fucking hotel, Mrs. Resnov.*"

"How did you know?" I'm doing it again. Attempting to keep him talking. This time it's another Resnov. This time, I'm not entirely sure if I have to try to save myself—shit, I didn't last time. "How do you—"

"I know lots."

I match his glare.

Simeon huffs. "Okay, Danushka liked to have Grigor watch. She is Anatoly's daughter. Same story. Different gig."

"Where's Vassili? Is he—"

"He'd be fucking pissed if he knew you were out so late too."

I stare at Simeon. Last and first time we chatted, he had very few words for me. He'd glared at me too. Now, he's glaring again.

"I made a mistake . . ." I murmur.

"Dah, worse mistake of your life."

———

He drives for over an hour. By the time we make it to a sand bed in the middle of the desert, my hands have stopped trembling. I've also grown content with Simeon's silence. I wait in the car for the longest as he digs a ditch. I've listened to a voicemail from my husband. Vassili has apologized while explaining Danushka's new low. I delete the voicemail and watch Simeon continue to dig. The entire process seems eerily peaceful—for him. Almost ritualistic.

While climbing into the SUV, Simeon continues sulking about the beauty of "how" he'd planned to murder his cousin. He's spent a good amount of time musing before I ask how he felt about Vassili—his *other* cousin. A phantom smile crosses his thick lips. I jokingly offer him a chance to do the deed, saying Vassili cheated.

Simeon said, "He wouldn't," and that was the extent to our conversation.

Another hour later, with the early morning giving the sky a lilac hue, Simeon pulls up in front of my father's home.

"This is where I leave you." Simeon nudges his chin toward the house.

My eyebrows pull together, and I ask, "Why didn't you drop me off first?"

His lips are so tense that they don't move. "Get some rest."

My heart begins to drum in my ears. All sorts of questions flit through my brain. My husband hates Simeon's guts —at least, I think. Yet, Simeon saved my life, and I guess, all I can muster is that I've become his alibi when it comes to Grigor's death.

No! I'm his accomplice. We stare at each other. Simeon's reading me well, but I'm not reading him in the slightest.

Damn, I have a feeling that this Resnov is substantially smarter than he lets on.

"My father . . ." I start pondering the notion of telling Simeon why I met with a federal agent. If I tell him the secret that I want to forgo with my husband, well, at least until my father is behind bars, maybe he won't be inclined to share tonight with Vassili. A married woman in a hotel room with *another* man is a bad combination. Hopefully, I can sway Simeon with the truth.

Without warning, Simeon gets out. He comes around and opens the passenger door.

My heart slams into my throat. "My father isn't a good person. I wanted to—"

"Go." Simeon gives me a two-finger salute like my words mean less than shit to him.

I groan as he backs away, then hustles to the opposite side of the SUV.

Part of me wants to slip off my shoe and throw it at the back of his head. Yet another part of me, the one raised by my momma, urges me to tell him to keep his eyes peeled for Five-Oh since I'm not sure Vassili and my antics let up with my father. Let's not forget, the part of me raised by Maxwell Washington. That devious side of me hopes Simeon Resnov disappears off the face of the earth.

I have the feeling that this Resnov is brighter than he lets on. I can't have Simeon's misguided intelligence working against me, but I stand there in a flurry of confusion as he sits in the SUV. Teeth gritted, he points to the door. Damn, even the devil has the nerve to be so chivalrous, but for how long?

30

Vassili

The next morning, a green slush twister spins around in my favorite blender. Simeon and Anatoly have settled down at the massive island in my kitchen. My father turns the illustrated pages of an old Russian fable about a kid with a pit bull. With a deep frown set on his face, Simeon drinks the coffee that I made him. I can't have the bastard walking around my own house getting comfortable.

Once my breakfast is the right consistency, I pour the contents into a large glass. Elbows on the marble ledge, I stand at the island across from their stools.

"Danny's dead," I share.

Simeon sips, Anatoly turns pages.

"Danny's dead, Horace too."

My father chuckles softly, pointing at a passage in the book and showing Simeon. My cousin grunts, which is proof that he likes what he sees.

"How is Chak-Chak?" His dark eyes glare into mine.

"Good, safe. I just said your daughter is dead, no need mentioning mine."

He smooths the orange lapel of yet another ultra-expensive clown suit. "Your daughter is my daughter, blood, *moy syn*."

"Stop calling me, my son!"

Anatoly's voice booms across the room, "I could call her a replacement for Danny! Chak-Chak is a fucking upgrade to all of you! All of you who have taken such liberties."

A replacement? An inferno scorches my skin at the thought of my last seconds with Danushka and Anatoly insinuating that Natasha *replaces* her. Shit, I down the green drink like it's a fifth of vodka.

"Kidding." Anatoly's teeth gleam.

I point a stiff finger at him. "Mention my kid again, and you're dead. I don't give a fuck if you're blood. Simeon, you take up for him, you're dead too. Matter of fact, where were you last night? I called the two of you as soon as I arrived at Danushka's. After that I reached Malich! Where the fuck were you, huh?"

A snarl of a smile flickers at the edges of Simeon's cheeks. "You want to know where I was last night?"

"Yes! If I hadn't called them—I . . ." Fuck, I'd be dead—dead in a compromising position with Danushka! But I refuse to say as much.

Simeon starts in a taunting tone, "Last night—"

My cousin's steely voice breaks off. He rubs a hand across his forehead; his middle finger begins to lift. He holds it out.

"Keep at it, I'll break that motherfucker off."

"Try." He tilts his hand until his middle finger is perfectly pointed in my direction. "Last night, I . . ."

"Simeon . . ." Anatoly stresses. I'm not sure if it's a threat to him for threatening me, or it has something to do with last night. Shit, I have no clue.

"Last night, I took a fucking life, but I did not enjoy a single second of it." He puts his middle finger down but holds up both his hands. "Blood, warm, beautiful blood is my life. I didn't delight in it, *last night,* Vassili."

"Whatever," I shake my head, though interested in what occurred *last night?* I stop myself from asking, fuck it!

"I killed your brat." With fire in his eyes, Simeon glares at me as if there's more to the story.

I chortle. "Oh, that's why 'last night' was the bomb you kept tossing? You murdered Grigor?"

"Dah! Your brother," he snarls.

"Good for you, because last night I was with my brother. Yuri. Mikhail. Those are brothers. Whoever you took out, good for you."

"You want to know why I had no fun?" Simeon stops wriggling his fingers around.

My father clears his throat.

For a second, I'm wondering what he's done that could've topped the whacked-out time I had. I snort. "You murdered Grigor, and I didn't so much as blink. The *sperm donor* of the idiot you murdered is more interested in reading a bedtime-story than reacting to you too. So, what makes you think I give half a fuck about what you're going to say?" I move away from the island as my father continues to flip pages, mumbling how much Chak-Chak will love her new book. With my now empty glass in the dishwasher, I glare at the both of them. "When is this meeting with the seven? Let's get it over with."

Anatoly places the illustrated book onto the table. He stands up. "There's no such thing as the seven."

I cast a glance at Simeon. His mother, who is also my father's sister, has a stake in their secret society.

"People are sitting at a table. Seven chairs. Sometimes more, sometimes less, that is how the world goes, my son," Anatoly grits.

"Then give me a fucking date, Anatoly. I have a belt that I want to get back." I huff. The second the light flickered out of Danushka's life, my love for MMA was returned. "I have a life with my wife and daughter!"

I start past him, but my father blocks my path. "Vassili Karo . . . You have my middle name, my son. You have your grandfather's middle name. Anatoly Karo! You took your first breath of air, and I vowed to God that you'd be safe. Simeon here, he loves you. We love you so much!"

"You love me?" I smile at my cousin. Mighty crazy how half my family is telling me they love me these days when we never said those types of words. Danushka was running around, crazy enough to believe she loved me. Anatoly is no better. I grit out, "You love me, huh?"

Anatoly replies, "Of course."

I stare at Simeon again. The flicker in his gaze tells me nothing. Aside from us fighting or him mentioning his love for blood every once in a while, I can't read Simeon. He'd make the perfect opponent in the cage, a fucking wild card.

Anatoly pokes at my chest. "You are my legacy. In 1 Samuel 8, the people begged and begged God for a king. They had God, but they wanted a mere man to rule. In another verse of the Bible, again, Israelites were divided about being ruled by the King of Egypt."

"What does that have to do with me?" I pound a fist at my chest.

Ignoring me, he laughs. "They preferred to stay under the thumb of an Egyptian king than venture into the unknown—venture into the freedom that God had for them. Throughout history, humans craved someone to rule over them. Not four, not five. *Not seven*. They craved a king!"

228

"I-am-not-interested," I growl. My eyelid twitches hard as I stare into Anatoly's eyes. If only he knew, Malich has come alive again. My uncle and Yuri want this. I don't.

"I've been that king, and you will be that king, Vassili. Fuck the seven, the only person who ever ruled was me. Now it will be you."

31

Zariah
Venice Beach

Out of habit, I attach a few photos of Natasha to a text message. It isn't until my thumb is hovering over send when reality dawns on me. Vassili isn't away from us while preparing for promotions. Danushka is gone. His story of how she'd pulled that move with the woman sucking my husband's cock hurts, but I have to believe it. Now, he's associating with Anatoly.

Instead of sending the photos of our daughter's recent vacation, I toss the phone into my purse. I look up at Samuel, who just might be staring at me. He clears his throat, eyes flitting across the spacious living room of his home and asks about a case.

We've had this conversation a thousand times over, based on my then client's needs. Yet, right now, something is between us, and I can't quite put my finger on it. I mention a psychological examination that my client's husband is forcing her to obtain. It's all about proving that your ex-wife is crazy when you've been cheating, and you want to keep the house, the cars, the kids.

"But she does have a few marks against her," I finish off, giving him the rundown on my latest case. Still, a plethora of uncanny feelings overwhelm me. I stare out the floor-to-ceiling window across at the choppy waters.

Vassili owned a beachfront home a few lots down from here when we first met. I begin to wonder if I'm projecting the jumble of confusion from my marriage onto us when Samuel clears his throat.

He asks, "What sort of marks?"

"Well, arson. My client found her husband and two other women in bed. She crept out of the house, took her rage out on his Porsche."

My mom starts into the living room, a bright beam on her face. She's carrying a silver tray with a tea kettle and tiny cups in her hand. Damn, my mom has the domesticated lifestyle down and this place fits her perfectly. Samuel's place, that is.

"So, you guys are talking work? We just returned from vacation," she says, voice all sing-song. "That reminds me, Zariah. I went to this boutique tea store. I have your gift somewhere. A few teas for calmness and peace."

Disregarding her concern about my Zen, I nudge my chin to Natasha. "Good thing Cutie Pie is sleeping, or she'll think we're playing teacups."

"She sure would, sweetheart."

My mom settles down onto the very chair Vassili sat when he glared at me while I questioned her over the phone. I'd been so concerned about the media's portrayal of Vassili the very day I'd learned she was being slapped around again.

Zamora adds, "Vassili was always big on teatime with her."

"Mom," I groan, scooting forward in my seat. With restless hands, I help pull apart the teacups. "Why are we . . . what's with teatime? I'm not a baby anymore."

The two of them exchange glances.

"Like you said, Momma, the three of you all are home from a vacation together. Let's forgo teatime and," I stop myself from saying 'anything revolving around happy.' Tension lines my shoulders and a dose of irritability tightens my lips. I glance at Natasha sleeping in the stroller since nobody was bold enough to take her out. With one look at her peaceful face, I decide that I need a happy moment. She's *my* happy. "Do you have more vacation photos, Mom? Because I know good and well that the ones you just Air Dropped aren't all of them."

She continues with the process of pouring us all tea. A gruesome amount of seconds past, and I bite my tongue. Momma didn't raise no fool. The only card I have left is patience.

"These past few weeks," Samuel begins taking his teacup from her, "have reminded me to slow down, to live a little."

Does he mean these past few days while on vacation? Or does he honestly mean weeks? Those thoughts pop into my head, then I wonder why I'm *wondering* about the validity of Samuel's words.

"Good. I'm happy for you," I say and smile. "You too, Mom."

"We have something that we need you to do for us, Zariah," he says.

Plucking up my tea, I forget that it's not a shocking dose of alcohol. Fire scorches my throat. Eyes wide, I gulp the little in my mouth.

"Are you okay?" Mom stutters.

Placing a hand at my throat, I nod. "Ye-yeah. That was very good."

"Better be, it wasn't cheap." She smiles. "Ahem, I got a few of your favorite loose-leaf teas and some toys for Natasha in Washington. Nevertheless, Sammy and I also purchased something else. It's not a tourist gift."

The two of them glance at each other. Samuel clears his throat and adds, "It's something I've been hoping your mother would allow us to do for some time now."

My eyebrows rise in confusion at the riddles they've tossed me. I'm livid with Vassili, regardless of my love for him and my intuition that Danny placed him in a compromising situation. So, I shrug. "Well, if it's a gift, I'll take it."

Samuel reaches over the side of his seat and grabs a brown paper bag. He, then, places the mysterious gift onto the coffee table. An eyebrow lifted, I reach inside and touch a box with bubble-wrap paper around it. I pull it out.

My very own words echo in my ears, "This is . . . this is a paternity exam."

"All these years, I never said a thing to Sammy," my mom shares. "He suspected, but I never said a word. Not until my heart began to break for Natasha. I want her around her father, and I-I want you around yours."

The truth slams into me. Samuel seemed nervous, staring at me earlier. He'd take subtle glances. Hell, our entire past comes to fruition in my mind. I can almost hear me telling Vassili that he's a father figure and to try to make friends with *him*.

The man who could be my father.

32

Vassili

I told them. The second the text message comes through from Zariah, I set aside this dark, traitorous world I've been living in. All the vindictive antics. All the bullshit. None of it means a thing because she told Ms. Zamora and Samuel that we are in the crosshairs of my father. The sea-salted air slaps against my face. Across PCH, the lights are blaring green in the dark of night. I open this bitch up. Had I no concerns about my wife, I'd enjoy this ride. I've taken it a million times before I sold the home I owned in the area.

After a while, I turn into the tiny alleyway behind the houses that line the ocean. Samuel's garage is open. I pull in beside his car. Fuck, I'm on alert. Maxwell might have someone on his team watching. Anatoly doesn't count at the moment. As long as I feign interest in becoming his successor until the meeting in a few days, we're good.

I climb off my ride, my eyes on the door as it opens. Zariah's chocolate brown orbs are wide; her tiny, curvaceous body seems to tremble like a leaf.

"The fuck happened?" I growl, ready to pounce on anyone who caused her harm.

"My dad . . . my dad . . ." she chokes on the words, fanning her face.

"Dah? Dah? What!" Her cheeks are between my hands. I crush her body against the door. "What happened?"

She gasps, "Samuel might be my dad."

"Shit," I mumble. It sounds like a good thing to me. Although my wife is too emotional to see the good in this revelation. I nod, reach down, kiss her lips and pull her up into my arms. I move toward the motorcycle, grabbing the extra helmet. I push her long strands from in front of her face and gingerly place them over her head. After shoving on my helmet, my leg swings over the side of the ride.

"Let's go, girl." I cock my head. "Hold tight. We have to keep my son safe."

She climbs on the back, and we ride. The freeway stretches before me as Zariah's arms squeeze tighter around my waist. Time passes by, and I can tell when she's calmed down. I zip back onto the onramp and return to Venice. Not ready for our time to end, I park at a dead-end a few blocks away from Samuel's place. When I remove Zariah's helmet, her eyes search mine. Again, I won't ask her any questions. We have time to catch up because though we've been worlds apart, she still belongs to be.

Another hour passes as we walk along the shore. I stop before her, look down and press my lips to her mouth. My hand clasps the back of her neck, tightening as my dick hardens. The kiss deepens.

Zariah steps back, breathless. She forks a hand through her fly away hair.

"You good?" I search her gaze. After I'd left the voicemail

about Danushka, Horace and the cocktail drug they'd given me, I expected her to hate me. Hate me for the situation I put us into. She had to know I'd never cheat. The video looked bad. Now the woman I never deserved smiles at me.

With a grin, Zariah shakes her head. "I don't know."

I rub a hand over my face. Shit, I guess if my Harley doesn't help me blow off steam then working out does. Sex does us both in too. Something in me doesn't want to fuck her happy tonight. Sure, I want to fuck. The big difference is, I've been so long without Zariah. The times we have been together all I'm doing is cutting deep into that pretty pussy. Tonight, I want her to smile at me because I've been there, not because my dick has been slamming through her body.

I rub the back of my neck. "How you feel?"

My wife chortles, sidestepping the waves that are coming in a little too strong.

Mouth hard, I say, "I said..."

She holds up her hands. "I'm sorry. Vassili, in the past, I've had to remove your teeth surgically. No anesthetic. When it comes to how you feel about your family, I'm an open book. Well, I guess I haven't always been the open book." Her eyes take on a faraway look as she mumbles about how I should've been a few good fucks when we met the second time.

"Zariah, girl." I clasp her shoulders and pull her out of an endless musing. "How do you feel?"

She sniffles. "Good. Happy. Sammy was all jitters when he walked out of the room, so Mom and I could figure out the test kit. He wants to be happy. I'll be his first and only child."

I sniff. "That is good."

"Yeah, although I started to feel guilty as she read the instructions. My dad . . . My dad is still *my dad.* Then my mom mentioned the first time she met," Zariah's voice starts to break, "the back of a man's hand, I was in her arms. That bastard hit her while I was a baby. That bastard will pay."

My hands shift into fists. I don't quite hear the last bit of Zariah's voice. It's carried off by the wind. The God honest truth is, I want Maxwell dead. I tell myself not to ask my wife to let me know the instant she finds out if Maxwell is her blood. She'll tell me. But my interest in that mudak would be too much of an implication if I ask her now.

Given the outcome, that piz'da is dead. I won't have the heart to *tell her* that he died by my hand. With her tiny hand in mine, we walk away from the shore. My wife shivers, and I'm out of my leather jacket in half-second. I tug it over the one she's wearing.

"Thank you, my Russian knight."

On the bicycle trail, I pull Zariah before me.

"It doesn't matter who's your dad, baby girl. We all know who's been there for you. Sammy. Your mom." When I look down at her, lust rises inside my chest. "Me."

I feel good about myself. I was there for my wife, and I didn't fuck her.

Now I can.

"Vassili . . . We," her voice trails off as she glances around her. I pull her up into my arms. I had noticed that one of these house's motion lights were out.

"Boy, what are you doing?" Zariah gasps, clasping at my biceps as I remember exactly which one. The four-story home doesn't have a single light on inside. Maybe they're saving energy. Shit, maybe they're out of town. I place Zariah over the waist-high fencing as she mentions the penal code for trespassing. I grab the ledge and hop over. There's a long, crystal hearth in the center of the area. I step over it. Arm around Zariah, I pull her toward one of the couches. It has a throw blanket on it.

"Vassili..." She tugs back on her heels.

"You were cold." I gesture toward the water. The sliding glass doors to the house are a fraction away from us. With the cove-like structure of the house, we're out of the wind. I grab both her hands, planting her fat ass on the wicker couch before me. I get on my knees. Zariah comes out of my jacket. The flurry of questions and anxiousness evaporates.

Moments like this are what life is made of. My hands claim her dark skin, fingers skimming up and down ample curves. Her thick, little frame no longer trembles beneath my touch. Those thighs, those hips, are sturdy perfection. I press my mouth against her forehead, tasting the salted sea. My mouth travels down to her nose and falls against her lips. Out of all the quickies, all the time I gave her hell and pain, tonight I want to give her nothing but goodness. Our tongues twine. I reach around, gripping more ass than is legal and pull her until the bubble of her ass is at the edge of the seat. Tongue gliding over her navel, I unbutton her jeans. This is going to be tricky—me fucking her with these jeans on. I push them down to her ankles.

"You still cold?"

"Hell, no," she purrs, trying to kick off one tight jean leg.

"Nyet, leave it." I claw at the flesh of her ass, then flick my tongue over her clit. I envelop that tiny bulb, letting my teeth rake over it. My thumb slams into her pussy to an instant gush. My cock roars against my jeans. Time for me to give her the world.

33

*Z*ariah

A whimper rushes through me. Although Vassili is digging in, the walls of my pussy are strained against his thumb, aching for more. My brain had lost all rationale for a second until I decide to try and use my big toe to kick off my other pant leg.

"Nyet, leave it," he growls. His lips press kisses against my tiny pearl that leaves the rest of me scorching. "I'm fucking with your legs closed. I want that pussy to choke the fuck out of my cock."

His words are hard. His Russian accent. It's all enough to kill me. I clasp at my hair that's in dire need of a conditioning treatment. With my legs pressed tight, all the action he gives leaves me clawing into a plush couch.

He settles back on his haunches and offers one of those smiles, the rare ones that I would beg a lifetime to see. With his index finger, he gestures for me to turn around.

"All that ass is about to bless my face," Vassili groans.

My pussy lips quiver in ways that they've never done. Thick, wet inner and outer folds convulsing. I'm tempted to go Hulk on my jeans as they restrain my ankles. The dynamic is all a mind fuck in itself.

I grip the top of the couch, press my knees against the edge of the seat and arch my lower back. The salt air tantalizes my wet folds until Vassili's warm breath trickles in.

His mouth sinks against my asshole, giving it a good Frenching. I reach between my legs and assault my clit, needing a little hurt to offset the scream of desire.

He eats the cake, and I grip at the couch until my nails tear straight through. I rock my ass back, and his tongue fucks that hole so well that I clutch tighter. Vassili grabs an ass cheek and rams his cock into my pussy. His girth stretches me so tight that I go beast mode on the couch. The scratches from my talon-like fingernails have nothing on my teeth gripping tight.

"Fuck," I hold in another scream.

With a hand on my ass, Vassili rockets in and out of me.

"Girl, you're so motherfucking tight. You want Daddy to cum." He beats my pussy until my back sags. "You want Daddy to cum all over you."

"Cum all over me," I groan, taking each pounding from his hard cock into my pussy with another bite of the couch.

Vassili slams into me like I'm his rag doll. The fighter's shaft assaults my insides. A wet sound becomes louder than the wind blowing in the background. It becomes music in my ears.

Vassili yanks my pant leg off. He flips me over until my back is against the couch, but I'm on top of him as he thrusts me up and down. He clamps his teeth down onto my throat as his cock burrows into the bottom of my stomach. His hot seed flushes into my pussy. Our heartbeats rock together.

"Shhhh…." he tells me. "You were screaming so loud."

A dizzy, little laugh floats through me. He kisses the heady smile from my face then asks if I'm cold.

I look up into Vassili's eyes. Those obsidian gems aren't their usual darkness, they're almost light. I love how he knows how to put me first at the precise second I need it.

"I'm not cold, Vassili. I have you."

———

We climb back onto the couch after I put back on my jeans and shoes. Hell, I understand how much strength Vassili has. He is able to yank off my boots with my ultra-tight pants. We lay on the couch, with the throw blanket over us.

Sleep claims us as we return to the beginning.

Our first night together, I was safe between Vassili's tattooed arms. We slept together, and nothing was ever the same. Seagulls squawk overhead. A rose-gold sun is beginning to rise. With my husband snoring, I decide to savor the moment.

Well, until . . . let's just call her Neighborhood Nelly, a middle-aged woman dressed in workout attire, stands on the opposite side of the gate. "I'm calling the police," she sneers. "*You people* are trespassing!"

I awaken Vassili, pawing at his massive chest. "Babe, wake up, we have to go."

He pops forward. Like two teenagers, we giggle and get up. Neighborhood Nelly steps back a few paces, eyes wide as she speaks into the phone.

"Oh, now you drifters want to get up! Just you wait. It's people like you who—"

Vassili roars at her in Russian. He hops over the fence, helping me over. I take off running, but he's not behind me. I glance back. He's moving at a leisure pace, with Neighborhood Nelly holding out her phone to record him. Fortunately, she doesn't follow.

241

"Why didn't you run?" I ask, a giddy smile on my face as he catches up.

"Run from a girl? Nyet."

"Hello, she was recording you, Killer Karo." I push at his chest, softly.

"And I'll deny, deny, deny."

I laugh as he takes me in his arms then hauls me over the side of his shoulder.

"Put me down, crazy!"

Vassili tickles my sides then place me down. "If there aren't bullets flying at your ass, you don't run, Mrs. Resnov."

I shy away from him as he pats the top of my head. I chortle, "Ha! I'm a Resnov, meaning too bad, too bold for bullets to go flying toward me—period."

"You make a good point," my husband retorts.

We walk hand in hand. Samuel's house comes into view. The serious chat we never had comes to the forefront of my mind.

"How are things?" I murmur. "Any idea where Horace is? I'd like to come home soon?"

"Dah. He's in the desert. Danny and the crew they were running with are all—"

"Six feet under." I sigh. Shit, because of Simeon, I have firsthand experience with a trip to the desert. Prior to that, it meant visiting Temecula, the worthiest orchards aside from the much further wine country. Or could mean a spa visit in Palm Springs. Now, with Grigor dead, it means a permanent stay.

Vassili adds, "Grigor too. They've all been put down."

I glance at him, a vein in my brain is on the verge of busting. Simeon hasn't told him . . .

"We go to Moscow this weekend. Me, you, Natasha."

I gulp. "Will we be safe?"

He stops in front of me. A runner glides by us. Vassili

clasps the back of my neck, massaging it. "Don't ask me shit like that, Zariah. Don't you ever wonder shit like that."

"Okay."

"We're having a meeting with the seven. We will be together throughout that meeting, Zar. When we're done with the meet and greet, me, you, my children are out of this life for good."

It sounds like a dream come true. Torn, I bite my tongue from the flood of questions.

"Let's go get her dressed. Take your mom and Sammy to breakfast, then we go home."

His words are heaven to my ears, though I don't follow him as he starts walking again. Since I'm rooted to the same spot. He stops and turns around. My husband's eyes wash over me. "Zariah, we need to put this all behind us. The day after the meeting, we'll head back. I prepare for Rhy."

"I... we... after we eat breakfast here," I stop stuttering and gulp. We set the entire scene for my father. I can't just douse water over the fire we started. I need to follow through. Blood or not, Maxwell Washington has to pay.

"Is there something you're keeping from me?" Vassili asks. When someone massive as a brick building asks such a question, it's only appropriate to look away. Terror courses through my soul.

I can't tell him about my angle with my *father*. Not yet. Vassili had this knack for grilling me on the background of all my previous clients. He calculates the threat of me defending any new potential clients. With Mrs. Noriega, it was all deception that helped me keep her case.

I can't tell him.

I look up at my husband. "Vassili, what are you talking about? Hello . . . Did you forget the entire reason we took a ride on your Harley last night? What do you mean *is there something I'm not telling you?* You should have an idea!"

"Shit. Your dad." His eyes blaze with sincerity, mine fall with guilt.

"Yeah. You say we leave this weekend. I can't come home with you tonight." I shift on my shoes. "Natasha can. I know you've missed her. On my end, can we let my father… can we let Maxwell stay in the dark for a little while longer?"

34

Vassili
   I'd asked my wife the very question my father never failed to demand of my mother. He'd have a million secrets. Too many to count. Too many to make heads or fucking tails from. His eyes would be enraged, paranoid. And he'd ask what she was keeping from him. His hands were at the ready, leveled out to strike her.

Now I feel like shit. Even as I recall the paternity test, something wrestles inside of me. The distrust drowning Anatoly has a hold on me.

My thoughts are on one thing. Zariah is going back to that other world. The one she had before me. The one she returned to after our first night. The one she tried to hold onto even though seven years have passed.

Fuck. I'm the one who can't live without her. I'm the one who had to have her. *If I hadn't gone after her, would we be together?*

Zariah's in my arms, asking me, "Can we let Maxwell stay in the dark for a little while longer?"

My fingers tangle in her hair. Her face is against my chest. In a split second, the ocean is a thousand miles away. Darkness surrounds us. I'm holding her, and she's crying into my chest. It's so fucking dark that all I see is the shape of the top of her head. I smell her lush scent and know that she belonged to me. Music is playing. An old Russian song about anti-love. Zariah starts pushing away. Fuck, she's not pushing but trying to, trying with all her might. My massive arms encase her. Her breath is warm against the inside of my chest. The sounds of her suffocating grow louder than the song. My love holds her there. I hug her so tight. The only thought in my mind is that I'd rather have her like this . . .

Still and dead, between my arms, than breathing and far away from me.

I cleave to her until the warmth of her breath at my chest runs cold, and she's limp within my arms.

The premonition fades right before my eyes. The darkness is gone. Early morning on Venice Beach surrounds us. I step back a few paces, my hand zipping from Zariah's hair. I'm no longer tangling her tresses with my fingers, no longer holding her, no longer a threat to her life.

Another runner zips past us.

I stare at my wife. She stares back in sorrow. "You're mad at me, Vassili?"

"Nyet." I stand there. After a beat, I take a few steps forward. The image flashes before my eyes as I hold her again. My body is the fucking weapon, my brain is the traitor. This time, I embrace my wife. I love her. "I'm not mad. I miss you. So, you want to spend a little more time with him while waiting for the test results?"

She looks up at me. "Yes. Not that long, Samuel says it may take a week or so. Though, I won't be there the entire time. All I need is a few days. Is . . . is that okay?"

"Dah." I let her go. My fingers are now tangling with hers, and we resume walking. Five minutes later, I hop over the ledge to the inside of Samuel's area. His isn't as elaborate as the one we'd slept at. As a matter of fact, there are bags of cement-like he's been preparing to update it all, but life got in the way. I pick up Zariah and help her over.

"Thank you." She's smiling at me, but I'm already looking away. I clutch a hand against the cross at my neck. Usually, I do this when I'm praying, right before a match. Now I need a moment with God, need Him to save me.

Zariah knocks on the sliding glass. Zamora comes down the stairs; she's all smiles. My daughter is in her arms. I set aside the fucked over, confused thought I had about her mother. I miss my baby. Unlike anyone else in this world, Natasha Resnov is my seed. She won't fail me.

35

Zariah

    I held tight to Natasha and Vassili two days ago. I got the best hug of my entire life. Natasha was pawing at my face with her thumb, wet from her gnawing on it. I cleaved to them in that moment. I miss them with a vengeance. Though I concentrate on my mother's beautiful face and all the times it was marred by bruises, a few images of Ronisha's abuse urge me on as well. This is not for me. This is for *them*, women who have endured pain at the hands of men.

Now, I'm in the lion's den. Candlelight flickers in my father's eyes as he holds up a glass of Pinot. "Too bad my other little princess isn't here celebrating with us."

I click my glass against his. A piano plays softly in the background. High-class, French food is set before us on a white linen table.

We are . . . celebrating. At first, it was us celebrating a Tuesday evening because nobody felt like cooking. It all wrapped back around to my failing marriage.

With a murmur, I offer another lie. "My mom is leaving

for ATL at the end of the week. So, she wanted a little more time with Natasha."

That's one of a horde of lies. My mom isn't leaving. Martin will be the one making that flight soon because our mom has all but moved in with Samuel.

"Ah, yes." Maxwell nods. "That mother of yours. Is she still enjoying her *girls?*"

"Yup." I also mention the friend that she had been staying at.

"Alright, she can have our princess for a few more nights. Then I'll have my daughter, my two favorite girls under one roof. Safe and sound."

Trying not to set off warning signs by sounding too agreeable, I steer the conversation to one of our differences. "Ha. Your woman was over this weekend. I'm sure since she's back in town I can expect that. Maybe Natasha and I should start looking for a place."

"Nonsense. I'm your father." He smiles.

My spine goes rigid. *Is he?*

Maxwell doesn't miss a beat with adding. "You're the angel from heaven I never deserved, still as innocent as you were when you met that Resnov. I believe the day you started seeing him, you wanted to move out. My casa is su casa. It will always be *su casa*. Far as I'm concerned, I want him good and out of your system before you and Natasha venture out into the world again."

It pains me to transform into the 'dummy putty' he prefers. "I guess I could save a little before Natasha, and I get a new place."

"Precisely." He holds up the glass again. "Save money. That firm you're working with won't have you anywhere near as safe as you need to be, with regard to location."

"Hey, LA is doing a lot better than…"

"Of course, I'm Chief. Listen, my beautiful daughter. If

things go my way, the next time you move, it will be with a worthy husband."

I blink a few times. How barbaric. My father refuses to let me take care of myself. He'd prefer I run from one man to the next. There's a big difference from the past, that if the world were tossing him favors, it would be to a man of his choosing. All those favors he banked in have been cashed out.

The next day, I can hear the garage door gliding shut when I slide off the stool in the kitchen. My heart starts to hammer in my ears.

This is the day.

Momma can stop with her attitude for me being at my father's house. I can get another good hug from my family; I can sleep in my bed with my man. I can argue with Natasha as she spills vegetables on the floors that I waxed and then love her.

This is the day. In fuzzy pajama pants and a camisole, I slip my phone from my pocket and dial Tyrese.

"I'm ready to check his safe," I share as soon as the call connects.

"Good morning to you too. Nervous?"

"Yeah." I start up the stairs, placing the call on the speaker. "He just left. Now, he's off to work, and I'll get a chance to check it."

"You think it's your birth date?" Tyrese chuckles through the receiver.

"Ha. I know Bernice's birthday. I'll start there. Thanks for the jokes, though. They kind of loosened me up." I open the double doors to my father's bedroom. The bed is made. I would be able to bounce a dime off the center of it. Everything is meticulous.

"Zariah, are you sure the evidence needed is in your father's safe?"

"I hope so. I'm checking now. Can you stay on while I do?" I ask.

"Hey, I don't mind sitting on the phone with you, Zar."

"Thanks," I gasp. "We already talked about me getting my head into the game but... thanks for being here. Give me a few."

"Roger that."

I set the phone down onto the dresser and move toward an acrylic painting that's hanging on the wall. With ease, I lift it. When my hands go over my head, my thoughts go straight to the baby in my womb. I smile at the notion of if my mom could see me now. She is a firm believer in old wives tells about pregnant mothers not raising their hands too high. I mutter a quick, silent prayer that's all thanks to God for keeping me safe so far. A nanosecond later, I hear footsteps at the walk-in closet.

The oxygen in my chest evaporates as I slowly turn on my heels.

Maxwell leans against the closet doorframe, a Glock in his hands leveled at my forehead. His dark face is dashed in anger. "Berenice came over late last night. I told her to catch an Uber here. She drove off in my car while you were plotting *and waiting.*"

Hands trembling, I lean the painting on the floor.

With an authoritarian voice, Maxwell orders, "Step forward. Keep your hands where I can see them."

I hold my hands out and take a few paces. My vision is on him and the double doors. "So, are you going to shoot your daughter in cold blood?"

"Who was that on the phone? Nah, it doesn't matter." He

251

gestures with the gun. "Didn't sounds like Russian hooligans. The cops are on their way. I'll tell them it was an accident while I was securing my own home. I live alone, and maybe I've had a slight case of PTSD in the past. At any old sound, I'm on high alert."

"Hmmm, I doubt any attorney worth their salt won't use your career for other reasons. Oh, such as you being a seasoned veteran. What about all the officers who were here?" I stutter. "They're aware that I've moved back in? What about my casa is your fucking casa!"

"C'mon, they're all on my payroll, *my beautiful daughter.*" He begins to cackle. "Awesome poker face. A minute ago, you didn't so much as fucking blink with my mention that you're my daughter. I'll have you know that I'm aware of Sammy's clout with the LAPD paternity unit. He had a rush order done on the test you took. *You are not my child!*"

The gun goes off . . .

36

Vassili

For the past few days, I've had these dreams. One where I'm plunged into the pitch. A darkness so thick I can fucking taste it. Zariah's there too. She's hugging me and kissing me. She's promised that she hasn't changed.

But things aren't the same, and I give her the same treatment my father gave my mother. Right before I can claim her entire life, I lunge into a seated position in bed. I run in my home gym, waiting for the sun to come up and for Natasha to wake up. After that, we hit Vadim's gym hard. A couple of times, he reminds me not to be so good, not to be the beast who left Kong in a coma.

Today, sweat glides over my tattoos and muscles. Natasha is on the sideline with Yuri. Every time he takes a call, she clamors over to the cage. Even with vicious thoughts on my mind, I'm able to pull out of them just to keep my kid safe.

"Little girl," I argue with her, heading from the door to the cage. After hustling down the steps, I yank up my daughter. Upon lifting her high in the sky, all of her few, tiny teeth come into view as she cackles. I sit her back in the folding chair. "Sit your little ass over here. No French fries later."

My one-year-old puffs her cheeks and shakes her head.

"Oh, you don't have words for Daddy?" I cock a brow. "I said no French fries."

"She doesn't believe the hype." Yuri grunts, settling back at Natasha's side. "Your pop is in Moscow. All of our aunts and uncles are en route."

"You've mentioned this." I nod.

"Dah. I know." Yuri waits for a beat as if doing so will give me psychic abilities. Rubbing the back of his neck, he asks, "Well, is Zariah coming? I chartered a jet for us all. I ..."

I bite a hangnail from my thumb. Malich and the rest of the family are still in shock that Zariah's at her father's and not here, with Natasha and me. I'll tell them of her concern about the paternity, pending the outcome. "Zar felt sorry for her dad. You sent that group text, Yuri. Of course, she will meet us before we leave— *like she said.*"

"I'm saying..." his voice trails off. The same concern he had for me in Italy begins to cloud his face.

"What the fuck are you saying?" I glare at him and almost laugh. We haven't had a chat about how he'll be king. That's a statement that they'll all present this weekend, to Anatoly and the rest of the seven. I can appreciate Yuri not backing down.

Waving him off, I move back toward the cage and another man is inside. Nestor vetted a new fighter for me to go head to head with. I've seen him around a time or two. Luckily, he was not here the few times I showed the locals my ass. The guy has a good head on his shoulders and all the patience I never had as a rookie. He knocks his wrapped knuckles together, deep in thought.

Vadim clings to the opposite side of the cage. "I want a good, clean fight. Vassili, Dima has an undercard in a couple of weeks. Go hard but be easy on him. Dima asked for this, and I appreciate the initiative. Dima, Vassili is old as fuck in the MMA world. Go hard but be easy on his grandfather knee."

I laugh at the old man. Dima has tunnel vision; his face is zeroed in with concentration that he doesn't respond.

Since Dima hasn't fought outside of a basement, Vadim had it all set up. The old man is good at preparing his team. We touch gloves, and a flash of adrenaline rushes through my ears. On my toes, I reach in to knock his teeth lose by way of his chin. Dima ducks just in time. I give a nod. He punches toward my nose. My wife has to kiss this face. Only the air from his powerful hands catch me. For the first half-minute, Dima and I test each other. He's got my kind of speed. Good for him. I'd tell him to reach back through his shoulder, but that's some shit I'll hold off on. I like his style enough to give him advice once I'm on *my way out of the game.*

I fake the takedown and come back with a right hook. Dima's fist slams in my side as his body is shaken from my hook. Fuck it; we're both on one. The rookie extends his arm in a cross. I spin around; the force drives through my knee, and the front of my foot batters his rib.

"You're a shit head," Vadim shouts at me in Russia for the move, which used my 'bad' knee.

I grunt. The blow left his teeth clattering. Yeah, that's the type of power the youngster has yet to garner. My hook claims the side of his ear. Dima comes back with a forearm that resets my entire jaw. I catch him with a left, right, left. That's the fucking thing. He takes the hits but needs a second to let that shit sink in. I've always dealt with the pain later. My motto is: if it cannot stop you, don't let it. Blood squirts from his nose. My fist hits the cage as Dima drops to the mat. I step back.

Dima jumps back up. He nods at me in approval.

255

His eyes are a little spacey. I look toward Vadim as to if I should proceed. Shit, I know good and fucking well that the hothead in me is always at bay.

"Chin down, eyes open, Vassili," Vadim shouts out.

I duck in the nick of time. Dima issues a cross hook that vaults out right over my head. Now, I nod at him in approval. That's some shit I would do. We go blow for blow. I take hits, he takes them too. When Dima becomes tired, he gives me space. He offers a kick to my shin, I jump it. I'm the fucking beast whose lungs don't drain of oxygen. Not anymore. Vadim called me old. I'm a vet in the cage and my belt is calling for me. Calling like it once did.

I slaughter his liver with bricks for punches. Dima's forearms come tight at his sides until one tosses up. I don't have a fucking machine gun on my forearm for nothing. I jump back, a hit that would've annihilated me is enough to remind me of Natasha's swats. My eyes spark, telling the rookie to come harder.

He does.

My mouth splits, I lick the blood. I'm in my fucking element the second Dima realizes that our bodies are falling. He grapples at the canvas, but the clinch isn't on his side. I flip Dima, pinning him in one of the most beautiful OG moves ever.

The rear-naked choke.

In this exact second, I know my life is back. My cousin and I aren't on the oust, as he shouts for Dima to offer a solid, tiny tap. My daughter is always in my sight, and I can ensure her safety. My wife promised to come home today . . .

Z ariah

I sigh. The blanks in my father's gun has all the sound effects. My bones are rattling damn near out of my body. A half-second later, the Feds are swarming up the stairs, along with their ringleader, Tyrese.

In a dark blue suit, Tyrese removes the gun from Maxwell's hand.

Although nerves buzz in my body, I offer a cold shrug. A second later, I hijack the conversation while he's being cuffed. "So, Dad, I knew Berenice spent the night. While you two were downstairs for a late-night drink, I changed out your bullets. Thanks, Dad, for teaching me how to reload a Glock. I couldn't have done this without you."

He begins to lunge at me, but my momma's blood runs deep in my bones. The time to gloat is now. There are too many agents around us for Maxwell to take the few paces he needs to put me in my place.

With a hand at my hip, I snap, "Oh and I never needed to get in your safe. All I needed was to plant this seed, make you wonder. Now, you've attempted to murder me. Scratch that, sounds a bit premeditated when you included Berenice into the fold."

He glares.

Tyrese is behind him, hiding half a smile.

"Since you taught me so well, I have a bit of advice for you too, Mr. Washington. I may not have lived up to your standards but FYI, you want an attorney that you can tell everything to. Not the one who does well on the contingency that he *does not want to know.* Nah, Pops," I roll my neck. "Your best bet is the litigator whom you can talk with, for hours about all your dirty deeds. As you can see a warrant to search this entire house is coming up soon. And that greasy fucking lawyer needs to not be blindsided by none other than *you.*"

Two agents pull Maxwell away as I lean against the post to the bed. All the sinew connected to my legs has shrunk. I place my head back onto the post to breathe. Damn, I don't have the slightest idea how my mom can mouth off under pressure, but I gave it my all.

Tyrese stands before me, patting my shoulder. "That was pretty good advice you gave."

"Thanks." I smile wearily. "Once I stop shaking inside, I'll pat my own back."

"So, I'm probably going to have fun opening Pandora's box." Tyrese glances around the house. In addition to changing out my father's bullets last night, I'd bugged his room. The agent and I had a really good chat after I came to him again. I boldly told Tyrese that I'd never sell out a Resnov.

I'm a fucking Resnov. He understands. I've told him everything, even shared how Samuel could be my father. Tyrese and I orchestrated this plan. As an agent, one accolade is as good as another. My father is the leader of a gang.

Tyrese is about to start the process of bringing him and his cronies down.

Tyrese licks his lips, asking, "Guess this is it then?"

I offer a two-finger salute. "It better be it."

More agents come up and down the stairs, and they don't need to be included in our sidebar conversation about the Bratva.

Maybe Tyrese will leave my husband's family alone. Maybe he'll give it a rest after putting my father away, then come back years from now. I give his hand a firm shake and then head out of the master suite. I round the ledge, glancing down the stairs where Vassili is so close to me, yet so far. All of my father's antics are against protocol, yet I have to believe that his actions today have left him wide open. There are secrets in this home. I can recall the exact step my mom busted a tooth on. The agents will find the rest of those secrets and hit him where it counts.

"Zariah," Samuel looks up at me from the bottom step. "Thank God, your momma would…"

"You're supposed to say *my* momma would murder *you* if something were to happen to me." I wink, taking the last few steps. He wraps an arm around me, and we head to the door, meandering around more agents who clutter the scene.

Outside, another notch to my father's psychotic ways comes to mind. Vassili had been arguing with my ex when Maxwell invited him over. We hadn't even gone a month into our honeymoon, and my father tried to test our love. I skip down the last few steps and turn around.

"So, is it true? Did the paternity test come back already?" I ask, heart slamming in my throat. My father was wrapped up with keeping tabs on Samuel. When he inquired about my mom leaving dinner the other day, he knew she shared the bed of his ex-best friend. That, coupled with the DNA possibility, blew his mind. He didn't consider that Billingslea firm utilizes a different DNA Testing location, not affiliated with the LAPD. We still had the test run through the company we outsource with. Samuel helped provide another variable by reaching out to a DNA technician at the LAPD. All the moves were made to blind, anger and further agitate Maxwell.

Samuel and my mom promised to call me in Russia once the results are back, and only open them at my insistence. However, I'm too antsy to wait. "Are you-you my dad?"

He takes a deep breath, then pats both my shoulders. "Too bad this isn't a crime show on CBS. We still have a couple of days."

I nod.

"Test results aside, Zar, I've always thought you were mine."

A bright beam breaks across my face.

"Albeit, it doesn't matter." His voice breaks a little. "What matters most to me is how you perceive our relationship."

Throat clogged, I reply, "You've always, *always* been there for me, Sammy. I love you, regardless."

Today has turned out to be a good, blessed day. After Samuel and I called my mom so she could have proof that I was safe, she hollered on the phone. She did a few freak nasty dances, elated about Maxwell's current predicament.

Now, I'm at the hospital to meet with my obstetrician. Vassili and Natasha are supposed to meet me here. He'd texted earlier, like around the same time I put our unborn child in danger.

I sit on the examination table, ass-out and cold by the way, and clinging to the thin material of my clothing. There's a knock at the door. Chewing my lip, I pray that it's not the doctor. Please be late and let my family come in her stead. These past 72 hours, I've never felt so alone in my life.

I huff, "Come in."

The door opens. The same smile I offered Samuel earlier, illuminates across my face.

"You came," I murmur as Vassili enters with Natasha on his forearm.

"Of course." He kisses me. Natasha quickly pushes her way into the center of our universe. Her fat cheeks puff out, and she purées out a juicy kiss.

"Okay, little bully, I saw you!" I kiss her. "How will you act when you have a little sis—"

"Brother," Vassili corrects.

"Hey, you're late, so I'm not believing it until I see it."

"I'm not late." He brushes a kiss on my forehead again. "Well, I wasn't. The second I started to get out of the car, there was an update on Kong on the sports radio."

"Did he wake up?"

My husband's heavy shoulders fall. "Nyet. He may have moved a finger, or his wife thinks he moved."

I clasp Vassili's bristled jaw. "We just have to keep praying for him."

"Dah. It's been a long time since I prayed with my wife."

"Well, it's in our best interest to appeal to God before we leave for Russia . . . Joking," I try.

He doesn't smile back at me. Not a second later, the door opens, and the doctor enters.

"Mr. And Mrs. Resnov, oh and Baby Girl Resnov," the doctor grins at each of us. "Sorry for the wait."

"Do we get to know if I'm having a son?" Vassili asks.

"Well, that's too soon. You're just shy of sixteen weeks. However," she honkers down to Natasha's level, "Do you want to hear your little sibling's heartbeat? Let's make sure it's loud and strong."

With all eyes on my daughter, I pull in a gulp of air. Vassili holds Natasha as the doctor explains the contraption to her. He casts a glance at me, his lips then press the side of my mouth. A bright smile warms my cheeks.

"Ready Mom?" the doctor says. Vassili helps Natasha guide the microphone-like contraption against my stomach.

A big, strong heartbeat blasts through the speaker. It's loud enough for Natasha to jump.

Vassili's whisper caresses my earlobe, "Nobody can tell me that's not my son. We made a beast."

I gasp, laughing too hard. "No, we made a baby. We made your son."

38

Vassili

We touch down in Moscow two days later. Anna, who has been a walking zombie on anti-depressants, begged to take Natasha with Albina to a Russian tea room. Being in our home country seems to have done some good for Igor's widow.

So, it's the first thing we do upon arrival. My little girl is dressed for royalty in a tweed dress that Zariah fussed over, red pea coat, and matching cap. My wife had even tried to put a puffer jacket on my child before we got off the jet.

Now, we stand just inside of the tea room. Golden walls, red tapestries, all the air of richness surrounds us as I place Natasha on her own feet.

"See, she would have toppled over and bust her head in that jacket," I tell my wife.

"Whatever, Vassili. I'll give you that, it's not as cold as last year. It could be warmer." She pretends to shake in her boots. Albina clasps our daughter's hand. Anna walks them toward an area where they can view even more expensive antiques.

I cup my wife's ass. "Nyet, you're not cold. You, also, have sturdy legs with hips that can and *will give me* ten kids. Most of them will be sons."

"Ha," Zariah presses away from me. "I might give you one more, Vassili. You're also in the wrong sport to demand an entire basketball team of children."

I nip her ear. "One can go pro NBA."

My arms dash around her body before she can flee.

"Not fair, Vassili. You should have gone to the drinking room with the guys." She presses her lips against mine. "This place is for uppity Europeans. You didn't make the cut."

My hard abdomen crushes against hers as I laugh. "All I needed was a fucking tie to play the part."

"Lies." Her gaze dances down my slacks and bomber jacket.

"Okay, so I can't wear a tie with this. I feel stuffy as fuck already," I growl, nipping her bottom lip. "But I'm wearing one tomorrow. If I had to do so two days in a row, you'd be in trouble."

"Why me?" She chortles.

"Because I like punishing you regardless." I start toward the table that Anna and the kids have claimed.

"I'll consent to that," Zariah murmurs, threading her fingers through mine.

A bejeweled highchair is placed at the table for my little girl.

"Look, Cutie Pie, you got the throne." I kiss her butterscotch cheek before claiming a seat. There are enough servants around us to imply that I'll be handing bricks of money over before we leave. I'm good with that. I'm home. Really fucking home. My beloved Russia, wife, and daughter —fuck this is the dream I always prayed for as a child. Nobody knows that aside from my mother's safety, I begged God for this.

Though Anatoly has ample room at his home, we all chose to stay at a hotel. The room is lavish as I kick off my shoes, bringing Zariah inside of the darkroom with me. I kick the door closed with my foot and the sound of the automated lock is enough for me. I haven't taken my eyes off her —my realized dream since we left the tea room. We'd also made sure that Natasha had enough clothing and essentials to stay with Albina.

Zariah moans in my mouth, then her twirling tongue pulls away from mine. "I want to see the room."

"It's expensive as fuck, like Anna's."

"But we have a view of the Kremlin and it's night and . . ."

"And you can see that view after I get some ass."

Zariah grumbles about how I always put her to sleep while a stiletto goes flying across the massive bedroom space. I yank her into my arms, walk the long length of the entryway and throw her into the bed. A goose-down duvet flutters around her shapely frame.

"Whoever gets undressed first is on top," I growl.

Though it's dark, light sparks shine in her eyes. She starts shoving down tights and tugging the buttons of her knit dress.

I'm out of my clothes in seconds. My cock salutes my wife. "I win."

"Aw, you're an asshole, Vassili," she groans, still playing with the buttons.

I climb in bed, snatch her fat ass and pull her under. Zariah's thighs don't readily wrap around mine. The shit is usually so miraculous as her thick thighs splay. The buttons down her dress clatter along the marble floor as I tear her out of it.

"You picked this dress, not fair," she pouts. Now, my

fucking miracle happens as her luscious thighs drape around my waist.

"Dah, I picked it." I toss a kiss along her protruding bottom lip before sucking it into my mouth.

"See? Not fair," she manages to say.

Shit, I picked the dress because my wife complains about being cold and this one, at least, fell over her curves.

"You want to be on top, girl. You want to ride this Russian cock?" My dick grinds against her.

"Mmmm, please let me ride your cock, Daddy," she purrs.

I bite the fuck out of her lip, grinding harder, then lick up the taste of copper. She took that pain. No complaints. I'm a proud mudak as I flip until Zariah's thick body bounces on my hard erection.

"Thank you, Daddy."

I lean up, my stubbled jaw scratching at her soft cheek. "Fuck me, girl."

The type of smile that would make any man buy a ring brightens her face. Zariah unclasps her bra. I grip her thong, slaughter her pussy and ass with it while yanking it up and shredding it off. Her wet pussy drags across my abdominals as she slides down.

"Lick that sweet cunt juice off me first," I order.

"Yes, Daddy." Zariah slides down until she's aligned with my knees. She kisses the head of my cock before dragging her tongue along my abs. "Damn, my juice tastes so good on your body," she murmurs against my eight pack.

I grip her hair, "Good girl. Suck my cock and lick my balls. I'll let you know when you can jump on my dick."

Grabbing the base of my shaft, Zariah engulfs one of my balls into her mouth. Pre-cum seeps at the top of my dick. She pulls my other ball into her mouth, swirling her tongue. An animalistic growl roars through me.

"Fuck," I groan. I'm not waiting for her lips on my dick.

That pussy sucks me in as professional as her mouth. I tangle her weave in my hands and bring her up.

"Squat, girl, and work that pussy for me."

She aligns the heels of her bare feet next to my hips, one hand on her breast while the other pushes back fat folds. Her clit is on display as I watch her cunt swallow my dick. My eyes roll back, and she's screaming my name the instant I shout hers.

39

Zariah

The lips of my pussy have never been so heavy. The sweet taste of it glosses my tongue, intoxicating me as my ass and hips slap down on his cock. I gain leverage, working Vassili's kingly erection. I twerk and twirl like I'm riding a bull. My husband reaches forward. The entire act stretches my pussy. His thumb makes circles on my pearl.

"Oh shit," I grunt, clinching his cock tight.

"Keep jumping my cock," he growls, his thumb and index tweaking my clit.

"Fuck, hurt me, hurt my clit," my voice is a low groan. I gain leverage again, sliding up and down. My breasts bounce, my ass pops, and my clit is tortured.

I look down at my husband and revel in his mass of muscles. My hands glide over dips, grooves, and masculine ridges. I gasp when I end up beneath Vassili.

"Hey," I groan.

"Shhh." My husband moves fast as lightening. He burrows his face in my pussy. The deep growl vibrates through my inner and outer folds.

"Vassili," I screech, marveling at the feel of it all.

The heaven he sent me to, breaks way into a second heaven as Vassili comes up. His hard body is on top of mine. The gentle scrape of his jaw rubs against my cheek until I'm kissing his wet mouth.

"That's my water," he groans as my tongue glides around his.

"Tastes so good," I murmur against his lips.

Vassili lines his cock with my slit. My heart pounds. His chest crushes my nipples. I exhale as my husband enters me. His eyes stay on mine. His dick strokes deeply inside of me, and I'm mesmerized by his intense gaze. He knows my body exceedingly better than I ever could. When I moan, he concentrates on that—growing my moan until my throat is raw.

"I'll never stop fucking you," Vassili declares, voice hoarse as he makes love to me.

"Don't stop, please . . . Don't ever stop."

He continues to lavish my mind, body, soul with attention while unraveling me with each stroke. I gasp, my treasure has become his ocean. Tears cloud my vision. He doesn't stop. He doesn't have words for my happy tears. Doesn't claim that he hates them. Vassili continues to ride me, his hardness delicious as it crushes my softness. His light against my dark. My light—goodness—against his perceived *bad.*

A wave of ecstasy crashes against the fighter and I. The world fades. All that's left is Vassili calling my name, I match him with my falsetto.

40

Zariah

Vassili gave me the best night of my life. That's a declaration I've made a thousand times before. Lord knows, he's
given me the best night of my life before. Each one exceeds
the last. It all started when we sat in my childhood bedroom.
Vassili showed me the power, the beauty, and the fearlessness
of my sex. Next, our wedding night left me breathless. As our
love grew, more perfect nights blurred with the last.

But last night elevated all that love and multiplied it. We
soared to uncharted territory. Loved each other so good that
the only place to go was . . .

Down.

I feel that shit in my bones as I get ready for the day. My
fingers tremble as I zip up yet another dress. This one is
black. Feels like we're heading to a funeral. My husband
matches me. The lapel of his suit is a white satin line, the rest
of his designer suit, his aura . . . It's all black.

I almost asked if he wanted to pray this morning. We had
one the night before leaving for Moscow, which has been the
norm before any of his matches.

But this isn't a match; it's *our* life. Our life is about to collide with the one that often leaves my husband's jaw clenched and his mouth closed. Though I know enough horror stories about Sasha and his mother, I'm aware that very few women in the Resnov Bratva mean anything. Not aside from Simeon's mother and Malich's departed wife, Anna is respected, and Vassili has done a stellar job giving the rest of his family the stiff arm. I'm not even Russian. Where do I stand?

"You ready?" Vassili's gaze washes over me. His face is unreadable until his lips caress along my jaw. "You look gorgeous, Zar. What are you thinking?"

I stare out of the ceiling-to-floor window and glimpse the Kremlin. "That I never got to see that last night all lit up."

There's no laughter at my attempt of a joke. Moreover, my husband doesn't tell me that I'll get my chance tonight. He's preoccupied with something so important that Vassili murmurs how gorgeous I look again. Like a muscular robot.

We don't share a thing with each other while heading out of the most opulent hotel room I've ever seen.

In the hotel lobby, Anna has her children and Natasha bundled up. They're not dressed for a "funeral." However, all the men are donning tailored suits. Malich is pawing Natasha's cheek while Yuri tussles Albina's pigtail.

Toying mindlessly with his cufflinks, Mikhail is seated a little way from the family. His demeanor seems a bit fore-boding and matches the dread I can't quite place.

"We will see you all later." Anna smiles at me. "I won't take my eyes off Natasha, not for a single second."

"I know you will keep my baby safe, Anna."

We all head out to two SUVs. I kiss Natasha a thousand times before Vassili places her in the car seat. Once again, Anna promises me that they'll all be having fun at a children's park. Yuri hands the driver extra cash, telling him to watch them all.

The men and I get into the second SUV. We're headed to Rublyovka. Needing to feel some semblance of normal, I find the town on Wikipedia. It's a suburb that models Beverly Hills, with similar lavish mansions.

A t the wrought-iron gate, armed men with red pinched noses stand to attention. I gulp, eyeing each one as the SUV is allowed to enter. Luxury supercars line a lap pool that can easily measure a few New York blocks. The home is even more dominating.

The scenario reminds me of a cartel movie with a trillionaire drug lord. Anatoly saunters down the steps with Simeon at his side. A few men follow behind them carrying automatic guns. On unsteady legs, I exit the car, contemplating who should I fear more: the man who ruined my husband's younger years or the man who holds my secret regarding a Federal agent and yet another hotel room.

"My daughter in law." Anatoly holds his arms out, disregarding his son and younger brother for me.

"You're not hugging my wife," Vassili growls. With my hand in his, I can only mumble a simple greeting while he guides me toward the house.

Simeon stares down at me. Not a glower of revulsion. Not a spark of familiarity or appreciation. Not a single sign of his thoughts. Yup. I fear him more. At least Vassili's father shows his true colors.

Mikhail and Yuri follow us, grunting their hellos. The two brothers, Anatoly and Malich, are unexpected in their affections and respect for each other.

"You know, that cousin of yours favors you." I try to calm the jitters in my belly with a smile.

"Who?" Vassili arches a brow.

"Sim," Yuri agrees. "I've been waiting for someone to say that. Meaning, if Simeon looks like the rear end of a dog—"

"Finish the statement," my husband grits. With him still holding my hand, I shuffle on my feet as Vassili squares off with Yuri.

"Therefore, you look like . . ." Yuri waves his hand as if to assist with the conversation.

Mikhail breaks a smile. "People who often resemble each other, do not get along."

Vassili grunts. Yuri's smiling, although it's not cocky. It's genuine, and he's staring up the stairs behind us. He says something in Russian; I think, auntie. Vassili and I turn around.

I glance toward the top of the steps and can't mistake the woman in a ball gown as Simeon's gorgeous mother. She mirrors Anatoly too. With the height difference, I'm instantly overwhelmed. I assume the woman, with alluring eyes and shocks of silver hair, is the most powerful woman in the Bratva.

"Sofiya," Yuri says, going toward her.

All the boys hug their aunt, Vassili last. He turns toward me. "Meet my wife."

Her brown eyes scoured me from top to bottom as she hugs Mikhail and Yuri. A faint smile is on her face as she hugs me. The Hallmark hug and kisses she bestows on men are dead to me. Feels like a jewelry box is embracing me.

"Nice to meet you," I say.

"Likewise," Sofiya grits. A half-second later, her face brightens considerably. My gut tells me that it wasn't due to our greeting each other.

"Malich," she nods to him.

"Sofiya," he nods back, slowly ascending the steps at the front of the home.

"If you don't hug me." A smile plays at the corner of Sofiya's lips then detonates into a full-blown grin like before.

The Hallmark preview continues. All warm, fuzzy feelings as she cries in his arms. One that leaves her body wracking. Malich wipes at her tears.

"Do you vouch for her?" Sofiya asks him, nudging her chin toward me.

"Dah."

She then takes a few steps over and hugs me too. Now, I'm smack dab in the middle of the feel-good movie.

"Oh, auntie," Yuri chuckles. "You asked me that."

"Me too." Mikhail shakes his head as she holds me tightly.

"I am elated to meet you," Sofiya says again. This time, my bones warm up. All the anxious thoughts choking at my soul from earlier have vanished.

I'm flabbergasted by her ways. Her rigidity has disappeared.

After she deftly rubs her eye ducts, she clasps my hands again. Sofiya wags a finger at them, saying, "Any of you tell the others I cried and your all dead. Now, Mrs. Resnov, I'll keep watch over you. Make sure the rest of the family doesn't try to eat you up."

"They won't," Vassili growls.

"Because the king is her father-in-law," Anatoly adds. My husband shoots him a dark, daggered gaze as we all start into the house. The ceilings reach the sky with murals lined in gold.

The lengthy foyer is lined with pillars and fresh-cut flowers on podiums. True to her word, Sofiya loops an arm with mine, and we travel through the mansion. We enter a room that makes the grand Russian Tea Room resemble Motel 6. Not one single inch of the room hasn't been polished. It's all incased in marble walls. The smell of wealth is sweetest here. She introduces me to more siblings and cousins. I expected to be overwhelmed by the entire dynamic of the mafia, but Sofiya is on one side of me, Vassili the other.

"Have we completed all greetings?" Anatoly asks. His gaze gleans with power.

A collective "Dah" resounds. He presses a button. A mural-like wall zips inward, revealing another room. In the center of the hidden room is a massive oak table. This is it. The secrecy of it leaves me in shock.

Sofiya kisses my cheeks before crossing over. Anatoly and a few other brothers I was just introduced to stand before the table.

"Malich, I beg of you," Anatoly implores. Although it feels like an order. Like there's no other choice.

Mikhail tenses. Malich heads toward them. They sit. All five of them, except for Anatoly. He stands behind his chair at the head of the table. I glance around at the rest of the Resnovs. There are a token number of men who remind me of "Horace" and are still in their good graces. Names that have titles, political and such. I notice Simeon in the fold. Why doesn't he have a seat?

"Moy syn." Anatoly pats the leather headrest of the head seat, staring at Vassili.

"Nyet. I don't want it."

The room seems to darken as everyone awaits the father's reaction to an insubordinate son. Vassili finds my hand, not saying another word, not making another move.

"This week, I lost a daughter and a son." Anatoly clears his throat, the head seat, though not claiming it. "I could say they would be missed, they *will not.* In time they will be forgotten. After today, they *will not* be spoken of again."

He used such a steel voice, I doubt there were no wounds, to begin with.

"I have a few more sons among you, the select few that are here today are important. Those that aren't, still serve their purpose. Make no mistake, *my son Vassili Karo Resnov* is my successor." He moves away from the unclaimed seat. He stops behind Malich, running a hand through his hair.

My eyes dart to Mikhail and Yuri, they're on edge.

"Contrary to everyone else's plans, mine will succeed," he continues. The king's slimy fingers rub through another brother's hair and then Sofiya's. "Though, I have my desires of one successor, I'll give my siblings the floor. They will all have a chance to convince me of *who* should be next in line."

Murmuring follows before silence descends. This is unheard of. Why is there even a table? It's like a boardroom with CEOs and it appears one man is accustomed to having it all.

Anatoly says, "Before I open the floor up to any such pitch to become successor, I must first make one last attempt. I'll ask *moy syn* again—"

"Nyet. Still nyet!" Vassili shouts.

Anatoly's eyes sparkle. *"I haven't asked you yet."*

He calls for Simeon. The man who is the ying to Vassili's yang locks gazes with me for a fraction of a second. All the blood running through my veins ceases its course.

I'll be the reason my husband becomes king . . .

41

V assili
Zariah stiffened. Why the fuck did my wife stiffen beside me? She should be assured that I'm not team Anatoly. Not now, not ever. My hand gives her fingers a reassuring squeeze. She's not close enough. I let her fingers go, clasping her at the waist now. I bring Zariah before me, my arms around my growing son. On the next doctor visit, my wife will know that she *is* having my son.

Simeon heads toward the table. My fingers thread through Zariah's again, my chin on my wife's head. She's my queen and none of these mudaks understand that I love her more than the power at their fingertips.

At the opposite head of the table, Anatoly and Simeon argue under their breath. It's all tensed jaws, hard glares. Simeon opens the left side of his blazer. Anatoly wrestles an envelope from his hands.

Teeth gritted, Simeon leans against the partition that would separate the two rooms.

Anatoly snatches open the envelop and pulls out an 8 by 12 photo.

"Nicks," Zariah murmurs.

"Special Agent Tyrese Johnson—presuming the alias of Tyrese Nicks, went on a wild goose chase," Anatoly declares. "The Feds have been infiltrated. The higher-ups allow lowly FBI agents to conduct investigations on us. We're all in agreement that nothing will be found."

My eyebrows pull together.

"Zariah," Anatoly inquires, "We must know *of your association to Special Agent Johnson?* I presume you knew him as Nicks when the two of you were—"

She blurts, "We never did anything."

An imaginary hook slams through me with enough force to floor me. I take a few unsteady steps away from my wife. Zariah spins around, and I look her dead in the eye. I command, "Who the fuck is he to you?"

"*Was,*" Simeon grunts.

"He's shark food now, by way of the Atlantic Ocean," Anatoly laughs.

Zariah looks up at me, her fucking face. Her beautiful motherfucking face is too much for me to stare at. "Who the fuck is he!" I tower over her.

"Vassili, hold it," Malich starts out of his seat, but Anatoly stops him with a hand at his shoulder.

Yuri comes to her side. "Brat," he lowers his voice, "Let's chat somewhere else."

"Nyet!" I growl at him. "She belongs to me, not you, Yuri!"

"I didn't say she did," he steps closer to me. "Zariah is family now, brat."

Zariah touches his arm. "It's okay, Yuri. I-I can explain."

He steps back a few paces next to Mikhail. I glower at them all.

My wife looks up at me, with a strangled voice. "Attorney Tyrese Nicks worked the Noriega case with me. I didn't know he was a Fed then—"

"You fucked a Fed?" I ask, begging myself not to be plunged in that place. The dark place where she's holding me, sobbing and crying tears at my chest. The place she goes to die.

Zariah moves closer to me. I'm too quick on my toes for that shit. "Talk!" I bark.

She speaks fast. She mentions her father and how I sent her home.

This time, she gets close again. I grab her biceps and shake her. "Skip that shit, Zariah! Tell me about you. Tell me about *you and another man.*"

My gaze lights with murder. She clutches her throat. What the fuck for? My hands are weighted at my sides.

"Vassili... listen to me. You tell Natasha everything. The night you came to see us at Maxwell's when I'd just gotten home—"

I laugh, "From out with another man."

"Don't do this, Vassili. Look at me, look into my eyes. Don't do this." She sniffles back tears. Her hands are out in an attempt to clasp mine. "What about the woman Danushka had screwing with you? I never held it against you!"

"Do not touch me."

Her hands shake as she pulls them away from me and across her chest. "Remember the night you came to see me? The night I was in the shower when you came to my father's home?"

Jaw clenched, I nod.

Taking a deep breath, Zariah murmurs, "That night I heard you. While you thought I was sleep, you spoke with Natasha. You tell our baby everything."

"Don't bring *my daughter* into this," I grit out.

Zariah wipes away the tears with a trembling hand. "You told Natasha you wanted a new life. No bad shit. You were making moves on your end. I wanted to get rid of my father for us. We were supposed to celebrate this news once we got back from Moscow."

I blink at her. Twenty of my family and associates are here to witness my wife make a fool of herself.

"I went to Tyrese for help—"

"You went to another man for help!" A vein in my neck pulsates. I push Zariah away again. She won't stop fucking trying to touch me.

"To get rid of my dad. Vassili, please believe me. In the beginning, when I learned Tyrese wasn't truthful, I assumed *Maxwell* was his target. You believe me, don't you?" Zariah's hands reach out for me. She's grazing my jaw when I step away from her again.

"Simeon," I growl. "*Lock her ass up.* Let's finish this meeting."

Zariah gasps. "Vassili, don't talk to me like that. I'm your wife!"

"Dah, *you belong to me.*" I step toward her now that she isn't attempting to place her silky, tiny hands on me. It makes my gut tie in knots that Yuri edges closer. My brat wants to save the woman who manipulated me! I point a finger at her. "Your biggest mistake is forgetting that I own you."

Simeon clasps her arm. She wrestles with him. Every fiber in my being wants to fight this mudak for touching my wife. But these are *my* orders. Yuri pushes at Simeon from the opposite side of her, Mikhail too. A resounding slap echoes across the room as Zariah slaps my cousin. Simeon growls. She wrenches her arm away from him.

"Vassili, I'm your wife. *You are not your father.*" Her fingers stroke my chiseled jaw. I clasp her hand on my face. Looking her deep in the eye, I notice her brown orbs softening. The pleading has become hope.

My fingers tighten around her hands, squeezing the fuck

out of them. "First, you talk shit about my mother? Now you compare me to Anatoly!"

"You told me to mention her," she shouts, voice strangled.

The entire room disappears as I continue to crush her fingers. I shake her body, growling, "You're comparing me to that mudak of a father of mine? Is that what you're doing."

"Vassili—"

Grabbing Zariah's face, I crush her lips harder than ever in a kiss that weakens her knees. Once she's putty in my hands, I toss my wife. She stumbles backward into Simeon's arms.

I declare, "You compare me to my father, big mistake. If you're right, Zar, then that means *I. Kill. You.* Simeon, lock her ass up while I make up my mind."

Zariah

    "You should stop crying," Simeon's deep voice dips with deceptive sympathy. We're in a dark room on the top floor of Anatoly's mansion. The windows are too high up for daylight to touch down on us. The gilded bedroom is strangled by dusk. On the edge of a four-poster bed, I sit with my legs at my chest, chin on my knees. Lips trembling, I glare at him. "When will he kill me. Oh my God! My husband wants to kill me."

    "He won't." Simeon pinches the bridge of his nose. "Stop crying."

    "Why? My crying pierces your evil soul?"

    The beautiful monster smiles. "Nyet. I like to watch people cry. It makes them real. I like it from a distance. Except, I'm stuck here with you, shit makes my head hurt."

    "You like crying from a distance? What does that mean."

    He shrugs.

    "What does it mean!"

    Simeon glares at me again as if to say I'm crossing the line for pushing. "I kill people. That's the job. Love the fucking job. Love it so much that when I'm done, I watch the dead man's family mourn. If they don't mourn—"

Unable to get a grip on my life, I taunt him with, "What? You kill them too?"

"Dah," Simeon chuckles softly. "I do. Even bad men should be loved. I can tell when a wife is breaking after her husband. Like Anna. I'd never kill her. She's family. Zariah, you are too."

I roll my eyes at him. "Oh, come on."

"You are. Anyway, those dead, rich men's wives that the Bratva need cleansing I'll watch them. Read them. Leave them or collect their lives too."

With nowhere to go but six feet under, I focus on Simeon. I was wrong about him. The only resemblance to my husband is by way of his looks. He's a friggen serial killer who doesn't know when to stop. "You're the grim reaper and then you play judge, jury, and executioner by way of going beyond the call of duty. Sounds like overkill. What about the wife who isn't ready to grieve? Some people take time before it all sinks in."

I pluck up a pillow, ready to suffocate myself, so Vassili doesn't get to do the honors. After a few beats, Simeon decides to respond.

"Zariah, it's best to cut off the vines. Say a husband is the root of the family, and if they truly follow his views on life, they should be cut down."

"What?"

His eyes sparkle. "You're a sophisticated being, Zariah. You're also listening, I know you are. Some women are trapped in relationships with vile, powerful men. Others are an equal threat—poison ivy. You cut the root—the husband— that vine will attach itself to something else. That parasite continues to grow." Simeon ceases his quasi-philosophical rant to shrug. "Zariah, expand your horizons. I don't just need another life to claim. There are various reasons that I do what I do."

"Okay, you're Robin Hood, who steals the souls of bad people so they're not harming good people?" I huff, for a moment forgetting my predicament.

"I appreciate your assessment." He nods. "Grim Reaper, Robin Hood of souls. Although it's not so complex. When I'm bored, I need an outlet."

"You're bored, try a book."

"I have an advanced reading collection in my home. I own one of the largest libraries in Moscow—amongst other locations, with large volumes of work." His voice grows far away as he adds, "I get restless . . ."

"Oh sheesh, genius serial killer." I lean back against the head post, gripping my hair. "With your skewed moral compass, you should be glad to watch Vassili mur-murder me. I'm cheating scum, right?"

He folds his arms. "You're not. The agent kissed you. You pushed him."

Eyebrows zipping together, I murmur, "How? How are you aware of this?"

"I'm the reason that Anatoly has photos. I took one of the kisses." Simeon bites his bottom lip. "Had Vassili not taken the bait on round one, a photo expresses a thousand variables. In certain instances, it tells everything aside from the truth."

Blood pounds in my ears, I growl, "You watched me that entire night! You watched Grigor—"

"Nyet. I was exiting the building across the way, the same as you. That shouldn't have happened. I apologize."

"Don't have the nerve to be sorry, Simeon! Try being

sorry about," my voice breaks. "Being sorry about Natasha and *my baby. I am pregnant!*"

"You *will* birth a Resnov baby." Simeon turns on the heels of his expensive loafers and exits. I hear a deadbolt click as a sob cracks through me.

My son . . .

43

Vassili

I claim the fucking seat. The one that my father has prepared for me and the opposite of him. While the meeting is commenced and the first issue at hand is on the table, I stare at nothing in particular. On my left, Sofiya scoots her chair close to me.

"Malich vouched for her," my aunt says under her breath. "Before you make any lasting decisions, Vassili, take everything into perspective."

"She betrayed me."

My aunt clasps the back of my hand, her thumb kneading over my skin. "Half the mudaks here will never have *half* the wisdom I do. How many times have I told you this?"

"Auntie," I groan.

"How many, Vassili?" she growls.

"A thousand."

"Try a million," Simeon's mother whispers wisdom. "Did I

appreciate anyone else's opinion regarding Natasha? Nyet. My brat, Malich, is the only man I'd ever trust without time and consideration. Yuri, Mikhail, and *Malich* all love your wife. You do too. Things are not always as they seem."

"Sofiya," Anatoly clears his throat from the opposite end of the table. "We're discussing the ports on the northeastern shore of . . ."

I sit back in my chair. The heads of the table chat and the surrounding family wait for outcomes and orders. All I hear is white noise.

I glance at my fists; the blood has gone from beneath them. The team is discussing Congress in the States. Names of senators are tossed around and how the petition will never see the light of day. Someone in the crowd confirms that he has the means to head this requirement.

Simeon returns to the room.

He nods at me, two hands fisting the finest champagne. Restless from even this short period of time sitting with the Bratva, I stand up from the table.

"Father, let's do this right. You've waited years for me to sit here. Let's set business aside to drink some champagne!"

Anatoly clicks his tongue, arising from the table. "I haven't properly welcomed you, moy syn. Good idea."

I nudge my chin, and he comes to my side. Like I've always done with Malich, I regard my father. My hand goes behind Anatoly's neck, our foreheads press together. I show him the utmost respect, a reverence he's never received from me.

"There will be two kings," I tell him, giving the back of his neck a pat.

Anatoly calls out, "There are two kings, long live *us*!"

. . .

O ne week ago, I was living the worse days of my life. Kong was in a coma—fuck, he still is. My wife and daughter weren't under my roof. I sat on stools with Simeon at the island in my kitchen. Two bottles of Resnov Water between us, because one wasn't going to cut it.

I mumbled, "My wife doesn't make it, you're dead."

"Brat, I'll keep her safe with my life."

I stared at Simeon; the motherfucker looked just like me. I needed to trust him. How could I? He spent more of his life beneath my father's thumb. Saw the bastard crazier than me. "You let one hair . . ."

"I don't need fucking threats, Vassili." Simeon glowered at me. "I give my word; you take my fucking word."

"I take your word?" I cackled, tossing back the entire bottle. "Sounds like you wanna fight this shit out. I'm not stupid, Simeon. I want more than your word to trust. You have always wanted to be ..."

"I want to be you?" He pointed a stiff finger at me. "That's your motto. Every time I look at you, mudak. All I fucking hear is 'You want to be me, Simeon.' Brat, grow the fuck up."

Giving my skull a few pops, I growled, "I—Fuck! I can't trust anyone with Zariah. She's my fucking life. She and Natasha are my life!"

"You're our father's son." He shook his head, then his eyes met mine. He was testing me to deny those words.

Our father's son.

I couldn't deny them.

Anatoly had raped Sofiya while Sasha was in my mother's belly. He'd been drunk out of his mind when my aunt tried to save my mom from another smacking. To my father, I can only fucking guess that he thought he was screwing his wife's best friend. Not his own sister. The two titles were given to Sofiya.

In return, she gave her brother a son.

"You think," Simeon groaned, "I'm jealous. Nyet, it's misplaced adulation when we were young. You were my big brat—you fucking idiot. I expected to work for you! I thought that I saw the same rage in your eyes for him. For OUR FATHER."

I patted his shoulder. There wasn't anything else I could think for us to do. We'd never been close and for this revelation to come out, the entire situation was awkward.

"Danushka said she had the same disease tonight before I killed her," I muttered. "I was about to strangle her, and she wanted me to stop. Like I wouldn't kill her."

"What did she say?"

"Right before I took her out, she reminded me of some shit. Fuck!" I rubbed a hand over my face. "I've always had time missing from my mind. Like I didn't want to remember certain things about the past."

"Defense mechanism," he mumbled.

"I'd forgotten about Anatoly raping Sofiya until Danny stopped me from strangling her. She and Grigor were there when our father raped your mom. Might be why those two . . . those two. . ." Shit, I couldn't say it out loud. That the siblings had been screwing each other too."Sim, the three of us, even my mom, tried to stop our father. We all watched him rape her. It's the first and only thing I ever did with them. They grew up to be two of the weirdest mudaks. They held that memory—"

"They weren't strong like you. Not strong enough to forget, brat." He patted my shoulders. "They were lost a long time ago."

I drank more of the liquid. "Why don't you hate me, Simeon? Why isn't this shit my fault? Everything else is your fault."

We sounded like true brothers for a second as he retorted. "You thought Igor was my fault when we went for blows at Urban Kashtan."

I shrugged. "We have a fucked-up life. Danny saw it. I saw it. Anatoly beat my mom! He raped auntie."

"Dah! He raped my ma!" he growled.

I huffed. "Dah, all of that made me not want anything to do with my siblings, you included. You hate me, you must. So, now I can't trust that you'll keep Zariah safe."

"Eh, you don't understand Vassili. Knowing what happened to my mom, your mom, it all made me work at being Anatoly's second." Simeon drank so much that it wetted down his chin and chest. "I should have noticed Danny and Grigor."

"They ended up more fucked over than us, brat." I shook my head. "She was so out of it when I choked her out that I had to remind her that I knew Anatoly raped your mother. Or maybe she had forgotten I was there. Maybe that bitch and Grigor thought they carried all this. The two of them... and it messed their brains over. Right before I killed her, Danny said she did this for you —for us!"

He roared. "She was so stupid, so fucked up. She was still our sister. Grigor . . . I didn't watch him enough!"

My eyebrows came together. Simeon is the youngest, but at that moment, he felt like the oldest. I knew what he meant by 'watch' Grigor. Not because he worried the little bastard would be disloyal. Simeon, the one who loves blood, would've been there, I wasn't. I muttered, "We didn't, Simeon. Brat, we didn't watch them enough."

"They may have been stupid, incestuous creeps, but we gotta right these wrongs, brat. Anatoly's abuse ruined them, Vassili," Simeon slurred. "We have to vindicate Danny, Grigor, Sasha." His eyes locked onto mine as he mentioned my sister's name. At that second, I knew that Simeon had spent years under the devil's rule to learn his ways. My calculating brat was a mastermind and more worthy to be king than all of us.

I pointed the neck of my Resnov Water at him and asked, "Sim, do you want the throne?"

L ike my father declared, there are two kings.
He isn't one of them.

From the back of the room, Simeon holds two bottles of champagne in his hand. They are symbolic that our plans are in order. He shouts, "I've got you all covered."

"*Moy syn!*" Our father accidentally slips with the truth. Over the years, I've always wondered why he didn't just let Simeon rule alongside him. That would bring his dirty secret to ahead.

At my side, my father glances through the crowd at the young man he's never claimed. The soldier that he could *only* ever be proud of and never give the crown to. The one who went above and beyond, while following his orders.

Anatoly says, "Simeon has learned under my authority for so long, he knows exactly what we should do. That's not enough champagne, though."

Simeon gestures toward another son who isn't aware that they're half-siblings and not cousins. My aunt is now married. Her husband believes Simeon is his, and he's such a fucking beta husband that he took the Resnov name. Some shit will stay in the dark, I guess.

Simeon places one bottle on the table and hands Anatoly the other. My father gives him a look. Or should I say *our* father? The look says to scat. This is the time for kings; Simeon isn't one of *us.*

My arm glides around Anatoly's neck. The chokehold is so forceful his face reddens on key.

"There is a new king among us," I growl. "It *is not me.*"

A knife zips out from the inside of Simeon's blazer. The blade plunges between our father's rib. The champagne bottle in Anatoly's hand crashes to the floor beside us. I grab the knife from his flesh and slide it from one side of Anatoly's neck to the other.

His body falls to the floor.

My voice booms across the shock-filled room. "Anatoly Karo Resnov Junior has completed his reign. My wife had the help of a Fed to get rid of another man, Maxwell Washington. I will not fault her for it. *Nobody will!*" I declare.

Father or not, I'm past the point of giving a damn. I stand before my father's corpse and continue with what must be done. "I'm aware of her faults. Betrayal of a Resnov is not one of them. The man she vindicated is now in prison, awaiting trial. I need him handled."

"What prison?" Someone says from the crowd.

I look to my brat, Simeon. He told me how Anatoly would persuade me to believe my wife cheated. He told me everything. Fuck, he had to use pictures of Zariah leaving her father's house with the Feds on the scene and Maxwell in cuffs. I loved her so much, too fucking much. My brother had to get through to me. I've never been so jealous in my life.

I did the agent in myself. Simeon disposed of his body somewhere in Florida before heading here.

Simeon might have a taste for blood, but his efficiency is more than enough to rule the Bratva. He mutters the name of the prison. A step ahead of everyone.

One of the crew has enough connections to confirm that it will be done.

"Thank you," I tell him.

Then I mention Noriega, his gang, and any affiliates. Another set that head various areas of the Bratva promise to deal with Noriega's closest friends. I'm making commands. Reveling in power while Simeon rubs at the blood speckled across his fingers. I haven't noticed crying. Nobody has.

I stare at the floor. My pupils widen, eyebrows snatching together. Embarrassment strains across Simeon's face. We all watch Sofiya on her knees, crying. Champagne mingles with the blood of my father on her palms. Shards of glass are around her too.

"Mama, nyet. There is broken glass. Please get up," Simeon implores. He holds out a hand to help her. He's like a father whose daughter took her first fall.

Sofiya slaps at his hand. Spits at her son, Malich, me. For a second, she reminds me of Danushka, lost and confused. Why is she crying for a rapist?

"*Why?*" Her voice strangles out the same question I have, but for a vastly different reason.

"You know why, mama," Simeon's hard voice lowers. He scoops her up. With the utmost care, he places Sofiya on a chair. Going to his knees before her, Simeon searches her over for shards of glass. He attempts at a smile while pressing his lips to her forehead. "It is best that you stop crying for Anatoly now, mama. He was bad blood."

For a second, my father's death is more real to me than I ever thought it'd be. Not because of my emotions, but the raw sadness emanating from Sofiya. Has she forgotten?

He caresses her cheek again then gets up. Anger and disappointment are in Simeon's eyes for a split second, then his face grows harder. Back to business. I hook an arm around Simeon. Her response to our retribution has to have killed him.

"My brat is king! I am not." I gesture toward Yuri, who hasn't glanced my way since Simeon removed Zariah from the room.

Yuri shakes his head, mumbling, "I don't want it, brat."

Simeon grabs my face. "It should be us. All my life, Vassili, it was us."

I can't fail him now.

44

Z ariah

The door opens, and Vassili enters the room. I'm already at the headboard of the bed. Nowhere is far enough away from the man who should be loving me. His shoulders are slumped. Haunted orbs land on mine. Not waiting to watch the hatred glean in his gaze, I fly out of my seat, hands hitting Vassili anywhere I can.

All too easy, my husband's arms wrap around me. "Stop, Zariah. Baby, I apologize. It was all an act."

His words go through one ear and out the other. In my fear, I toss my knee up. "I won't let you hurt me or my baby," I shout.

Vassili blocks the blow by swooping me into his arms. He plants me on the bed and kneels in front of me.

"I married for love, Zariah," he grits. "I married a woman I admire. A woman who I planned on building a life with, a life of mutual respect."

"Don't hurt . . ." My lips tremble.

His head lowers. He kisses my belly. "We're done. Done playing Danushka's game—"

"She's dead!" I cut in.

Vassili's eyes connect with mine. "Anatoly's game. We're done, with all of it."

Throat constricted, I ask, "Did you?"

"Baby, I'm sorry," Vassili declares, his voice breaks. I look into his eyes, noticing the struggle there, the fear. "I had to treat you like Yuri when it came to my father. You had to be left out, Zariah."

"You scared me," I murmur.

The back of his knuckles stroke my cheek as if he's reminding himself that I'm real. "I hurt you, Zar. It had to look real, I'm so fucking sorry, baby."

An imaginary grip continues to hold my throat siege.

Vassili's hands engulf mine. "Anatoly's dead. Simeon and I did it."

"How?" I huff. Although, I'm actually wondering *how* my husband feels about what he's done. My voice is too strangled to continue.

"A life of privilege was what too many people believe I was born into. I don't give a fuck what people believe. It wasn't a privilege, Zariah, you know that. I faced more hardship than some of those same doubters. You were my happiness." His voice lowers as his eyes lock onto my lips. He offers the same taste that he had earlier. A good, pleasing taste. This time, Vassili's hard body is tangible between my legs as he hugs me close. Our lips meet, a warmth blossoms across my chest, ridding the chill of anxiety. Heat spreads through me, tingling in ripples. All the love we've built floods back into my heart.

Again, I'm reminded of the breakthrough after the depression I felt when Vassili tore his patella. Life isn't meant to be perfect, but we've fought for each other and persevered.

O n jittery legs, I stand at the door of Samuel's beachfront home, waiting for it to open. My mind was clear for the past few weeks, now it's not. We'd extended or stay in Russia. I saw my husband cry for the very first time.

Then he declared his love for me and promised to never let me go.

The very next day, Anatoly's body was placed in the dirt. There was a family reunion of sorts. Not like the one my mom had for us in the A after we married. No ribs. No oldies blaring through the radio. We ventured throughout my husband's wonderful country and learned so many things. Now, Vassili has Natasha in one arm and he's clutching a manila envelope with the sex of our other child. We arrived in Los Angeles this morning, with just enough time to attend our doctor visit.

I stop my leg from moving, ready for two revelations, one of which I already know. We are having a son, but who is *my father.*

The door swooshes open, Samuel's wearing a black apron that reads, "The Grill Father." He rubs his hands together as he often does when boasting with Vassili about his steaks. His eyes land on me. A flicker of hope is there as my mom comes from behind him, hands on her hips.

"All of you look so refreshed and lively." My mom pulls me into a hug first. She hugs each of us, saying, "My baby girl is glowing. Cutie Pie, you have this European flair about you. Son, look at you! After all the food we plan to eat today, you better get prepared to put an ass whooping on that little boy!"

"What do you know about that little boy, Mora?" Samuel asks her. He, too, hugs us all. He's nervous when he gets to me and mumbles about steaks. Damn, I never thought I'd see the day that the brilliant attorney was at a loss for words. I gulp back trepidation too.

We all head into the kitchen. Seated at the breakfast nook, overlooking choppy gray water is my brother, Martin. He's pulling at a bottle of beer when a smile brightens his face. "Good news, the witch is dead."

"Martin," I sigh as he pulls me into a hug. Our mom is in the background huffing beneath her breath. "You're in HR, have a heart."

He clasps my cheeks. "You okay?"

Our father died a few days ago. He had a heart attack while in prison, isolated from the general population. Or should I say Martin's father? My brother and mom Facetimed with the news. Part of me thinks Martin was still blindsided by the fact that I might be related to Samuel. While I'll always have a history with Maxwell, I can't bring myself to look around. Today we learn if he's my father, and for more reasons than not, I'd feel slimy crying over the man who raised me.

"I'm okay," I murmur.

My brother removes his glasses, chews his lip. "All right, maybe that wasn't the best way to greet you all. I could use the therapy I'm always harping to y'all about."

"Preach," our mom says, bumping him with her hip. "You sure you're all right, Zar?"

"Yeah," I murmur.

"We're taking a walk along the beach, girls," my mom's cheeks brighten. "Give these men a chance to finish dinner. I expect dessert."

"I second that." I chortle, reaching over to kiss Natasha, who's comfortable on my mother's hip. "Cutie, would you like pie?"

"French Fry," she counters, with juicy lips.

"Daddy will make you some French Fries," Vassili says. He pulls me against him. I look up at his deliciously dark eyes and fall in love. Maybe he had something to do with Maxwell Washington's death. Maybe he didn't.

For now, I'm content with the fact that my husband owns the cage, and his *brother*, Simeon, owns the Bratva.

———

While we walk along the beach, my mother explains something that's been nagging me all this time. Martin is my older brother. Why not test his DNA as well? She explains that Samuel had only slept with her once. She gives this dreamy example that only die-heart lovers like Zamora Haskins does. One that includes another dark chocolate man who she once had a humongous crush on. Wesley Snipes. Also, it includes the *Waiting to Exhale* movie. Similarly, Samuel's wife/her best friend is dying of cancer. When she began to explain the bitter-sweet sex scene in comparison, I drown in laughter. Honestly, mom has always hoped that their one single time together conceived me.

This afternoon, my family and I sit around antique patio furniture that has my mother's name written all over it. Martin is on one side of me while Natasha and Vassili are on the other. My mom canoodles with Samuel, cutting his steak and being her usual super lovey-dovey self.

"Can we get to the envelope?" I push aside my plate.

Vassili reaches over, placing a hand over my slightly protruding belly. "Is my son full?"

"Not until the cake is on the table." My mom gushes. "A little cake, a little bubbly. Zar, you've got room, right?"

"Bubbly?" I cock a brow. "Momma—"

"You can have half a sip." She gestures toward the men. Samuel, Vassili, and Martin all rise to leave the room.

I bite my thumbnail. "Damn . . ." I murmur.

"What?" She cocks her head, Natasha follows suit.

Leaning back in the chair, I groan. "Depending on the outcome of the test, I'm wondering if I should've felt—acted more distraught when it came to Dad's death. Damn! I don't even want to call him Dad anymore." I place my hands over my face and rub. My daughter begins to paw at my shoulder. My eyes pop open, and I reach over to make sure that she's not about to fall off Vassili's chair.

But something catches me from the corner of my eye. A cake! A *pink* cake! Vassili's holding it. Martin has saucers, with champagne flutes, while Samuel holds a few more flutes and a bottle.

Scooping Natasha into my arms, I plant her into my lap and groan. I place my hands over her ears. "Oh, Vassili, we can't have another girl yet. I need a son. Someone to keep this one in check when they're out and about without us."

"What?" My husband starts to place the cake in the center of the table.

Eyebrows pulled together, I ask, "You opened the results? We're having a girl."

"Oh, yeah, we did open the results, sorry." Vassili's pleasing lips slide into a panty wetter smile.

Samuel clears his throat. "Vassili's ready to whoop Rhy's butt and retire, then he'll spend the next 18 years coaching in a new MMA era, with his Junior."

Martin pulls something from his pocket. A plume of blue confetti bursts in my direction. With tiny blue pieces of paper shimmering around me, I stare at the three of them.

Natasha giggles in my lap, clutching at a few blue particles from her face.

"This is quite confusing. Pink cake, blue confetti?" I mumble.

After a beat, Samuel says, "You're having a son, Zar. Someone else *had* a girl."

My jaw drops. Vassili removes Natasha from my hands. With a voice that has failed me, I start up from the chair on shaking legs and realize my mom has been recording us.

"Momma . . ." I mouth.

"Daddy . . ." She mouths back, holding up her iPhone.

"Maybe not daddy," Vassili murmurs.

Laughter bursts through me, laughter and tears as Samuel and I hug.

"You're my . . ." I stutter.

"I am."

I stare up at my father, the sparkles in my gaze mirroring in his. The man who did his best to help raise me the right way embraces me with the same reverence.

For the first time in my life, I can say, "I love you, Dad," and that completes the sentence. It also completes the sentiment because I'm not in shame for caring for someone who has given me life and given my mother the worst pain ever. I'll never say it out loud, but if Vassili had something to do with Maxwell's death, then I'm numb to that. My entire soul is alight with happiness right now, and not a damn thing can take that from me.

VASSILI
Half a Year Later

Gray cement slabs for walls surround me. I'm standing
in sweats and an A-shirt with my Killer Karo brand. I
watch ESPN on the television bolted to the wall. All the
channels are sports oriented; all focused on me. The shit has
never gone down like this before. Especially not at the start
of football season.

Killer Karo versus Rhy the Russian Rampage. My limbs
are warm. Every part of me is ready to tear him apart. Some
of the commentators are calling me a vet and the favorite.
Others are calling Rhy the new, improved me, since he'd
started under Vadim. None of their predictions will sway me.
This is my fight. But I can't stop doing one thing.

Thinking about my wife.

"Vassili, if I'm not at my seat, baby . . ." I rub the back of my
neck, letting it sink in. The first time she left the seat, she was
having my baby. The second time, that bitch of a friend of

hers brought her back to the stadium, when I fought Tiago. The first match after my torn patella. Fuck, guess I can't hate Taryn for Yuri's sake when she understood how I felt about my wife always being there.

I'll give the world the match they came to see. Let Rhy feel me out in the first round. Round two, I take his ass out, all too easy, just because. Or, round two, I take his ass out because I have to get to the hospital. It's Kentucky Yum Center all over again. Except, this fight is being held in Long Beach, California. This time too, we have a chopper on standby because my little king is coming into this world. He's been baking for a little over 40 weeks.

I press the mute button, get to my knees, and thank the Man Upstairs. When I stand up, there's a knock on the steel double doors.

"Dah?" I head toward it, fisting my cross at my neck for a moment.

"You have to keep warm, son." Malich pats my shoulder as I enter the outer room where my entire team is standing.

We have new members. Dima is representing Killer Karo clothing. Not in this world would I even dream that Simeon would don one of my shirts. Even Malich has my shirt over his polo.

The old man grips my shoulder. "You have a belt to get back, Dah?"

"Fuck yeah!" I growl.

"You get that fucking belt." Simeon takes my other shoulder. "Or I do it for you, the Resnov way."

Dima, whose been sparring with me recently, gulps.

"Nyet, brat." I pat the back of his neck. "This will be easy."

His face is all a sinister mask until he grins. "Khorosho."

"Dah, no Resnov way. Not today." Vadim hooks his arm around both of us. "But that little shithead, Rhy, was on my team, Karo. You gotta kill 'em."

"The fuck happened with the saying, Kill 'em, Karo." Nestor snorts. "What's this, *you gotta kill 'em?* It doesn't have the same spark."

"The old man is going senile." I shake my head. "Vadim said it backward."

The coach wags a finger at us all. "Tonight, Karo will lay Rhy to rest, and he's going to do it so good. He's going to do that takedown so flawlessly that none of you bastards will ever have anything to say about Karo or me. Dah, we're old as fuck. Karo, you're a vet now. Seasoned... old."

"You said that," I tell him. We all roar with laughter.

"Yeah, I'm old," I nudge my chin to Dima. During our last practice, I gave him a few pointers. Advice that a powerhouse doesn't give until they're ready to leave the game.

I'm ready to put MMA to rest in my life, for a little while. I've got a wife, a daughter, son on the way. And I've got Simeon, my real brother. We have the Bratva. That shits in our blood.

EPILOGUE

Zariah

A letter to my husband:
—Vassili
First and foremost, I could never be so happy for
you, for us, than I am right now. When I was
young, I was on the outside looking in when my
mother had to keep invisible masking tape over
her mouth. My father showed her love with the
back of his hand. That was the type of love I
could never desire.
Then you found me.
I should say, I found you. I came into a gym under
the blessing of a Resnov. You found me, you held
onto me when all I did was doubt. You loved me
before I understood the meaning.
Vassili, you taught me to be a fighter. You taught me
how a man should love a woman. You taught me

304

wisdom, guidance, and adoration for our
children and us. Sheesh, you and Natasha are
the type of father/daughter goals that I will have
with my dad, Sammy.

Now, I have to let you know, Vassili, if I'm not at my
seat, baby, it's because I'm doing something for
us. I'm bringing our little king into the world.
You called our Junior a king once. While I didn't
say anything, the symbolism is everything to me.
Maxwell called me 'princess.' (Forgive me for
mentioning him right now, in a letter that should
be totally, and utterly beautiful—like you.)

No matter how many times Maxwell said it, I never
felt like a princess. Never wanted it, if it
encompassed Maxwell's version of the word. We
have a princess, we have Natasha, and you've
never treated her any other way. We have a
prince, a king. If I'm not seated at the event
tonight, it's because I'm fighting to bring our
king into the world.

With every fiber of my being,
Your wife

T he letter to my husband roams through my mind. I'd snuck it into his duffle bag before he left yesterday morning. Although his match is local, we chartered a chopper to take us to the hospital tonight—if necessary. I've done everything I could to make our Junior come a little early, but we're covering all the bases the best we can.

I suspect Vassili's just now seeing the letter in the compartment that is solely for his lucky socks. He wears the darn things all day before a match, then stows them away for me to wash later. Shaking my head, I let the bright grin on my face fade into a pleasant smile.

Family surrounds me. Taryn is at my side. Yuri is on the opposite. She's appealed to him; said she'd never be used to love. With time, I guess we can see where that goes. Yuri is such a good man. I'll never forget how he tried to stop Simeon and Vassili when the two of them were setting the perfect scenario at my expense. Mikhail is here, with dark-rimmed eyes from a hard double in the ER. My mom and Dad are seated right behind us. Everything is as it should be.

"Killer Karo!" my mom screams, her voice loud enough to pop my eardrums. "Killer Karo!"

"Momma," I whip my neck around, my "super preggo" braids slapping me in the face as I turn. "You just *eloped* with an affluential black man. Don't mess up his rep with all that down south shouting and clapping. This is not a brothel," I joke.

She pulls me into a hug, my very swollen belly making it awkward. Samuel adjusts Natasha on his shoulders so that she can see over all of us, then leans forward a little. "Your mom is all the sauce in my life."

"The sauce?" I chuckle as my almost-two-year-old daughter attempts to jostle over his shoulders and into my arms.

"Cutie Pie, you're too heavy for momma." I smack a kiss on each of her cheeks before Samuel wrestles her back onto his shoulders. "Dad," I begin, feeling so refreshed to give him that title. "You sure you're ready for the boy version of Natasha?"

My dad chuckles. "The day I met Miss Mora; I was ready for anything."

During the pre-match festivities, commentators mention how a 'well-rested' Kong and his wife will be watching the

match this evening at home. He'd awoken from a coma a few
weeks after we returned from Russia.

———————

A woman in a bikini, holds my husband's belt high
above her head, strutting around the cage. My eyes
peer about twenty yards away, coming from the side of the
cage is Simeon. He's the GQ version of my husband. Yet
today, he's wearing a Killer Karo t-shirt that's straining
across his bulging chest. Tattoos that I hadn't noticed, since
I've only seen him in button-downs, are inked down his
throat. His deadly gaze fades into liquid thoughtfulness as he
stares at something. At first, I believe he's salivating over the
chick in the bikini, but as she continues along, his eyes are
steady. His lips tense before his eyes connect on me, and he
starts over.

"Hey," I wave a small hand at him. "You okay?"

His lips hardly move, "*Khorosho.*"

"You sure?" I can't help but ask. Although I doubt I'll ever
consider him on the same level as Yuri or Mikhail, I play nice
because he could murder me. Very easily.

"Dah." He rubs the back of his neck. "I saw someone—
assumed that I did. It's nothing."

"Someone on your list?"

"Not in the same terms as you're thinking," he mutters,
taking the space next to me.

What does that mean? Grim Reaper terms? I don't know.
I move over a little, letting him near Taryn. I inch over to
Yuri. "Is your cousin, okay?"

Yuri shrugs. "Who? Vassili? He better be. I have the shoe
division of Nike ready to—"

I chuckle. "Yuri, I know, boo. You haven't been playing
any games since scheduling this fight. Our little King Karo

and Natasha will be set for life at the rate you're going." I edge closer to the man who was once a teddy bear. "I mean Simeon. He seemed a little depressed, walking over here."

"Sim? Sad, ha. He's too evil genius for that, Zar." Yuri puts an arm around me and whispers. "You start having labor pains, hold his hand this time."

"You mean squeeze," I reply, tilting my head.

"Dah," he chuckles.

"I can hear everything the two of you are saying," Simeon clears his throat. "Zariah, Vassili says that he has a gift for the King. *His belt*. If you need to squeeze my fucking hand off at any time during this fight, that's fine with me. Squeeze until you can't take it. Hopefully, Vassili can grab that belt first."

"Alright," I chuckle. Leave it to Vassili Karo Resnov Junior to enter this world when his father is hustling for *his* belt. Shoulders squared; I breathe in deeply. I need to be fearless, right now.

VASSILI

L ike I said, the first round is for my fans. I'm humble enough to know that I wouldn't be here without their support. My heart drums in my chest, sweat drips down my skin. I glare at Rhy as he sits across from me. On the first round, we tossed bricks at each other. I blocked some, took others. While he gave it the best he had, I came with all quickness and half the power in me. The little bitch didn't know he was being taunted. He will soon.

Vadim is in my ear, telling me things I already know. I chug down the water Nestor hands over and flick the water cup. My eyes are still on Rhy. His blue ones are confident. Confident that if we continue at this rate, the mudak will tire me out. Fat fucking chance. I sneer at him.

We all know the drill. TKO's are pretty, but submission is king. My wife is bringing a new king into this world, possibly this evening or sometime soon. So, I could only match that love she has for me.

This is my last fight. I'm going out with the MMA industry, calling my name. The Gogoplata choke requires a flawless technique. It's such a difficult, rare submission that the entire arena will be left talking. Fuck yeah, I let my fighting speak for me. The bell rings.

I bounce onto my toes. Rhy and I come at each other like bulls ready to lock horns. A look of murder is in my eyes, but behind Rhy, I notice Zariah's seat.

Fuck!

It's.

Empty.

Damn, I told Simeon to sit with her. He was supposed to text Nestor if she got up. Yeah, I'm supposed to keep fighting. I told Yuri the same thing. The dude doesn't listen. If Zariah told him not to text me, regardless of what I told him, then he'd listen to her.

I have anticipated setting up the Gogoplata about a minute in, give my fans a little more before the takedown.

But there's no time for that. I have to get to my wife. My left hook swings out, connecting with Rhy's jaw. There's fucking ammunition in my bicep this time because he clobbers back on his heels. Dah. The ESPN commentator on my side was right. No way in fucking hell Rhy is accustomed to a hit like that. His right arm begins to swing. I spin to my side, bringing my knee out and kick him in the ribs. The force is enough to batter his liver.

Punching my hand at my chest, I give Rhy a chance to

catch some air. That's the confidence he needs to bring us down to the clinch. He falls on top of me, fists flying. Commentators are in our ears, mentioning how the tide has turned—

A second later, my forearm hooks over his before he can assault my face. I brace my calf around his waist, then twist until my legs are locked around Rhy's body. The armbar submission is too fucking easy for this wannabe. Next, I'm on top now. I press my shin against his throat, choking him in a perfect Gogoplata. The crowd screams so loud my eardrums rock. From my peripheral, Rhy taps his trembling hand against the canvas. I jump up to my feet, straddling the cage. My gaze latches onto Zariah. She's walking around. She stops, presses her fingertips to her lips, then blows me kisses.

"Stay," she mouths.

With a nod, I clamber back down the fence. The referee has Rhy at one side. I move to the other. My belt, the first love I've ever known, is shiny and calling out to me. The belt is placed around my waist.

This one is for my son. One day, I'll be back under all the lights of the octagon. I'll be the man Vadim and Malich taught me to be. The new King Karo learns that all the aggression he's ever needed to take out is right here. Right in the motherfucking cage. For now, I'll love and worship my wife as we continue to raise our children. As we continue to be fearless for each other.

THE END

Thank you for reading!

SUBSCRIBE

Consider joining my newsletter to stay up to date on new releases and super discounts (especially during these holiday times). You'll also receive a free book for subscribing.

AUTHOR'S NOTE

Hey, you made it! You finished Vassili and Zariah's roller-coaster love story. Your thoughts mean a lot to me. Your response tells me if a particular character was exciting, and should I continue with another character's story. For the past three books, Vassili and Zariah were as real as flesh and blood to me. And being the person I am (all over the place. Yup, I've read that a few times via reviews), I enjoyed creating a puzzle of a story in an attempt to lead them back to each other. For now, I believe they're strong enough in their relationship for me to set my sights on someone else.

I know, I know, Yuri has been mentioned in so many reviews. He and Taryn still might make a good story. But that's not where my heart is, LOL.

Simeon Resnov is ev-er-y-thing. Yeah, I had to stretch out that word. I gravitated toward him. I had so much fun with Vassili mentioning how "dog's ass" ugly he was throughout the series. Then to find out they resemble each other, ha! Who doesn't know people in their family that they resemble and clash with? Well, so Simeon. . . Do you want more of him? Please include so in your review.

315

In the meantime, I've got you covered. Met Sim the guy Zariah dubbed as a serial killer. Even more than that, he's now the King of the Bratva, and he murdered his father. That sounds bad, but hey, I doubt too many people had a problem with Vassili killing their dad ;)

Turn the page for Sim and Asya.

But before you do, just a quick disclaimer. #Lawless is a lot darker than Fearless. Sim had a much harder life than Vassili.

Asya had a harder life than Sim.

But *he* saved *her*.

CONTACT ME

Before we get to the sample of LAWLESS, I wanted to cover a few things.

The best way to chat with me is in my Facebook Group. I'm a bit on the shy side, but I'll open up there the most. The readers give me so much good insight. Often, I'll get ideas about what to write next from my group. They get to see all the sexy ideas I come up with first! And I'll be sharing some new Fearless news with them first . . .

But check out the various buttons below, and feel free to connect with me on whatever platform you prefer.

Give a few of my buttons a click and say hi! Then, turn the page to meet Asya and Sim!

Blessings,
Amarie Nicole

ANASTASIYA (ASYA)

Merriam-Webster explains invisible (noun) as someone or something that cannot be seen or perceived. Based on that definition, I'm not sure most children would ever pick that as something to daydream about having. Other children's innocent fantasies revolve around becoming a superhero or a pretty, little princess.

Not me, though. I wasn't your ordinary child; I'd take invisibility any day over anything in this dark, dead world. Though no matter how much wishing on a star I did, my beauty refused to fade. My body, curves, full lips blossomed instead of withering . . . Invisible.

I resided in a gilded cage in a mansion in Moscow. On display for the world to see, for my future owner's delights.

At least I wasn't alone. The place operated as an orphanage. Every young girl could take a grown man's breath away. We, the trinkets that adorned the walls, came in shades from obsidian to porcelain doll.

My mocha-colored skin was curtesy of a faceless set of benefactors, which included a model who was away from

South Sudan. I suspect she's dead now. Mothers never last in this business.

This business, my life.

I had a father, who was Russian, had to be handsome too. Perhaps dead, fuck it, maybe living his best life.

Parents posed no definition in my brain, had no place in my heart. The rainbow of non-blood siblings I had was moya sem'ya--my family. We understood each other, the need to survive tethered us.

Nanny's raised us. Their gazes not quite meeting ours because they knew our impending demise.

We were chattel of the Resnov Bratva.

Those all-powerful Bratva scum ruled the world.

They made us the most beautiful part of sex trafficking, if you could be bold, or fucking heartless enough to say so. Before we were touched, we had a structured life. It included exceptional etiquette, a prestigious education, and we adhered to all caveats on golden-leaf paper. Those papers were our bibles. The writers of said bibles were the men who owned us even in the womb. Our owners came to the mansion and staked claim to us when we had an ample pair of breasts, hips, or an ass. In other cases, the sadistic fucks claimed us, sullied us younger. Whatever those rich men fancied, well, that constituted when we left the mansion, for our last time. That was when our innocence bled out.

Only, I left the intricate marble walls too soon.

And the Resnov's never made the standard 15 Mil off me.

Some girls go for more.

But I became a trophy, a Resnov possession.

So, if you're curious as to which of us girls were worth the most.

Unfortunately for me . . . It was me.

SIMEON (SIM)

My heart lurches in my fucking chest. Palms accustom to squeezing the life out of mudaks is sopping with sweat. Me, the king of the Bratva. King of Russia. Next stop, the world.

All because we found her.

Has to be her.

No other woman in the world compares to her. Light skin. Innocent honey eyes mask all the sin that she's lived in. A hypnotic body meant to ride cock. Only my cock. Damn that pretty mouth of hers. Those lips know how to take.

While I steal lives, her lips steal hearts with hard kisses and angry words. Her mouth stole my fucking heart. The inside of my chest has been empty for four years since I last set my sights on her. Held her tight like a treasure nobody should see, touch, nobody but me.

She has to be here.

If not, I have one real fear. Not dying, that shit is in the cards. I have my hopes too--that my demise is far the fuck away from now. But what I fear? That I would be molded into the image of my father at the thought of her not being here. I fear that I'll put two slugs between the eyes of Luka.

321

The bastard said he'd gotten the word about her . . . Here. Luka is loyal. Nothing trumps loyal in my book when life and death follow you each day. Luka is also blood. Unlike my father, I rather not spill the same life force running through my veins.

So she's here.

This fucking shit hole of all places.

A dented in, steel door swings open. The base bumps against my chest. A bouncer eyes us. Six of my soldiers are at my sides. We look like money, donning the best Russian suits. We look like death follows in our wake, and we are the sole survivors. And he's dead if he doesn't let us in.

The bouncer licks his in lips in trepidation, knowing that we're all Resnovs. Remembering he has a job to do, he sets terror aside and sneers. "Packing heat?"

"Dah," I nod. "Nyet, we don't leave our guns in the car."

I sniff. The goon to my left opens a duffle bag and moves around the bricks of cash. There's nothing else there — the solider hands one over to the bouncer.

"You see nothing?" I raise a brow.

"I didn't see shit." The bouncer steps to the side.

The music is louder, the smoke putrid. Neon lights zip around, skimming over stripers' flesh. I can't lie, my country has worse places than this club. But the day I met her, I knew all the dirty delights of the dark clung to her—only in the fucking night. In the light, what surrounded her could only attempt to rival her beauty.

Blood becomes venom in my veins. I eye my cousin. Damn, I'd prepared myself for the self-control of not killing Luka because she is not here. Now, part of me wants to slit Luka's throat, feel his warm blood spray across my face— stop the numbness for a while— because she is. That other men have seen her beauty.

"Boss, I promise you. Anastasiya is here," he says in

Russian.

If she's fucking here . . . We burn this place to the ground. I'm thorough, so that means my thoughts are running rampant. A list is in the making. Said list includes all the patrons who's ever walked into the building while my Asya was present. Every man who laid eyes on her. Their deaths are mine too.

I don't express my thoughts. I rarely need my men to murder for me. Even when my father treated me like shit, and I increased my numbers—body count—I relished it. The small comfort in taking a life. The warmth in blood.

I sink onto a sticky, fake leather chair in the center of the seedy strip club. The women on the stage flock toward my seat, they smelled me through the thick of horny fucks. They scent my power, my money.

I slide a brick onto the wooden paneling before me. A stripper's legs o opens wide while my gaze continues to scan the room. I'm searching for Asya as I've done since she left me. Left us.

"How about a private dance?" The girl purrs into my ear.

I lean back a little. Never trust a bitch you don't know.

"No," I switch over to English. "I'm looking for someone."

"I can help," another woman says, crawling over— her ass beckoning other men to follow. My glare stops them. This conversation is for my ears only.

The two strippers clap their asses against each other while offering me all their attention.

I address the girls, "You can both help. Her name is Anastasiya."

The first one smirks. "Oh, that's the real name of the stuck-up bitch?"

My eyelid twitches. "My Anastasiya isn't stuck up." She's an asshole. And it's cute.

The other one tries, "Mixed chick who wants to . . . ?"

323

I weed through half the bullshit these catty cunts say. My peripheral still scouring the room. So far, I'm not sure they're talking about my girl.

One of them says, "Sometimes she sounds ... like you."

"Foreign," the first one says, plucking up the brick.

"Sim," Luka whispers.

I glance in the direction that he nudges his chin.

An imaginary grip is at my throat, and then I'm standing on my own two feet before I realize. On a side-stage, is my hard-on, my fucking heart. I hate Asya for this. Crave her like the trance that builds in an inferno of fire. Under a spell, I step forward again.

About twenty yards from her stage, I stop, stare up at her, drink in her form. A bra clings to her chest. Between her thighs, a tiny silver triangle covers my treasure. A star tattoo sits gracefully on her shoulder. A lace garter and Desert Eagle tattoo she had to have in Vegas years ago, wraps around her thigh. She's stopped dancing. Beneath a fury of lashes, her eyes lock onto mine. Shapely, muscular legs hold her curvy hips steady. A thin waist juts out for the soft flesh of sweet ass, begging for my hands to pluck her up.

My eyes consume her. I starved in the desert for a thousand years, and she's my sustenance. My drink, my food, mine to demolish. We're both fucking paralyzed, staring at each other. My prey is calculating her next move. How the fuck she'll flee my sight. I made that mistake before—letting her out of my sight. Not again. Asya has my heart locked away somewhere. She doesn't have one; those are her words. My gaze gleams with the notion of how I'll snatch the soul right out of her bones and own that shit forever—time to take my heart back too.

Between us, two horny mudaks stand from their barstools, unaware of our connection. They lean over the ledge, reaching for Asya.

One shouts, "Dance, bit—"

I grip the mouthy one by the back of the neck, slam his forehead into the stage. His body slides to the ground.

"What the fuck you do that for?" The other guy starts to turn around.

My hands clutch his shoulders, and my knee slaughters his liver. He crumples forward.

I grit out, "Because I fucking can, bitch."

Since his friend with the big mouth went down too easy, I snatch him back up. My forearm slides across his throat, shoving him back. He yelps as his spine smash against the edge of the stage. With his throat constricted, his Adam's apple attempts to bob up and down. His heart hammers against my arm.

Getting in his face, I ask, "You touch her?"

I apply pressure, twist my forearm until the bone connects with his Adam's apple. The music may be loud, but I relish this moment of dishing out pain. Usually, I'm not this possessive with Asya. Men are going to look at her; it's a given. So, I let his unconscious body slid to the ground.

"You have got to go!" I turn to see a man in a cheap suit that hardly fits him.

"I'm not leaving yet." I bite out, glancing back. Now, why the fuck did I do that? She walked out the second I assaulted the first guy.

"You have to go," he starts for me.

I pull a wad of cash from my pocket. "Not until I dance with your girl."

Your girl—those idiotic words that I said jar my eardrums.

Never in my life would I say such words. Let another man claim her. I taught her better than that when I saved her from the mansion in Moscow. Anastasiya is infinitely better than being owned by someone. Even me.

ASYA

"What the hell are you doing, dressed!"

A hard voice beckons me back toward the present. Bright lights blare down from around a full mirror. Hot, funky pussy mingling with Bath and Body Works assaults my nose. Sweaty women are on either side of me, plucking tassels from their tits, wiping grime from their faces.

I'm fresh from a two-minute shower, with soggy flip flops on my feet. I'm not bold enough to touch those stalls with my toes. A red, faux silk robe is around my body.

"Asya, I said, what the fuck are you doing dressed?"

I look into the mirror. The boss's reflection glares down on me.

Lips taut, I growl, "I pay you for stage time, Jimmy. I'm leaving early, should I ask you to prorate tonight?"

"Prorate? Can you even do that math? Dance for the Russian, or I kick your ass out!" Jimmy's hand starts for my shoulder.

You can kind of expect that I'm not good with touches. My shoulder dips, I slip off the stool.

I stand eye to eye with him. The knot from my robe clinched in my hand.

"Kick me out," I snap each word. "Kick me the fuck out. Do me like you did Tara last week!"

His hand becomes a fork through his hair, but his unruly wisps don't follow. "Oh, because a man wants a few minutes with you, you think your hot shit?"

My eyelid twitches. Damn, I swear it never happened to me until the first time I saw Simeon murder. A smile spreads across my face.

I pat his jaw. "Jimmy, you're free to have your perception of me. Hot shit, whatever. You. Should. Try. Me," each word slithers from my lips, sexy and lethal.

"G-go," he stutters.

The taste of blood that's laid dormant inside of me is prepared to rear its head. I could snap his fucking turkey neck, but I don't. I stalk past him and toward the rooms. Behind each door, women sell the rest of their souls for a few dollars that are a little crispier than the ones tossed on the stages.

I've never given a private dance. Screw the extra money. I'm not as tame as the rest of these chicks believe. There's no middle ground for me. It's either indifference or the next World War.

At the right door, I stand still, unable to graze the knob.

Maybe Simeon Resnov wasn't a million-dollar baby, who had a life of wealth set before him. He sure as fuck wasn't the beloved of the Bratva. Although when he walked in earlier, I wondered what had occurred since I last set eyes on him. He'd always had a way to polarize me toward him.

Now, it appears that the unwanted son of Anatoly Karo Resnov Junior, that fuck off King of theirs, has more of the reigns. What I perceive as newfound power means that I can't have a brain inside of my head if I open this door.

328

My palms press against the chipped paint; I shovel out a deep breath. My spirit is wrestling the thought of running. My body flushed hot with the notion of consenting. Fuck it. I'll leave Simeon again tomorrow . . .

Confidence squares my shoulders, and I push the door open. A soft smack sound comes from the inside as the knob slams into the weathered wallpaper.

At the furthest wall, I make out Simeon's shadow looming in the dark. Good. I've already done what dumb girls do when they stare at a man so intensely attractive that drool slides down their chin. At the sight of him tonight, I died, and I loved every second of it. I wasn't at much of an advantage at an elevated position. He stood taller than I could remember.

Light bleeds between us. The room's focal point is a pole that's seen more ass than is decent. Darkness surrounds him and I. Through the haze, my gaze roams over sharp plains of shoulders, a Russian god of a face, all angles. A fucking Russian fallen angel of a body, even more, cut angles.

My breath ghosts over my parted lips as I cease from breathing him in. Damn, I clung to that scent for years — heady, masculine, sweet death. While I lived a jaded, crummy life, I conjured the smell of Simeon Resnov. It enveloped me, reminded me that while I ran, he was still there, which was a good thing. He made me fearless. When his intoxicating scent began to fade, part of my body magnetized toward Russia, toward my now enemy.

I meander past the light meant to be the focal point of the room. Mounds of muscle engulf the low seated chair. Simeon's glorious muscles are wrapped in designer digs. His hair is darker than midnight and cropped short. A flicker of a smile tries me as I recall how his curly hair once shaded over eyes sparkling with genuine intelligence. I reminisce about my time where I laid, lazy, innocent in his arms. His breath

tickled my cheek as he read to me. That was the innocent
Simeon, who I sometimes prayed wasn't a Resnov. Not all his
family treated him as such anyway.

Simeon doesn't have a one-note demeanor. He's somewhere between heaven and hell. So good it hurts, so bad it
hurts.

Scholar. Maniac. Lover. Depraved.

His father made him a maniac. I stole the honors of
further corrupting him.

Simeon pins me with a glower. Though I played mute
when we met, he often studied me in silence too. It was deliciously unnerving--still is.

I grip the knot of my robe, undo it, tighten the strings.
God, my actions are stupid, anxious. Why did I do that?
Those intense dark eyes pair with rich lashes, tanned skin.
My eyes flit over the opening of his linen button up at the
tattoos inked across his hard flesh. From his throat, traveling
to places I've loved, touched, kissed, licked. I dare not let my
eyes continue to fall. I might be weak for him, but I'm not
that much of an idiot to remember how my kryptonite
resides in his pants. He has a stiff, thick piston.

His fingers flex at the edges of the fake leather chair.
"ASYA" on the knuckles of his right hand and "MINE" are on
the other.

Scrawled on my knuckles are "SIM," with a heart on my
index knuckle. "MINE" is tatted on the opposite hand.
Clearing my throat, I peer into his eyes. A sly grin curves his
lips. Simeon has me in the precise spot, a lion pawing at his
victim.

Before I glance away, I force out, "How the fuck did you
find me?"

"You were supposed to pick me up from Black Dolphin,"
he mutters, matching my English for Russian.

I sigh. Black Dolphin is where our criminals go to serve

time. No cutesy American prison accommodations. "That was almost three years ago."

"Four. You left me with half a year into my sentence." Again he reverts to Russian like I've lost touch.

I shrug. "Didn't feel like playing rideshare, Sim. I'm sure you had someone pick you up."

"You left me for this?" He observes me through the lenses of a genius. Dark eyes lightened in curiosity, only to spark into an inferno. That wisdom parts ways, as the beast snarls. "You fucking left me. For this!"

I clutch the walls of my pussy lips together in a sharp Kegel. The man has this way about him, such as he's drop-dead sexy twenty-four seven. Don't let him get angry. The sweetest parts of you die in hunger, craving that death only his cock can give.

"Not this, per se," I murmur. Damn, I'm a master at indifferent.

"Get over here, Asya!" He cocks his head.

I give mine a quick shake. Moving back a few paces, I'm drenched in light. My flip flops twisting as I stumble past the pole. Darkness claims me again, but my heel collides with the closed door. Who shut the motherfucking door? Must have been my stupid boss.

"I," the word tremors from my voice, "came to say one thing."

Simeon presses his fingertips to his lips. My gaze wavers away.

"What?" he grits. "What would you like to say, Asya?"

"For your to, ahem, leave me alone. Never try to find me again. Please." With the distance between us, I search the darkness for his shoulders and the rigid angles of him. To see if he's softened to my request. "Fuck, Sim, I said please! We both know I'm not the begging type. So agree."

He starts off the chair. Light from the center of the room

hits the tips of his loafers. My eyes adjust to him now. Simeon gestures toward the pole. "First, you dance. Then we talk."

"I don't dance for the Bratva."

"I'm one man, not the fucking Bratva, Ana—"

"Don't."

"Stasiya!" His voice slams against my chest harder than pristine bass. "Since you're a brand new girl, should I proposition you first?"

My eyebrows creased. I follow Simeon's gaze to the rumpled carpet. The duffle bag one of his men was carrying is on the floor. It's teeming with more money than I've seen in a while.

"The woman I loved never needed monetary persuasion." He taps his massive chest where his heart is. His knuckles bruise across my name. "She had me. I had her. The fucking world shifted axel for us. I fucking fixed you!"

Every word he says is accurate. The mansion in Moscow was consigning me to live under someone else's rule. Simeon mended my broken heart and gave me a better future. But I reach between my hips, concealed beneath my robe is a .38 Special. Hey, can't have a tat on my thigh and not back it up. Unstrapping the gun, I level it out before me. "Sim, I've said please more times to you today than I've said in my entire life—we both know that. Now, I'm telling you to go about your life—"

"You won't be the first to point a gun at me, krasivaya," he growls. The light washes over him, offering me the perfect mark.

"You won't be the first to die by my hand, Simeon," I smirk. "You taught me well."

He. Does. Not. Stop. Walking.

"Khorosho—okay, we're doing this. You're shooting me," he tells me. His finger goes to his forehead. "Nyet, Asya. Not my chest. You've got my heart, snatched it out on day one, girl."

"I—"

"My head, Asya." He thumps between his eyes. "Teflon is a way of life for me. Make sure I'm de—"

"Sim!" I gasp, unwilling to hear him complete the sentence. If I could massacre a million Resnovs, I'd spare Simeon. If I could have Simeon Resnov, this world wouldn't be such a dark place.

The gun twirls around my index finger; the trigger is pointing downward. My mind creates a feeble fail-safe. As long as we aren't in Russia, I'll survive. I can thrive off the love he once gave me.

Simeon slips the gun from my hand and into the back of his waistband.

His fingertips glide down the center of my chest, between my breast. We had this thing between us when we were kids. His palm settled atop my chest. It was innocent until it wasn't. But when it was, he felt for a heartbeat and murmured that I was alive. Though I never spoke a word when he did so, he was the first to touch me there.

His hand is massive, fingers callused. Fire sparks across my skin, jumpstarting my dead heart.

His hand roams over my heated skin, and he cups my breast over the silk of my robe. My heart slaughters at his palm, beating harder than it ever has. Carved stone and full of confidence, Simeon holds steady. His other hand wraps around my neck. My lips tremble apart, lust pooling into the pit of my stomach as his warm body crushes against mine.

My brain is screaming for him to touch me with his lips. Even the scariest corners of my mind have powered up for this. Simeon has known me almost my entire life. He knows that one touch from him ignites my soul. Shivers crash down my spine, my throat is dry.

His cold gaze scouring over my chest and stopping where my harden nipple spears against the thin material. My eyes snap tightly closed. For a half-second, I pray for his lips to kiss, to bite, to worship, and punish. Why the fuck is he waiting?

Nerves frazzled, I look Simeon deep into the eyes. Since we met while I was mute, he knows very fucking well how to read me. He can decipher the pleading in my light brown orbs. In silence, I beg him with every fiber of my being because uttering the words aloud would make me tupoy —stupid.

Please kiss me . . .

SIMEON

"Sweet dreams, moya milaya," I tell her as my hand slides around her neck, finding that delicate spot. The pressure on her artery is enough manipulation to send Asya's sexy curves and limbs slipping into me. Her breathing tickles against my neck. Those gorgeous, deceitful eyes flutter closed. Now, she's vulnerable, weightless in my arms. I press my lips against hers, offering the kiss her eyes have begged for.

Asya's heart becomes steady by the second, and she snores softly. I smile, remembering when she was in a deep, good fucking sleep. Moya milaya snored to the heavens. I kicked her ass out of bed once.

It took one instance to learn my lesson. A jagged knife nicked the side of my neck. After that, I placed blankets and pillows in the tub, then slid Asya's loud, sleeping ass inside of it. She liked that. But she didn't snore at all during bad dreams. For those, I held her, sang an old Russian song. It's a wonder my awful voice never awoke her. My crooning rivaled her snoring. No matter how dead sleepy I was, I'd sing a soft tune until that good, loud snoring returned. At those times, I couldn't bring myself to place her inside the tub.

With her in my arms, I kneel some, grab my money and head for the door. I haven't the slightest idea why Anastasiya left me, and I won't be figuring it out in America. She won't speak Russian. She denies me, though her body draws near.

We have to figure out why. Together.

I press my lips to her forehead. Almost all my life, I've kept Anastasiya safe.

"Moya milaya, you are my everything," I murmur against her forehead. I pull out my phone and dial Luka. In Russian, I order, "Bring the car around back. Fuel the jet."

"Where too, boss?"

"Home." I breathe easy, impatient about our beautiful land and the place where our paths first collided. Home is where she'll open up to me.

The fucking shakedown.

I did my first ride-along at age ten. I was unstoppable after that. The only thing that fit better in my hand than a book was a gun. Sometimes the shakedown ended in money, always ended in sweet death. That was the Resnov way. The wise never asked for a coin. The foolish borrowed and returned our money before we found them. Then there was the idiot, who needed money, begging for fucking death.

We come looking for you; only blood would suffice.

Today, there'd be something more beautiful than death.

I was almost fifteen, seated on a rickety chair at the kitchen table of my next mark. The bitch owed a betting house that belonged to us. I'd woken up early that day and thought fuck it; I'd have my first kill of the day before dawn. With a proclivity for murdering unexpecting people during their regular daily routine,

I'd gotten into the woman's flat and would do her in when she woke up.

A pot simmered on the stove, with leftover borscht that I'd found in the refrigerator. The sun hadn't slammed across the horizon yet. A tiny lightbulb flickered on the ceiling, glowing down on my Glock as it rested on the table beside my bowl of soup. While flipping through the pages of Wuthering Heights, I took my first bite.

I spat the borscht back into the bowl and swiped it off the table. The food had ruined this calm element that I needed for torture. Seconds later, shuffling came from the bedroom. Illumination from the hallway bled across the soon-to-be-dead woman as she clicked on the light. She was clutching a rusted pipe. Her form of protection clattered to the ground as she eyed the Glock weighing my palm.

Her skin turned a shade of gray. Before she could question me, I spoke.

"You owe Bogdan." I leveled the gun.

"I-I . . . Dah. I do. You don't work for Bogdan. You're a Re-re-res . . ."

With a wave of the gun, I helped her out, "A Resnov, dah. Bogdan runs the betting house. He doesn't own it, we do. Regardless, it's disrespectful not to pay your debt."

Her head lowered. "I-I respect all Resnovs, even you."

I laughed a little. "Even me, eh? The bastard prince?"

Now her fingers trembled toward her chest. "I'm nervous. I didn't mean—"

"Nyet? Was it a slip of the tongue. It's psychological, given that those are truer than not. Let's be honest. You wish you hadn't offended me?"

"Dah." She shuffled back a little. "I will go get your money—"

The chair clattered to the ground. I was up and across the area. I stood eye to eye with the mark. My shoulders extended double hers. After all the heavy lifting I had done, she'd be an easy death, with my bare hands. But we weren't to that part yet.

"You look at me," I said — the nozzle skimming the tears gliding down her cheek. "You think, I'm the Resnov that nobody gives a shit about, but his ma. Dah, a ma should always love her child."

"I'm sorry—"

"I haven't finished making my point." I gritted. "Aside from being an unwanted Resnov, you think, this kid is fucking stupid. Right? We're at the part where you don't lie through the teeth that you plan to keep—even in death."

"Please. I promise. I have your money!"

This should've been the point where I murdered her. Something stopped me. "Miss, I was here yesterday morning. I took my time, went through everything for my payment. No hiding spots for money, no fucking money! That pistol you have under your mattress won't suffice. Or did you think you'd shoot me with that shit if I allowed you to search for your phantom money?"

"I—"

I squeezed the trigger. The gun went off a fraction away from her face. Blood trickled from her eardrum and down the side of her cheek.

It was a pain that I knew well. My father did the same thing to me--just because, and my ear rang for days. Sometimes my ear still acts up.

The woman gritted, folding over. I reached down, grabbed her by the back of the neck, and went to the other ear. "Since you lied, I'll make a call to the doctor. Lady, you will die a thousand times today, for me."

I stopped talking at the sound of rustling in the room. The other door led to a bathroom. These things I already knew because the shakedown meant infiltrating someone's life first. Going in guns blazing wasn't me. I was invisible enough to catch someone off guard.

"Who is that?" I asked. My fingers chewed further into the back of her neck.

"A little girl. A stupid, da-daft little girl."

I looked up, keeping my hand on the back of the woman's neck. My eyes collided with a honey gaze, full lips. Even in jeans and a long-sleeved floral shirt, I knew she was one of them. The girl that could've been a handmade matryoshka doll on a marble mantel was from Moscow. She lived in one of the mansion's—a Resnov mansion. Hating the fact that the blood coursing through her body meant we owned her, I tried to turn away. The intensity of those eyes held me captive.

The beautiful, little thing was skinny, no tits yet. The girl had to be maybe eleven or so. Too young for me, but worthy of more than the life forced upon her.

The mark wriggling at the side of me straightened up, and our connection crashed. She said, "The girl's just a dumb kid. Please don't harm her. I'll owe more than—"

"Dumb," I snarled, insulted by her choice words. The look in the girl's eyes didn't signify that she was unteachable.

"Milaya, why are you here?" My voice softened as I removed my hand from the back of the woman's neck. The kid glared at me for a fraction of an instant. Her glower was enough to deduct that 'milaya' and other sweet nicknames were out. She couldn't care about the woman before I'd addressed the girl; she had a look of indifference about her. "Are you okay, girl?"

Those honey eyes pinned me, warning any help I offered her would be all wrong.

"Why is she here?" I asked the woman again. "She has a beautiful home to live in." I cleared my throat, uncomfortable with the inference — a beautiful home to blind her from a lack of future.

"I'm her nanny."

"Tell me about her," I growled, knowing protocol at the golden mansion. The girls went out with their owners. Mostly they left and never came back. It sickened me how young some were taken.

"She doesn't speak anymore. She was brilliant, loved the arts. She could tell you everything about a painter, even the dead ones from history. Um-um, the French renaissance, was her favorite.

Now, she's an idiot. She has a cold, and the new headmistress hates germs."

That was a little more than I needed to know. I only meant to decipher why the trophy had left her mantel. They never did. I let the woman's words sink in: don't speak, very smart.

She had secrets. I wanted in.

Stepping down the hall, I stopped before the girl.

"Trust me," I said, placing my hand flush against her face. Her skin was hot to the touch — her teeth sank into my palm.

"I won't hurt you, kid," I said. My calm voice and touch didn't lessen the pain.

"These are the things you shouldn't see," I murmured in her ear as she struggled to be free of my touch. I let off a shot on the mark — a single shot. The kid didn't so much as jolt. And here I was, attempting to save her from a nightmare by covering her eyes.

"You have medicine? Go get it," I said, removing my hand from her face. She tried to look. Why wasn't she afraid, but more curious and challenging.

"You shouldn't see shit like that, milaya—girl," I stopped myself from calling her sweetheart again. "Get your shit."

She glanced at my hand. I hadn't noticed I was still touching her arm. I let go. The jaded girl went to the bedroom. Fuck, she could've been grabbing the gun. It was empty anyway. I dragged the nanny into the bathroom because a woman or a girl shouldn't see death even if it was just a bitch.

When the girl came out of the bedroom with a handbag, she swung at me. I dodged, slipped around her, hugging her from behind. "Stop—I'm here to save you," I growled. Save her? How? I hadn't the slightest idea.

She slaughtered my forearm with pinches. The vampire of a girl was about to sink her teeth into me again. I flipped her around, crushing her body against my chest. She couldn't breathe, but she could fucking hear me.

"I'm taking you now, milaya," I snapped. Why had I told the kid

this? She came into this world marked with an owner. But stopping myself was impossible. I added, "Come willing; I'll give you back your life. Act up, and I'll take your ass back to the mansion."

Warmth spread across my chest; she was breathing hard. No, she was laughing. I rested her against the wall and watched as she cackled. The laughter was torture to my ears, torture, and disbelief. Her eyes flickered, saying all the words she refused:

There was no saving her.

"Girl, you don't bite me, pinch me, then this," I said, holding out my hand, "is all we have between us. An agreement."

A last bit of laughter bubbled over, then the kid chewed her lip, wresting with the one choice she had. My mind a whirlwind of how I could save her. I'd have to go to the man who had all the rights to her: the devil, my father.

She took my hand.

We headed toward the door. I grabbed my book off the table and slid it into my back pocket. Then my shoulders squared with more confidence than I'd ever had in my life. I'd need that to convince the mudak that I hated with all of me . . .

To give me her.

The bastard hadn't given me shit in my entire life though he asked a lot of me. In return, I had given him bodies. A cemetery full of the dead.

Now I was determined that a river of blood would be my leverage.

I wake up on the jet, neck stiff from sleeping on a leather chair. For a moment, I wonder why I hadn't gotten my ass up and headed to bed. My lips press into a smile. Asya. A vibration from my cellphone in my pant pocket trills one last time. A call woke me up from the first day I met the only woman I'd love.

Coming to a stand, I yawn, then pull the phone from my pocket. Vassili's 'house phone' flashes across the screen for a split second. Fuck, I head toward the bathroom, brush my teeth, then return to the center of the jet. The door to the bedroom in the back is closed, giving off the faint sound of snoring. She hates me enough already, so I'll let her sleep. After opening the tiny window shades on either side of the sitting area, I sit back down and press redial.

"Hello, brat," another woman is answering, speaking in my native language. Her words are unsteady. Not from fear, unlike when we first met. But from an attempt to get the dialect right.

Though she can't see it through the cellphone, I smile. "Dah, you are getting better, with your pronunciation, Zar. Where is my brat?" I reply, alternating from her native language to mine.

"Ummm," my brother's wife begins. "The nursery," she tries out in Russian. "Alright, that's enough learning the language for today. Aren't you supposed to be helping Vassili plan our son's first birthday? What happened to ensure we incorporate your family customs?"

Clouds warp into smoke, gliding by outside of the tiny jet windows. Last night, I was closer to my brat, Vassili, and his family. Los Angeles was my destination until Anastasiya. I groan, "Something came up,"

I can hear her bare feet and how they stop moving through their house. She's hesitant, asking, "Oh, like dead bodies?"

"You're bolder than usual, Zariah."

"You seem to be less . . . Cold and calculating." She chuckles. "Here's Vassili."

Vassili's first words are, "Give me a sec." Now more footsteps. The piz'da is fleeing from his wife so that we can have a real conversation about the Bratva. As the oldest, Vassili was worshipped by our father. They could shed each other's blood from Russia to Australia and still that mudak sperm donor loved him. What Anatoly Resnov did wrong, he treated everyone else like crap. Even our individual mothers.

Waiting for my brat, I tap an old warn copy of Fyodor Dostoyevsky's "The House of the Dead," against my thigh. Most people pass on this bit of work from Dostoyevsky, saying it's not his best. I say fuck that; this book is the godfather of all prison memoirs. All Dostoyevsky's novels are haunted; this one has a bit more truth that hooks me in. I've highlighted passages all the way through. Damn near every line holds meaning to me.

"I'd say business first, but that means you're on your way?" Vassili huffs.

"Nyet." I stop myself from glancing at the bedroom door rear of the jet. "Listen, nothing will stop me from my nephew's first birthday in a few weeks. For now, I'll have an assistant at your place within 48 hours to . . ."

He chuckles softly. "Simeon, I almost prefer your Mumbo jumbo about bloody fucking hands, you mudak. I'm giving my son a party. Zar is antsy. Half the reason she's in the dark about it is that she knows you've got a few more brain cells than—"

"Than you?" I counter, eyebrow arched.

"Fuck, you had to finish that sentence. I was saying: than you let on, Simeon."

"That's fine too. Since we're throwing shots, I should add my IQ is higher than yours, brat."

"Ha, shots. Sim, guess I'm planning this party all by myself. I'm good with that, really good. There'll be an octagon. MMA memorabilia. The works."

I sigh. "Poor kid."

"Hey, you convinced Zariah to step aside so that we could plan this birthday party. Now, you're backing out."

"Not for long. But I promise, you sing that fucking happy birthday bullshit song, Vassili, I'm pulling out my guns."

"That was my compromising factor, Sim, for Zariah to not be apart of party planning. We have to sing it."

"Alright, then. Empty your swimming pool. I'm bringing vodka." The smile disappears on my face. "Vassili, we need to talk about Dominicci."

All the laughing ceases, Vassili clears his throat. "So, you mean war? War with Don Roberto Dominicci."

Face shaded of all emotion, I grit. "Dah."

"Okay, so he was a pawn when our half-sister, Danushka, orchestrated a coup against our family, Simeon. I'm not downplaying the situation, but Don Roberto gave us a peace offering."

"Danny aside, he was disloyal to our father."

"We fixed that problem," Vassili snaps.

"Brat, nobody can infiltrate this conversation, just say it. We took that bitch out. We murdered our father. Anatoly was a disease, the type of man who would screw over his mother. He got what he fucking deserved. Even still, we have to vindicate our blood, show our strength."

"Almost a year later, and you're still angry Sim? Dom Roberto gave us ports lining the west coast of Italy, access to museums . . ."

"A horde of shit, Vassili, dah. That's what he did to pay penance for choosing our little sister, Danushka, over the entire family. Her greed was the end of her. His greed must end him, as well." I growl.

Vassili did the deed with Danny; it had to be done. She was beautiful and dumb and blinded by power. The Resnov Bratva didn't sanction Danny's actions when she tried to make a deal with the Italians. She put those roaches parallel to us. That's blasphemy. "You forget one thing, Vassili. I abhor disloyalty with a passion. The only reparations

344

allowed are that person's last breath. All the crawling he's done on his knees since Danushka died was to lead to the same conclusion. You know that."

"Let's chat this out after Junior's birthday," he tries.

I hear shuffling around in the bedroom, which is good enough for me. Anastaysa waking has stopped me from making a baseless promise, so I reply, "Brat, I've got to go."

"Sime—"

I hang up.

One reason can cease me from setting out a plan once it's toiled in my mind. Dominicci is safe for now. I'm a man of many skills, and what takes precedence has just awakened. Right now, I'll set aside vengeance for an academic nature. I need to observe the woman I love, get in her head. If I remember correctly, it took ages for her to open up for me.

ASYA

My eyelids lull open then closed. The clouds I'd slept on disappear beneath me as my ears pop.

Fuck. High attitude.

Where am I? Crap.

Who am I with? Double crap.

Where am I going? Forget crap. I'm dead.

Sliding into a seated position against the pillow-soft headboard, I flick the lamp on the right side of the bed. A faint glow casts across the room. The tiny jet curtains are closed. On the dresser opposite me is two chrome Colt 1911s. The pearl handles gleam. They're gorgeous enough to send my tongue sliding out and over my bottom lip. The platinum engraved with moya milaya—my darling.

Damn it, Simeon. We had his and her guns. Falling for him expanded my horizons. Books for days. Death too. We were two psychotics who fucked mad, loved sensually, murdered together.

The handles fit snug in my palms.

"Where have mama's babies been?" I mutter in Russian. Okay, so I don't use the language aloud to anyone else. It hurts Simeon that I don't speak our native language. He's sentimental. He should worry, because if he's not in pain by my hand, then he's claiming my heart again. He's better than my shitty ass heart. There are only two people who ever truly loved him. One is his mother. The other is an asshole. Yup, that's right. Me.

I press one of Mama's Babies into the band of my new cotton pajama pants. The tags for my clothes are on the floor. Friggen Simeon. If he wasn't wearing tailor-made, he was tossing price tags in annoyance.

I start out of the room. Simeon is seated, facing the cockpit. He gave me guns and dares to have no fear about me using them.

Ever so often, a hum comes from his abdomen. He's deep in contemplation over a book; too comfortable around me.

My hand slips to the handle of the Colts in the back of my cotton pants--sits there. The familiarity is right for me, yet another ghost of the past settles into my thoughts while I watch Simeon read.

I was about fourteen when Simeon switched gears from one literary subject to psychology. Simeon was researching the Electra Complex. He was always educating himself and sharing his knowledge with me. Sometimes, Simeon would bait me with what he'd learned. He knew the reason I'd gone mute was because of my connection to someone else. A man more than double my age. Still, at that moment, I flipped out and tried to smack him over the reference.

We were in front of other Resnovs. They didn't lift their blessing. His mother's cold eyes took an interest in my reaction. She filed my response away for later. The Electra Complex sort of reminded me of the relationship I had with the man who often took me from the mansion, Volk—Wolf. (Which is honestly not his name. He comes from a prestigious family, which I refuse to mention.)

The only thing innocent between Volk and I was my tender age. The Electra theory went that I was supposed to be in love with my father.

Nevertheless, he was just Volk. Not my father. Only one of the richest men on planet earth. Or rather, a grown-ass man that offered me indecent thoughts, emotions, caresses . . . A man I'd never see after Simeon took me from the mansion.

Though, I had noticed the similarities between Simeon and Volk when I first met the boy. The attractiveness, the intelligence. The willingness to share some parts of their beautiful mind. I know that one would've owned me until every ounce of my body was used up. The other freed me— and look at how I've repaid him.

I cock back the hammer and nudge the Colt 1911 at the back of Simeon's head. I order, "You cannot force me to return to Russia, Sim."

Without removing his gaze from the book, his voice is deep, lush, dreamy in response. "Squeezing the trigger in here is deadly for us all."

Simeon turns the page of his book. There are highlighted sections; it must be a favorite of his. He's crazy about highlighting the best shit. "Come sit on my lap, Asya."

"No."

"Nyet, you mean?" His huge index finger continues to glide across the lines. He drapes an arm over the back of the chair, and I step back a few paces. "The guns were a peace offering, Asya. You're capable of murdering any man on this earth. Not me."

"Sim," I hastily unclick the hammer and step around him. "No, Russia, that's all I'm asking."

"Nyet to our beautiful country, our home?" A dark streak shades across his face.

"No," I beg.

"It's Nyet. Easiest word ever, Asya. Nyet. Nyet. Nyet." Simeon arises before me.

"No. No. No," I huff, standing my ground.

"I taught you so much, Asya. How to numb the pain," he growls. His thumb traces across my lips. "How to lose yourself in someone else's adventure." He slams the book into my hand.

"True. You brought me back to life," I murmur, tossing his book over my shoulder. There was a time I preferred death. I'd just learned that Volk was the reason for my existence. I can't tell Simeon that, though. Doing so would sound like I'm an unappreciative brat.

Simeon went to his father the day I no longer had to return to the mansion. In my sick little mind, father's meant nothing. If life were a puzzle, Anatoly Resnov would've fit into that scheme of parents being the scum of the earth. Simeon owed the boss the day I went free because nothing is ever free.

"You saved me, Sim." I let the words float out, and hope they sink into my bones. After years apart, I hope they remind me not to regard him as any other Resnov.

"That's correct. I brought you back to life, Anastasiya." His hands skim down my bare shoulder, locking my wrist, Simeon spins me around until my back is flush against his hard chest. His mouth caresses my earlobe a fraction away from kissing it.

"When you were ready to set aside childish things, moy milaya, I taught you how a man pleasures his woman." His fingers slide along the shape of me, sending my pulse on a race. My taut nipples ache against the thin camisole I'm wearing. When Simeon grips the inside of my thigh, on instinct, my legs plant wider.

A lightning bolt of pleasure zaps through the center of me. That should be his next stop. Has to be. His thumb rubs over his nickname at my knuckles. Simeon brings my hand up and presses my fingertips reverently to his lips. "I never thought for you to please me, krasivaya, not until you're body had firsthand experience with pleasure. You will always be my treasure."

"Yes," I murmur, then shake the hypnotism prepared to cloud my judgment. I slip away from Simeon's touch. Turning around, I look him in the eye. "Correction, you taught me that I didn't belong to any male. No one."

Inside the walls of my head, I shout: I belong to know one. Not them. Not you, Simeon. Not . . . Volk. My chest crashes as I breathe heavy.

A smile washes over the edges of his lips. "That might have been the biggest lie I ever told, Anastasiya. You have always belonged to me. The only difference between me and that mudak from when you were too fucking young is . . . I belong to you too. He took!"

"Shut up!"

"Nyet. With us, we give, and we fucking love taking from each other. Tell me, I'm wrong!"

My palm burns like fire against his jaw. Simeon never mentions Volk. Not ever. Unlike the pleasant deception at the hand of Volk, Simeon offered me some semblance of control as much as any female can in a man's world. He forced the Bratva into my freedom, so the mere mention that he has rights to me pisses me off.

Yeah, I'm crazy in the head. Were we from any other planet, I'd cling to the obsessive love Simeon offers me what Volk offered placed stars in my eyes. When that fairy tale crashed and burned, it ruined me for the boy I shouldn't have loved — a fucking Resnov.

"I belong to no one!" A red mark mares the area of his chiseled jaw. I drop my hand at my side, palm stinging from the slap.

Simeon grabs my wrists and yanks me to him. "Like you said last night, you do nothing for the Bratva. But for me, you will do— you will . . ."

He stops. The hatred that burned my skin is doused. Fuck, even when we first met, I'd cross the line. Pissed him off enough for him to snap. He should've snapped at me then. Over the years, I'd taken it too far, and he'd cling to his demons, not unleashing a single one of them on me.

"You don't say that you own me, Sim. You never say that." I mutter. Long forgotten tears blur my vision. Simeon's mouth catches a tear as it falls from my jaw. His lips press against my wet cheek, tasting jaded proof that I'm still a little bit human. The thought of being 'owned' by any other frightens me to my core.

"Fuck, Asya, krasivaya, you have to know I didn't mean it like that. I said we own each other. I'm fucking telling you I'm in love with you. You're in love with me! That's it!"

A ghost has a talon-like grip on my throat. I'm the bag lady no man should take a second glance at. Fuck looks. Stone line my bags. One day, I'll resemble a tiny babushka, with worn leather skin, frail bones. None of my stripes will indicate the honor of caring for a vast family. All the wear and tear on my body will be because of my bags.

Simeon loves me so much I'm drowning in it. It's a pleasant warmth that envelops me, yet I can't swim strong enough, can't reciprocate it.

Simeon's fingertips skim over the center of my chest like he's done a thousand times before. The act always lifts the ghost, always sends an exhale sparking through my body. His massive hand paws of my breast, he dips down. My nipple erupts in a static of pain and pleasure as he nips and licks.

"Just tell me you belong to me, Anastasiya," he murmurs.

This is him settling when I should give in. But I can't. His essence is perfection--exceeds it. God should've molded a girl for him, a good girl who shined a light and washed out the darkness.

I fed off the small seed of evil, caused it to decay. Probably even more than the Bratva ever could.

"Wait . . . Sim," I groan, my fingers rushing over his short hair.

"Nyet," his growl sparks across my breast. His teeth sink into the side of my cleavage and my lower back bucks.

"Okay," I purr. While Simeon sucks, licks, and plays my nipples through his teeth, I mouth my love of him. Too stubborn to let him hear the words; instead, they evaporate between us. This is me delirious and forgetting the danger that awaits me in Russia.

And this is us.

The madness as we crash into each other. I climb into Simeon's lap, my hands weaving across his face. I lock my palms around his chiseled jaw. He isn't going anywhere. Our lips catch in a kiss that could kill us. Neither of us is sane enough to desire oxygen more than we crave each other. Kissing the way we do could lead to our deaths. I let the burn in my depleted lungs spurt me on, my tongue soft and slick against his.

His hand slams down on each of my hips, cock spearing the flesh between my thigh. The pain sends my mouth wide in a yelp and offering all the air I desperately needed.

"Naked," I mutter in Russian at a loss for anything more intelligible to say. Hell, the hindsight of my brain is only active enough to crave him.

With a firm grip of my flesh, Simeon is up. He carries us back to the bedroom. I'm clawing at his biceps when he kicks the door shut with his heel.

Simeon places me at the edge of the bed, descending onto his knees before me. His hands shred the camisole from my heated skin. I hardly let out a yip of glee when the pajama pants I'm wearing rip from my skin in much the same way.

He settles back on his haunches, wrestling the tie from his Adam's apple.

While his gaze sends a fiery of goosebumps across my flesh, I yearn for him. Throat too taut to beg for the slightest touch—my orbs do.

Beg.

I never begged for it until I pissed Simeon off.

"How did I go a day, a minute, half a fucking second," he murmurs, "without setting eyes on such beauty?"

"No sweet words, Sim. I've hurt you." I reach for him, but he's out of my grasp. "You should hurt me now."

My legs part ways. Simeon's hand travels up my calf. His lips are tasting places that only he knows as he works his way to the inside of my thigh. He swings my leg over his shoulder, then the other.

"Sim," I murmur, reminiscing on the first time he touched me like this.

Fingers skating across my damp pussy, he pushes the thick lips wide and breathes in my sex. The beast in him gives an intoxicating groan.

His tongue sweeps along my slit. Shivers race over my spine, the inferno building like fireworks igniting from my hair follicles to my toes.

"Sim!" My voice breaks.

Lifting his head, chuckle low, his intense, masculine gaze shines with satisfaction. I point downward, mouth too tensed to speak. Simeon shakes his head in another laugh. That smile is enough to liquefy my insides and obliterate my heart. My eyes narrow a bit, but the happiness and contentment that I'd lost touch with now flood through me.

His massive palms slide over my mound, covering my saturated sex. I'm so wet that Simeon's palm makes a smacking sound each time he softly slaps at my pussy. My lips are begging for a beating and my core yearning for attention too.

"Dripping wet," Simeon growls.

A deep luscious groan comes from the depth of my body. I concentrate with all my might and gasp, "Wha-what, are you doing?"

His thick shoulders rise, eyebrow cocked. His hands framed my pussy, spreading me wide so that fresh air licked at my clit. I suck in oxygen, dying for action.

"Ohhh . . ." I wriggle as Simeon's lips touch my clit with the barest pressure. Then suddenly, his mouth is every, planted around my labia, kissing and sucking.

My back arches. His tongue darts into me. Fingers dancing around in Simeon's short hair, I growl and buck. My hands tug at his hair as if I could bring him even closer. A cry of ecstasy builds in my throat.

His tongue leaves my folds and coaxes the tiny nub with titillating flicks.

"I'm going crazy," I pant, licking my lips. The orgasm torpedoing through my body continued its ascend.

Fuck, the finesse of Simeon between my thighs is killing me!

Once more, his tongue swirls around my pearl before showing the rest of my sex attention. His lips clamped around my folds, teasing licking, fucking.

I clutch the sheets, surrendering myself to him. The high from the climax rising, ready to climb over the edge, is enough to shatter my soul.

The second I detonate, a falsetto tears past my lips. Simeon's tongue slams straight through me. I pant, sing praises, and pant until my voice breaks.

My hips shimmy further down the bed, greedy for the thrusts of his powerful tongue. He clasps my ass in his hands, licks and stuffs me with his tongue while my heart hammers out of my chest. The love of my life presses his mouth against my valley, claiming my pussy as his feast.

The finesse in how he stroked me with his tongue disappears, tempo crashing.

I had lost control.

He, no doubt, lost it too. With my legs spread eagle, Simeon slaughters me with his mouth.

"Sim, Sime, Simeon," I pant, legs shaking so hard I feared I never would walk again. The walls of my brain are jarring with the words: I love you, I love you, I love you. Biting down on my tongue, I stop myself from the reckless, truthful declaration.

The high from my orgasm dusts across my skin like the best cocaine I've never had.

Simeon comes up, his glossed lips locking on mine.

"That's how fucking good you taste when you're really fucking wet for me, Asya," he murmurs against my mouth.

"So fucking good," I breath against him before taking us under in another lung crushing kiss. "Sim, break me, baby. I miss your cock breaking me."

Crushing my lips with his, Simeon pulls out his cock. So heavy that it sinks against me. Cum laden and ready to burst. I lick my lips, desiring a taste.

"Nyet," he mumbles, peppering my mouth with the sweet taste of my cunt. "I got you wet for my dick; you will clean me later."

Lust pools into my mouth. I delight in my taste again. Later, his cock will be swimming in the feeling of us, and I'll taste that too.

Simeon lines the head of his massive erection at my tiny apex. As my heart thunders in my chest, he pins my wrists loosely above my head. He leans forward as if to kiss me, his mouth a breath away. All the nerves in my entire body unravel as he asks, "Are you ready?"

———————

Thank you for reading this sample!
Asya is soooo ready for him. The real question is . . . are you?
Preorder your copy today and the book will appear on your Kindle on release day.
And by all means, please don't forget to leave your review of Fearless III.

Made in the USA
Monee, IL
19 July 2020